DENDERA

YUYA SATO

DENDERA

Written by **Yuya Sato**

Translated by **Nathan A. Collins** and **Edwin Hawkes**

HAIKASORU
SAN FRANCISCO

DENDERA by Yuya Sato

Original Japanese edition published by SHINCHOSHA Publishing Co., Ltd., Tokyo

This English language edition is published by arrangement with
SHINCHOSHA Publishing Co., Ltd., Tokyo in care of Tuttle-Mori Agency, Inc., Tokyo

Cover and interior design by Fawn Lau

HAIKASORU
Published by VIZ Media, LLC
P.O. Box 77010
San Francisco, CA 94107

www.haikasoru.com

Library of Congress Cataloging-in-Publication Data
Sato, Yuya, 1980–
Dendera / written by Yuya Sato ; translated by Nathan A. Collins and Edwin Hawkes.
pages cm. — (Dendera ; 1)
"Original Japanese edition published by SHINCHOSHA Publishing Co., Ltd., Tokyo"
[2009] — Verso title page.
ISBN 978-1-4215-7173-7 (paperback)
1. Older people—Japan—Fiction. I. Collins, Nathan, translator. II. Hawkes, Edwin,
translator. III. Title.
PL875.5.A85513 2015
895.63'6—dc23

2014042414

Printed in the U.S.A.
First printing, February 2015

TABLE of CONTENTS

PART 1

PART 2

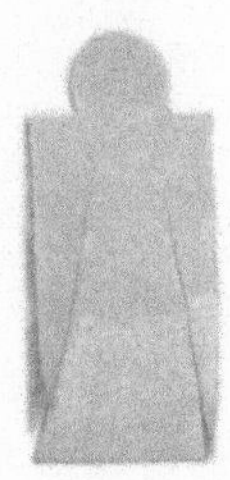

CAST of CHARACTERS

(AGE)

Kayu Saitoh (70)
Makura Katsuragawa (88)
Hatsu Fukuzawa (74)
Somo Izumi (85)
Hono Ishizuka (86)
Naki Sokabe (88)
Nokobi Hidaka (88)
Itsuru Obuchi (94)
Mei Mitsuya (100)
Kotei Hoshii (79)
Maka Kikuchi (83)
Ate Amami (81)
Chinu Nitta (84)
Hikari Asami (85)
Soh Kiriyama (81)
Shigi Yamamoto (87)
Inui Makabe (82)
Matsuki Nagao (91)
Ran Kubo (71)
Kuwa Kure (79)
Sasaka Yagi (88)
Kyu Hoshina (87)
Tai Komaki (72)
Koto Onodera (84)
Kaga Kasugai (67)

Guri Togawa (78)
Tsugu Ohi (77)
Tsuina Kamioka (68)
Tahi Kitajima (69)
Ume Itano (74)
Kan Tominaga (73)
Mitsugi Kaneda (62)
Shima Iijima (68)
Usuma Tsutsumi (84)
Hyoh Hamamura (74)
Tema Tsukamoto (81)
Mumi Ohara (85)
Tamishi Minamide (81)
Tsusa Hiiragi (75)
Masari Shiina (89)
Kura Kuroi (71)
Seto Matsuura (91)
Sayore Nosaka (92)
Noi Komatsu (76)
Hotori Oze (87)
Ire Tachibana (87)
Kushi Tachibana (87)
Hogi Takamiya (75)
Shijira Iikubo (75)
Maru Kusachi (75)

Part 1

Chapter 1

At Death's Door

Once upon a time, Kayu Saitoh was abandoned on top of the Mountain. This was only natural. She felt fine about being abandoned. This too was only natural. In fact Kayu Saitoh had been looking forward to this event for some time, so the day held no fear, and indeed when it came she faced it with serene equanimity.

Now, the living cannot know what happens after death, so nobody knew for certain whether the stories that they were told from a young age, about Climbing the Mountain and the Paradise that awaited, were entirely true. So Kayu Saitoh stopped thinking about the stories, and she was now standing contentedly at the Destination in the middle of the snow-covered Mountain.

When a person reached the age of seventy, no matter who they were or what their circumstances might be, the custom of the Village dictated that, come winter in the new year, they were to be taken one by one to Climb the Mountain. That was how it was for everybody. And as this was the custom, it never occurred to Kayu Saitoh to think too hard about it.

The snow was still falling; it covered the Mountain in a thick sheet of white. The ground and the withered grass were completely buried in the snow.

That was how snowy it was.

Such was the season when Kayu Saitoh found herself standing at the Destination in the heart of the Mountain praying. Yes, her body was thoroughly chilled through, and her legs had turned purple, and even her white robes were saturated by the snow, exposing the bony limbs underneath to the freezing wetness. But she never stopped praying. Kayu Saitoh didn't know why she prayed so devoutly under the circumstances. She had never been taught why she should pray, and she had never thought about why she should pray. She just prayed and continued praying.

Kayu Saitoh's thoughts were not of the Village, not of the place where she had spent her entire life without once leaving. Her thoughts were not of her son, for whom she had suffered through months of a painfully swollen belly so that she could deliver him into this world, her son who had just a moment ago brought her to this place in the Mountain. Her thoughts were not of her seventy years in this world.

Her thoughts were of nothing.

It was not that Kayu Saitoh's mind was empty. Rather, she did not need to think. All she had to do was put her hands together and pray and she felt complete. She felt no sorrow, no suffering, no regret.

Ever since she was a little girl Kayu Saitoh had been told that old people Climbed the Mountain for a clean departure from this world so that they could enter Paradise. Of course, there had been some people in the Village who murmured in hushed tones that Paradise didn't really exist, and Kayu Saitoh also understood how the practice of Climbing the Mountain conveniently reduced the number of mouths the Village had to feed. But thinking about these things got you nowhere, so Kayu Saitoh had decided not to think about anything. Some old people refused to Climb the Mountain and instead ran away from the Village, but Kayu Saitoh knew these people were depraved—a side effect of doing too much thinking. People who let their thoughts run wild. People who tried to find the answers to questions that were too difficult to answer. What those people should have done, what anyone should do before they were tempted to confusing conclusions, is to just put their hands together and pray. That was what Kayu Saitoh believed, and that was why she was now praying. Indeed, she felt positively virtuous that she was Climbing the Mountain after a year when the crops had been so lean, and her prayers were tinged with a trace of pride.

Years of meager living and hard labor had rendered Kayu Saitoh's body frail to the point that even the simple act of joining her hands together in prayer was a struggle. There was no strength left in her fingertips, her snow-buried legs were numb, her nostril hairs were frozen solid, tiny white crystals formed every time she exhaled, and her white hair was hard with frost, but Kayu Saitoh did not succumb to fear. In her judgment, there was no reason to fear anything, because she would soon disappear from this world and arrive in Paradise, and then all the people who had Climbed the Mountain before her would be waiting to welcome her with open arms.

Night fell.

Kayu Saitoh stood firm as the Mountain dissolved into darkness. She prayed. Excepting her head, which was feverish from effort and lack of food, her body was now thoroughly frozen through, and she no longer even shivered. This was a sign that her heart and body had given up on their task of keeping her alive.

Some crows had noticed Kayu Saitoh and were circling the sky immediately overhead. They were waiting for her to become a mound of dead flesh. The old people who died Climbing the Mountain were food for the wild animals that roamed the Mountain during the winter months, for the crows and the foxes. And so a body that was nothing more than a drain on the Village's limited food supplies would, ironically, become a food source for others. You will not be too surprised to learn that Kayu Saitoh did not think too hard about this fact either. She just waited for her body to shut down.

The birds cawed louder now and drew nearer. One particularly bold one came low enough that its eyes met Kayu Saitoh's eyes. She saw a lucid image of herself reflected clearly in the crow's jet-black pupils. Perhaps this was a hallucination, and perhaps it was not. Either way, Kayu Saitoh did not so much as blink. She simply stared straight back into the crow's eyes. If you were to look at her now you might imagine that she would have even been smiling were she not frozen stiff. In truth Kayu Saitoh was by now past the point where she could imagine what her own reactions would be, and soon enough, the last of her remaining energy deserted her, as was only natural, and she toppled over backward. When the snow started to settle on her she felt no cold, and when the crows started to peck at her with their greedy beaks she felt no pain.

In this state Kayu Saitoh was unable to see the moon as it appeared in the sky to gleam down its faint blue rays. But the hint of warmth that the moonlight provided was just enough to revive her, infinitesimally, and her frozen eyelids popped open. She figured that Paradise was on its way, and that the last remaining traces of her spirit were about to depart this world. She was content with this thought, and she closed her eyes again.

Time passed, and then there was a sound of footsteps in the snow.

Kayu Saitoh listened intently and decided that these were not the footfalls of wild beasts. Beyond that, however, she had no idea as to what they might be. The rules of the Village prohibited anyone from entering the Mountain during the hours of darkness. This was so even when someone was due to Climb the Mountain. In fact, the ritual of the Mountain Climbing Ceremony was clearly laid out: early in the morning the Village Headman would come to the house of the old person destined to Climb the Mountain, and the *sake* put aside for the special day would be passed round the family, and after all had partaken of it the old person would sit in the center of the house along with the family member appointed to take them to their Destination atop the Mountain, and the Village Headman would solemnly explain again the precepts of the Mountain Climbing Ceremony, and then all would drink again, and then when the sun reached its zenith in the sky above, the appointed family member would place the old person on his back and carry them up the Mountain to the Destination. Such was the custom.

In other words, there really should not have been the sound of peoples' footsteps at this time of night.

The beating of the wings of the night crows grew faint, and the footfalls drew nearer. This much Kayu Saitoh perceived, just enough for her to understand that events were taking an unexpected turn. Her consciousness might have been fading fast, but this much she knew.

Then there was the sound of breathing.

Women breathing.

Now, women were forbidden from entering the Mountain. Women who bled from their loins were an abomination to the Mountain, who was herself a woman, and it was known that a woman stepping foot on the Mountain risked bringing a curse of fire and brimstone upon her family home. The only time a woman was ever permitted on the Mountain was after her role as a woman was completed and there was no danger of her monthly curse defiling the Mountain. The only time a woman ever set foot on the hallowed slopes was when it was time for her to Climb the Mountain.

The sound of footsteps surrounded Kayu Saitoh.

By now Kayu Saitoh was completely immobile, and she could not even flutter her eyelids, much less think about running away. A number of hands reached out and touched her, but she could not open her eyes to look at them. The hands radiated warmth, and one reached down to feel her cheeks, but Kayu Saitoh could not even feel it as it touched her. Even so, her ears still seemed to work, and she just about heard a phlegmy voice rasp excitedly: "She's alive!"

It was the voice of an old woman.

At this point Kayu Saitoh lost consciousness completely.

2

She drifted in and out of sleep throughout the next day. The first time she awoke her head was groggy and she could only see red light and indistinct images, but she was conscious enough to realize that her hearing was shot—from strain—and from the dull lethargy that gripped her body she surmised that she had a fever, and then she passed out again.

When she next awoke she realized that she was being lowered into some sort of straw bedding, although she did not understand how or why this was happening. She wondered whether she might be dreaming, but as Kayu Saitoh was a young girl again in most of her dreams she dismissed this idea. Before long Kayu Saitoh lost consciousness again, and this time she really did dream. As was to be expected she was now a girl, in a time before her face and neck were wrinkled and her palms and soles were riddled with cracks and her teeth and ears were enfeebled with age, a time when she was beautiful and lived beautifully. In her dream Kayu Saitoh was running through an open field, laughing for the sheer joy of laughing, even though in her actual past there had been precious few scenes like this one, if any. Her actual past had consisted of tilling half-barren fields, sitting in her house sorting beans, babysitting her younger brother, and reaching maturity so that she could bear a child. That was how her actual youth had gone. There hadn't been time to run through the fields laughing. Still, Kayu Saitoh never thought of herself as unfortunate.

The dream having finished, Kayu Saitoh consciously opened her eyes.

First she saw the ceiling, and then she saw her own body covered in straw. Kayu Saitoh lifted her right arm out of the straw. She should have recognized her own arm, but for some reason it seemed alien to her. She didn't understand why such a familiar part of her own body now seemed detached and irrelevant.

Kayu Saitoh stood up. She was unsteady on her feet, and her joints ached, but not enough to trouble her at this point. She took a few steps across the dirt floor. She still felt detached from her body.

She ventured outside.

Her first thought was that she was back in the Village. There were houses, and people, and the snowcapped Mountain stood in the distance, so it was an understandable first impression. Within the space of a few steps she had cause to revise her first impression. This wasn't the Village. The reason for this new thought was simple. There were far fewer houses, and the only people she could see were old women.

One of the old women noticed Kayu Saitoh. The old woman gave a hearty yell, alerting her surroundings to the fact that Kayu Saitoh had woken up. Faces turned to Kayu Saitoh. The faces seemed surprised, almost angry, even. Not blank. Kayu Saitoh looked at the faces one by one, and a realization hit her.

She had seen all these faces somewhere before.

Kayu Saitoh thought for a moment that she must therefore be in Paradise and felt a sweet sensation, but this passed as quickly as it had come. It occurred to her that if this were really Paradise then it was no different from the life that had preceded it. The thought made her despondent.

By and by, one of the old women approached her. It was Makura Katsuragawa, whose house in the Village was right behind Kayu Saitoh's. Childhood memories flowed back to Kayu Saitoh of Makura Katsuragawa as a young woman playing with her, Kayu Saitoh, as a little girl. The same Makura Katsuragawa was supposed to have Climbed the Mountain eighteen years ago. She was supposed to be dead, but instead she was here, standing right in front of Kayu Saitoh, older and thinner than before and with a nose that looked like it had suffered from frostbite.

Makura Katsuragawa's mouth crinkled up at the corners in what seemed to be a friendly manner. "You're awake, then," she said, and "It's been a while," and her breath came out white. Kayu Saitoh thought that she should really say something in return, but she could only move her parched tongue from left to right, and not even a sound emerged from her mouth, let alone coherent words. Makura Katsuragawa continued speaking. "Yes, it's certainly been a while." Kayu Saitoh realized she was being pushed to say something, to respond, and that nothing would happen until she did, so she forced herself to focus on wetting her lips and mouth.

"Where am I?" Kayu Saitoh finally managed. It felt strange, speaking, and she realized how long it had been since she had last done so.

Makura Katsuragawa placed her hand over her nose as if to cover up the ravages of frostbite. "You've been saved," she said.

"Saved? What does that mean, saved?" Kayu Saitoh asked.

"Well, this isn't Paradise, if that's what you mean." Makura Katsuragawa grinned. "We're on the other side. Of the Mountain, that is. The Mountain's between us and the Village. So the Villagers won't find us here. It's a good place. Now isn't that a comfort?"

Kayu Saitoh had never thought about life outside the Village during the seventy years that she had resided there, so Makura Katsuragawa's words gave her a new shock. She understood vaguely on a theoretical level that there were places outside of the Village, of course, but the idea that she herself was no longer in the Village was beyond her comprehension, in the same way that she understood that birds could fly but couldn't imagine flying herself.

"So you Climbed the Mountain too, right, Kayu?" Makura Katsuragawa lowered her face. "I was mighty sorry to see you in the state you were, collapsed in a heap at the top. But everything's all right now. We dragged you along to Dendera."

"Den...dera?"

"That's what we call this place. When I was dumped in the Mountain eighteen years ago I was all afeared and cold, the crows were pecking at me, but then the people of Dendera saved me, just like you. Sasaka Yagi and Naki Sokabe and Nokobi Hidaka all Climbed the Mountain that year too, and all of them were rescued as well."

"This place...has been here since before you Climbed the Mountain?" Kayu Saitoh asked.

"Just take a look around. Plenty of familiar faces, right? Of course, there are some who die here, and there are plenty we can't get to in time to rescue, but there's plenty that *do* survive, and here we are. And now you're one of us! You're one of the lucky ones! How does that feel?"

"What have you done?" Kayu Saitoh hurled herself onto Makura Katsuragawa, knocking the older woman to the ground. She wrapped her hands around Makura Katsuragawa's neck and squeezed. "Why did you do this to me?"

The very idea that you could Climb the Mountain and not die offended Kayu Saitoh. And even worse was to make a place like Dendera and live there. It was unforgivable. Makura Katsuragawa was supposed to have gracefully parted from this world eighteen years ago. She was not supposed to be eking out a miserable existence on the other side of the Mountain. The very idea was sacrilege. Kayu Saitoh felt defiled.

If Kayu Saitoh were to go back to the Mountain now, even though she had never meant to come back down again, even though she had been brought down without her consent, the Mountain would *know.* It would know, and it would not allow her to move on to Paradise. The path to the next world was closed off to her forever. The thought of this had made Kayu Saitoh boil with anger. And she had needed to take the anger out on somebody, and that somebody was Makura Katsuragawa.

Makura Katsuragawa was struggling to push Kayu Saitoh off her, but she might as well have been a rag doll for all the good her resistance was doing. Kayu Saitoh squeezed harder, digging all ten digits into Makura Katsuragawa's neck. The other old women were watching the fray, though, and two of them leaped out and restrained Kayu Saitoh, pinning her to the ground.

"Let me go!" Kayu Saitoh shouted.

The two old women holding Kayu Saitoh down were Hatsu Fukuzawa, who had Climbed the Mountain four years ago, and Somo Izumi, who had made the journey fifteen years ago. Kayu Saitoh's anger was now directed at them. Weren't they ashamed to be still alive after Climbing the Mountain?

"Calm down, Kayu. What do you think you're playing at? I thought you only just woke up?" said Hatsu Fukuzawa, her foot planted firmly on Kayu's back.

"Maybe she thinks she's still dreaming," said Somo Izumi.

"Don't you dare talk about me as if I'm one of you!" Kayu Saitoh howled. Her body was starting to work again; she was starting to feel again. She could feel the snow, cold, underneath her. She wasn't *supposed* to be able to feel anything...

"Ka—Kayu," Makura Katsuragawa sputtered out eventually between heavy coughs. She clambered up and looked at Kayu Saitoh warily.

"What's this 'Dendera' shit?" Kayu Saitoh said. "Why are you all in a place like this?"

"What do you mean, 'why'?" said Makura Katsuragawa, rubbing her neck where Kayu Saitoh had been choking her. "Because we don't want to die. Why else?"

"Have you no shame?" Kayu Saitoh's voice was full of hate, and Makura Katsuragawa scurried back into the crowd without listening to the actual words. Kayu Saitoh wanted to chase after her; she made a renewed effort to throw off the two old women who were restraining her. At the same moment a new figure arrived on the scene. She too was an old woman. She wore dog pelts over her grubby white robe. Kayu Saitoh recognized her. It was Hono Ishizuka, the old lacquer-tapper's wife. She too had Climbed the Mountain—sixteen years ago. She too was supposed to be dead. She too was a gutless coward. Kayu Saitoh glared at her.

"Ah, Ms. Kayu. You are welcome here." Hono Ishizuka looked down at Kayu Saitoh. "Violence, however, is not permitted in Dendera. The next time there is a violent outburst from you, we will place you behind bars. You shouldn't cause such a scene. It makes problems for people. For yourself too. Now, you have been granted a new lease on life. Shouldn't you show some gratitude for this?"

"Who asked you to bring me back to life?" Kayu Saitoh snarled, still held in place. "Hono Ishizuka! You used to be important in the Village. I used to respect you! Now you just disgust me."

"You were prepared to roll over and die just because they told you to," said Hono Ishizuka. "You are weak. Your opinion of me doesn't mean anything."

"You were supposed to have Climbed the Mountain! You were supposed to be dead! What are you doing *here?*" Kayu Saitoh asked.

"Living," said Hono Ishizuka.

"That's what I'm saying! *Why* are you still living?" Kayu Saitoh said.

"Ms. Kayu. I live because I don't want to die. Do *you* need a reason to live?"

"Shut up! I don't need to talk about this! Now order these two women to release me!"

"Release you?" Hono Ishizuka sniffed, as if Kayu Saitoh had finally touched a nerve. "Why would I want to do a thing like that? What a stupid notion. If they were to release you, you would no doubt simply kick up another ruckus. In any case, I do not have the authority to give such an order."

"Then get the person who does!" Kayu Saitoh shouted.

"Oh, you'll be meeting her soon enough," said Hono Ishizuka, nodding. "In fact, as you are a new arrival, Ms. Kayu, we'll be taking you to the Chief right now."

"The *Chief?*"

"Yes. Someone you know well, I think you'll find."

3

Dendera was similar in size to the Village, in terms of its boundaries, but once you considered the fact that Dendera was comprised of nothing more than sparse clumps of crude huts, it paled in comparison. It was through this meager landscape that old women, wearing white robes topped with rough straw overcoats, flitted like withered leaves drifting silently. They were caked with dirt and grime that made each one indistinguishable from the next, at first glance, but when Kayu Saitoh looked more closely she began to see that they were all old women who had once upon a time lived in the Village. These old women were now looking at Kayu Saitoh through bloodshot eyes, with a mixture of wariness and anticipation. Kayu Saitoh registered all these stares one by one as she was marched off under guard by the three women holding her captive. All the while she was thinking about what pathetic creatures these old women were. After a while walking, though, Kayu Saitoh had occasion to revise her view somewhat, when she found herself in front of a larger building. They were still wretched, shameful creatures, of course, but she understood for the first time that they really were making a go of *living*.

She stood in front of a two-story wooden building.

It certainly wasn't anything that could have been described as fancy, but it was surrounded by a rudimentary persimmon-colored earthen wall, and there was even a crude balcony jutting from its second story, the effect of which was that it stood conspicuously apart from the other buildings. Hono Ishizuka, who was leading the way, stopped, and Kayu Saitoh thought she saw a smile emerging from underneath the wrinkles on her face.

"Ms. Kayu, the rest is now up to you. Just be sure to think for yourself before making up your mind," Hono Ishizuka said.

Kayu Saitoh didn't really know what Hono Ishizuka meant by that, but even so she found herself walking toward the entrance to the two-story wooden building.

Once inside she found herself in a room with an earthen floor, and she saw three more old women milling about. There was Naki Sokabe and Nokobi Hidaka, who had both Climbed the Mountain the same year as Makura Katsuragawa, eighteen years ago. And then there was

Itsuru Obuchi, who had Climbed the Mountain twenty-four years ago. Kayu Saitoh was surprised by the fact that Itsuru Obuchi was still alive. After all, if she was still alive (and she was) that would make her ninety-four years old.

Inside the musty room the three old women were busying themselves with sundry tasks: carving wood ornaments, boiling water, hanging pelts to dry, and generally keeping themselves occupied as if their pride were at stake. So they paid no attention to Kayu Saitoh, and, much to Kayu Saitoh's relief, she was able to slip past them and start climbing the ladder to the second floor. The second floor was smaller, more cramped, but the walls were lined with real wood panels now, somewhat rough-and-ready ones perhaps, but it was more impressive than the usual mix of straw and twigs that was used in most houses.

And in the middle of this room sat a solitary old woman.

She wore a mask that framed the edges of her face while leaving her features visible, as well as robes that were so dirty that they could be called white in name only. She sat atop a pelt of some unidentifiable animal, and beside her was a well-used walking staff.

Kayu Saitoh peered at the face framed by the mask. It was a heavily sunburned face, and she had no memory of it.

"What's this? Don't say you don't remember me? Or perhaps you're going senile in your dotage, hmm, Kayu Saitoh?"

As soon as Kayu Saitoh heard that ugly rasp the mystery was solved, and she was brought back half a century. The old woman's looks might have become gnarled beyond all recognition, but that distinctive braying voice immediately gave her away. It was Mei Mitsuya. Mei Mitsuya, who had entered the Mountain thirty years ago. Due to their age difference Mei Mitsuya hadn't really played much of a direct role in raising Kayu Saitoh, but Mei Mitsuya had been an important figure in the Village for a number of years, a *de facto* leader of the women even, so Kayu Saitoh naturally knew who she was.

"Mei Mitsuya, is it," Kayu Saitoh said briskly, without any ceremony. "Well, you can tell me what's going on, I'm sure. What's this all about, this—"

"So, how do you like my Dendera?" Mei Mitsuya blurted out, drowning out Kayu Saitoh in her usual loud, unrestrained manner. "Anyhow, sit. Relax. Make yourself at home. We may have a hierarchy here in Dendera, but we don't stand on ceremony. Every woman is as good as any other."

Kayu Saitoh was still none the wiser regarding her new situation, but she did as Mei Mitsuya ordered and sat down in front of her.

"So, Kayu Saitoh. It's been a while. I remember when I last saw you, you were a mere stripling of forty. Yes, you've aged quite nicely, ripened to maturity. Life in that shitty Village has taken it out of you, all right! So how do you like my Dendera? Great little place, no?"

"Are you one of the founders of this place?" Kayu Saitoh asked.

"I asked you how you liked my Dendera, *girl*!" Mei Mitsuya snapped and then appeared to reconsider her outburst almost immediately. "Still, just this once. Just this once I'll answer your little question for you. Yes, I founded this place. I Climbed the Mountain thirty years ago, but of course I had no intention of dying. So I climbed down the Mountain, down the other side, away from the Village, and found myself here, in this place. Back then there was nothing here. Nothing here, nobody here!" Mei Mitsuya was shouting now. "I had no tools. I knew nothing about survival. Oh, it was something all right, it was something! The rains! The storms! No people. No food. But I never gave up the fight, not for one moment. For the first year I must have survived on anger and bile alone. Then, the next year, when Mountain Climbing Season began, I staked out the Mountain, waiting to rescue the abandoned, the discarded, and make them my friends, my neighbors. And with these new friends, together we built this place. What you see around you. A refuge for the abandoned. That's what this place is. *Dendera*."

"Thirty years..." Kayu Saitoh mused aloud. It was an incomprehensible length of time to be in this place.

"And so I turned a hundred. A hundred years old! How's that for a freakish life span? Sometimes I feel more like a devil than a person, I can tell you." Mei Mitsuya laughed, a demonic cackle emanating from her large red mouth.

"So, how many?" Kayu Saitoh had finally started to regain her composure. "How many of you here in this *Dendera* of yours?"

"Forty-nine," Mei Mitsuya grinned, her toothy smile disconcerting. "And you bring it up to a nice round fifty!"

"What have you done, Mei Mitsuya? What have you been doing?" Kayu Saitoh asked, her voice full of reproach.

"'What have I done?' Come, now, I'm sure you can think of a better way of phrasing that. How about 'What have you achieved?'"

"No. I mean what have you *done*?" Kayu Saitoh hissed.

"Kayu Saitoh. I can tell that you're still delirious. That's plain for anyone to see. You're confused by your own feelings. You're feeling embarrassed that you're still alive. Survivors' guilt."

"*I'm* ashamed?" Kayu Saitoh was incredulous. "*I'm* ashamed?"

"Of course. But you're one of us now. You're one of the survivors. One of Dendera's own. Try not to dwell too much on silly thoughts of the past. Starting today, you're one of the fifty old women of Dendera!"

That confirmed the thought that had been nagging at Kayu Saitoh. "So there are no men. That's right. I haven't seen any. I must have seen most of the village, but I only saw women."

"Of course there are no men! Why the hell would I want to save any men?" Mei Mitsuya jumped up and slammed her wooden staff against the floor like a woman possessed.

Kayu Saitoh couldn't find a suitable response. But she didn't need to. Some things can be left unsaid. Some things are just understood by women, women who have had common experiences, who have experienced common emotions, who have suffered common hardships.

"I'll never allow a man in this place. Never! Dendera is *ours*! How do you like *that*?" Mei Mitsuya said, her anger transformed into a warped triumphalism.

How *did* Kayu Saitoh like that? Quite well, if truth be told. The words pierced her, filled her with a sense of satisfaction—before she remembered to suppress those feelings, by retorting that she could have died properly if Mei Mitsuya and her people hadn't interfered.

"Die *properly*?" Mei Mitsuya asked. "What's that supposed to mean?"

"It's supposed to mean," Kayu Saitoh replied, "that if we had just Climbed the Mountain properly, seen it through to the end while we had the chance, we wouldn't have to be in this miserable place. We could be in Paradise by now."

Silence prevailed for an instant, and then this was broken by Mei Mitsuya's laughter. It was rough, raucous, close to a roar, and it was derisive, a laughter directed *at* somebody, a somebody who would not or could not use her head, and that somebody was Kayu Saitoh, who stood there in silence, accepting the scorn-filled laughter and words. "Kayu Saitoh! You surprise me. I never took you for such an ignoramus." Mei Mitsuya was still laughing as she settled back down into a sitting position. "Paradise, huh? You really believe in that fairy tale? *Really* believe it? What are you, a child?"

"You don't know what happens to us after we die," Kayu Saitoh said defiantly.

"And because I don't know, that means there must be a Paradise, hmm?" Mei Mitsuya asked.

"All I wanted was to Climb the Mountain properly and then disappear from this world properly. That's what's best. That's all I'm saying."

"What? You're saying it's better to freeze to death in the snow? Hoping that you'll find your way into a Paradise that you don't know even exists? That's better than making a life for ourselves here, is it? Horseshit, Kayu Saitoh! You're deluding yourself. You're a half-baked washout, and that's all there is to it!"

"What? How dare you?" Kayu Saitoh said.

"I'll tell you what's really going on. You grew tired of living, that's what! You just wanted to die and *get it over with*."

That's not it at all, Kayu Saitoh wanted to scream back, but she found that her mouth wouldn't open to form the words. She realized that perhaps what Mei Mitsuya said wasn't so far off the mark. Kayu Saitoh was shocked at herself.

Maybe that *was* why she had wanted to Climb the Mountain so desperately, and why her dreams had been of a Paradise to come. Maybe her obsession with Climbing the Mountain had simply been a nice, clean pretext for a nice, clean death.

Kayu Saitoh reflected on this, whether it was true, whether she had simply been fooling herself all along. Rather, she tried to reflect on it, she wanted to, but she didn't know how to go about doing such a thing.

"Thirty years," Mei Mitsuya continued. "Thirty years Dendera's been going now, and you know what? You're the first one to think like that. Normal people want to live, to carry on living, no matter how hard that life is." She looked positively bored by Kayu Saitoh now.

Kayu Saitoh, on the other hand, was still struggling to find a way to gather her thoughts, to articulate the conflicting mass of ideas and emotions that were now swirling around inside her. She couldn't do it. During Kayu Saitoh's seventy long years in this world, she had never really used her mind. After all, there had been no need. She had never had to think while she lived in the Village, and besides, the backbreaking daily grind of work and chores had never left her with any time or energy to spare.

That was then, though. Now, things were different.

This was a new land. It operated under new rules. And for the first time ever, Kayu Saitoh needed new words to express herself. She needed new ideals. She needed new principles. All those things that she had never had before (and even if she *had* had them she would have felt terribly ambivalent and uncomfortable thinking about them), she needed now—she needed *something* to make sense of her new situation, even if that something might turn out to be nothing more than half-baked half lies.

"What's the matter," Mei Mitsuya goaded, "cat got your tongue? Nothing to say for yourself, eh? Nothing? Eh?"

"It's true..." Kayu Saitoh eventually forced herself to say, "true that maybe I was just fed up with living. Maybe I did just want to Climb the Mountain and die without thinking too hard about whether there really is a Paradise."

"Oho! So you admit it! You confess! What a weakling!"

"But," Kayu Saitoh continued, ignoring Mei Mitsuya's interruption, "I still can't help thinking that this place is an abomination. The very idea of making this place called Dendera and eking out a miserable existence, it's shameful. You live like beasts. Like monkeys. You could have had a clean, elegant death in the Mountain, an honorable ending, and you chose to throw that away. There's no honor in this. There's no human dignity. It's just...a *disgrace*."

"And that's what you really think, is it?" asked Mei Mitsuya. "That's the reason you want to die?"

"I don't know," Kayu Saitoh said, suddenly aware of an acute, painful dryness in her throat. "It's the first time I've ever put it into words."

"You just spoke, girl, about honor. How important it is. Pretty words. Well, do you know what? I agree with you. On that one point, at least. Honor *is* important!" Mei Mitsuya's wrinkled face was trembling with excitement. "And one more thing. You've got us wrong. We're not monkeys. We're people. Want to know why? It's because we have *plans*. We're *planning* our next move."

"Your next move?"

"Do you really think, girl, that I made Dendera just so I could while my days away in peace?"

"Didn't you?" Kayu Saitoh said defiantly.

"No! *That's* what a monkey would do, not me!" Mei Mitsuya said, staring straight back into Kayu Saitoh's eyes. "No. I built Dendera for the sake of honor."

"Then why not just go back to the Mountain now and—"

"Stupid girl! There's *nothing* honorable about dying atop the Mountain. That's not how honor works. Honor is something you have to win for yourself!"

"Oh?"

"We're going to attack the Village," Mei Mitsuya declared.

"Attack...the Village? What do you mean? You and your army of one-foot-in-the-grave hags?"

"What's the point of just living in peace safely tucked away from the Village?" Mei Mitsuya continued. "Where's the satisfaction in that? No, as long as the Village is standing, as long as the people who abandoned us are living their smug little lives, there'll be no true peace for us here. We're going to overthrow the Village. We reject them. We're going to destroy them! Annihilate them!"

Mei Mitsuya's face flushed redder and redder as she spoke. Kayu Saitoh observed this and realized that she was talking to a woman who was well and truly overcome with hatred. You could almost boil a kettle on that hot face, Kayu Saitoh thought. Mei Mitsuya had done all this because she was driven by a desire to confront her old family and friends who had abandoned her. *How do you like that?* Kayu Saitoh could see that Mei Mitsuya was consumed by one-sided, unrequited hatred that only the truly abandoned could cultivate. And Mei Mitsuya called that hatred *honor.*

"What's that face for, girl? Are you *mocking* me?" Mei Mitsuya turned her wild, watery eyes on Kayu Saitoh again.

"It can't be done," Kayu Saitoh answered simply. "You can't cross the Mountain in winter. You'll freeze to death along the way."

"Use your head. How long have I been living in exile from the Village? Thirty years! You don't think I've learned a thing or two during that time? I've been up and down the Mountain so many times I know it like the back of my own wrinkly hands."

"It's still a stupid idea," Kayu Saitoh said. "Desperate. What do you think a bunch of old women, worn out by the journey, could do even if you did manage to reach the Village? They'd just beat the crap out of you or use you for target practice for their hunting rifles."

"That's why I said use your head! Do you think I haven't thought of that? Hell, these last thirty years I've thought of nothing else!" Globules of rank spittle were now spraying from Mei Mitsuya's mouth as she spoke excitedly. "We plan our route carefully. Take breaks along the way. Arm ourselves. And we time our raid for when the Village is fast asleep. Those bastards have forgotten all about us—they won't be expecting us! They'll be lying there all cozy, and then *bam*! They won't know what hit them!"

"No way. No way that'll work," Kayu Saitoh said, calm in the face of Mei Mitsuya's fervor. "They'll send you packing. Or just slaughter you all."

"Maybe. Maybe they will at that." Mei Mitsuya's face was still scarlet with exertion, but her words were now calm again, matching Kayu Saitoh's demeanor. "Which is why we need every bit of help we can get right now. That's why I'm asking you, Kayu Saitoh. Won't you join us? Help us win back our honor?"

"Go ahead and win back your honor on your own, all forty-nine of you. Leave me out of it," Kayu Saitoh said.

"If only there *were* forty-nine of us," said Mei Mitsuya, "maybe we'd be able to. But not everyone sees things my way. Some of the people here are happy to be monkeys. They just want to live and let live. What the hell do they think I built this place for in the first place?"

"How many? Who opposes you?" Kayu Saitoh was starting to find that she could use her head to think after all.

"Almost half! Given up the fight before it's even begun! Cowards and ingrates, the lot of them!"

"Mei Mitsuya. I've listened to your story. I understand why you founded Dendera and how all this works," Kayu Saitoh said with a calmness that she barely felt, fighting to quell a rising tide inside herself. "But I still think you've got it wrong."

"What? You... useless—"

"Attacking the Village won't change anything," Kayu Saitoh declared, her first truly confident declaration since her arrival at Dendera. "It won't win you any honor."

"Well, we're doing it anyway. I don't care what you think, and I don't care whether half of Dendera refuses to come with me," Mei Mitsuya said, her voice unwavering. "As soon as we're ready, we attack the Village. We *massacre* them. We're going to turn their twisted little smug lives inside out. Twist their heads inside out too, and their bodies. *Turn them inside out!*"

Chapter 2

Down Blind Alley

It was the third day of Kayu Saitoh's life in Dendera.

Kayu Saitoh had at first imagined she would be living an aimless existence wallowing listlessly in the mud and grime. But the workload she had been assigned was so heavy that she barely had time to snatch a breath. It brought back memories of the drudgework she had done as a young woman back in the Village.

Kayu Saitoh must have been about fifteen when she was wed to the paper-miller. Her day as a fifteen-year-old girl had gone something like this: First she had to fetch the water. She would awake while it was still dark, then draw water from the river that ran two fields over. Of course, one trip a day was not enough for a full household, and the paper mill used copious amounts of water in the course of business, so a number of round trips were involved. Seven trips to get enough water for work, three trips to fill the household cistern, and another six trips to fill the bathtub. She had to prepare the morning meal, work the fields, and then the day would end and she would wake up again the next morning so that she could fetch more water and start the cycle again. When her body aged and she was no longer fit for such tiring work, she was transferred to other duties—minding the grandchildren, looking after the chickens, and weeding the garden. Not quite so strenuous work as when she had been younger, perhaps, but physically exhausting all the same, due to its relentlessness (there was always some mindless beast or child to run after, to catch, to tidy up after, to clean, to look after...) And then she would have to have everything neat and tidy and ready for dinner by the time the younger adults returned home from their toil in the fields, and everything would have to be up to their exacting standards. Then, before she knew it, before she had a moment's respite from the daily grind, she found that she was seventy and it was time to Climb the Mountain as the new year dawned.

That should have been the end of her toils, when she finally entered Paradise, but instead she now found that her work carried on unabated.

The majority of the working day of the fifty old women was taken up with sourcing food supplies.

Nothing could be grown under the blanket of winter frost that covered the area, so food had to be found in the Mountain. As no plants, fruits, or nuts were available during winter, that meant hunting game. To Kayu Saitoh, who knew only how to fetch water and work the fields, this was a whole new world, and she was as ignorant of its workings as a newborn babe, and so it fell to others to teach her the necessary skills and know-how. This morning she was under the wing of the hunting party that consisted of Hatsu Fukuzawa, Somo Izumi, Kotei Hoshii, and Maka Kikuchi. The men of the Village often employed a technique called *wadara* hunting to catch wild coneys. One woman was familiar with this method, and so it gained predominant use in Dendera. The wadara was a ring-shaped bundle of sticks and straw that when thrown would be mistaken by the coneys as an attacking hawk. The animals burrowed into the supposed safety of the snow, from which the women could easily pluck them. Kayu Saitoh tried throwing a wadara, but with no result. The sound the disk made as it cut through the air was crucial to its effectiveness; having failed to produce this noise, Kayu Saitoh might as well have tossed a clump of straw, and as such she hadn't been able to alarm the coney.

"Watch how I do it," Hatsu Fukuzawa said as she spotted a single coney perched some distance away. She maneuvered herself downwind so that the coney wouldn't pick up on her sound or smell, and then skillfully threw the wadara up so that it danced through the air, spinning and emitting a whirr that startled the creature. Twice, three times the lure went into the air, and meanwhile Kotei Hoshii and Maka Kikuchi nimbly closed in on the coney as it frantically burrowed into the snow.

Back in the Village, women were not permitted to eat rabbit flesh. It was said that a woman who ate the meat of a coney would bear children with cleft lips. This was a baseless superstition of course, but the whole of Village society was governed by baseless superstitions and myths. And so Kayu Saitoh did not know what rabbit flesh tasted like. She hadn't even been allowed to taste it after she was past childbearing age.

"Hoho, got it!" Kotei Hoshii cried as she grasped hold of the fear-struck coney's trembling hind legs.

"Well done!" Maka Kikuchi grinned broadly, and Kotei Hoshii grinned back. Kayu Saitoh knew that the two women hadn't been particularly close back in the Village, but now they were all smiles. Dendera had evidently brought them together, forged a new friendship in a new place. The thought made Kayu Saitoh shudder.

"Don't worry, it won't take you too long to pick up the knack," Hatsu Fukuzawa said to Kayu Saitoh, misinterpreting her contemptuous stare and placing a hand on Kayu Saitoh's shoulder in friendly encouragement. "Why, four years ago, when I first arrived at Dendera, I couldn't do *anything* for myself."

"Yeah, and I was the one who showed her how to throw the wadara. She was useless at first, and now look at her!" said Somo Izumi, her breath visible in small white clouds. "Even teaching others!"

Kayu Saitoh observed with detached contempt as the other old women talked excitedly at the scene of their triumphant catch, but then a stabbing, painful realization hit Kayu Saitoh: that she was *not* detached, she was now one of them; she was along for the hunt, doing the same work for the same reasons.

Upon her return to Dendera, Kayu Saitoh was tasked with butchering the coney. Kayu Saitoh hated the idea of being idle more than anything else in the world, so she immediately set about her assignment. However, Dendera was utterly lacking in anything that could be described as proper tools or even the technology to make them. The old women of Dendera had, back in their Village days, spent their working lives in the fields and never had the opportunity to pick up any useful skills. That was why the "houses" in Dendera were worse than crude stables.

Still, it had been thirty years since Mei Mitsuya had founded Dendera.

That was thirty years' worth of accumulated knowledge.

That was thirty years' worth of accumulated skills.

Working under Hatsu Fukuzawa's supervision, Kayu Saitoh hung the coney upside down, then peeled the skin from its body down to its head before pulling off its limbs and using a jagged piece of black flint—Dendera's version of a knife—to open the coney up. Kayu Saitoh was entirely inexperienced at butchery, and the crude blade wasn't up to much, so it wasn't long before the area was a mass of blood and a foul odor permeated the air, as Kayu Saitoh had accidentally ruptured the animal's innards.

"Not bad at all for your first effort," Somo Izumi said with approval in her voice.

"Yep, you've definitely got the knack," Hatsu Fukuzawa said, nodding. "You're a quick study, you are, Kayu."

"I just don't like the idea of not being able to pull my weight, that's all," Kayu Saitoh mumbled.

"Ha, don't you worry about that! You're still a youngster!" Hatsu Fukuzawa said. "Why, so long as you've got your five senses, you're fine and dandy!"

"Five senses?" Kayu Saitoh asked.

"Yep. Dendera's full of old women, don't forget. Some of them can't even move anymore," said Hatsu Fukuzawa.

"What happens to them when they get like that?" Kayu Saitoh asked.

"Happens? What do you mean, what happens?" Hatsu Fukuzawa replied. "We take care of them, of course. What else?"

What else indeed? How could they possibly abandon those who had already been abandoned? The fifty old women who lived in Dendera couldn't Climb the Mountain. Their path to Paradise was blocked forever. If the inhabitants of Dendera started forsaking their own when they could no longer fend for themselves, why, that'd make Dendera no better than the Village. No, that would never happen here.

As Kayu Saitoh used the snow outside to wash the coney blood off her hands, she acknowledged to herself that in this one thing, at least, Dendera had got it right. Then, another entirely different thought occurred to her. A thought that now seemed so obvious that she wondered why she hadn't asked about it before, however unused to using her head she might be.

"Did you lot, by any chance, rescue Kura Kuroi from the Mountain?" she asked, raising her head from the snow.

"Kura Kuroi, huh? The one who Climbed the Mountain last year, right?" Somo Izumi said, brushing her white hair away from her face with her hand. "Sure we did. No worries. I was the one who discovered her, in fact."

"But Kura was—"

"Yeah, she's still bedridden," said Somo Izumi. "Can't be helped, I suppose, if she was like that back in the Village too."

"That's not what I'm talking about!" Kayu Saitoh hissed.

"Huh?"

"Kura was like me. She wanted to Climb the Mountain. She couldn't wait. She believed with all her heart that she'd enter Paradise. That was all she wished for," Kayu Saitoh said. "And you had to go and mess all that up for her."

"Huh. You think I'll believe that someone actually *wanted* to die? For real?" Somo Izumi responded without missing a beat.

"Kayu?" Hatsu Fukuzawa spoke now with a startled expression on her face. "Are you telling us that you *actually believed* in all that stuff? That you weren't just delirious from the cold?"

"Yes! That's what I've been trying to tell you all along! And you should all be ashamed of yourselves for clinging to your pathetic little lives!"

"Say that again, why don't you?" Hatsu Fukuzawa growled and lunged for Kayu Saitoh, but Kotei Hoshii thrust an arm out to hold her back.

"What are you doing?" Kotei Hoshii asked reproachfully, locking arms with Hatsu Fukuzawa. Then she turned to Kayu Saitoh. "And you. Listen to yourself. So you really wanted to die, huh? That's a sneaky way of putting it. It makes you feel better to tell yourself that, does it? And yet here you are. Don't kid yourself. You're just as much part of Dendera as anybody else here. You're one of us now."

"One of you? Who *asked* you to save me?" This time it was Kayu Saitoh who raised her arm ready to lunge, and as she did so Maka Kikuchi barrelled into her, knocking her to the ground.

"Hey. I already told you once. No violence," Maka Kikuchi said in an uneasy voice as she sat on top of Kayu Saitoh's back. "If the others catch you fighting there'll be hell to pay."

"And let me tell you something else," Somo Izumi said to Kayu Saitoh, looking down at her as she lay pinned to the ground. "Kura Kuroi was grateful that we rescued her. She thanked us!"

"You're lying!" Kayu Saitoh spat.

"She's not lying," Hatsu Fukuzawa answered. "I heard Kura say so too with my own ears. She said 'thank you' as she was being carried to Dendera."

"Lies..."

Back in the Village, Kayu Saitoh had always kept her interactions with other people to a bare minimum. There were hardly any people around to spend time with anyway, and Kayu Saitoh had never been one for talking much in the first place, and besides, she was so busy with her daily chores that there simply wasn't time to stand around gossiping. She was able to snatch and savor rare moments of blank respite in between chores perhaps, but other than that it was a case of work until time for sleep and then work again. That said, once she had grown too old for fetching water and she'd been assigned to household chores, she did then finally have a little spare time to her self. Not much, but more than before, certainly.

That was when Kayu Saitoh finally made her first-ever friend, Kura Kuroi.

Kura Kuroi was only a year older than she, so Kayu Saitoh had been aware of her since girlhood, but Kayu Saitoh had never really had the opportunity to get to know her. Owing to a sickness of the organs, Kura Kuroi spent most of her days asleep indoors. As an invalid unable to perform any useful work, Kura Kuroi was seen as something of a burden by the other Villagers, who had to shoulder her share. As Kayu Saitoh grew older and found that her own body was slowing down, she found that she could empathize with Kura Kuroi's incapacity, and one day, when she finally had some free time to herself, she went to pay Kura Kuroi a visit, the first of what became many. During these visits Kayu Saitoh would listen to Kura Kuroi talking with joyous expectation of the time when she could Climb the Mountain and finally be free, and then one day Kayu Saitoh discovered a new emotion stirring inside her that she had never experienced before, although she couldn't quite put her finger on what exactly that emotion was. She was old by then, you see, and when you are old it's hard to truly accept a new idea, even when you want to. As a result, Kura Kuroi ended up Climbing the Mountain before Kayu Saitoh had the opportunity to understand this new, recently awakened feeling that now dwelled inside her. Usually, whenever an old person was about to Climb the Mountain, Kayu Saitoh would be filled with envy and impatience for her turn, but when Kura Kuroi's time came about it was different, and Kayu Saitoh found that both her mood and thoughts were disturbed, ugly. She felt like she had been left alone. That her husband had Climbed the Mountain three years earlier was a factor in her newfound loneliness.

Kayu Saitoh had no idea how to react to the news that Kura Kuroi was still alive, living in Dendera, and, moreover, grateful for being rescued. So she did the only thing she could, which was to throw off Maka Kikuchi who was sitting on top of her.

As she did so, Kayu Saitoh heard a gaggle of voices coming

up from behind. The fishing party, comprising Ate Amami, Chinu Nitta, Hikari Asami, Soh Kiriyama, and Makura Katsuragawa, had returned.

"Oh my. So you were only able to catch two?" It was Ate Amami who spoke first, eyeing the spoils of Kayu Saitoh's hunting party and seemingly oblivious to the bad blood in the air.

"We were teaching her the basics as we went along. That takes time," Hatsu Fukuzawa shot back defensively. Kotei Hoshii and Maka Kikuchi had also taken up guarded postures, their hackles raised at the implicit criticism in Ate Amami's breezy remark.

"Oh, no, please don't misunderstand me," Ate Amami hastily corrected. "I meant no disparagement. You see, we had something of a rotten time of it ourselves. Hardly *anything* was biting today. All we really have for our troubles is sore, freezing legs."

She showed them the contents of their rough wicker basket. Four measly fish.

"This is turning out to be a lean year. Nothing's coming easy," Hikari Asami said, fiddling with the half-frozen flask of water that was dangling from her crude straw overcoat.

"As long as we don't have to eat those shitty millet-husk dumplings again, that's all I ask. I can hardly keep those bloody things down," said Somo Izumi.

Somo Izumi's words gave Kayu Saitoh a jolt. Kayu Saitoh had been used enough to eating millet and chestnuts back in the Village but never the actual millet husk. The reason for this was simple: it wasn't a foodstuff fit for human consumption. Kayu Saitoh realized that she had been underestimating just how precarious the food situation was in Dendera.

"Have you even got any stores for the winter?" Kayu Saitoh asked, concerned.

"Do you see those storehouses over there?" Ate Amami pointed out two comparatively sturdy buildings in the distance. Kayu Saitoh could see some ears of corn hanging out to dry and noticed that the two buildings' entrances faced directly opposite each other, and that each entrance was guarded by an old woman acting as sentinel. The sentinels both held wooden spears in their hands. Kayu Saitoh had noticed before that both buildings seemed to have a permanent guard day and night, but she hadn't had the opportunity to ask about them before. "We've got dried fish in there and whatever grains we've been able to rustle up. Though nowhere near enough to comfortably feed fifty old women for a whole winter, of course."

"But why have two storehouses?" Kayu Saitoh asked. "And what's with the two guards? They look like they're watching each other."

"You don't miss a beat do you, Ms. Kayu," Ate Amami said, craning her grimy neck. "We had storehouses in the Village too, to guard our food from wild beasts and thieves, of course. But you have to remember that food in Dendera is even scarcer. What's to say that the sentries won't start raiding the stores that they're supposed to be guarding, unless there are other sentries to watch *them*?"

"It's just the kind of place Dendera is during the winter," Makura Katsuragawa said, covering her flared nose with her hand. "Nothing for it except to grit your teeth and tough it out until the ground frost thaws and we can start planting again."

"That's how desperate you are to eke out your miserable little existence, huh?" said Kayu Saitoh bitterly.

"Kayu..." Makura Katsuragawa's voice was trembling again.

"Women eating coneys? Setting guards to watch the other guards?" The bile inside Kayu Saitoh was rising again, and she snorted, causing a whistling sound to emerge from her frozen-over nose. "I just don't understand you all. You run away from the Mountain and make this little Dendera, but so what? What's this all *for*?"

"I thought Mei Mitsuya had explained that all to you. We're going to attack the Village. That's what we live for," Hatsu Fukuzawa answered.

"Pathetic. So this is what you call revenge..." Kayu Saitoh muttered.

"You're one of *them*, then, are you, Kayu? One of the weaklings who just wants to fritter away the rest of her days in Dendera?" Hatsu Fukuzawa said.

"No! How dare you lump me in with *those* wretches. I'm not like them. I'm not like *either* of you! And I won't be staying here forever, that's for sure."

"Well, what *are* you going to do, then?" Hatsu Fukuzawa asked harshly. "You're not going to attack the Village. You won't be staying in Dendera. So, I ask you once more, Kayu—what *are* you going to do?"

What Kayu Saitoh *had* been going to do, of course, what she had *wanted* to do, was to Climb the Mountain and enter Paradise. But it now seemed that what she wanted didn't have anything to do with what she was going to get. She was now an inhabitant of Dendera whether she liked it or not, and the road to Paradise was closed off forever. So what *was* she going to do next? She simply didn't have an answer. Kayu had to find a new path for her life now, but she hadn't thought about it yet, hadn't been able to think about it, and she still had no idea, not an inkling. Her face contorted in frustration and shame.

"Ah, ladies, it seems it's time." Ate Amami changed the subject when she noticed movement in the distance.

Figures were emerging from the two-story wooden building—from Mei Mitsuya's house. Three women: Mei Mitsuya herself, with Nokobi Hidaka and Naki Sokabe in tow. They were moving unsteadily toward the clearing in front of the house. Soon, the area was full of old women clutching wooden spears.

"Time for drill," Makura Katsuragawa said breezily, as if all of Kayu Saitoh's objections to this lifestyle were now answered.

Drill. It wasn't a word that Kayu Saitoh had ever heard used in the Village. It had a lazy, wasteful, decadent sound about it. Once more, Kayu Saitoh felt deluged by a wave of shame. She wished it could wash her and all the others away and kill them all instantly.

"Well, *we're* going for our drill," Hatsu Fukuzawa said. "Are you coming?"

"Am I . . . ?" Kayu Saitoh was at a loss for words.

Before she could answer, a new voice was heard on the scene. "There's absolutely no need if you don't want to, you know." It was an old woman who wore a dog pelt. Hono Ishizuka. "It's a savage idea and pointless to boot. Rather than squandering our time and energy on such nonsense we should be focusing our efforts on something constructive, such as finding all the food we can."

"Oh, looky here. The yellow-belly's come to try and recruit another to her cowardly ways," Hatsu Fukuzawa said, squaring off with the new arrival. "What an embarrassment."

Hono Ishizuka didn't flinch at the challenge and coolly shot back that it was Hatsu Fukuzawa's way of thinking that was the true embarrassment.

"And what's embarrassing about what we're doing, pray? Can't you see how serious we are?" Hatsu Fukuzawa said.

"Yes, and *that's* what's so embarrassing," Hono Ishizuka said. "Expending time and effort on such folly. Why not actually make yourselves *useful*? There's food to gather and buildings to build—"

"This isn't the Village!" Hatsu Fukuzawa barked. "Stop trying to make things like they were! We've got a different task now!"

"Have you forgotten what happened in Dendera ten years ago as a result of your obsession with your new little *task*?" Hono Ishizuka asked. The question evidently hit a nerve, as Hatsu Fukuzawa, whose expression remained unchanged, took this as her cue to go silent, and she retreated to join the other old women who were practicing with their spears.

"Hono Ishizuka," Hikari Asami said, brushing her white hair, "what you say is . . . correct, of course. But . . ."

"You don't need to say any more," Hono Ishizuka said, her tone gentler.

"But I still . . ." Hikari Asami's words trailed off, and she walked toward the clearing where the drill was starting. Somo Izumi, Ate Amami, Kotei Hoshii, Maka Kikuchi, Chinu Nitta, and Soh Kiriyama all followed her. Only Makura Katsuragawa hesitated, but eventually she too went to take up a wooden spear.

"And what about you, Ms. Kayu? Will you be joining the drill? Will you practice whirling a spear around?"

"I heard that there was a faction who were against the idea of attacking the Village. Are you their ringleader, then?" Kayu Saitoh responded with a question of her own.

"Ringleader of a faction? My, that's a rather harsh way of putting it," Hono Ishizuka said with a wry smile. "It's true that there are some of us who consider that we'd be better off working on making Dendera a better place to live, rather than worrying over attacking the Village. *Doves*, they call us. No, I do my bit, but our real leader, if you want to call her that, is Masari Shiina. I'm sure you'll remember her? She Climbed the Mountain nineteen years ago now, it must have been."

"Shiina? You mean the Shiina from the salt merchants?" Kayu Saitoh asked.

"Just so."

The incident of the salt merchants had happened when Kayu Saitoh was only a little girl, but it was etched into her memory as if it had happened only yesterday.

The salt merchant himself had been a serious and conscientious man in every respect until one day when he became possessed by a hunger demon. He gobbled his way through his household's food supplies in no time flat, and soon he was reduced to desperate measures such as chewing weeds, shoving his face straight into the river to drink water, and even sucking on pebbles. The salt merchant's wife, deprived of food, grew so thin that her skin started clinging to her skull, and the children of the household soon starved to death. As the salt merchant had eaten his household into abject poverty, the Village had to provide the rice for the ritual offerings for their graves, but the salt merchant snuck into the graveyard at night and ate the offerings as well. And then the incident happened. The salt merchant was discovered in the fields of another household, chewing on a pile of raw potatoes that he had dug up with his bare hands. The salt merchant was immediately apprehended, blinded, and lynched. Then his wife was tied up and brought out into the open to join him, as was Masari Shiina, who had married into another household. After that, the entire populace of the village, excluding the young babes, gathered in the open, and the Mountain Barring began.

Mountain Barring was the punishment reserved for households that broke taboo. First, the offending household's possessions and livestock were seized and distributed among the rest of the Village. Then, the house was razed to the ground. Next, pieces of wood were taken from the debris and used to beat the members of the household. While this was happening the Villagers would take up a ritual chant: *We won't let you Climb the Mountain.* A household so lacking in shame that it couldn't uphold the ways of the Village had no right to Climb the Mountain. Furthermore, it would be a terrible thing if the Mountain were ever to know of the existence of such embarrassments, and so it was up to the Villagers to destroy their shameful secret before it ever got out. So the salt merchant and his wife were both ritually cudgeled to death. The twenty-seven-year-old Shiina was beaten to within an inch of her life too, of course, but the Villagers were more merciful to her as she had entered the Shiina household and taken their name. She wasn't killed, but only blinded in her left eye.

After the Mountain Barring ritual was complete, all trace of the salt merchant was removed from the Village, and no one ever spoke of the household again. Food was always scarce in the Village, and in actuality any sort of theft, let alone the stealing of food, was crime enough to warrant the annihilation of an entire household. The young Kayu Saitoh who had witnessed the Mountain Barring vowed to herself that however hungry she became she would never, ever resort to stealing, as the prospect of being denied the right to Climb the Mountain and enter Paradise was a fate worse than death.

"Of course you remember her. How could anyone forget a Mountain Barring?" Hono Ishizuka said softly, as if she were reading Kayu Saitoh's thoughts and memories. "There's every chance that something just as barbaric could happen here in Dendera, you know, given the chronic shortage of food. *That's* what we're about, the Doves. Our priority is to make Dendera a place where that sort of tragedy never happens."

"With Masari Shiina and you leading the way?" Kayu Saitoh said.

"Yes."

"Fine. So once Dendera is a nice, peaceful place with a nice, stable food supply, then what? *That's* when you attack the Village?"

"Heavens, no." Hono Ishizuka shrugged her shoulders. "Why would we go out of our way to disturb our hard-won peace and stability? Not that I don't have plenty of ill feelings toward the Village, of course, but the idea of *attacking* it is sheer folly. As if a gaggle of raggedy old women stood a chance of winning in the first place!"

"Well, I'm in complete agreement with you on that point," Kayu Saitoh said, nodding. "So, according to Mei Mitsuya, you—*Doves?* You're about half of Dendera? How many of you are there exactly?"

"There are twelve of us who you could say have declared for the Doves," Hono Ishizuka said.

"That's nowhere near half!"

"No. I imagine that Ms. Mei Mitsuya conflates all those who haven't made up their mind with those of us who have declared against an attack on the Village. There are twenty-eight Hawks in total—that's those who plan to attack—and twelve Doves. The other nine are either undecided for the time being or not in any state fit to make decisions."

And so it was that Kayu Saitoh learned how Dendera comprised three distinctly different groups: the Hawks, the Doves, and the undecided. Not everyone in Dendera was cut from the same cloth. Not that their differences were enough to cause them to descend into outright hostilities, of course—their common bond of all having been abandoned, all being outcasts, was enough to ensure *that,* Kayu Saitoh decided, but nonetheless there was a definite uneasiness to their truce. Yes, this was still a land of shameless, pathetic creatures, Kayu Saitoh thought.

"I must admit that the Hawks do have the upper hand at the moment, unfortunately," Hono Ishizuka said, almost apologetically. "I suppose it's inevitable, as Ms. Mei Mitsuya herself is the faction leader. But what about you, Ms. Kayu? What is your position? Which side will you take? Are you a Hawk or a Dove?"

"Neither."

"So what does that mean?"

"I won't be attacking the Village. And I won't be working to make Dendera a better place."

"So what will you do?"

"Why don't you die?" Kayu Saitoh said.

"I'm sorry?"

"I'm saying you should die," Kayu Saitoh said, glaring at Hono Ishizuka. "We're all over seventy. We shouldn't be alive. Don't you feel ashamed? Haven't you let yourself down?"

"That's a pretty mean-spirited attitude to take," Hono Ishizuka said quietly.

"No. I'm not being mean. I just think it's a terrible shame that you don't all just die. Hawks, Doves, the lot of you." With that, Kayu started walking away.

"Where are you going?" Hono Ishizuka asked.

"To watch this so-called drill."

"Well, take care," Hono Ishizuka said. "I'll look after your coneys for you."

2

The Hawks, or rather the twenty-eight old women, were gathered in the clearing. They were lined up in three rows, practicing thrusting their flimsy-looking wooden spears in rough time to Mei Mitsuya's count. Once again, Kayu Saitoh was embarrassed on their behalf at the pathetic display.

When Mei Mitsuya noticed Kayu Saitoh, she ordered the women to continue and then turned her gummy, brown-toothed smile to Kayu Saitoh to ask in her usual barking voice whether Kayu Saitoh had come to practice with them.

"No, I'm just here to watch," Kayu Saitoh said.

"Just look at them! My brave little soldiers," Mei Mitsuya said, surveying the stick-wielding old women with pride. "This is my army that'll bring down the Village."

"Mei Mitsuya. Do you remember the Mountain Barring we had in the Village?"

"Mountain Barring, eh? That brings back memories," Mei Mitsuya said.

"I was only a little girl when it happened, but I still remember every detail," Kayu Saitoh said, vivid memories flooding back to her as she spoke. "The Villagers who destroyed the salt merchant's house and beat the couple to death were determined. They were strong."

"What're you trying to say?" Mei Mitsuya asked.

"This group of half-dead hags don't stand a chance against them,"

Kayu Saitoh said. She ignored the half dozen or so pairs of eyes that were now glaring at her.

"You're forgetting that I was the one who roused the women of the Village at the time! They didn't want to go through with the punishment at first! Yes, *I* was their leader. And I'll be leading the attack again, except this time against the whole Village. How can we possibly fail?" Mei Mitsuya was in an elated mood. "At that time, all the people in the Village felt was anger, anger that their food was stolen. Anger can be channelled! It gives people strength. Strength enough to run riot through the Village!"

Mei Mitsuya opened her large mouth and laughed triumphantly. Kayu Saitoh couldn't think of anything to say back, and she just stared at Mei Mitsuya's open, red-raw mouth.

The twenty-eight women continued their drill. Their movements might have been stiff, a farcical parody of a real army, but Mei Mitsuya was right at least about the anger that dwelled in their eyes, smoldering away and driving them on. Kayu Saitoh didn't think that would be enough to affect the outcome of an attack on the Village, though. Kayu Saitoh knew all too well that back in the Village life was hard, that there was an undercurrent of resentment and anger running through everybody's lives, whether they were old or young, man or woman, and that even so nothing ever changed. The old women here should have known for themselves that anger alone was never enough to change anything. Perhaps they had forgotten or were willing themselves to try and forget, for there was nothing half-hearted about the effort that these women were putting into the drill, even if the outcome was risible. Kayu Saitoh had seen enough, and she turned away from the drill to go back to the home that she had been assigned to.

They called it a home, at least, but although it might have been big enough to be called a house, it was basically just a makeshift shelter consisting of planks of wood and straw—nothing compared to Mei Mitsuya's residence or the storehouses. This particular excuse of a house was residence to Kayu Saitoh, Ate Amami, Shigi Yamamoto, and Inui Makabe.

Only Shigi Yamamoto was in, sitting in front of the fire in the center, muttering something unintelligible to herself under her breath.

Kayu Saitoh removed her straw shoes and sat down by the hearth, opposite Shigi Yamamoto, and picked out a potato from the embers. Food was strictly rationed in Dendera, and each person was allowed one potato a day. The potato was hot and brought a twinge of pain to Kayu Saitoh's frozen hands where it came into contact with them and thawed them out, but even that pain felt good as Kayu Saitoh split the potato open. A warm, savory cloud of moisture rose up, making Kayu Saitoh's stomach rumble, and she took a big bite. Having said that, Kayu Saitoh had lost most of her teeth, so it was more a case of trying to crush the potato between her dribbling gums.

Kayu Saitoh glanced over at Shigi Yamamoto as she ate the potato, but Shigi Yamamoto simply stared into the fireplace without appearing to notice her. Shigi Yamamoto was always lost in her reveries. She would feed herself occasionally, but other than that she hardly did anything—never talked, never went outside the house. She just waited for the days to end. Even so, Kayu Saitoh thought she understood why Shigi Yamamoto acted the way she did.

Kayu Saitoh had decided that Shigi Yamamoto must have wanted to Climb the Mountain.

Shigi Yamamoto was about seventeen years older than Kayu Saitoh, and Kayu Saitoh remembered her from their Village days as a lively and articulate person. Her memory of Shigi Yamamoto was that she married into a household with a fine herb garden and that Shigi Yamamoto took great delight in cultivating it. Not that you would have known any of this to look at her now.

The sun set, and it was time for dinner. Rations in Dendera were never enough, so to make what little there was go further, everything was thrown into a communal pot on the fire. There were no such things as iron pots in Dendera, of course, so it was more like a makeshift stone bowl, hollowed out using bone and flint. It was a poor substitute for the real thing, and it took a long time to heat up, unevenly. The broth itself was made of water, the day's catch of coney (both the flesh and the bones), a few vegetables, and corn dumplings. The old women huddled around the fire, scrunched up from cold and fatigue from the days' exertions, and all went calm as they focused single-mindedly on the task of slurping up the bland, tasteless broth. An eerie quiet fell on Dendera.

After that, the old women all went to sleep before the next bout of hunger pangs had time to fall on them. Kayu Saitoh tried to do the same and burrowed herself into the straw, but the biting cold that gnawed at her fingers and froze her rump was too much, and she opened her eyes. The cold had never been too much of a problem back in the Village, but here it was a matter of life and death. The only clothes the women had were the gossamer-thin white ceremonial robes they had worn to Climb the Mountain, supplemented by whatever straw overcoats they had been able to rustle up without real tools, and the huts they lived in were so flimsy the roofs had to be regularly cleared of snow lest they collapse under its weight. The cold was ever present. It suffused their lives.

Because Kayu Saitoh lacked the fiery determination of the Hawks who lived for revenge on the Village, or even the quiet resolve of the Doves who were passionate about turning Dendera into something safe and stable, she could not comprehend what possessed people to put up with this level of suffering and hardship just so they could extend their miserable lives that little bit further. She needed to consider how she would choose to live her life from now on. It was the first time ever that she was faced with such a choice. When she lowered her eyelids again she saw the figure of Kura Kuroi floating up in her mind's eye. *I must find time to go and see her tomorrow,* she determined, and by and by she was overtaken by a death-deep sleep that won out over the ever-present thick cold. She dreamed no dreams.

The next morning Kayu Saitoh awoke amidst icy air that seemed to sap away at her very soul. She flicked away the frost that had almost glued her eyelids shut and emerged from the straw bedding. Ate Amami, Shigi Yamamoto, and Inui Makabe seemed to have grown used to the cold, for they were blithely asleep amidst the chill air that was enough to freeze solid the remnants of last night's broth still in the pot. Kayu Saitoh felt a painful, raw swelling at the back of her throat and realized that she must have some sort of cold coming on. She dragged her miserable, maladapted body out of the hut and into the still-dark breaking morning. Snow had settled where it had fallen during the night, more snow. The promise of the new day was in the air, and when Kayu Saitoh exhaled, crisp clean puffs of crystal emerged, but the beauty of the scene was lost on her.

Then her nose picked up a strange odor.

It was a cloying scent, dense, and it puzzled Kayu Saitoh. It might have been different had the women been walking around and going about their business, but nobody had stirred, as far as Kayu Saitoh could tell, so there should have been nothing to pollute the fresh morning air. Kayu Saitoh lifted her nose and sniffed, and she followed the scent. The two storehouses came into view. Kayu Saitoh noticed that the ears of corn that had been hung out to dry were now scattered on the ground in ruins, and she hurried toward them to investigate. As she grew closer the smell became worse, much worse, assaulting her senses and forcing her to stop using her nose to breathe, but still she pushed forward.

The women at the scene had become chunks of meat.

Blood. Entrails. Teeth. Clumps of hair with pieces of scalp still attached. All scattered about the entrances to the two storehouses. It was impossible to tell which body part belonged to which person. Furthermore, one of the storehouses had a hole ripped into its side. Agitated, Kayu Saitoh tried to consider what to do next, what her next step should be, but she couldn't think; her head wouldn't work. She couldn't link one idea with the next. The next thing Kayu Saitoh was conscious of was sitting on the ground being kicked in the back by Mei Mitsuya, who had somehow arrived on the scene.

It took a few such kicks before Kayu Saitoh snapped out of her daze. She looked up to meet Mei Mitsuya's eyes. Mei Mitsuya's wrinkle-etched face was trembling, and she looked about to collapse, but she kept herself propped up using her wooden staff and sheer force of will, speaking the names of the old women who had been brutally dismembered. Kayu Saitoh learned through this that the dead were Matsuki Nagao, Ran Kubo, Kuwa Kure, and Sasaka Yagi, but as none of the victims had been particularly well known to her, this new piece of information did nothing one way or another to affect her already-shattered mental state.

"It was a bear!" Mei Mitsuya hollered.

That was the only explanation, of course, for what other creature could have performed such an act of brutality? Still, hearing it spelled out in so many words made Kayu Saitoh shudder. As the Village had been equipped with rifles, bears had simply not been a real issue there, and Kayu Saitoh had never heard of one actually attacking the Village. Bears were supposed to have been responsible for desecrating cemeteries, for killing and eating horses and cows, for attacking people while they harvested vegetables in the field, but that was just rumor, closer to legend than reality. Here, in Dendera, it *was* reality. Kayu Saitoh realized, once and for all, that she had just understood the crucial, decisive difference between the Village and Dendera.

Mei Mitsuya looked at the broken wooden spears and then entered the storehouse through the hole in its wall. Kayu Saitoh followed her and, as soon as she entered, saw the chaos inside. The stores of dried fish, potatoes, and beans had been well and truly eaten, with debris scattered around the floor. When Kayu Saitoh realized the implications of the sudden loss of so much of their valuable stores, her fear of the bear was replaced with a sense of despair at how they would possibly survive the morrow.

"Ludicrous!" Mei Mitsuya banged her staff against the ground. "What the hell is this? It's ludicrous! Why would it do a thing like this? A bear! What have we ever done to hurt *it*? So, you think you can get away with ruining all our plans, do you? You? A mindless *beast*? Well, you're wrong. I'm going to kill you for this! *Kill* you!"

3

A beast cannot speak the language of men and has no such thing as a name. Nevertheless, as the hair on this particular bear's back was notably reddish, let us call her "Redback." Let us say that Redback could speak the language of humans. What would she say if she were given the opportunity to explain herself? No doubt, she would angrily growl that the mountain was her territory, and that the Two-Legs had no right to be here. The reality was that Redback's ancestors roamed the mountain for many a generation, long before people even arrived on the scene to start calling it "the Mountain." And yet these Two-Legs had the temerity to appear on the scene and start cutting the trees down with their tools and shaping the mountain according to their will, carving what they called their village into the landscape, preventing

Redback from roaming freely around what should have been her birthright.

Redback knew what a powerful beast she was.

She knew that she was the strongest, proudest beast in the area, as did the other beasts of the region, who all deferred to her might and kept out of her way. That was the rightful way of things. And yet when the two-legged intruders ignored this natural order, and when Redback decided to teach them a lesson by going to that place that they had claimed for themselves, Redback came across a group of these Two-Legs on the way down the mountain, and they had pointed those strange sticks at her that spat fire, and she felt a pain like no other as her rear leg went limp. After that Redback decided never to appear before the Two-Legs again. That was the law of nature, the logic of beasts. Avoid confrontation with that which is stronger than you.

Circumstances, however, conspired to cloud Redback's usually sound animal instincts.

It was winter. The very fact of a bear roaming the mountains during winter was, in itself, an anomaly. Redback should have been hibernating, as she did most years. Most years she would eat her fill of salmon from the streams, and strawberries and lingonberries from the fields, and then settle into a comfortable, fatty, torpid stupor, but this year had been different. Food had been scarce, and she hadn't managed to eat enough to acquire the necessary layer of insulating body fat. And so the cold winter wind had sapped away at her body heat, and when the snow began to fall and her stomach began to rumble, Redback sensed that her life was in danger and emerged prematurely from her winter hideaway.

So far she had managed to scavenge just about enough nutrients to survive by gnawing at roots and other such meager offerings, but the miserable forage left her in a bewildered, disturbed state close to anger. Why should she—whose rightful territory this was, who was supposed to be stronger and prouder than every other creature in the mountain—be reduced to such misery?

On top of that, Redback had given birth to a cub the year before last.

Like her, the male cub had missed his opportunity to hibernate. Suffering extreme hunger, he followed his mother in short, weak strides. Whenever she looked at him, her maternal instincts heightened—in terms of human emotions, she wanted him to somehow survive. But the winter wouldn't end, and food wasn't to be found, and the mother and cub weakened further with each passing day. When they searched for it, they could find fir trees with inner bark to scavenge and paltry remnants of decaying plants buried beneath the snow, but none of this would fill their stomachs. Such was their existence, when one day, her cub became too emaciated to walk steadily, and her normally sound animal judgment went awry.

There were two places where the Two-Legs seemed to congregate. One of those was where Redback had tried to enter and received the awful wound from those strange fire-breathing sticks. But she had not yet tried the other one, so that was where she was heading. It wasn't a risk she would have taken under normal circumstances, but it was clear that there just wasn't enough food anymore, and besides, the fact that all of this should have been *her territory* was starting to gnaw deep. She drew on her remaining reserves of strength and raised her hackles.

Night crows resting on a nearby tree branch flew away, sensing the disturbance in the air caused by Redback's new sense of resolve. Redback was a female and slightly past her prime, but she had an unusually large head for her kind, and her build was exceptionally muscular, and her fangs and claws were all in good order. Redback had, after all, only ever lost one fight in her life, and that was to the Two-Legs with their strange spitting sticks. Redback wasn't exactly calm at the prospect of having to face those things again, but her four legs carried her forward nonetheless. Redback—that is to say, a bear—is able to move through mountain terrain at speeds that are quite remarkable considering its short, stubby legs. So it wasn't long before Redback arrived at that other place where the Two-Legs lived.

This place seemed quiet. Redback could remember that sharp smell those hateful sticks gave off when they had hurt her back leg. Well, that smell was nowhere to be found now. Still, Redback was taking no chances. She moved stealthily through the night, using the trees for cover, scouting out the whole area. Eventually she saw some of the Two-Legs. There were four of them with sticks in their hands, standing still in front of two of those strange dens that the Two-Legs made. There were ears of corn hanging from the walls of the dens. Redback sniffed the air once more, carefully, to check again if she could detect that sharp smell of those pain-sticks, and when she confirmed she couldn't, she started advancing, slowly, toward the Two-Legs.

Redback moved boldly now. After all, there was nothing underhanded about what she was doing, not from her point of view. She was just taking back what was rightfully hers. This wasn't an invasion—she was just claiming bounty that had been harvested from her territory. Unlike smaller, weaker animals that tried to sneak in to steal from under the Two-Legs' noses, Redback simply walked up to the corn as if she had every right to do so and began to furiously devour it. The Two-Legs just stood there at first, dumbstruck, at a complete loss as to how to deal with this new arrival. Having said that, they couldn't simply watch in silence as Redback ransacked their stores, so eventually one of them plucked up the courage to swing her stick at Redback's rear. At this point it would have been easy for Redback to take a lazy swipe with one of her massive paws and rip through the offending Two-Legs' flesh and bone, but instead Redback chose to make a show of standing erect on her hind legs and facing her attackers, as if to show once and for all that this was *her* territory, not the Two-Legs', and that she would take down any interlopers face to face, anytime, anyplace. Then, Redback decided it was time for a little experiment. She gave one of the Two-Legs a little exploratory jab, fully expecting the counterblow of the painful sticks and bracing herself for the pain. It never came. Instead, the Two-Legs' head just flew off into the air, and blood spurted from the place where its head had been attached to its body. The remaining Two-Legs were rooted to the spot in fear, but in her own way Redback was even more fearful and confused than they were. She tried poking at another one of the Two-Legs with her claws. Its belly ruptured and its innards poured forth as it crumpled into a heap on the ground. Redback really wasn't sure what to make of this complete lack of resistance, so she charged at one of the two remaining Two-Legs, slamming her into—and then through—the wall of one of the dens, as both the Two-Legs' body and the wall were pulverized. Redback's face poked through the wall too, and she had been a little slow in removing it to face the final Two-Legs, and when Redback finally did look back she realized that the creature was aiming its stick at her, ready to stick it in her anus. Redback was vulnerable there, she knew, so she shifted her rear end, and the Two-Legs' stick bounced off her hind leg instead, snapping instantly. Redback jumped onto the Two-Legs, shoving it to the ground with her massive front paws and then, not really knowing what else to do, decided to take a big bite out of its head. Redback's giant jaws and fangs made light work of the creature's skull. The Two-Legs gave a short scream from inside Redback's mouth and then was silent. Its flesh and blood and brains splattered viscerally onto Redback's tongue.

That instant, Redback's instincts and experience informed it of two facts.

The first was how weak these Two-Legs were.

The second was how delicious these Two-Legs were.

After finishing off the head, Redback moved on to the flesh on the Two-Legs' body. It had been a long time since she had felt the exhilarating taste of fresh meat, but Redback managed to contain her excitement long enough to raise her head and look around to check that no other Two-Legs were drawing dangerously near. Her mouth half open and dribbling with fresh blood, she sniffed, confirming to herself that nothing was coming and, even better, that there was more food nearby. That new smell came from inside the den that she had crushed the Two-Legs against. Redback deftly used her claws to enlarge the hole she had made with her charge, and then she forced her giant frame inside. There she found dried fish, beans, and grains. Redback ate and ate to subdue the hunger that had been driving her half mad. Once her belly was finally full, she went back outside, selected the Two-Legs that looked like it had the most eating on it, and picked it up in her giant mouth before sauntering back into the Mountain, satiated and proud once more, having eaten her deserved fill and restored her honor as the rightful master of all she surveyed.

Chapter 3

Before Terminal Point

"We will now form an expeditionary squad to kill the bear."

Mei stood on her balcony, surveying the forty-one able-bodied old women gathered in the clearing below. The day had started with the terrible news of the ransacked stores and the mangled bodies, and Mei had wasted no time in hastily assembling the inhabitants of Dendera from their respective houses.

"This hateful beast has declared war on Dendera! It ate our supplies and killed four of our friends," Mei declared. "It must be killed. We must have a bear hunt!"

"Ms. Mei. It's a fine thing to see you so lively this early in the morning, and an expeditionary squad is all very well, but can we actually win against this bear? That is my question." Hono had stepped forward from the crowd and was looking up at Mei. The sun had only just risen above the peak of the Mountain, casting a light on Hono's back.

"Don't be a coward. It's just a dumb beast! How can we lose?"

"But we have no experience fighting bears. We don't know how to fight them. We have no rifles."

"We have the numbers!" Mei rasped, licking her crusty lips. "There are enough of us. What chance does a bear have if we are united against it?"

Her war cry seemed to have a rousing effect on the rabble of old women assembled below, and there were shouts of agreement, one after another, until it seemed they were all speaking with one voice. The old women had nowhere to run and nowhere to hide, so perhaps it was only natural that, when backed into a corner, their decision was to fight.

Kayu Saitoh kept her cool amidst this fighting spirit, but she agreed with the idea of a do-or-die expeditionary squad. She understood that Dendera was the only place that the old women—herself included—could survive, and that if a bear threatened its existence then it was only natural to resist. She also agreed to some extent with Hono, or at least understood where she was coming from. However much the inhabitants of Dendera might have wanted to stand strong and united, the fact was that they didn't have any rifles, or the strength of the men of the Village, only their pathetic makeshift weapons and the weakness of old women.

"If we're going to hunt down this bear then let's do it quickly, before it gets the chance to eat Sasaka's body." Kyu Hoshina's voice rose from the throng.

Kyu had Climbed the Mountain seventeen years ago, the same year as Shigi Yamamoto, but unlike Shigi she had not been immediately rescued by the inhabitants of Dendera. Neither had she simply died on the Mountain. Instead, she survived by herself for three full years before finally discovering Dendera on her own. As such, she was a credible voice among the Hawks, second only to Mei in terms of her influence over the others.

"That's right. We need to bring Sasaka's corpse back before it's too late. So that we can give her a proper burial along with these others!" Mei looked down pointedly at the basket at her feet.

It was full of the remnants of the bodies of the old women killed by the bear.

Kayu Saitoh couldn't see the fleshy remnants clearly as they were hidden by the basket. It all seemed so pointless to her. The women had endured, they had suffered, they had fought, and then they had been eaten by a bear that had no conception of what they had been through. And that was all, a meaningless ending. Kayu Saitoh felt something akin to sympathy for those women, and it wasn't an unpleasant feeling.

"Yeah, we need to find the rest of Sasaka as soon as we can," Kyu said.

To say that Sasaka's corpse was incomplete was an understatement. The other corpses had also been chewed to the point of desecration, but they could at least be identified. In the case of Sasaka, however, only her head had been left behind, and there had been a trail of blood leading away, so the prevailing verdict was that her body had been dragged off into the Mountain. Kayu remembered being told by the menfolk back in the Village how a bear would always take its fresh-caught prey to a safe place before it started feasting on it.

"I don't even care whether you're a Hawk or a Dove!" Mei yelled. "Our Dendera has been attacked! This thing decimated our food supplies, killed four of our number, and dragged Sasaka's remains into the Mountain! So who will step forward? Who has the courage to lay their life on the line? Raise your hands!"

Kayu Saitoh's hand was the first to shoot up, causing quite a stir.

It might have been only her fourth day in Dendera, but she had already acquired quite a reputation for herself—and not in a good way—as a complainer, unhappy with the very existence of Dendera. The other old women were understandably surprised, then, when Kayu Saitoh was the first to volunteer for a mission that was potentially suicidal. Hono looked at Kayu Saitoh as though she were being betrayed.

"This has nothing to do with Hawks or Doves, right?" Kayu Saitoh said, defiantly meeting Hono's gaze, then looking up at Mei.

"I'd like to volunteer too," said Kyu, jumping forward. She smiled at Kayu Saitoh, and her face, as sun-blackened as the chief's, possessed such intensity that Kayu Saitoh could hardly believe this was a woman seventeen years her senior.

The expeditionary squad ended up consisting of Mei, Kayu, Kyu, Makura, Somo, Hatsu, Kotei, Ate, Chinu, Hikari, Soh, Tai, Koto, Naki, Nokobi, Itsuru, Kaga, Guri, Tsugu, Tsuina, Tahi, Ume, Kan, Mitsugi, Shima, Usuma, Hyoh, Tema, Mumi, Tamishi, and Tsusa, numbering thirty-one in total. Hawks and Doves alike were welcomed, and members of both volunteered, but the final numbers were skewed toward the Hawks. Hono held out till the end, flatly refusing to volunteer.

As the series of steely-eyed, determined women stepped forward one by one to coalesce into the expeditionary squad, Kayu Saitoh noticed one woman out on a limb, going against the flow. This woman had long white hair that hung over her face, obscuring her features. The woman stood straight and was dressed well enough, by Dendera's standards, but the way her hair just fell over her face was incongruous to Kayu Saitoh—it made her look weird, unnatural. As Kayu Saitoh thought this, a sudden burst of fresh air blew through the clearing, lifting the woman's fringe up so that Kayu Saitoh managed to catch a fleeting glimpse of the face underneath.

It was Masari Shiina.

Masari Shiina, who had lost her left eye in that ugly Moutain Barring affair, seemed equally as unconcerned by her thick fringe as she did the expeditionary squad, and she simply walked back toward her house.

Once the expeditionary squad was satisfied that the sun had risen far enough in the east, they made their way into the Mountain. It was Mountain Climbing season, of course, but the actual Climbing always took place between noon and evening, so the chance of accidentally running into a Villager was minimal, and the hastily taken straw-poll consensus of the old women was that this slim chance was a risk worth taking given that time was of the essence, and that a sudden flurry of snow could cover up the bloody tracks at any time to make pursuit impossible, and that furthermore it was already a race against time if they wanted to recover Sasaka's corpse while it was still in a semblance of good shape. And so it came to pass that the expeditionary squad charged eagerly up the Mountain without the women even taking the time to partake of their morning gruel, without even taking the time to stop for water. It was hardly surprising, then, that the pathless climb was quick to take its toll on the even-more-than-usually-famished Kayu Saitoh, whose breathing became ragged and uneven. She used her wooden spear as a walking stick as she pushed herself along through the white mountainscape following the red blood tracks, but that could last only so long, and soon she found that her legs would no longer carry her, and her feet slipped away beneath her, landing her on the soft snow. As Kayu Saitoh watched the rest of the expeditionary squad charge ahead determinedly, a memory from her past floated into her mind.

Last year had seen crop shortages in the Village, but that paled into insignificance compared to the great famine of ten years ago that had brought the Village to its knees. The Villagers had resorted to desperate measures, surviving on thin soup with tiny dumplings made of vegetable scraps and the flour left at the bottom of mortars, or by chewing on roots like wild animals. Before long the last of the Village's livestock had perished, and the last ounce of nutrition had been wrung out of their withered carcasses, and then the Village had faced the real prospect of mass starvation. It was against this backdrop that a decision was taken to relax the normally rigid rules surrounding Climbing the Mountain. At a household's discretion, its elders could now be sent to Climb the Mountain even if they had yet to reach the age of seventy. Kayu Saitoh had been sixty at the time and had wanted to go herself, but her son and in-laws refused to send her. Other families were quicker to take advantage of the new rule, however, and that year had seen ten women—Tai, Kaga, Guri, Tsugu, Tsuina, Tahi, Ume, Kan, Mitsugi, and Shima—all Climb the Mountain, even though they were all technically underage. All ten of the premature Climbers were here now on the hunting expedition. Even with the ten years that had passed, Kaga was only sixty-seven years old, and Tsugi was still only sixty-two. From her prone position amidst the thick snow Kayu Saitoh couldn't help but feel a pang of envy at their relative youth, but then she considered that most of those who had to Climb the Mountain that year were now older than she, and she pulled herself together and forced herself to stand up again and push on.

The expeditionary squad was moving through the Mountain at a fair pace, and before long Kayu Saitoh started to notice things about the way the more experienced women moved, how there seemed to be a knack of sorts. They were lifting their legs in a way that allowed them to spring against the ground, to utilize the momentum of each step rather than allow it to be absorbed into the ground. Kayu Saitoh attempted to follow suit and found that it made an immediate and noticeable improvement. This discovery lifted her spirits, and she sped up, only to trip and fall again—her earlier exertion had taken its toll. A figure ahead doubled back and appeared beside Kayu Saitoh, holding out a hand to help her up. It was Kyu.

"I can stand on my own," Kayu Saitoh snapped, hastily gathering herself back up. She wasn't about to let an eighty-seven-year-old rescue her.

"Sure, I know where you're coming from. You want to *pull your weight*, right?" Kyu, stinking of sweat and grime, grinned at Kayu Saitoh. "Ms. Hatsu told me all about you. That's the spirit, kid!"

"But I'm not pulling my weight. I'm a burden," said Kayu Saitoh, disgusted with herself.

"Hey. Before you start kicking yourself, isn't there something else you should do?" Kyu said.

"Huh? What?"

"Why, *walk*, of course! Lift your legs! First one and then the other! You can wish all you like, but you won't get anywhere until you start walking! Now, come on. With me!"

Urged on by Kyu, Kayu Saitoh managed to get some of her breath back. The clouds of white vapour emerging from her mouth flowed more steadily. She moved one leg and then the other, and soon she was walking at a decent speed again.

"That's it. Remember, take it at your own pace," Kyu said from behind, gently encouraging her. And then, "By the way, Ms. Kayu, I've been wanting to ask you. Why are you always so *angry* all the time?"

This new line of conversation stopped Kayu Saitoh in her tracks. She certainly hadn't considered herself the angry sort before. Certainly not compared to the hot-blooded Hawk faction of Dendera. Indeed, she had always thought of herself as one of the reasonable, levelheaded ones.

"The word in Dendera is that you were actually looking forward to Climbing the Mountain, Ms. Kayu. That you wanted to go to Paradise. Would that be the reason for your anger, perhaps?" Kyu was walking right beside Kayu Saitoh now. "I do believe that you are the only one who thinks this way."

"Yes, well," Kayu Saitoh said, breaking her silence in spite of herself, "that's what gives you a reason to live, isn't it? You wouldn't want to live on if you believed in Paradise."

"Actually, speaking for myself, I do believe in Paradise," Kyu said.

"What? Really?" Kayu Saitoh's tone betrayed her surprise.

"Sure. Your body may disappear, but what happens to your thoughts and memories? Where do they go? Where do they fly to? I can't imagine they hang around here on the ground, can you?"

"So you're saying we fly away to Paradise?" Kayu Saitoh asked.

"Well, yes. Paradise is the name given to the place to where the memories of the dead travel. That's what I believe, anyway."

"Kyu. Answer me this then. If you believe in Paradise, why didn't you accept your death?" Kayu Saitoh said, her tone now uncomprehending, more than angry. "I heard that you somehow survived for three whole years on your own in the Mountain."

"Why didn't I accept my death?" Kyu said. "Why, because I didn't *want* to go to Paradise, of course."

"Even though you believe in it..."

"I survived by eating worms and weeds, Ms. Kayu, worms and weeds. It was a... harsh time. My face went black from sunburn, as you can see, and I lost all my teeth. Why do you think I put up with all this? *Because it's better than having to go to Paradise,* of course. That's what I think, anyway. You're in pain? Suffering? Fine, you're still *alive,* that's what matters, that's what's important. When you're alive you can walk, like we are now, or talk, like we are now."

Kyu laughed loudly, and as she did her mouth opened out into a gummy, toothless grin. Presumably malnutrition had claimed whatever of her teeth she still had on the day she entered the Mountain. Then Kyu's face turned serious again, and she solemnly whispered that not being able to speak anymore was the thing she feared most of all. Kayu Saitoh realized that Kyu was talking about her friend Sasaka Yagi. Kayu Saitoh recalled how close the two women had been and remembered the day Sasaka had Climbed the Mountain, how Kyu, younger than Sasaka and left behind, had bawled her eyes out right in front of the whole sending-off party, even though such a thing was considered unseemly on what was supposed to be a joyous occasion.

The memory was not enough to make Kayu Saitoh's next words any more sympathetic, however. "Well, Sasaka's not going to Paradise now, is she?" Kayu Saitoh blurted out. "She had her chance to Climb the Mountain, but she ran away from her fate, and now she's been killed by a bear."

"Ms. Kayu, why must you always be like that? So harsh and unyielding?" Kyu asked, still walking beside Kayu. "You know, when I first discovered Dendera, I was overjoyed, truly I was. I would be able to live with everyone again, and damn the Village and its rules. Don't you feel like that at all, Ms. Kayu? Not even a little bit? Weren't you *happy* when you discovered that the people you thought were dead were actually still alive? Didn't you feel any *joy*?"

Kayu Saitoh was a human being, of course, and the truth was that she couldn't deny that she had felt something like that. When she first saw Makura again, or Mei, she had been almost overcome with feelings of nostalgia, of memories of good times past, and Kayu Saitoh supposed that these feelings could be called *happiness* or *joy*, if you had to put a name to them. No, it wasn't that Kayu Saitoh didn't feel happy. Rather, it was that her other feelings—disappointment at not reaching Paradise and anger toward the cravens who insisted on defying the tradition of Climbing the Mountain just so that they could scratch out a few more miserable years—these feelings were stronger, and they crowded out her positive emotions. The very fact of these women's continued existence riled Kayu Saitoh; they made her feel filthy, unclean. And anyone who can make you feel like that, well—it's easy enough to suppress any feelings of sympathy or love that you might otherwise have felt toward them.

Unable to articulate all these conflicting emotions, though, Kayu Saitoh simply said, "When you get to Paradise you are granted eternal happiness."

"Eternal happiness? As if such a thing could exist," Kyu fired back. "So you believe that once you are in Paradise you'll be perfectly happy forever and ever. You really believe that?"

"Well, won't I?" Kayu Saitoh said, defiant.

"As far as I can tell, Paradise is just a place where people's thoughts and dreams go, so it'll be just as full of hope and despair and anger and wishes as anywhere else. Can you really call that happiness? No, when you die, nothing changes and nothing ends."

"So when are we going to be able to finally rest in peace?" Kayu Saitoh asked.

"There's no peace. No rest. *That's* why we all have to carry on living, as best we can." And with that, Kyu disappeared off into the distance.

It was an irritating conclusion to a disturbing conversation—there was no closure for Kayu Saitoh, no satisfaction. It would have been far easier to deal with if Kyu had simply denied the existence of Paradise, but no, she had to go and decide what Paradise was *like*, and it troubled Kayu Saitoh; it gave her thoughts she didn't want to have. Determined to banish the unease from her mind, Kayu Saitoh concentrated on picking up her pace as she ascended the snowy slope in an effort to catch up with the rest of the expeditionary squad ahead of her.

At the plain at the top of the slope, the squad were standing still, focusing intently on their surroundings, bristling at every flurry of snow falling from the branches of the surrounding trees. They were fixed intently on their course: to recover the corpse of Sasaka. Now and then, Mei advanced nimbly forward, giving signals to the others to follow or to spread out. The expeditionary squad had been divided into smaller units, and Ate, Hatsu, Somo, and Naki clustered around a fir tree on an outcrop up front, with Makura, Soh, Kaga, Guri, and Ume positioned at another fir tree some way away from that one, while Kotei, Hikari, Tai, Tahi, and Tamishi stood next to a creeping pine positioned some way behind the two fir trees, while Chinu, Koto, Shima, Hyoh, Tema, and Tsusa were in a linear formation with Nokobi, Itsuru, Kyu, Tsugu, Tsuina, Kan, Mitsugi, Usuma, and Mumi forming another line behind them. Mei herself was positioned sideways on, giving her a full view from which to survey and command her assembled troops. When Mei saw that Kayu Saitoh had finally arrived, she narrowed her eyes and grumbled how Kayu Saitoh was late.

Kayu Saitoh ignored Mei's comment and just asked, "Any sign of Sasaka, then?"

"This is where the trail of blood stops. Kayu Saitoh, you go line up over there with the others."

Kayu Saitoh made to move toward the rear wall that she had been assigned to, but suddenly Kayu Saitoh sensed an immense, looming presence somewhere behind her, causing her to tremble. It happened so quickly, without warning, out of nowhere. Kayu Saitoh hadn't seen anything, hadn't heard anything, and hadn't understood anything. And she didn't need to.

A mass of blackness emerged.

It appeared from the direction of the creeping pine. Kotei, Hikari, Tai, Tahi, and Tamishi all just about managed to leap or roll out of the way of the black bundle as it charged at them, but the ferocity and the suddenness of the attack, combined with the uneven, precarious surface of the ground, meant that they all ended up collapsed in heaps on the snowy earth. The black mass's momentum continued unabated, however, and now it was charging toward the old women posted at the fir tree on the outcrop. Makura, visibly disturbed by this development, was waving her wooden spear to and fro and shouting some incomprehensible war cry, and then the black mass split in two, and the smaller half barrelled into Ume, tossing her body into the air as if it were a child's doll.

"Bear!" someone cried.

Kayu Saitoh had already ascertained that much for herself, of course, but was nevertheless surprised, both by the fact that the bear that had assaulted Dendera yesterday had a cub and by the implication that therefore the bear must have been female. She had heard that with bears, as with humans, it was the female that weaned the child. But this bear was so big! Even on all fours, it was easily as tall as a horse.

Its legs, like logs.

Its shoulders, towering like a mountain range.

Its belly, thick and strong.

Its claws, hook-shaped and black as treacle.

Its head, looming massive, even compared to its already huge body.

Its fangs, fully bared, menacing.

Its eyes, small, deep-set, the color of night.

And its red hair that sprouted down its back.

The last vestiges of night had disappeared, and morning had fully broken, but that didn't change the fact that somehow this awesome creature had been living in the Mountain and with a child to boot.

The creature roared.

The roar was a challenge and a declaration. *Submit to me, you weaklings. I am stronger than you by far. There is nothing you can do to stop the carnage that is to come.*

The old women, startled by the creature's sudden appearance, were in disarray, screaming and scrambling to get out of the she-bear's line of fire. The beast paused for a moment to scan the scene with its beady eyes and then charged again toward the two lines of old women. In an instant the lines crumbled as the women dispersed as quickly as they could, some running to try and scramble up a nearby tree, others tumbling down the mountainside, and yet others discarding their wooden spears and rolling themselves up into tight balls. Pathetic whimpers and cries echoed throughout the Mountain as the she-bear roamed as she pleased, treating the old women like so many playthings.

Kayu Saitoh started to clamber up a slope to her side and found that someone was tailing her. It was Kyu. Kyu was using two wooden spears almost as crutches to help propel her along. The two women's eyes met, and although neither of them made any signal, a mutual understanding somehow seemed to be formed. They acted in tandem. They turned to stand their ground between two trees and blocked the path. Sure enough, the she-bear appeared in front of them, bearing down powerfully, throwing chunks of snow into the air in its wake. Its movement was also surprisingly fast, nimble even. Surprising to Kayu Saitoh, that is, for she had never known just how agile a bear could be, and this cruel new discovery imbued her with a fresh sense of dread, but even so she managed to hold her nerve and keep her wooden spear firmly outstretched in front of her, bracing in anticipation of that moment when the she-bear finally barrelled into her. The she-bear closed in on her and closed in again, but the impact never came, for the she-bear stopped suddenly in her tracks in front of the two old women. Kayu Saitoh was now barely a spear's length away from the she-bear.

The she-bear's nose twitched, and she seemed to be evaluating the two women that now stood in front of her. Behind the she-bear was the cub, anxious and wary. The cub's eyes showed not anger or hostility but something closer to fear. Kayu Saitoh decided that the cub was not what she needed to be worried about now and focused her attention on the much more imminent threat of its mother.

The she-bear stood tall on its hind legs and outstretched its front legs.

Standing tall, the she-bear was now over twice as big as before. Kayu Saitoh's entire field of vision was now dominated by russet-brown fur.

"What did you do with Sasaka..." Kyu's voice was trembling, but she too managed to hold her ground.

The she-bear, of course, didn't answer. Kayu Saitoh looked at the animal's sturdy paws, huge balls of flesh from which five thick claws protruded. An image flashed through Kayu Saitoh's mind of the scene of carnage this morning by the food stores, and she felt like she wanted to shrink away into nothingness, but then she thought of how Kyu was using her righteous anger toward the she-bear to bolster her courage, and Kayu Saitoh tried her best to do the same. But the fact was that unlike Kyu, Kayu Saitoh did not truly belong to Dendera, and in her listlessness she still even now couldn't help but feel somewhat detached, not truly angry. No, she was living in a void. She could survive all right, but not truly draw strength from her surroundings, not when she believed in nothing. Kayu Saitoh didn't know what to do next, and that sense of unease welled up again inside her. She knew full well that any sign of weakness would be pounced upon by the she-bear—figuratively and literally—but still she could do nothing. Her spirit had been broken once, and who could spring back from that on command, as if nothing had happened? Kayu Saitoh's ears were filled with an uncomfortable clattering sound, and she realized that it was the sound of her own teeth chattering together. She would die now, she thought. She would die and never reach Paradise, but rather she would be cast into the void forever.

The she-bear stood there, on its haunches, staring at the two women, but then it placed its front paws back down on the ground and abruptly turned away before heading off into the mountains, its red back rapidly becoming a distant memory as its cub scurried off to follow.

The immediate threat had dissipated, just like that, but Kayu Saitoh remained rooted to the spot, frozen. The same was true of Kyu. Both of them remained that way until the other old women finally caught up to them and tapped them hesitantly on their backs and shoulders to help Kayu Saitoh and Kyu snap out of the daze. Once Kayu Saitoh regained her faculties somewhat, she noticed in the distance the figure of Ume being dug out of the snow. Ume, the sole casualty in the recent attack, turned out to be miraculously unscathed—the soft snow seemed to have cushioned the blow after being hurled through the air.

Mei raised her staff into the air, declaring that now was their chance to find Sasaka's body. The rest of the women, however, were overcome with helplessness in the face of the she-bear's might, and they were now more a disorderly mob than a fighting unit capable of taking orders. No one seemed to hear Mei's command, and instead they started huddling together as a mass, each woman jostling for a safer place in the center. It was only when Kyu took action that the disorderly squabbling finally stopped. Kyu forced her still-wobbling body onward and started on an unsteady course after the bears, disappearing deeper and deeper into the mountains. Hatsu, seeing this, sternly admonished the others, asking if they were going to just let their sister go off and get killed, and then she followed after Kyu. Eventually, the rest of the women started to pull themselves together and went after Hatsu.

It was Mitsugi who, before long, gave a loud yelp as she was searching near a fir tree. She had discovered a large mound of snow and blood scattered all around. Mitsugi started brushing away at the snow to reveal pieces of cloth and chunks of flesh. The white robe, soaked in blood. Pieces of straw that had once been an overcoat. A right arm, hand missing its ring finger. Two legs, covered in deep bite marks. That was all that could be found. The rest had evidently been eaten.

"Sasaka..." Kyu burst forward, ignoring the women around her who tried to stop her from seeing the grim remains of her friend. The moment Kyu set eyes on the dismembered pieces of flesh, her face went white, her eyes blank, and she collapsed, insensible, to the snowy ground.

It was just after noon when the expeditionary squad returned to Dendera, carrying with it the unconscious body of Kyu and the remnants of Sasaka.

2

"I need you all to listen to me while you eat!" Mei Mitsuya said from her balcony.

Immediately after the expeditionary squad arrived back at Dendera, the chief gathered to the clearing the forty-one inhabitants who could still walk. Not even having been given time to eat, they squatted uncomfortably, faces and lips wind-chapped, eating potatoes, looking up sullenly at Mei Mitsuya on her balcony.

"I've decided that we will postpone our plans for attacking the Village. Killing this bear has to come first." The chief's voice sounded reluctant, as if she were admitting defeat. "As such, we will need a new expeditionary force."

There was no response. The old women were, to put it simply, exhausted, and they had nothing more to give. It was all they could do to pick away at the sprouts on the cold potatoes and shove the rest into their mouths. It was no time for thinking, let alone making difficult decisions.

"Next, food," Mei Mitsuya continued, visibly irritated at the lack of response. "The storehouse was raided and we lost almost all of our potatoes, corn, beans, dried meat, and fish."

"Is there nothing left?" This question that emerged from the gathering was enough to cause the hitherto lethargic women to perk up. Starvation, after all, was their biggest fear. Even the new threat of the bear paled in comparison with the all-pervading reality of dying through a lack of food.

"The other storehouse is fine. But the reality is we've lost half of our supplies. So, as from today, there will be no more daily potato ration. There'll be less to go around from the communal pot too. And it's all the bear's fault—don't forget that! Until we do something about this creature, there will be no attack on the Village and no hope for Dendera's future."

The potatoes in the women's hands now felt scarce, valuable, and where many of the women used to wolf them down, now they started nibbling at them gingerly, savoring the taste, not knowing when they would have the chance to experience it again. Their sense of unease about the bear started to crystallize into something stronger.

"You should all know that there will be no peace here until we kill the bear. No one will be able to sleep safely at night until the creature is dead." Mei was making sure that righteous indignation, fueled by a healthy dose of terror, was now the dominant feeling. "There is only one priority for us now. *Kill the bear.* The expeditionary squad will be on hunting detail every day! The other able-bodied women, gather food! And there will now be six guards posted to the storehouse at all times. The invalids will all be sheltered in the house at the west end of the village. That's far away from the storehouse, so they should be safe there. Be sure to move the invalids and their belongings promptly. Now. What else?"

Kyu Hoshina, who had recovered somewhat, stood up quietly. "When do we give Sasaka and the others their funerals?"

"This evening. We'll be busy hunting the bear from tomorrow, and we should do it sooner rather than later in any case. Kyu Hoshina, Hatsu Fukuzawa, Hikari Asami, Soh Kiriyama, Ume Itano. We'll use your house. Kyu Hoshina, you lead the ceremony. Anybody who wants to help with the funeral, speak to her directly. That's all for now. Now, nobody else get themselves killed!"

Having said what she wanted to say, Mei Mitsuya turned on her heels and retired to the second floor of her house.

What Kayu Saitoh really wanted to do now was eat her fill and then get some sleep, but she knew full well that the thin broth she had just finished eating was nowhere near enough to assuage her hunger pangs, and that in any case even if she were to try to close her eyes she would just be tormented by visions of her recent encounter with the bear. So she decided to lend Kyu Hoshina a hand with preparations for the funeral. Hatsu Fukuzawa, Somo Izumi, Itsuru Obuchi, Ate Amami, Tsugu Ohi, and Tamishi Minamide also offered to help. In truth, there wasn't much work actually involved. Suppressing the urge to retch at the odor, they separated the piles of flesh into four mounds, removed the roundish specks of fly-eggs that had accumulated on top of the tissue, and placed the pieces of the women into makeshift baskets. That was all there was to do. None in Dendera knew the sutras, and they had no white rice or ceremonial sake in any case.

"Kayu, come along with us, why don't you?" Hatsu Fukuzawa and Ate Amami called for her to join them as she tried to leave after the work was done. Then, for the first time since her arrival, Kayu Saitoh was given a proper tour of Dendera. Dendera ran lengthwise along the base of the Mountain. Mei Mitsuya's manor occupied the center, with the clearing directly in front. To the east stood the two storehouses, behind which continued five huts, each with some space separating it from the others. To the west, another four huts dotted the settlement. The women led Kayu Saitoh to the west, with the Mountain on their right-hand side. Passing the huts, they continued farther, into virgin snow. Just as Kayu Saitoh began to wonder whether she was still in Dendera or on the Mountain, she saw them.

A row of large stones jutted out of the snow. Next to them were wooden planks with names crudely etched into them.

Gravestones and stupa, Kayu Saitoh realized.

"This is where the people who died in Dendera rest," Hatsu Fukuzawa said, coming up beside her.

"Thirty years is a long time, after all. People die. Especially old people," Ate Amami continued. "Twenty-seven rest here in all. Well, it'll be thirty-one from tonight, I suppose."

"That many..." Kayu Saitoh was genuinely surprised.

"That's right, Kayu. All those people, people you knew, lived and worked here in Dendera. They gave their blood, sweat, and tears to help build this place up to what it is today. Dendera has history."

"What are you trying to say?"

"Can you really not tell? I'm simply trying to get you to see Dendera in a more favorable light." Ate Amami brushed snow off one of the gravestones. "You see, I always hated the idea of the Climb. It always seemed strange to me. You work hard all your life, you give your body and soul to growing food, bringing up your family, working for the Village, and then at the end of it all, just when you should be able to sit back and finally enjoy the fruits of all your labors, they take you to the top of the Mountain and dump you there. Does that really seem right to you?"

To Kayu Saitoh, though, the woman's words were little more than tiresome grumblings. "But you've always known!" she said. "You've always known you would Climb the Mountain once you turned seventy! How can you talk about it like it was somehow unexpected? Do you think you're fooling anyone?"

"You can think what you like," Ate Amami replied. "I'm just saying that the structure of the Village—and the Climb—seems strange."

"If the old people don't Climb the Mountain, the Village will run out of food. Our families would all suffer. Isn't that right?"

"I suppose so, but..."

"And while we're at it," Kayu Saitoh continued, "there's something I wanted to ask you Hawks."

"What is it?" Ate Amami asked.

Kayu Saitoh wanted to find the extent of their resolve. "Are you planning on killing your own children? And their families? That's what's going to end up happening if you attack the Village, right?"

"We—that is, the Hawks...have discussed this in some detail, of course. And we came to a decision." Ate Amami lowered her voice. "None of us will touch our own families or friends."

"So you'll have your family killed by someone else and return the favor, that's the idea?"

"Are you mocking us?" Ate Amami asked, her face serious.

"No," Kayu Saitoh said, equally serious. "It makes perfect sense. Who would want to kill their own children or their friends, after all?"

"When my son brought me up the Mountain, he was crying. He was a good boy." Ate Amami's expression was one of pure anguish. "That was eleven years ago. He'll be sixty-seven, now. He'll Climb the Mountain in three years."

Unrelenting, Kayu Saitoh said, "And because he's a man he won't be welcome in Dendera. Rejected by the Village *and* Dendera. In the end, everyone just becomes a burden. Why couldn't we have just died properly on the Mountain?"

"My son...is he well?" Ate Amami asked.

"Yes, he's fine." Kayu Saitoh nodded. "He's a hard worker, always looking out for the Village."

"That's good," Ate Amami said with a genuine smile. "And Kayu, how about your son? How old will he be now?"

"Fifty-five. And I suppose you lot want to murder him too? I won't allow it, you know!"

She was seething with anger now, but there was also something else—all the memories of her son and her family, all flooding back to her. It was overwhelming.

"As you say, Kayu. The more you think about it the more complicated it gets." Ate Amami looked up at the sky and then gradually back down to earth, gazing at the gravestones. "When I think of Dendera, what has happened here, and the thirty-one people who have died, it fills me with hatred, and I want to destroy everything, kill everyone. But then I think of the Village, and the children who live there, and I wonder whether perhaps I'm the villain."

"Then *don't* kill anyone. Just die yourself." Kayu Saitoh felt a reaction to that phrase—*villain*—but she covered it up. Why she reacted, and why she covered it up, she didn't know.

"The problem, Kayu, is that we are no longer the same people that we once were. Our world is no longer limited to just the Village and the Mountain. We are in Dendera now. Things are different. We can think in new ways."

"Oh, is *that* what it is? A *new way*? And here's me thinking you just want to attack the Village that brought you into this world and looked after you all these years. Disgraceful! You should be ashamed of yourself," Kayu said.

"Come on, Kayu." Hatsu Fukuzawa broke her silence. "Look at

where you are. Standing before these graves. Can you really still say that, here of all places?"

"I'll say it wherever I am," Kayu Saitoh said.

"These people, they all wanted to *live*. They didn't want to die. They survived, best they could. Who are you to deny them that?" Hatsu Fukuzawa squatted down in front of one of the graves and brushed away some of the snow that had settled on it. "Look, it's so cold here that even the stone is cracking."

It's not like I killed her, Kayu Saitoh thought, but she couldn't find the right words to say it out loud. She felt as if her throat were jammed with jagged little pebbles, and she realized it was becoming harder for her to proclaim her thoughts and beliefs with confidence. She still wanted to Climb the Mountain, she would try to tell herself in her heart of hearts, but there was something about the words that rang false now. She didn't want it to be false, of course, not for one moment, and she was still disgusted by the cowardliness of the women who chose to live in Dendera, but she found that when she put those thoughts into words they seemed too simplistic, almost glib. She realized that she herself was now tarnished with the same brush, and she thought again about Ate Amami's *villains* and realized that even though she herself was hardly in the same category as the others, perhaps the label could be applied to her too.

"If we attack the Village, I may have to end up killing Ate's or Somo's sons and friends," Hatsu Fukuzawa said, standing up. "In truth, it'll probably be hard."

"Then *don't* kill anyone. Just die yourself." Kayu Saitoh found herself using the same words again.

"You can say that, but I'm *going* to kill them. And I'm *not* going to die." Hatsu Fukuzawa met her stare. "Do you know why? Because I'm a part of Dendera. I don't belong to the Village anymore."

"Well look at you, with your new life and new creed, all full of yourself."

"I'd say the same to you. You're even more dishonest than we are. You're even more conceited than us. You don't take a stance on anything and just complain about everything. *You* should be ashamed. You're the villain. Why don't you try making a decision and acting on it?"

Hatsu Fukuzawa's words hit the mark, but Kayu Saitoh didn't intend to change the way she thought, so she left the two old women and the twenty-seven gravestones. She thought about life and death and allowing people to live or killing them instead. In the end, she wanted to hear from people who lived as if they were dead, and so she walked to the westernmost hut. An emotion whirled about in the back of her mind, neither elation nor anxiety.

Six women were in the hut. Two were Mitsugi Kaneda and Shima Iijima, three she couldn't quite place, and the last was Kura Kuroi.

Kura Kuroi was nearly skin and bones. She had become even more gaunt than when Kayu Saitoh last saw her. Her head, its cranium bulbous, seemed oddly large, and her body paper-thin. The white robe truly suited her.

"Oh, Kayu," Kura Kuroi said from where she lay on the hard floor. She turned her head with apparent weight. "I thought you'd come visit me sooner. It took you so long. Well? What's wrong? Why are you so quiet? It's me. Look, I'm alive, aren't I? I'm no corpse yet. I'm still all here. You have nothing to fear. You have no reason to be sad. You have no reason to be so quiet."

Finally, with considerable effort, Kayu Saitoh forced herself to say, "You can talk, that's for sure. You're in good spirits."

Spreading out straw on the floor, Mitsugi Kaneda said, "You, give me a hand. We have to prepare their bedding."

Kayu Saitoh nodded, and as she helped pull apart the piles of straw left near the dirt-floor entrance, she looked around at the women. One of them she hadn't recognized at first, due to the woman's advancing age and the grime that caked her hair and skin, she now saw was Seto Matsuura. The woman's Climb had taken place twenty-one years earlier. Back in the Village, the younger women had sought her advice. Now, she appeared to have gone completely senile, huddled over like a monkey, her mouth hanging open for no reason. Thinking her unsightly, Kayu Saitoh focused on pulling apart the straw. A cluster of straw slid off the top of the pile and hit the back of one of the sitting women, who flailed and fell over more than was strictly necessary. This too was unsightly, so Kayu Saitoh told her to get out of the way.

"Ah, she can't," Shima Iijima said. "She's blind."

That meant the woman was Sayore Nosaka. Then Kayu Saitoh remembered the last one. She was Noi Komatsu, who hadn't the mind to count beans, let alone remember anyone's face, but she could draw beautiful pictures in sand, and paint with crushed-flower watercolors. People like Sayore Nosaka and Noi Komatsu, if without husbands or children, were allowed to live together in a house outside the Village, but no matter their mental faculties or any other personal circumstances, all had to go to the Mountain once they turned seventy.

"So these are the cripples, then?" Kayu Saitoh asked.

Mitsugi Kaneda nodded and said, "The woman in your hut, Shigi Yamamoto—she's the same way, but she doesn't ever leave there."

Still lying on the floor, Kura Kuroi grinned and said, "Kayu, even in Dendera, you're the diligent worker I always knew. I'm impressed. I've never seen you complain about anything, not once. You go about each day with this serene look about you. I don't know how you do it. It's a mystery to me."

"And I've never seen you complain," Kayu Saitoh said, continuing her work. "Even though you've always been stuck with that body."

In her weak voice, Kura Kuroi replied, "I got used to it, that's all."

"What about the bear?" Sayore Nosaka asked, looking nowhere near whomever she was addressing. "Can it be killed?"

"Ah, we'll be fine," Shima Iijima said, wiping at the base of her neck. "The chief is committed to bringing it down."

"It's too bad I can't help. If only my eyes worked, I would give that bear a licking."

Mitsugi Kaneda chuckled. "There's more than your eyes that's clouded. Keep quiet and get some rest. Leave the bear to the young and able. Once we've killed the beast, you can have your fill of meat."

"I'll be looking forward to that. Since I've come here, I haven't had a single piece of meat bigger than my fingertip."

"That bear was incredible," Shima Iijima said. She turned her head toward the ceiling, as if looking up at the giant in her imagination. "It was *that* big. There'll be enough bear to fill all of our stomachs."

"That'll be a relief," Kura Kuroi said. "I've been so hungry that any one of these days now my old belly will be gone."

Mitsugi Kaneda joked, "I think your stomach's the only part of you that works right."

A wave of modest laughter spread through the women. Only Kayu Saitoh and Noi Komatsu didn't join in. Noi Komatsu swiftly arranged the straw on the floor into a depiction of the river that flowed just beyond the Village's fields. Kayu Saitoh had gone there to fetch water many times each day.

When Kayu Saitoh had finished her task and was about to leave, Kura Kuroi called to her.

"Kayu, what do you think? How do you like living here?"

"I'd rather not answer."

"Yeah. I thought you'd say that," Kura Kuroi said. "I *knew* you'd say that. But this is our new life. You can accept it, you can reject it, you can ignore it, but you have to use your head. You're resilient, and you've got spirit, but you're not bright. When faced with the unfamiliar, you go this way and that. I know that about you."

"Kura Kuroi, are you a Hawk?"

"Certainly not." She shook her head. "I could never attack the Village. My little brother, who took such good care of me, lives there... Though I'm no Dove either. What about you, Kayu? Are you the same way? Have you thought about it?"

"I'm a Dove," Sayore Nosaka said. She unfolded her legs and tilted her head, favoring her ears over her eyes. "I don't know anyone in the Village, and they never took care of me right, so I wouldn't mind if the Village went away. But I'm blind; if Dendera is destroyed by the fight, I won't be able to survive on my own."

Kayu Saitoh looked into the woman's unseeing eyes. "I envy you, Sayore Nosaka. Everything's so simple for you. The rest of us have it complicated. It's hard for us to kill and to live."

"Nonsense. It's easy for you; you can see." There was an edge in Sayore Nosaka's voice. "I couldn't kill anyone without help, and neither could I live. It's a hardship. Well, I suppose it's the people who can't speak for themselves who really have it tough."

Seto Matsuura remained seated in silence, and Noi Komatsu was rearranging the straw into a new picture. As Kayu Saitoh looked to these two women who couldn't speak for themselves, she realized that she was avoiding what she had been wanting to say.

She glanced to Kura Kuroi, and when she spoke, she was surprised at how the words caught in her throat. "Can I be honest with you?"

"Sure," Kura Kuroi replied. "I won't mind."

"Kura Kuroi...after you went to the Mountain, I felt alone. My husband had already gone, you see. I had my son and his wife, but that's not what I mean. I felt *alone*. And yet...I was at peace. I was relieved because I could Climb the Mountain." She looked away from her friend. "I wasn't afraid of it, and I didn't resent it. All I wanted was to reach Paradise, and all I had to do was Climb the Mountain. Do you understand?"

"I do."

"But we're all still alive," Kayu Saitoh said.

"We are," Kura Kuroi said. "We have failed to die."

"I talked with some of the Hawks, and while they're conflicted about certain aspects of it, they seem like they really do want to attack the Village. They're going to kill everyone they know, even their own children." She thought to her conversation with Hatsu Fukuzawa and Ate Amami. "I wanted to go to Paradise. That's all. I won't join the Hawks."

Right away, Kura Kuroi said, "But you also won't join the Doves. You want to die, so that much is obvious."

"But you changed your ways; you want to live now."

"Changed my ways? What an odd way to put it."

"When we were both in the Village," Kayu Saitoh explained, "you told me you wished you could Climb the Mountain even sooner. But when you were rescued, you were grateful, weren't you? What a change of heart!"

"This is a nice place. Unlike the Village, here I don't feel guilty about being in this condition. Everyone here is equal. Everyone's an old hag with an empty belly. We're hungry ghosts. And we all know it about ourselves, so the able naturally help the disabled, and the disabled naturally accept the help."

Sayore Nosaka nodded. "That's how I feel. No matter what else, we're all simply nothing more than old women."

Summoning a feeling akin to courage, Kayu Saitoh looked to Kura Kuroi. "What you both said is true. We're all the same here. We're equally elders. We're equally women. And we're equally frail. But is that really all you have to say, Kura Kuroi? Be honest with me."

Kura Kuroi's eyes locked on to her, and their intensity didn't diminish as she answered. "In Dendera, to want to die is to be a villain," she said. "From your perspective, raiding the Village and living peacefully in Dendera are both wrong and shameful acts. I understand that. But I have to repeat myself: whoever believes that here is the greatest villain."

"And that's why you started wanting to live? Ridiculous. I can't change the way I think so easily. Kura Kuroi, are you...really happy to be alive? Are you fulfilled?"

"I am happy," Kura Kuroi said, and nothing more.

And so Kayu Saitoh needed to leave the hut.

Night came, and the funeral began.

For a funeral, it was a simple affair. The women could afford the ceremony no extravagances, and shared not a drop of sake nor lit a single stick of incense. They merely lined up the four baskets that held the victims' remains, clasped their hands in their respective ways and with their respective thoughts, and then left the hut. Ten remained until the end—Kayu Saitoh, Kyu Hoshina, Mei Mitsuya, Hatsu Fukuzawa, Soh Kiriyama, Inui Makabe, Ume Itano, Hikari Asami, Itsuru Obuchi, and Somo Izumi—and in the silence, they built a fire in the sunken hearth together. The flames turned the chief's face, already dark red with anger, into an even deeper red. Kyu Hoshina clasped her hands and didn't speak, while Ume Itano cried, her throat occasionally twitching. The only other sounds in the room were the popping of the fire and the women breathing out their noses to keep the stench of the remains at bay.

"Unforgivable," Mei Mitsuya said, breaking the silence.

Kyu Hoshina nodded in agreement and said, "I want to get that bear as soon as we can."

Itsuru Obuchi reached with her wrinkled arm and added a fresh log to the fire, then said, "Right, we won't be able to raid the Village until we kill the beast."

"Feh!" Mei Mitsuya exclaimed. "I bet that makes you Doves happy."

Her voice hoarse, Itsuru Obuchi said, "You always have so much energy. You're only six years older than me, yet you haven't changed a bit since you were a little girl. Are you really a hundred years old?"

Baring her yellowed teeth, the chief said, "I'm a demon now."

"We're all old here. No one would be mad at you if you took it easy."

"I'd be mad. And listen, Itsuru Obuchi, you're not old yet. You're on the expeditionary force, aren't you?"

"With a brown bear about, we can't idle. But anyway, why has the bear come in the middle of winter?"

"Maybe it doesn't have a den," Hikari Asami said, standing beside the earthen-floor entryway. "Bears typically hibernate through the winter, but if they're unable to store up enough fat, or if they can't find a hole the right size for their bodies . . . they will roam and forage."

Itsuru Obuchi asked, "And that bear hasn't found a—what was it, a den? The humans and the bears are all starving. It's tragic."

Hatsu Fukuzawa folded her arms and said, "But still, I've never heard of a bear attacking a place where people lived."

"The creature might think us weak," Itsuru Obuchi explained.

"After all, there's no one in Dendera but a bunch of old hags who have outlived their deaths."

"Itsuru Obuchi, that's enough of your crass remarks," the chief snapped.

"No, she might be right," Hatsu Fukuzawa said. "I've heard that bears are clever. Maybe it's figured out that we don't have any hunting rifles here."

"Like that damned brute has that much brains," the chief said.

"Bears," Hikari Asami said, "have sharp noses. And rifles smell of oil and gunpowder."

"Hikari Asami," the chief bellowed, "what is all this? How do you know so much about bears?"

"My husband...was a bear hunter. I've heard most all there is to know about them."

"I remember that now," the chief said, her expression calculating. "So, do you think we have a chance?"

"It'll be tough..."

"Why?"

"We don't have rifles," Hikari Asami said.

"But we have spears!" the chief countered.

"It's true that people used to hunt bears with spears before there were rifles, but even then, the hunters had steel spearheads. All we have here is...wood."

Somo Izumi cut in, saying, "What if we set a trap? We can dig an enormous hole and lure the bear to it. When the beast falls in, we clobber it."

"That's idiotic," Hatsu Fukuzawa said with a smile on her lips but nowhere else. "Why don't you try tossing one of those straw wadara rings of yours at it?"

"Stuff it," Somo Izumi retorted. "If a pit won't work, we can poison the thing."

"Poison it? With what? Where do we have anything like that?"

"Who cares what we use to kill it," Kyu Hoshina said, her hands still clasped, "as long as we do."

Hatsu Fukuzawa clapped Kyu Hoshina on the shoulder and said, "Let's avenge them together, Kyu."

"I'll be dead soon either way." Kyu Hoshina smiled weakly and separated her hands. "A bear's head won't be a bad prize to bring to the other world."

The chief said, "A bear's head, you say? That's a good one!" Arising, she stood before the four baskets and proclaimed, "We'll bring you the bear's head in offering. That should please you. You'll be able to rest in peace."

Kyu Hoshina said, "I hope they can reach Paradise. They didn't complete their Climb, but they were killed by the bear. I think the Mountain will forgive them."

Hatsu Fukuzawa said, "Right now, they're in Paradise eating all the bear meat they can fit in their stomachs," then shared a laugh with Kyu Hoshina.

The women had begun to regain their spirits, but Kayu Saitoh remained wordless. Her conversation with Kura Kuroi remained in her head, but that wasn't what bothered her—a strange noise had caught her attention for a little while now. She could hear it coming from the other side of the wall. It was a rustling. Something was moving out there. At first she thought it was snowflakes hitting the walls, but it wasn't snowing and the skies were clear, the moonlight illuminating the snowy ground. She stood to go see, when a rumbling came like she'd never heard, and a black shape burst through the wall, scattering the four baskets and their grisly contents. The black mass tossed Ume Itano aside and kicked over the hearth.

The moment the fire went out, Kayu Saitoh saw the clear image of the bear's face and forelegs.

3

After eating of the Two-Legs meat that she had brought back, Redback's stomach was finally full again. Together with her similarly full cub, she hid in the bamboo grass and slept. The cold air clung to her, but the food in her stomach warmed her body, and she was so very tired. Both she and her cub should have been hibernating in a den until spring's coming. Out here, even the simple act of breathing consumed their energy.

Whether bears dream or not remains unknown, but in Redback's slumber, she recalled the time when the mountain was bountiful. *Spikenard. Wild parsley. Grapes. Acorns. Salmon.* She thought of the time when such sources of nourishment abounded. As the products of nature, these foods weren't necessarily to be found in the same amounts each year; but Redback had never seen a year as mean as this one. The prolonged rains that had come at summer's end were the primary cause, affecting even the rivers. The cold currents rose, and not even the spawning salmon swam upstream, for the changes in water temperature and volume had sent the fishes' paths astray. Redback's food supply had vanished. Frustration at her empty stomach turned to rage, which then turned to hatred against the Two-Legs.

In truth, Redback feared the Two-Legs.

They could fell trees using some kind of strength unknown to her. They could inflict terrible pain upon her with those strange sticks. But without those strange, fire-spitting sticks, the Two-Legs were weak. They crumpled at a single blow.

Two-Legs were weak without those strange sticks.

And their meat was remarkably delicious and came in such volume that she couldn't finish it in one sitting. Even better, the Two-Legs were far easier prey than salmon or deer. Ruminating over these many blessings, Redback slept.

The next morning, she awoke amid feelings of satisfaction. Digging at the base of the fir tree, she unearthed her leftover meat. She touched her snout to her cub's cheek, awakening him, and coaxed the little bear to eat. With a joyful roar, he ate of the Two-Legs' meat, bones and all. As her cub was engrossed in his feast, Redback kept a protective watch, surveying their surroundings.

He was still young, having been birthed during her hibernation the winter before last. He had come out no bigger than a mouse, and she fed him her milk and consumed his excrement, and when the snow melted, his eyes opened, his teeth grew, and his body covered over with soft underfur and bristly guard hairs. He had started as a mouse but grown into a bear's body. Mother and son crawled out from their den, and she began raising him to be the next ruler of the domain. But this year, she had been too busy securing food to attend to his upbringing. Redback and her cub had trudged across the infertile mountainside. The seasons passed, and snow fell earlier than in most years. For the two to have missed their hibernation would have typically fated them to die of starvation. Such was the way of the wild. But Redback had battled the Two-Legs and won. Until now, Redback had lived on nature's bounty alone; this victory was the first step of her new life.

Her nose caught a scent. She signaled her cub to stop eating. He recognized the situation but didn't know how to properly react. As bits of saliva and gore dripped from his mouth, he sought shelter in her underbelly. Redback forced him away, returned the meat to the base of the fir tree, and dragged her cub into hiding within the bamboo grass.

She saw the Two-Legs climbing the mountain's slope.

They walked slowly enough that she needn't keep an eye on them. She signaled her plan to her cub, who was trembling, his ears pinned back. He twitched his nose and snorted, but Redback was resolute. Though sluggish, the Two-Legs were approaching. They seemed to have followed the blood trail, and Redback realized they had come to steal back her catch. When several of the creatures drew near to the bamboo grass where the mother and cub hid, Redback turned her resolve into action, spurring every muscle in her massive body into movement as she and her cub charged the group. The Two-Legs scattered into confused flight, clumsily tumbling down the slope. Next, Redback turned upon a cluster of Two-Legs that were wandering near the fir where she had hidden her meat. One was late in making an escape and flailed a stick about, not looking where it was swinging. To Redback, this was nothing to shy from, but she had taught her cub to fear the Two-Legs, and he veered from their charge. He crashed into a different Two-Legs but kept on running, seemingly oblivious. Redback pulled away from her attack and got her cub under control. He had been howling, overcome by confusion and discontent, but when he saw his mother, he was able to regain most of his composure, and he took his plump behind into hiding.

Redback turned to the Two-Legs and roared. Her voice resounded across the mountain, and when the echo died off, she could hear the forest's little creatures flee and resting birds take flight. The Two-Legs were no exception, and struck with fear, they let out weak cries and ran in all directions. Instead of moving to attack, Redback observed them. If her thoughts had words, they would have been this: Why had she been so frightened by them until now? How had they acted with such arrogance? For what reason do they exist?

Suddenly, she understood.

Again Redback charged. She charged, filled with even more confidence than before. Unwavering, her legs kicked against the ground and her head faced straight ahead. Redback was one life, with one will, in which dwelled one incredibly clear thought.

Kill and devour.

Keeping true to this thought, Redback displayed her power in a relentless rampage. The Two-Legs were no longer a threat but mere pieces of meat moving slowly about. Guided by instinct and her sense of supremacy, she pursued the Two-Legs as they climbed up trees and ran in circles screaming.

But then something happened that forced her to reconsider her actions toward the Two-Legs. It happened when she was charging up an incline after two of the fleeing creatures. She thought she had them cornered, when they turned on their heels and stood, taking a fighting stance, holding their sticks at the ready. Redback halted her charge. She recalled the fear she'd originally felt toward the Two-Legs. Hesitation began to take root within her. She tried to shake it off, standing upright on her hind legs to intimidate the creatures. But they didn't run. Redback and the Two-Legs faced each other, clashing in determination and pride. Her cub came up from behind. Distressed, he buried his nose into the side of her hindquarters. He still feared the Two-Legs and seemed deeply affected by the Two-Legs' menacing aura.

Redback had been the one to call the temporary truce. But she didn't simply retreat; she lowered her guard and her forelegs, and she turned, leaving her back exposed, and marched away with dignity. By exposing her rear and moving without urgency, she was signaling exactly how much she outmatched the Two-Legs. At the same time, she was testing the women's might. If they truly were strong, they would attack her when she was defenseless. But the Two-Legs didn't move. Once she was out of the creatures' sight, she ran at full speed, pulling her cub along, until they had built up a good distance.

Redback had cautiously taken her cub deep up the mountain, but when night came and she was hungry again, she returned. She intended to finish off the meat she'd hidden at the base of the fir but found that her food had been unearthed and stolen. Rage spread within her. The red fur on her back stood up, and she exuded her animal scent. The theft of her meat, her food, *her possessions,* was a violation of her sovereignty. If they stole from her, she would steal back. The rage filled her now, and with her hackles still raised, she once again set out for the land where the Two-Legs dwelled.

When she arrived, she cloaked herself in the darkness and observed. She saw one of the buildings where they kept their food, but she hadn't come to satisfy her hunger; she was here to reclaim her meat. The Two-Legs needed to be punished for breaking the order of things. She attuned her sense of smell to the wind. Among the smells to which she was accustomed—those of snow; the expanse of wet earth beneath; trees, sticky; the animals of the mountain—she found a putrid scent. It too led to a building. The structure looked weak, like it would give against a single solid strike. From within came the rotting smell—and the voices of the Two-Legs.

She struck the building head-on. The wall opened up even easier than expected, and her momentum carried her through. She ended up scattering the baskets of stolen meat that had been her objective. Seeing the fourteen Two-Legs clustered around the central fire, she decided to display her strength by tossing aside the nearest one, then immediately kicking out the flame. Deciding that this must have completely subjugated the Two-Legs, she moved her eyes and saw one of the Two-Legs staring at her straight on.

Redback was an animal of the wild, and she found this creature's gaze so incomprehensible that she reflexively stopped. Those eyes showed no panic, no anger; no fear, no awe; but were incredibly calm, as if they had just found a counterpart.

Chapter 4

By the Gallows

Everything happened quickly. The nine women aside from Ume Itano, who had been sent flying, might have been startled by the bear's appearance, but within an instant they understood they needed to fight rather than flee. They each gripped their weapons: Kyu Hoshina and Mei Mitsuya held their wooden spears; Hatsu Fukuzawa, Soh Kiriyama, and Hikari Asami picked up pieces of firewood; Kayu Saitoh and Inui Makabe picked up stone knives, while Itsuru Obuchi and Somo Izumi balled their hands into fists. Their actions were cool-headed and true. Only one problem remained: how to go about the difficult task of killing the bear. Worse yet were the conditions inside the hut: the fire had gone out, sinking the room into darkness. The women's eyes had been acclimated to the light, and now they couldn't see anything around them, let alone the bear itself. Kayu Saitoh was no exception. Frozen in her mind's eye was the bear's face, the last thing she had seen before the light was extinguished. But now, seeing only darkness, she was unable to swing the dagger in her hand.

But unless they took action, nothing would happen.

Even if one of them knew exactly what to do, the action would be meaningless unless she could communicate it to the others, both in and outside the hut. Only those who realized that could move.

Kayu Saitoh slashed the darkness with her knife. She didn't hit anything, but one of the others mistook the sound of the moving air for the beast and charged at her. In the next moment, a sound rang through the darkness. Something had struck the floor. Then came a scream. And another scream. It was Hatsu Fukuzawa. Soon, a wet, sticky sound mixed in with her screams. It was a gruesome sound, and one that did not bode well for the woman's survival. As the noise continued somewhere nearby, Kayu Saitoh stood blind and motionless, irritated at her inability to act. But then, suddenly, one small part of what had been complete darkness lifted. A small but forceful light had appeared.

It was a torch.

And Mei Mitsuya held it. The torch was just one small light against the oppressive darkness, but it peeled back the shadows enough to reveal what had happened to Hatsu Fukuzawa. Her body had been ripped apart, bones and all. Her entrails had spilled out, and her neck was twisted in an unnatural angle. The torch moved, and its glow fell upon on forelegs that lifted her body up as if it weighed nothing. The sight of the bear, whose body was far too massive to be fully illuminated by a single torch, would normally have sent waves of terror through the women in the hut, but they were gripped by the call of battle. Kyu Hoshina held out her spear and ran at the beast, while Soh Kiriyama and Hikari Asami moved to flank it, and Kayu Saitoh and Inui Makabe swung their knives. The bear reacted calmly, tossing Hatsu Fukuzawa's corpse into Kyu Hoshina, Kayu Saitoh, and Inui Makabe, whose forward charge dissipated as their legs tangled up in the body and its tumbling entrails. Even as her feet slipped on the still-warm viscera, Kayu Saitoh managed to stand back up. The bear moved quickly, pouncing onto Soh Kiriyama and Hikari Asami. The beast bared its fangs and tried to sink them into Hikari Asami, who was underneath its chest. But its fangs didn't reach her, stopping partway even as they dripped with hot saliva. Soh Kiriyama was wedged between the bear's chest and the woman, and her body seemed to be preventing the bear from being able to reach. The bear persisted, chomping at Hikari Asami, but the woman remained safe by a hair's breadth.

The torchlight moved.

Mei Mitsuya ran forward and whacked the bear's rump with the burning torch.

In truth, Kayu Saitoh hadn't expected that something of that degree would unnerve the bear, but contrary to her belief, the bear jumped up with its back legs and scrambled out the hole from which it had entered. Its departure was as sudden as its arrival and left the women in stunned silence. The chief was the first to move. She waved her torch about and shouted something. It was "something" not because Kayu Saitoh couldn't make it out, but because it wasn't in words. It was nearly a shriek. The noise jolted Kayu Saitoh out of her horrified paralysis, and she wiped away the viscera clinging to her body and ran to Soh Kiriyama and Hikari Asami.

Hikari Asami looked up at her and said softly, "I'm . . . not injured."

Soh Kiriyama, who also appeared to be unharmed, looked down at Ume Itano, who had fallen on the ground. The woman groaned painfully but didn't have any outwardly apparent injuries. If she had been wounded by the brown bear, she would have met the same fate as Hatsu Fukuzawa, dead with her guts strewn about.

Glaring at what was left of Hatsu Fukuzawa, Kyu Hoshina said, "It got her."

"It killed Hatsu Fukuzawa," Kayu Saitoh muttered, confirming the truth. "We were powerless again."

"That damned bear!" the chief said, her torch lighting her dark red face. "What happened? Why did the bear come here?"

Hikari Asami said, "Maybe it thought we stole its catch."

"Its catch?"

"Matsuki Nagao, Ran Kubo, Kuwa Kure, and Sasaka Yagi . . . from the bear's point of view, they're its rightfully gained catch." Hikari Asami straightened her white robes, though she couldn't brush off the bear's smell. "We . . . took back Sasaka Yagi's remains. The bear might have decided that we stole its food."

"Doesn't that beast know what a funeral is?" the chief asked, but a sound came from the outside, and the women immediately tensed and crouched down, on their guard.

"What happened?" A voice called out to them. "Did something happen? Oh, it's me—Hono Ishizuka."

The women stepped outside where Hono Ishizuka stood torch in hand. The woman's dog pelt, worn slung over her shoulders, had Kayu Saitoh seeing visions of the bear, so she averted her eyes.

"You sap-for-brains!" Mei Mitsuya bellowed. "Don't startle us like that!"

"I could say the same to you, Mei. You came barging into my hut and stole my torch. So... what happened?"

"The bear."

"I thought so."

"You thought so?"

"Well, I got to talking with the others in my hut, and that's what we came up with. It was the look on your face that did it."

"If you thought that's what it was, why didn't you hurry up and help us? Where are the rest of you?"

"They're scared stiff," Hono Ishizuka said as if it couldn't be helped. Then she looked to Kayu Saitoh and Kyu Hoshina, who were soaked in blood and guts, and she gasped. Kyu Hoshina told her Hatsu Fukuzawa had died, and she lowered her head.

Kayu Saitoh couldn't be sure, but she assumed the heavy silence would continue for quite a long time. They had a death to mourn, but more than that, the bear's attack sank their spirits. She thought this silence would last the whole night. But something unexpected came to shatter it. Here, Kayu Saitoh would learn that tragedy came not only sudden and unexpectedly, but in succession as well.

It was a scream.

Mei Mitsuya lifted her head and said, "What was that?"

Hono Ishizuka pointed to the western side of Dendera. "I think it came from over there."

"It couldn't be," Kayu Saitoh said. She took a step forward without realizing it. "Over there, that's where . . ."

Speaking quickly, Mei Mitsuya commanded, "Hono Ishizuka, fetch the others. Hurry. The rest of us will go straightaway. Got it? We're going to save them. We're going to save them!"

2

Everything was already over by the time they reached the hut to where the bedridden women had been evacuated. A hole had been opened in the wall, and a deep stench emanated from within.

Mei Mitsuya, torch in hand, stepped through the hole without pause, and Kayu Saitoh and the others followed after. Straw from the busted wall was strewn about, and the hearth had been destroyed. Blood and flesh and organs covered everything. Kayu Saitoh couldn't tell what had belonged to whom. Fighting her urge to vomit, she kept looking, and eventually she recognized Mitsugi Kaneda's and Shima Iijima's remains. Their bodies had been torn to shreds; their faces alone remained intact. More problematic were the four women who had lacked free use of their bodies. What hadn't been eaten had been trampled into slurry. Despite a painful prickling that came to the back of her eyeballs, Kayu Saitoh surveyed the carnage. She found a piece of skin that appeared to have come from Seto Matsuura's face. One part of the floor caught her eye as particularly unusual. There, the pattern of gore felt artificial, and artfully arranged. Kayu Saitoh quickly realized why—it was a painting of the Village made from blood, a vivid depiction of a typical day's end, with the houses, the sky, the river, the liveliness, the people, and all. It may have been a rough sketch, but anyone who had lived long in the Village would have instantly recognized the scene. An arm was splayed out beside the painting, its pointer finger covered in blood. Kayu Saitoh realized what had happened. As her head reeled, she realized that this was Noi Komatsu, and that the talented artist had painted this scene until her final moment.

Looking up at one of the ceiling beams, Itsuru Obuchi said, "What... is that?"

Something was wriggling about.

Mei Mitsuya held her torch aloft. It was Kura Kuroi, but only the top half of her.

"Kura Kuroi!" Kayu Saitoh yelled, running directly below the crossbeam where the woman's torso had gotten stuck. "Can you move? How did you get up there? What happened to the bear?"

"So many questions," Kura Kuroi wheezed. She seemed to be trying to form a wry smile, but her muscles appeared to be largely inoperative, and her expression hardly changed.

On Mei Mitsuya's orders, the women pulled Kura Kuroi down. The lower half of her body had been ripped away, leaving bones and shredded organs exposed. It was a wonder she still lived and strange that she wasn't dead.

"I want... water."

But even if they were to give her water, she lacked the half of her body needed to receive and contain it, so they instead wrapped her in her white robe and some straw. No one expected this would save her, but at least it slowed her rate of blood loss, and they could give her water without it simply draining out the other end.

"My head is still clear," she said, trembling. "But I can't . . . talk much."

"Don't talk," Kayu Saitoh said quickly.

"The bear's claws caught me," Kura Kuroi said regardless. "The next thing I knew, I was tossed up to the beam, and my legs were gone. It's big . . . that bear."

Kayu Saitoh watched over her, while Kyu Hoshina, Soh Kiriyama, and Hikari Asami searched about the room, taking stock of the scattered viscera.

"Kaneda and Iijima had a chance to escape, but they protected us." Kura Kuroi coughed blood. "Go and fetch that straw mat. Kaneda . . . hid her beneath it."

Hikari Asami flipped over the mat. Sayore Nosaka lay beneath. A deep gash ran down her back that penetrated down to her spine. She was unmistakably dead.

"Kura Kuroi," Kayu Saitoh said, ignoring everything else as she squeezed the woman's hand. "Hang on. Don't die."

"First you say I should die, and then you say I shouldn't die. You need to make up your mind, Kayu. I only have one body."

"Don't die."

"I can do what I want."

"Don't die."

"I'm all right," Kura Kuroi said weakly. "I can still live. I . . . feel that I can."

Carrying torches and spears, a number of women—Hono Ishizuka, Makura Katsuragawa, Kotei Hoshii, Ate Amami, Kaga Kasugai, Guri Togawa, Tsugu Ohi, Tahi Kitajima, Kan Tominaga, Usuma Tsutsumi, Nokobi Hidaka, Hotori Oze, Hyoh Hamamura, Tema Tsukamoto, Tamishi Minamide, and Tsuina Kamioka—poured in through the hole the bear had made. The women gasped at the scene in which they suddenly found themselves. Once again confronted with the gulf that separated the bear's strength from their own, they held expressions somewhere between terror and frustration. The women did what they could to treat Kura Kuroi's wounds, but without needle or thread, all they could manage was to tighten and secure her bindings. Showered by her spurting blood, Kotei Hoshii, Tsuina Kamioka, and Hyoh Hamamura tried to stop her bleeding. When they finally raised their heads, their expressions were those of surrender.

Kayu Saitoh pleaded with them, moaning, "Do something for her. Please save her."

"I wish we could," Tsuina Kamioka said with a deep sigh. "There's nothing we can do for an injury like this."

"Lies! Spare me that nonsense. You *can* save her." Kayu flung Tsuina Kamioka back down and again took hold of Kura Kuroi's hand. "They'll save you. Don't let a little thing like this get your spirits down. They *will* save you."

"Quiet," Mei Mitsuya said, her voice low. "We'll use her as meat."

"What?"

"We can be sure that bear will return," the chief said. "It'll come back to eat the rest of its catch. We can lure the beast with Kura Kuroi's body and kill it."

"I see," Guri Togawa said.

Makura Katsuragawa touched at her nose where the frostbite had taken part of it away, and with a nod, she said, "That's good. That's a good idea."

"Hey," Kayu Saitoh objected, "what are you all talking about?"

"Don't you get it?" Mei Mitsuya grabbed Kayu Saitoh by the collar and pulled her to her feet. "The bear ate the bottom half of her body. Kura Kuroi is part of its catch now. We know that the bear will come back for the rest of its spoils. So we will wait in ambush, and this time, we *will* kill the beast."

Her head spinning, Kayu Saitoh muttered, "You're going to use her as a decoy? She's still alive. We can fix her."

"She's been shredded apart from her stomach down. It's hopeless."

"Shit!"

Kayu Saitoh pushed away the chief's hands and looked over her shoulder to Hono Ishizuka, whose expression remained unchanged.

"I have no objections to the idea," Hono Ishizuka said.

"What kind of Dove are you?" Kayu Saitoh snapped. "You're a hypocrite."

"I am no such thing. The Doves are called Doves because our utmost priority is to make Dendera a better place to live, and so—"

"Shut up!" Kayu Saitoh interrupted, leaping for the woman. She couldn't tell if Hono Ishizuka tried to resist her or not, but with the force with which she threw herself at the woman, it didn't matter. She toppled the woman and pinned her to the floor with ease. Just as she got the idea to split open the woman's stomach so she'd know how Kura Kuroi felt, Kayu Saitoh was peeled off and got pinned to the ground herself. As the other woman held her down, Hono Ishizuka quietly arose, looked down at her, and told her that she mustn't use violence.

"What you all are trying to do," Kayu Saitoh shouted, "*that's* violence." But her words didn't resound within any of the women, nor did it impel them to reflect upon their thinking.

Instead, Hono Ishizuka continued, saying, "Kayu, I already explained to you that Dendera has several rules, one of which is that violence is forbidden. Violence threatens destruction upon Dendera's fragile order."

"*Violence? Destruction?* Last time I looked, Dendera is about to be destroyed by the *bear's* violence!"

"Please don't change the subject. We're talking about you, not the bear."

"I don't want another word from you murderers!"

"Kayu, enough," Kura Kuroi said, her voice a shadow of a whisper. "We can catch the bear by surprise. With my body, we can do that. That's something to be happy for. I never thought this inferior body could be of such use."

Still in shock, Kayu Saitoh muttered, "Happy? Are you stupid? Has life among all the fools of Dendera turned you stupid? How could you talk like that?"

"Kayu Saitoh!" Mei Mitsuya barked, thrusting her torch in front of the pinned woman's eyes. The heat felt searingly hot against Kayu Saitoh's eyeballs, but she didn't close them. "You broke the rules," the chief said.

"How can you talk about rules at a time like this?" Kayu Saitoh said.

"A time like this? Yes, we are in a state of emergency. And you'll ruin us by butting in with your tiresome feelings. You're deplorable. Take her away."

Kayu Saitoh was to be forcibly removed from the hut before she was finished. But she had resisted all she could, and it had been for nothing. She decided to hold her tongue.

Then she heard Kura Kuroi feebly say, "I'm not stupid. I've found honor, far more than I'd ever known in the Village."

Kayu Saitoh was taken to the manor.

Kaga Kasugai held her right arm, and Hotori Oze restrained her left, while Nokobi Hidaka and Tahi Kitajima blocked her escape to the front and behind respectively. Kayu Saitoh had no choice but to obey. The first time she'd been inside the manor, she hadn't noticed the hole in the ground toward the rear of the earthen-floor entryway. Dirt had been dug and packed into ten steps leading belowground, and as the five women descended them, Kayu Saitoh felt a cool, moist breeze. At the bottom of the steps was a tiny room barred by six wooden poles. It was a jail. Kaga Kasugai wiggled the rightmost pole forward and back, releasing it, and tossed Kayu Saitoh inside. Then Kaga Kasugai and Tahi Kitajima went back up the stairs.

"Kayu, stay in there a little while," Nokobi Hidaka said from the other side of the bars. "I understand how you must feel, but you mustn't use violence."

Choosing agreement over sarcasm, Kayu Saitoh said, "Apparently not." She knew she needed to use her head now. "How long will I be in here?"

"Usually it's for ten days, but I think you'll only have two or three days this time, circumstances being what they are."

"But the bear might come back today."

"Not with how much it ate," Nokobi Hidaka said. "We'll be safe for today." She scrunched her eyebrows, seeming to be picturing the bloody leavings of the brute's feast and unable to decide if she should feel sickened or saddened.

"Tell me, why is violence so taboo here?" Kayu Saitoh asked. "I hardly did anything, and now I'm stuck in this cage."

"Hono told you. The day we allow violence to happen here, everything will be destroyed."

"The Village had violence."

"It did." Nokobi Hidaka sighed heavily, her breath white. "It was awful."

Violence occurred often in the Village, though not between individuals. As the Mountain-Barring demonstrated, such incidents had been cleverly replaced by violence between individuals and the Village as a whole. For example, if a man had his romantic advances spurned by a woman, and he tried to vent his pent-up frustrations by spreading false claims against her, a violent act called the "Slack-Mouth" was permitted. The man was made to stand in public, while the woman and the members of her family could each place one stone in his mouth and punch him one time. For the next few weeks, the people of the Village made much merriment in exaggerating tales of the broken, sorry state of his teeth. Similarly, if a married person committed adultery, the "Slack-Groin" was sanctioned, and the guilty party and his or her partner were made to stand in public, where they were forcibly stripped, whether it was summer or winter, then ordered to have intercourse, while the people of the Village could cheer and applaud as they threw rocks at the couple.

When violence came, it was blind to the age and sex and social standing of its subjects. The judgments were as coldhearted as they were absolute, as if the Village itself was committing the act. Violence served to wipe away the people's weariness and frustrations and made the Village function as one entity. It served both this purpose and to educate as well. The children were not only shown these many violences, such as Mountain Barring, the Slack-Mouth, and the Slack-Groin, but they were taught to enjoy them. Because they wanted to see something fun, children would report infractions, and because they didn't want to become targeted, they behaved themselves. The Village was managed through violence, and Climbing the Mountain was the foremost example.

Nokobi Hidaka said, "Mei has no intention of running Dendera through violence like the Village does. I've lived here for eighteen years now. I'm an old-timer. So I know how Mei does things. She forbade all forms of violence. She didn't even make an outlet for it."

"And yet everything has worked out?"

"We're so busy scrounging for food each day that we don't have time for violence in the first place."

"Nokobi Hidaka, I think you're hiding something," Kayu Saitoh said, pointing a finger at her. "You know the real reason violence is forbidden in Dendera, don't you?"

"That's enough," Hotori Oze said, stepping forward.

Nokobi Hidaka placed her hand on her stooping back and climbed the stairs.

Hotori Oze watched the woman go, then wedged her face between the wooden bars, locked eyes with Kayu Saitoh, and said, "No more prying. That's an order, Kayu Saitoh."

Kayu Saitoh was always quick to accept any challenge or provocation, but this time she averted her eyes and sat down on the bare floor. Even in the Village, she hadn't wanted anything to do with this woman.

Sixty years ago, Hotori Oze had married into the Village from her home in another land. Kayu Saitoh didn't know from where she had come, not then and not now. The woman had appeared suddenly, showing her unfamiliar clothes and talking about unfamiliar things. Her disdain for the Village, apparent in her attitude, galled Kayu Saitoh, and when she advised the woman to correct her manners, Hotori Oze coldly replied that she didn't have any desire to listen to Kayu Saitoh's childish envies. Kayu Saitoh's dislike for the woman may not have been the direct result of that incident, but it didn't help. When Hotori Oze Climbed the Mountain seventeen years ago, Kayu Saitoh had been glad to be rid of her, though she certainly didn't speak such thoughts aloud.

She shook off the recollection and tried to think of seventy and eighty-seven as not that far apart. Then she said, "I'm not prying. I'm just worried about the bear."

"This is a time for self-reflection," Hotori Oze said. "When you're sorry for what you've done, you can get out of there and kill the bear. My life is not to be wasted on some animal."

Despite her efforts, Kayu Saitoh's tone turned belligerent. "What did you say? Are you some coward?"

"My life exists to attack the Village," Hotori Oze replied. "To destroy the Village. To destroy the Village. To *destroy* the Village. The place where I was born was nothing like it. It was a good place."

Saying no more, Hotori Oze disappeared up the stairs.

Kayu Saitoh was alone. With the torchlight gone, she was beset by darkness. The light of the hearth upstairs reached her so faintly that it might as well have not, and she could only barely perceive her own outline against the shadow. But even worse was the lack of heat. The cell was nearly as cold as the outside, and her nose ran, and her teeth chattered. Soon she could bear it no longer and tried to force herself to sleep. But sleep wouldn't come, and she remained awake until Nokobi Hidaka returned and provided her some straw. Normally, the prickly roughness of the stuff bothered her, but not today. She burrowed into the straw like a spoiled puppy, and gave herself over to sleep. When she awoke, neither the cold nor the dark had changed, and she hadn't the slightest notion of how long she had slept. She sank back into the straw, deciding that even fitful sleep was preferable to thoughts of the bear and of Kura Kuroi as she suffered her continued imprisonment. She wished for a dream. She wanted to wear a kimono with beautiful colors. She wanted to have a smile on her face, a face without a wrinkle or even a single blemish. She wished for a dream of the time when she could dance and leap about in youthful exuberance. Perhaps because she wanted it too strongly, she didn't dream at all.

Suddenly, she felt warm, and the pleasant feeling awoke her. Torch in hand, Nokobi Hidaka and Makura Katsuragawa were looking down on her.

Her voice listless, Makura Katsuragawa said, "Hey, Kayu. Looks like you're awake."

"Can I finally get out of here?"

"It's only the first night," Nokobi Hidaka said, moving her torch to direct more heat onto Kayu Saitoh.

"Then why are you two here?"

"Your dinner." Nokobi Hidaka handed her a single potato through the prison bars.

"That's all there is? You shouldn't have bothered waking me."

"Why, were you eating something nice in your dream?"

"My dream," Kayu Saitoh said, the word carrying a sweetness. A part of her responded to the thought, trying to grab at it but failing, and in its place reality came crashing down on her. "Wait, what's happened to Kura Kuroi?"

"She's alive," Nokobi Hidaka said.

"She is?"

"We were able to use snow to cover, you know, below her stomach," Makura Katsuragawa explained. "But the blood keeps coming and coming, so the snow turned red. And the warmth of her blood keeps melting it, and—"

Growing irritated at the woman's endless, graphic description, Kayu Saitoh cut in, asking, "And she's fine like that?"

"I wouldn't say she's fine. We've slowed her blood loss, but we can't save her life."

"You all want to use her for bear bait, so you don't *need* to save her life. If that's all she is to you people, then end her misery. Why needlessly prolong her life? She must be suffering. She must want to die."

Kayu Saitoh punched the bars that separated herself from the two women, but all it did was make her hand hurt.

"We have a message from Mei Mitsuya," Nokobi Hidaka said, ignoring the display. "'You will be released early next morning. I want you to join the ambush with haste.'"

"I'd do that without being told. What I want to know is, is Kura Kuroi—"

"Let me finish," Nokobi Hidaka interrupted. Her voice carried the cool composure only possessed by those who had learned to let go of what they couldn't change. "'There is but one plan. Kura Kuroi's body will be the decoy. The ambush party will hide in the hut with her and wait for the bear. When the beast comes for Kura Kuroi, we will charge the bear and stab it with our spears. Kura Kuroi consents to the plan with enthusiasm.'"

Kayu Saitoh waited, but when the woman didn't continue, she said, "Is that all?"

"That's all."

"I don't understand. Why would Kura Kuroi be enthusiastic?"

"Do you really not get it?" Nokobi Hidaka asked.

"Huh?"

"Then I pity both of you."

"What's that supposed to mean?" Kayu Saitoh asked, but Nokobi Hidaka didn't respond, instead departing with Makura Katsuragawa.

Kayu Saitoh thought about going back to sleep, but she wasn't tired. On the other hand, she recognized that twisting in her thoughts inside the jail would be pointless. And so, without eating her potato, she sank back into the straw and closed her eyes.

Things not wished for will come; Kayu Saitoh dreamed. Wearing a kimono of vivid reds and yellows, her younger self frolicked, her wanderings eventually leading her to the monthly hut that stood at the boundary between the Village and the Mountain. During menses, the women would be moved to the monthly hut, which stood a distance from the Village. When they moved in, they brought rice with them, and each day they worked the fields, returning at night to eat their cold rice as blood smeared their nether regions. Kayu Saitoh was of the age where her first menstruation could come at any moment. She hadn't intended to walk here, and she regretted finding herself nearby the shack. But she felt that to leave would be like running away, so this time she purposefully approached the structure. The smell of blood grew heavy, and she could hear women talking. Their conversations were typical gossip: this man in that house was kind; this woman in that house was miserly; those sorts of topics. Kayu Saitoh found it distasteful that these women, who did nothing in particular to relieve their affliction, cheerfully chatted as if nothing were out of the ordinary, while they sullied their thighs and their plain kimono. She thought of how in the not too distant future, she would be inside there, chatting casually and shoveling down cold rice as her unclean blood flowed freely, and she reviled that future self. But back then, she hadn't been able to think of what would come later. She couldn't imagine what she would be like when her menses stopped coming and her teeth fell out from old age. All of the problems that came with dotage were tidily resolved in a turn of phrase: Climb the Mountain. Even as she gained in years, this remained unchanged. The only thing that changed this outlook—the thing that had forced her to change it—was her failed Climb and the beginning of her new life in Dendera.

A voice awoke her, and she opened her eyes to see Kaga Kasugai, Tsuina Kamioka, Kyu Hoshina, and Makura Katsuragawa standing outside her cell. Kaga Kasugai announced that Kayu Saitoh's punishment was over and then released the rightmost pole in the same manner as before, freeing her. Outside, the snow glittered under the morning sun. Kayu Saitoh bathed herself in the warm light and fresh breeze that had seemed long absent. She hadn't walked for a while either, and her joints felt off, each step producing dull aches, and her hips throbbed painfully. But if anything, she enjoyed these sensations. Her body was in working order, such as it was—except from her neck up. Her head felt heavy with sharp, painful pressure, as if it were filled with muddy water sloshing about. She approached the hut where Kura Kuroi was to be used as bear bait, and when she entered, it wasn't with a cheerful heart.

The interior remained largely unchanged from its state two days earlier, with the destroyed wall, the blood and flesh and organs strewn everywhere, the choking stench, and Kura Kuroi lying on the floor. The stump of Kura Kuroi's torso had been wrapped in a white robe, but the cloth was stained black and—perhaps her bleeding hadn't stopped—glistened wetly. In the sunlight that came through the opening in the wall, Kura Kuroi's skin appeared as pale as clay. Her eyes were unfocused, and purple spots flecked her lolling tongue. At first glance, Kayu Saitoh couldn't see if the woman was alive or dead. But then she saw the barely perceptible rise and fall of her chest, the singular substantiation of her survival.

"Kura Kuroi!" Kayu Saitoh called out. "How can it be? You're alive!"

Kura Kuroi's chin and mouth remained still, but her throat faintly trembled out the word, "Kayu."

"Incredible. You're nearly a corpse, aren't you. You're bait."

"Is that a... compliment? I expect... we'll fool that b-bear."

"Kayu Saitoh, you're here!"

It was Mei Mitsuya's voice, but when Kayu Saitoh lifted her eyes, she couldn't see where the chief was. Kaga Kasugai pointed to the ceiling. Kayu Saitoh looked in the direction and saw the chief and Hikari Asami lying flat on one of the ceiling beams.

"You didn't notice us!" Mei Mitsuya said with pride. "Hikari Asami, Hyoh Hamamura, Mumi Ohara, and I are hiding here."

Hyoh Hamamura and Mumi Ohara popped out from the mountain of straw piled in the corner by the entrance.

"So this is your plan," Kayu Saitoh said to the ceiling.

"Exactly. The bear will come. When it does, we'll strike at once and kill it."

"And you'll sacrifice Kura Kuroi."

"Kayu Saitoh," the chief said, "do you only see her as bait? Is that all you can see in her?"

"What are you talking about?"

"Kura Kuroi is part of our ambush."

Kura Kuroi moved her right arm just enough to reveal a sharpened, sturdy-looking stake, the same length and width as the arm that held it. "If that beast comes in," the woman managed, so softly that it was hardly a voice at all, "and opens its big mouth to eat me . . . I'll run it through. I don't think bears . . . are so tough on the inside."

Kayu Saitoh realized she stood alone. Everyone else had prioritized their goals over sentimental compassion or kindness. For the women who longed not for the Mountain or Paradise, that choice came naturally. Whether or not she should choose to follow that course, Kayu Saitoh regarded herself a villain to have viewed Kura Kuroi only as bait, and she felt ashamed of her behavior.

"All right," Kayu Saitoh said, "what should I do? I'll do anything."

"Hide in the straw and wait for the bear to come," the chief said.

A second pile of straw towered a few paces away from Hyoh Hamamura and Mumi Ohara's hiding place. Kayu Saitoh watched Makura Katsuragawa, Kaga Kasugai, and Tsuina Kamioka take positions on the ceiling beams, then she plunged into the straw and found a wooden spear waiting inside.

Once Kayu Saitoh had situated herself, Mei Mitsuya explained the current situation. In the westernmost hut where they were, nine women waited in ambush, while similar groups—six in the adjacent hut where the funeral had been, and nine in the storehouse where the bear had first attacked—lay in wait around some of the remains as bait. Nine others watched Dendera from locations nearby. The chief had spared no women to forage for additional food, so they all had to live off their current reserves. They would hold their positions for as long as ten days. If the bear failed to show, they would lift the ambush and return to their lives. None had objected to the plan. Some had expressed concern over their dwindling provisions, but the plan was deemed far preferable to living under the continued threat of the beast.

Here, Kayu Saitoh began her new life, with slaying the bear her priority. But her foe was an intelligent living being, so it would not simply act as she expected. The beast didn't come. When the designated messengers Ate Amami and Inui Makabe arrived bearing potatoes and water, they reported with bitterness that the bear hadn't come to the other locations either. Kayu Saitoh ate her potatoes amid the stench of rotting flesh. Kura Kuroi no longer possessed the strength to eat, but she had the women moisten her lips. Night came, but in order for the ambush to work, the women had to remain alert at all times, so they slept in shifts. When dawn came, Kayu Saitoh hadn't yet had her turn to sleep.

With the second day, this new life became routine. She had just about gotten used to the way of things, except for her empty stomach. In the Village, she had been no stranger to hunger, but it had been a long time since she faced such naked starvation. Her thirst was so severe that just by swallowing her saliva, she could feel her guts churn about to reclaim the moisture.

When the next day came, Kura Kuroi hardly moved at all. She

ceased talking, and her breathing became faint. Kayu Saitoh called out to her again and again, but received no response.

Kayu Saitoh stuck her head out from the straw and said, "Kura, Kura Kuroi, she's—"

"I don't care if you talk, just keep hidden," Mei Mitsuya admonished from the ceiling.

"She's not moving."

"I can see that," the chief snapped. "Hey, Kura Kuroi. Are you still alive? If you're alive, give us a sign."

Incredibly slowly, Kura Kuroi moved her head, but that was all.

Mumi Ohara said, "I can't say I have high expectations for her attack."

"Nonsense!" the chief barked. "Moving or not, alive or dead, Kura Kuroi is doing her best. I won't allow you to talk about her like that."

Silence enveloped the room.

The listless quiet persisted through the day. When darkness joined the torpor, tension, hunger, and stench that permeated the space, Kayu Saitoh was no longer in any condition to think about anything; she simply imagined her body melting into the shadows. Only her stomach carried on its workings.

The next morning came with a change.

Kura Kuroi's energy had returned.

"Wow, I feel really good today," the woman said with a gentle smile. "It must be sunny outside. I bet that's it. I feel like my old self again. If I still had my legs, I'd go for a walk." She kept on talking. "You know, I've never taken one step in my whole life. I always wished I could walk just once before I died. But I won't be walking now. I'll die without being able to. I think that's wrong, you know—for a person to die without ever having walked. I wonder. Maybe I'm wrong about that." And still she talked. "To walk, yes, to walk. None of that for me. The only parts of me that work are my belly and my mouth. I guess that's why the Village was so cold to me. I only caused trouble for my parents and younger brothers. If only I could have walked. If only I could have moved. I wanted to work. Kayu, are you there?"

Kayu Saitoh responded, but Kura Kuroi seemed not to notice, continuing to ramble as she pleased.

"You know, you were just about the only person I knew in the Village. Why were you such a good friend to me, Kayu?"

Again Kayu spoke, but Kura Kuroi again didn't notice.

"I really did want to die," Kura Kuroi said. "I wanted to die. I wanted to die and be no more. To vanish without a trace. After all, I'm a nuisance, aren't I? I was a nuisance to the Village. So when I turned seventy, I was happy. I was happy to repay my debt to the Village. My younger brother carried me up the Mountain on his back. I was so joyful that I cried. Then, when I was waiting to die on the Mountain, I was saved. And when Mei explained everything to me, I again cried tears of joy. And I realized that the tears I was crying in Dendera were better and more precious. Kayu, I wanted to live in Dendera forever. I didn't want to die."

Kura Kuroi spoke with more conviction and spirit than Kayu Saitoh had ever heard from her in the Village.

"But now I'm in this state," Kura Kuroi continued. "It's a shock. I never thought anything like this could happen to me here in Dendera.

I thought I'd be able to go on enjoying life. But I'm fulfilled. You might not believe me, but I'm fulfilled. I can finally die. And I can do it while helping Dendera, not the Village. I've never felt this good before. But Kayu, you're still alive. Live life embracing death, and keep life in your thoughts until you die."

"Don't die!" Kayu Saitoh said, leaping from the straw. "You're making no sense. Do you want to live or do you want to die? Which is it? And don't feel fulfillment at dying! That's not what I meant when I asked you. Why can't you understand that? You're happily dying, and you don't even understand."

Without answering, Kura Kuroi closed her eyes.

Thankfully, the woman's chest continued to rise and fall. But Kayu Saitoh couldn't accept a single word her friend had said.

That night, all of the women sensed the animal smell that had worked its way into the air.

Each in their places, the women tasted a thickly simmering stew of fear, tension, anticipation, and unease as they awaited their moment. They knew the bear was near but couldn't predict if it would truly come, which hut it would enter if it did, or what actions it would take upon arrival. Inside the straw pile, Kayu Saitoh tightened her grip on the wooden spear, her palm moist with sweat.

She didn't know how much time passed like this, but eventually two noises approached: the rustling of thick fur and the crunching of footsteps in snow. Suddenly concerned that her own breath might be audible outside, she held it. Her heart pounded and cold sweat ran between her sides and her arms.

The outside thing cautiously circled the hut three times, then returned to where it had started and put its head inside. Kayu Saitoh again held her breath. The bear's head was so massive that she couldn't tell how far away it was; but either way, the beast was incredibly close. It was close enough that if she jumped, she could have reached it. The beast stepped its front legs inside. Without any light, Kayu Saitoh only saw the outline of its head and forelegs, but that was enough to make her more aware of the beast's mass and weight than she cared to be. The stench of its breath grew oppressive.

Again the bear moved, advancing its bulk into the room. Passing in front of Kayu Saitoh, its body moved with real grace, the fur on its back vivid and red. Despite the darkness, Kayu Saitoh saw the crimson fur more clearly than when she had faced the beast in the Mountain. She fought to keep her strength from draining out from her feet.

As she stared at that red fur, she wondered if the women could really win, though it was far too late for such doubts. The answer came to her almost immediately. *We can't win. We can't win. We can't win. We can't win. We can't win. No matter how many spears we prepare, no matter how many women we bring together, we can't win.* But even as quickly as the answer came to her, the time to escape had passed. She desperately tried to banish her despair, renewing her grip on the spear—the spear, she told herself, that very well might be the one to kill the bear.

Having squeezed itself into the room, the beast focused its gaze on Kura Kuroi. The bear's hindquarters blocked the view from Kayu Saitoh's hiding place, and she couldn't see what was going on. But she knew Kura Kuroi was going to be eaten. She heard joy in the bear's fierce snorts and enthusiastic grunts. The grunts built into a fierce roar. Kayu Saitoh recoiled, but the movement hadn't drawn the beast's notice. Instead, the creature raised its head, ready to fling itself onto its feast.

Kayu Saitoh didn't know what had happened, but the bear suddenly collapsed, landing on its rear, while Kura Kuroi's body was hurled against the wall. Along with the sound of the woman's impact, Kayu Saitoh heard someone shout, "Now!" It was Mei Mitsuya's voice. Simultaneously, Kayu Saitoh saw the chief, Hikari Asami, and Tsuina Kamioka leaping down, spear-tips first, onto the bear. Kayu Saitoh joined the charge. She ran ahead without thought. The beast's red fir was visible even in the dark, and that was where she thrust her spear. At least, that was where she tried to thrust her spear. Instead, she bumped into Hikari Asami and Tsuina Kamioka.

The battle was in turmoil.

Cries that could have belonged to either beast or woman echoed in the space.

Quickly, she got back to her feet. The first thing she saw was Mumi Ohara and Tsuina Kamioka's heads flying off. Next, claws pierced through Kaga Kasugai's back. With a flick of the bear's arm, the woman tumbled to the floor.

"Kill it!" Mei Mitsuya was shouting. "Kill it!"

Whether the bear was reacting in panicked surprise or in calm measure, Kayu Saitoh couldn't tell; either way, the beast swung its paws again and again. Each swipe generated a gust of wind sending Kayu Saitoh's hair and robe flapping. Makura Katsuragawa fled through the open hole with tears and sweat running down a face contorted in terror.

Reacting to the sudden movement, the bear turned, and its eyes and Kayu Saitoh's eyes met. At least she thought they did. A chill crept along her spine. She checked her grip on the wooden spear and flung herself forward at the bear's face.

She pictured the left side of her body being ripped away.

The image came only as a flash.

It came not as prediction or premonition, but in a vision.

But she was already in air; her feet were off the ground. Having seen the vision or not, it was too late for her to do anything about it aside from thrust her spear forward. She felt an intense hot wind. She saw the bear swinging down its front paw to kill her. Kayu Saitoh had moved first, but the bear's claws were moving quickly, overtaking her. She twisted her body midair. She felt two things simultaneously: something struck her head, and her spear sank into something soft. She fell, her body slapping against the ground. Pain threatened to take her from consciousness, but somehow, she managed to look up.

Something long was sticking out from the bear's right eye.

Kayu Saitoh realized that she no longer held her spear.

The bear let out a terrific roar and flailed its forelegs about. Someone shouted, "Run, run!"

Using only her arms, Kayu Saitoh dragged herself away until she thought she was safe. She looked at the bear. With the spear still lodged into its right eye, the beast opened its maw to its fullest and cried out, then fled through the hole, leaving vast amounts of blood and body parts behind.

Hikari Asami scrambled to her feet and began checking on the women. Shaking, Hyoh Hamamura appeared from the straw. Kayu Saitoh crawled forward, shouting, "I'm alive!" She repeated, "I'm alive, I'm alive!" Mei Mitsuya pulled her to her feet, but Kayu Saitoh's hips had dislocated, and she collapsed back down on her rear.

"Can you move?" the chief said, pulling her up again. "Don't give up!"

"I—" Kayu Saitoh said, her voice sounding not like her own. "I'm... alive. I'm alive. I'm alive."

"Are you?" the chief asked.

"What?"

"Your head's split open."

Kayu Saitoh touched her hand to her head and felt something wet as pain jolted her.

Her palm was covered in red.

Hikari Asami said, "The bear is injured. It fled. I'm going after it," then left through the hole, and Mei Mitsuya followed after.

Kayu Saitoh wanted to join them but couldn't see through the blood. In frustration and anger, she wiped her eyes, grabbed a piece of nearby cloth, and wrapped it around her head. Immediately after, she realized the scrap was part of Kura Kuroi's robe, and she saw her friend's severed head where it had rolled to the floor.

When she went outside, Dendera was in complete chaos.

Kayu Saitoh didn't know what had happened, but confusion heaped upon confusion, and an extraordinary uproar unfolded under the moonlight. Shrieks, cries, and shouts came from all directions. Kayu Saitoh ran alone through the madness. In the snow, a blood trail led up the Mountain. It seemed to belong to the bear.

"This way, everyone!" Kayu Saitoh shouted. "The monster has fled to the Mountain! It's injured. If we're going to catch it, and if we're going to kill it, we have to go now!"

But her voice didn't carry over the uproar. As rage filled her, a tiny spray of blood spurted from her head wound.

She saw several women emerging from the adjacent hut. She yelled at them as loudly as she could, and they came toward her. There were six women: Kotei Hoshii, Maka Kikuchi, Koto Onodera, Nokobi Hidaka, Tamishi Minamide, and Tsusa Hiiragi. After Kayu Saitoh filled them in, the two torch-bearing messengers, Ate Amami and Inui Makabe, came with Mei Mitsuya and Hikari Asami in tow.

"Why is all of Dendera in such chaos?" Kayu Saitoh asked Inui Makabe. "The bear came into *our* hut. What happened?"

"Well," Inui Makabe said, embarrassed, "the women watching over the cemetery started screaming that the bear had come, and—"

"Who cares about those fools?" Mei Mitsuya said, adjusting her headscarf. "We have to hurry. If we let that thing escape far up the Mountain, we'll have trouble later."

Eleven women set out in pursuit: Kayu Saitoh, Mei Mitsuya, Hikari Asami, Kotei Hoshii, Maka Kikuchi, Koto Onodera, Nokobi Hidaka, Tamishi Minamide, Tsusa Hiiragi, Ate Amami, and Inui Makabe. With only one torch, navigating the shadowy Mountain proved difficult, but all save for Kayu Saitoh proceeded with experienced movements. Kayu Saitoh gave up on leading the group and settled for trying to at least not hinder the others.

At some point, the sky over the Mountain had changed, delivering a snowstorm, but the group pressed on, following the scattered blotches of wet blood beneath the top layer of snow. The thickening fir trees and intensifying storm blocked the moon, leaving the single torch their only real light. Then further misfortune struck. The blood trail vanished.

"Impossible!" Kayu Saitoh said. "The bear's wounds were far too severe for the bleeding to stop."

"Don't worry. Its footsteps remain. And look at how clear they are. It's shameful, really."

The beast's footsteps indeed remained, leading higher up the Mountain. Refusing to let feelings of unease get the better of them, the eleven women forged ahead. The bitter storm froze them to the bone, but this was of no bother to the women excited by the prospect of slaying the bear. They kept walking. But they were forced to stop when the bear tracks abruptly ended.

Hikari Asami brushed away the snowflakes clinging to her face, and her expression was dumbfounded. "It doubled back." she said.

"What?" Mei Mitsuya groaned.

"The bear...knows we're following its tracks. It's used its trail against us—to confuse us."

"To confuse us, you say?"

"The bear purposefully left this trail," Hikari Asami explained. "Then along the way, it jumped to a tree and escaped in some other direction."

"It's just a dumb brute!" the chief said. "How could it fool humans?"

"This is definitely a false trail. The bear could be anywhere by now." Hikari Asami shook her head. "What should we do?"

The chief clearly wanted to keep moving, but she looked back and forth between her torch and the untouched snow, then ordered a withdrawal. The women were forced to return empty-handed. Amid the bitter taste of humiliation, Kayu Saitoh and the others went back down the Mountain. Their excitement melted away, leaving only the cold, and no one said a word as they dragged their legs in an anemic descent. Having lost their quarry, the hunting party was reduced to skin and bone and disgrace.

The weary group arrived back in Dendera to find that the commotion hadn't calmed but rather had intensified. Despite the ill-spent exhaustion that had taken hold of her body, Kayu Saitoh jogged ahead to see what had happened. For a moment, she pictured the bear having returned to Dendera to massacre its inhabitants, but the women's shouts carried a great joy.

A group had gathered in front of the burial ground.

Several graves had been unearthed, wooden grave markers snapped in half, and gravestones tossed about in every which way. A few corpses—mostly bleached-white skeletal remains—had been dragged out and appeared to have been partially eaten. And yet the women had circled around these desecrated remains and shouted and cheered with delight.

Guri Togawa raised her hands in the air, cackled, and said, "We did it! Don't mess with us!"

"Don't mess with us!" Kan Tominaga repeated.

"It was me who did it," Makura Katsuragawa said. Her body was covered in blood, and she jumped up and down in excitement. "I killed it! I killed the bear!"

Hearing this, Kayu Saitoh sprinted the rest of the way, pushed through the circle of women, and put her eyes on the lifeless brown-furred animal.

It was the cub.

3

Redback hadn't lost because she had underestimated the Two-Legs. Rather, her defeat came about *because* she understood their strength and remained ever cautious. They didn't have those strange, fire-spitting sticks, but she fully expected them to attack her using some different method. When she came back to fight to reclaim the food that had been stolen from her, she felt something hot strike her rear. Despite its not being a serious injury, she fled out of caution that it was some new form of attack. And even as the abandoned meat lingered in her thoughts, she endured her increasing hunger and waited, inviting the Two-Legs to lower their guard.

But despite all her prudence, she was now fleeing through a blizzard, her right eye destroyed.

Her backtracking had successfully thrown her pursuers off her trail, but she still had lost her eye. To a creature of the wild, the loss was dire. And when she had found that her cub, who always clung to her so, hadn't followed her, she knew she had lost him. She had lost he who was to carry on her blood, her experiences, and her ways, and that, to a creature of the wild, was the greatest possible loss.

The Two-Legs killed the cub she had been raising to rule over her domain. As she fled, Redback thought about what had happened and where that left her. Had she human emotion, she would have been angry and sorrowful, but she felt nothing at the killing of her cub. Creatures of the wild were endowed with no such emotions. Her offspring had been her priority, and she had protected him with her life, but now that he was gone she felt nothing. Even if she did, the emotion would have been expressed by a small, single howl.

What Redback needed now was escape and recuperation, and she had secured one of those when the Two-Legs gave up her trail. To a creature of the wild, the actions of the Two-Legs had been an error, nothing more, made in total disregard of the rules of nature. They should have either kept searching for her on the mountain or gone back to secure more numbers and better equipment and then resumed their pursuit. If, hypothetically, they had taken either of those measures, nature would have judged her death a fair outcome. But the Two-Legs let their resignation rule them. They descended from the mountain, and Redback achieved her escape.

Having successfully eluded the Two-Legs, recuperation became her next goal. Her measures were simple: she found a hole to shelter her from the wind and settled in to endure the pain and blood loss. Humans would offer a helping hand to their injured, but the creatures of the wild, and bears in particular, lived solitary existences where injury and death were in direct relation. Animals understood far better than man what an injury meant. Redback's fangs chattered and her back fur drooped, and she did her best to survive.

After three full sleepless days, she had endured the worst of it, and her wound had closed over. When she dislodged the stick from where it had remained, it came out with a clump of coagulated blood, to which clung tufts of ripped-out fur and bits of what used to be her eye. The injury was far from completely healed, but nevertheless, she crawled out from her hole. Outside, the snow was thick, but the sun's warmth soothed her frozen body. She stretched her back and began to walk just to see if she could. The right side of her vision had been lost to darkness, but she was a creature of the wild; to stop for such a minor reason equated to death, and so she kept her four legs moving.

Redback knew injury better than humans, and she had battled against it and won. Inside her, the fires of vengeance blazed.

Vengeance was not only the domain of mankind.

Wounding an animal was to invite vengeance.

Inside Redback, a new goal began to blossom.

She would survive this winter and carry a new child. To do that, she needed to secure food—in the form of those weak Two-Legs who acted as if they ruled over the domain that was rightfully hers.

She would beat the Two-Legs.

She would kill and devour.

She would kill and devour and survive.

She gave the land where the Two-Legs dwelled a single glance with her left eye, then proceeded deeper up the mountain. After that, she didn't show herself again.

Chapter 5

IN DEATH THROES

At first, the women wrestled with uncertain fears, but after five days passed with no sign of another attack, they concluded that the bear had succumbed to its wounds on the Mountain. That same day, they celebrated their victory. Casting aside their typical frugalities, they lit scores of fire baskets, brought food out from the storehouse, sharpened their stone knives, and boiled water over a bonfire in the clearing. There, they had buried the bear cub's carcass in the snow to keep it from spoiling. Thirty-six women had survived the attacks, and all gathered in the clearing—save for Shigi Yamamoto, who never left her hut—where they unearthed the cub and gazed at it in the midday sun. The animal was still small, only about as long as a person was tall, but its stout, muscular body, thick legs, and sharp, amber claws demonstrated that even at its age, the cub had been a fierce creature.

"Listen to me!" Mei Mitsuya said, standing on the balcony of her manor, raising her cane overhead. "The bear hasn't shown itself for five days. We've won! We are victorious against the beast. And we have the meat of its cub. Our victory is total. So come, let us celebrate. Let us eat meat. Let us feast until we can feast no more. This is our vengeance!"

The women raised a triumphant cheer.

It might have been the first outcry of optimism in the history of the secret settlement.

Kayu Saitoh later heard what had caused the mayhem the night of the attack. The group keeping watch near the cemetery saw the cub unearthing the graves, while a separate group saw the commotion and mistook the cub for their target, and in the end, Makura Katsuragawa, having succumbed to her fears and fleeing for her life, stumbled into the fracas and ran her spear through the cub, killing it. Since the women had obtained so much meat through her actions, none rebuked Makura Katsuragawa's flight, and instead regarded her as a hero. But it was Kayu Saitoh who had garnered true respect. All praised her for destroying the beast's eye, even as she suffered a vicious head wound. She was proud to have been of help to Dendera, but amid unease over the lack of confirmation of the bear's life or death, and heartache over having let Kura Kuroi die, Kayu Saitoh didn't speak, instead placing her hand on the bandage made from her departed friend's robe cloth. With meat on the menu, none in Dendera would criticize her silence.

Mei Mitsuya came down from the balcony, joining the women in the clearing, and in the light of the sun and the fire baskets, the celebration began.

First up was the butchering of the cub. Hikari Asami was the one to wield the stone dagger. She had volunteered, asserting that she had never taken apart a bear before, but had seen it done and might be able to imitate it. The woman held the knife in a reverse grip, then pushed its tip into the black fur, plunging all the way into its groin as fat spilled out jiggly and milky white. The stone blade kept catching on the animal's thick hide, but she pushed it deeper. A stench arose, not an animal smell, but something closer to rotting fish. But none of the women cared. Hikari Asami wiped her arm in the snow to clean away the clinging bits of fatty tissue, then switched to a fresh knife. Inserting the knife into the same place, she finally opened up the cub's abdomen. Next, she ran the knife to the ends of the animal's humanlike feet and arms. She cut the lines around the cub's genitals, separating them from the carcass.

Hikari Asami looked up, sweat covering her face, and said, "I'm going to pull off its skin. I need help."

Kayu Saitoh, Kyu Hoshina, and Nokobi Hidaka stepped forward and helped remove the hide. It wasn't as easy work as with a rabbit, but the skin came off with little resistance, revealing pink flesh beneath a film of fat. Their eyes trembling in fury and hunger and curiosity, the women stared at the carcass in wordless silence. With the cub's hide and flesh separated, Hikari Asami next began carving into its chest. Once she had cut through the tough, fibrous pectoral muscles, she turned her blade to the cartilage of its ribcage, then directed Kayu Saitoh and the others to follow suit, and the four of them removed the ribs from either side and left the bones in the snow. Hikari Asami severed the arteries around the cub's heart and placed the heavy-looking organ on the ground. The women proceeded to pull out the trachea, esophagus, lungs, and other bits and parts one after another, meanwhile instructing Kayu Saitoh to scoop up the blood that had settled inside the chest cavity. Kayu Saitoh filled up a soup bowl with the thick, grape-colored liquid.

"Drink it," Hikari Asami said to the women. "Fresh blood will warm your bodies and give you strength."

But none moved, the corners of their eyes and lips trembling in quandary. Then one woman stepped forward, cackling. It was Mei Mitsuya. The chief pulled a chipped sake cup from her breast pocket—where she'd found the thing remained a mystery—and told Kayu Saitoh to pour. Kayu Saitoh poured. The chief downed the cup as if to drink even the fumes, then displayed her blood-streaked teeth, cackled again, and said it tasted great. She extended the cup to Ume Itano and instructed the woman to drink. Ume Itano's expression was one of flat refusal, but when the chief added that it might heal her hips, the woman took the cup. Ume Itano had crashed into the bear once in the Mountain and once in the hut, and the battles had taken a toll on her hips and back. Kayu Saitoh filled the cup, and Ume Itano closed both eyes and drank it all. At first, the woman's face contorted in distaste, but the look gradually faded. Seeing this, the other women stepped forward one after another to ask for blood, forcing Kayu Saitoh to keep pouring. As she served the other women, she surreptitiously licked some blood that had spilled onto her finger. The taste of it stimulated long-neglected taste buds, and she began to salivate. This was the first time she'd tasted anything salty since her arrival in Dendera. The women drank of the blood, rich with salt and nourishment, and became lively. Someone started making noise, and that kicked off a merry clamor of voices, lilting somewhere between conversation and song. Meanwhile, Hikari Asami continued silently butchering the cub. Now she was working on the digestive tract. She pulled out its long intestines, squeezed the waste out from one end, pushed a narrow branch through the tube, used the stick to turn it inside out, sprinkled snow on it and washed it clean, then told Kyu Hoshina to fill it with blood. Taken aback, Kyu Hoshina asked why and received the curt reply, "For eating." Next Hikari Asami began removing the cub's head. This was an important step in the celebration, and the women cheered on Hikari Asami, who stabbed into the side of the cub's neck and circled the blade around it. She pulled away the bones connecting the head to the body, then grasped the head and yanked it off. The women beamed with great satisfaction as they gazed at the cub's severed head.

"I'm ready to carve out the meat," Hikari Asami said, out of breath. "Does anyone want to help?"

The women pushed themselves forward and crowded around. Hikari Asami made several incisions in the animal's back and instructed the others to follow the cuts and remove the limbs, and the women eagerly got to work. Gripping their daggers with hunger and rage, these drinkers of blood picked at the carcass with more efficiency than a flock of starving birds, and the cub had soon been dismantled, no longer a figure of dignity and awe, but just meat now.

"It's time! It's time!" Mei Mitsuya shouted, blood smeared on the edges of her mouth. "Let's eat. Let's eat it all. Let us starving women consume this bear. It cannot stop us now!"

The women tossed the meat chunks into several stone pots that had been brought to a boil over the bonfire. They stirred in potatoes and other vegetable scraps from their storehouse, and soon steam rose, giving off a fatty aroma. In another pot they simmered cut-up offal in blood for more flavor, and in yet another, they boiled Kyu Hoshina's blood sausage. The smell of cooking meat entranced the women, and their throats trembled in rapture, and their stomachs rumbled. Kayu Saitoh was no exception. Her stomach pulsated and her mouth overflowed with saliva.

The food was ready a little after midday. "Line up!" Mei Mitsuya ordered. "I'll divide up the meal." The women had been watching the meat get tender and smelling its aroma, and when the chief gave the order, they lined up like intelligent dogs. Kayu Saitoh joined the line.

Some hadn't.

Six women refrained: Hono Ishizuka, Naki Sokabe, Masari Shiina, Hotori Oze, Ire Tachibana, and Kushi Tachibana.

Normally, Kayu Saitoh might have wondered why, but hunger ruled her thoughts now. The moment the bear broth hit her bowl, she forgot all else. Mei Mitsuya smiled, told her she had done a great service, and gave her an exceptionally large piece of meat.

The women formed a circle around the cub's severed head. As they watched over what remained of the bear while eating of its flesh, the head sat there in what seemed like humiliated silence.

When her teeth sank into the meat, Kayu Saitoh's mouth filled with grease. As she swallowed the mixture of fatty juices and saliva, the hot broth passed down her throat and into her stomach. She eagerly chewed the tender meat, and the taste of it, so strong as to be nearly overwhelming, filled her mouth and her nose. Not even in the Village had she ever eaten so much meat. The Village had bear and deer hunters, but most of the meat and offal ended up elsewhere, and what remained was usually claimed by the hunter's family. Having married into the house of a paper-miller, Kayu Saitoh wasn't sure how to manage more meat than she could fit in a single mouthful, but she polished it off and moved on to the offal stew. Her tongue rejoiced at this new texture, and as she chewed, the grease coated her mouth. Much in this same way, the women all emptied their bowls.

After the meal was finished, the ring of women around the cub's head raised a victorious shout. Some danced, some sang, some laughed, and some cried. As the festivities continued, Mei Mitsuya raised her cane, called Kayu Saitoh and Makura Katsuragawa over, and said she would bestow them each with part of the pelt and a bowl of stew with the bear's genitals. Kayu Saitoh forced down the bitter soup, and her insides felt feverish, and sweat formed all over her body. Makura Katsuragawa seemed to have trouble as well, following the stew with a coughing fit that continued until tears had begun to form in her eyes. Sharing a dose of ribald humor long absent from Dendera, the other women joked about how she was probably just upset because the food had gotten her libido going again while she was stuck with only old women around.

"The sun has set," Mei Mitsuya announced. "It's time to bring this celebration to a close. The funerals will be held tomorrow morning.

Sleep well, and don't be late! Sleep while the bear is in your bellies."

With the daylong festivities at an end, Kayu Saitoh dragged her feverish body back to her hut. Ate Amami and Inui Makabe came home in high spirits, while Shigi Yamamoto sat, as she always did, in front of the hearth in mute disinterest for the lingering revelry—or for that matter, for the party itself. After a little while, Hikari Asami arrived carrying a piece of the cub's pelt, which she gave to Kayu Saitoh. When Kayu Saitoh wrapped herself in the fur and lay in the straw, she was able, for the first time since she'd arrived in Dendera, to sleep without feeling the cold.

She awoke the next morning and felt refreshed. Between the nourishment and fat of the bear's meat and genitals, and the deep sleep granted her by the fur's warmth, Kayu Saitoh was stronger than ever. Her arms moved freely and with vigor, her joints didn't hurt, and even her skin had regained its luster.

"Good morning, Kayu," Ate Amami said, emerging from the straw beside her. "How was it, the fur?"

"Warm," Kayu Saitoh replied frankly.

"The straw was terrible, as you know." Ate Amami's tone carried no bitterness, only the truth. "I hope you'll let me use it sometime."

"Sure. Anytime."

"Kayu, your face is so bright and cheerful now. You look like you've found acceptance."

After a moment, Kayu Saitoh responded, "I haven't accepted the way of life in Dendera."

"I know," Ate Amami said. "That's not what I meant." She brushed the straw off the back of her head. "If you don't care for that word—acceptance—let me rephrase it. You've found resolve."

"Resolve," Kayu Saitoh said softly. "I still haven't figured out how to live in Dendera. Now that the bear has stopped coming, I'll be thinking it over every day."

"Today is the funeral. Maybe you should think about everyone who died in this fight, and everyone in Dendera who has died before, as you make up your mind."

Ate Amami went to the water jug. Half watching her, Kayu Saitoh realized that the woman's advice was sound, and even though Ate Amami wasn't watching her, she nodded. But then she felt that someone *was* watching her, and she looked around. Shigi Yamamoto's eyes were open. The woman wasn't looking directly at Kayu Saitoh, but her head was turned in that direction. Her eyes had been full of life back in the Village, but not anymore.

"Shigi Yamamoto," Kayu Saitoh said, "what are you thinking about all the time? You move hardly at all. You didn't care when the bear came. You're always thinking."

Shigi Yamamoto didn't answer.

"You... were always so good to me," Kayu Saitoh continued regardless, "all the way from when I was a little girl. You were kind. All the women liked you. And envied you. You married into that herb garden. You weren't stuck with some lousy husband who couldn't feed you. You know, I've been thinking, and I've wondered if maybe you wanted to die on the Mountain. I wonder if life in Dendera is just unbearable for you. I wonder if you wish you were dead."

"It doesn't matter what you say to her," Ate Amami said, having finished her water. "Shigi won't respond to anything. You really should know that by now, Kayu."

"Even so, I wanted to ask. I was curious if *she* had thought about everything and made up her mind, and that this was the result."

"Yeah, I understand. She used to be so lively and cheerful."

Ate Amami and Kayu Saitoh held their eyes on Shigi Yamamoto. Even under their combined stares, her mud-smeared face showed no reaction at all, and she merely kept on with her unintelligible mumblings.

Kayu Saitoh wrapped the fur around her shoulders and stepped outside. The bright and clear morning sunlight announced a new day for Dendera, but to Kayu Saitoh, who had only just recovered from the celebration's fever, the glare was blinding and painful. She scooped up a handful of snow and washed her face with it, but the snow only left a lingering coldness on her skin. She set forth for the western end of the settlement.

As she walked, enjoying the fur's warmth, she saw Ire Tachibana and Kushi Tachibana leaving their hut. The twins had Climbed the Mountain seventeen years ago. Here in Dendera, as in the Village, the two lived inseparably, never interposing themselves into the world around them. Here, as in the Village, they looked only to each other, sharing their laughter.

They gave Kayu Saitoh the creeps. She swore to herself that she would never let herself behave as they did, and she scurried away.

Kayu Saitoh arrived at the burial grounds.

The graves were still in disarray. Beneath a thin layer of snow, the wooden markers and gravestones were scattered about, and the unearthed remains remained unearthed. The chief had delayed the cleanup, having decided either through pragmatism or compassion not to spoil the celebration by reviving memories of the horrific events. Kayu Saitoh brushed away some of the snow and revealed bones just as white. She didn't know to whom they had belonged, but seeing the remains, she came upon a cruel truth that seemed to dwell within the bones. The dead could do nothing for the living, and the living did not live in service of the dead. She continued into the desecrated cemetery and focused on clearing snow from the bleached skeletons and the rotting deceased. As she worked, she realized that the dead no longer had any responsibilities. The thought warmed her heart, but she disregarded the sentiment, judging the sympathy an indulgence she mustn't allow.

Beside one of the splintered markers, she found another set of bones, a ribcage with backbone intact. Seeing the nearly complete ribcage, Kayu Saitoh again felt that tenderhearted sympathy, and again she ignored it, concentrating solely on cleaning away the snow.

But then her fingertips felt something abnormal.

It had been only the slightest feeling; had her bare fingertips been even a little colder, she might not have noticed. She ran her finger over the place she'd felt the minute anomaly, and finding it again, she looked down. On one of the ribs was an unusual flaw. She held the bone in the light and inspected it closely. What she had felt wasn't a dent or a chip, but was as if something sharp had scraped the bone. It was so incredibly tiny, that had Kayu Saitoh not taken interest, nothing would ever have come of it. But the crack nagged at her thoughts. She doggedly pursued any theory that would explain its existence but came to no conclusions. She did, however, manage to put together a supposition. Carrying the ribcage, she left the cemetery.

She came to the manor. As she entered, she heard what sounded like an argument, but she considered it no concern of hers as she crossed the earthen entryway. Nokobi Hidaka and Itsuru Obuchi, who shared the manor with the chief, lifted their heads, noticing Kayu Saitoh carrying the ribcage, but the two women said nothing. Kayu Saitoh climbed the stairs to the second floor, which wasn't an easy task with the bones cradled in her arms.

Upstairs she saw Mei Mitsuya flanked by two women whose backs were turned to the staircase. On the left was Hono Ishizuka, and on the right, Naki Sokabe.

"Come now, Mei," Hono Ishizuka was saying, disappointment in her tone. "It's too early for that. You hold Dendera together, so please, use your head."

"The women are energized from our victory," the chief said, confidence presiding in her voice. "It's the perfect time! We will attack the Village. It's the right move. Why can't you see that?"

"But look," a flustered Naki Sokabe interjected, "so many have died. The Hawks—no, Dendera as a whole—we've lost so many. We had fifty, but now only thirty-six are left. We can't hope to attack like this—"

The chief laughed. "So that's why you interfere. You've been a Hawk for a long time now, but you've given in to defeatist delusions. You've lost your spine."

"But, Mei Mitsuya," Naki Sokabe pressed, "think about it, please. We just don't have enough people. Why don't we take a few more years, rebuild our numbers, and—"

"And wait?"

"What?"

"Are you telling me to wait?" The chief's face turned red, and her voice rose to a fierce roar. "I've waited for thirty years! I'm one hundred years old! I'm at the end. I can wait no longer."

With great patience, Hono Ishizuka said, "Mei, I understand how you must feel, but you're our leader, and right now, your duty is to rebuild Dendera. We need to rebuild from the bear's destruction."

"No. We need to attack the Village with what strength we have left."

"Then Dendera will be destroyed."

"You don't know that," the chief said. "And frankly, it doesn't matter. I built this place for my own reasons. Dendera is mine. You have no right to tell me what to do."

"Is that how you truly feel?" Hono Ishizuka asked.

"You must not be taking me seriously," the chief said, looking up at Hono Ishizuka. "It's not my 'true feelings' or any such rubbish—it's what I set out to do from the beginning."

"Why do you spurn peaceful life in Dendera and instead seek war? We have no connection with the Village anymore. At the very least, they've forgotten about us all."

"It's not over until I say it's over. *There's* your connection. As if you know what the Village thinks." Undeterred, the chief smiled with only her mouth.

Having observed the scene in silence, Kayu Saitoh spoke up. "Mei Mitsuya, I found these at the burial grounds. They're cracked. It's not the work of a bear's claws or fangs, but rather something with a sharp edge. What is this? How did this person die? Or should I say, why was she killed? Who killed her?"

2

Mei Mitsuya didn't speak. Kayu Saitoh asked the same of Hono Ishizuka and Naki Sokabe, but they didn't speak either. Their silent reactions caused Kayu Saitoh to begin doubting her theory as a product of pure fantasy. But the bones cradled in her arms gave her a feeling akin to courage, though harder to describe, and she managed to retain confidence in her intuition.

"You won't fool me," she said. "I believe the crack in these bones more than I believe you. If you won't talk, I'll take matters into my own hands. I'll show these ribs around until I find someone who will tell me what happened."

"Don't," Hono Ishizuka said sharply. "Any actions that would bring further disorder upon Dendera will not be permitted."

Kayu Saitoh didn't yield. "Who won't permit it? *You?* I'm not afraid of you one bit. You know, Hono Ishizuka, I've been in Dendera for sixteen days now, and I haven't seen you do even one bit of work. You only complain."

"I won't respond to your provocations."

"I'm only stating the truth," Kayu Saitoh said.

"In that case," Hono Ishizuka said, "you're worse than me. You complain about every single thing. Really, you should be ashamed."

"Trying to nitpick your way out of a losing argument, are you?"

"Kayu Saitoh," the chief said, looking straight at her, "nobody knows about that crack. If you forget about it, it'll be as if the crack never existed. It'll be like nothing happened."

"Enough," Kayu Saitoh said. "I don't need your help."

When she turned to leave, she heard the scrambling footsteps of Hono Ishizuka and Naki Sokabe running after her with violent intentions. Quickly, they restrained her and pinned her to the floor.

"You bastards!" Kayu Saitoh shouted. "The moment the bear goes away, you act in arrogance! The moment we feel safe, you make your big move! I was right about you people who didn't go to the Mountain—you're all a bunch of feckless good-for-nothings!"

Kayu Saitoh tried to struggle free, but the women had her arms and legs and even her back pinned firmly. She was helpless.

The chief sat down on the floor, looked Kayu Saitoh in the eyes, and said, her voice low, "We gave you a chance, you fool. Shall we put you in the jail again?"

"If you're going to kill me, hurry up and do it. Stab me in the ribs and do it."

"The more you fuss you make, the more you isolate yourself. You must understand that by now."

"I'm not afraid of being isolated," Kayu Saitoh said.

The chief stood in resignation, then kicked Kayu Saitoh down the stairs. Reflexively, Kayu Saitoh grabbed for one of the steps, then pulled herself up to run away, but Nokobi Hidaka and Itsuru Obuchi surrounded her, and when she saw Hono Ishizuka and Naki Sokabe coming down the stairs, she knew she had lost any chance of escape.

For the second time, she was led belowground and tossed into the jail cell.

"Kayu," Hono Ishizuka said, her face expressionless, "you've put yourself in the worst possible situation."

"What is that crack in the bone?" Kayu Saitoh asked, beating at the wooden bars. "What has you all in such a panic?"

Hono Ishizuka didn't respond. Neither did Nokobi Hidaka, Itsuru Obuchi, or Naki Sokabe, who disappeared up the stairs.

Not threatening, but only stating the truth, Hono Ishizuka said, "You might be killed. You really might be killed." Then she departed, leaving Kayu Saitoh alone in silence and gloom.

As before, Kayu Saitoh didn't feel like escaping into slumber. This time, she had the fur to help her endure the cold, and she quietly waited, left without an outlet for her energy. The air cooled further, and the gloom settled into utter darkness, and she knew that night had come. Yet no one had delivered her dinner. As her head wound ached, she grew angry at having missed the funeral and having been unable to pray before Kura Kuroi, instead being abandoned in this cold cage. She stewed in the intolerable irrationality of being locked away like some villain when she had only done what she felt was right.

She lost all sense of pity and sympathy for Dendera, instead blaming the settlement for all her ills. Wrestling with a sea of emotions, she put her hand to the bandage she had made from Kura Kuroi's white robes.

After a while, she grew tired of feeling angry. She gathered a pile of straw in which to sleep, but just then, she felt a delicate disturbance in the stagnant air.

She froze and listened.

She sensed a nearby presence.

Someone was cautiously approaching the cage.

"Who is it?" Kayu Saitoh asked.

"Keep your voice down," the woman said. "If I'm found out, I'll be in serious trouble."

"Who is it?" Kayu Saitoh repeated, softly this time.

"It doesn't matter."

"I have a problem with that."

"And I have a problem with telling you."

The voice seemed to belong to one of the old women, but Kayu Saitoh couldn't place it. The mysterious woman seemed aware that this was the case and gave no indication that she would reveal herself. From the pungent body odor that assaulted her nostrils, Kayu Saitoh knew the woman was just on the other side of the bars, but in the dark, she couldn't discern even an outline.

Kayu Saitoh tried a different question. "Why are you here?"

"You're still too loud. The others are sleeping upstairs. If you won't keep quiet, I'll leave."

"All right. I'll be more careful."

"What did you do, Kayu Saitoh?" the voice asked. "In the span of a single day, your infamy has spread through all of Dendera."

"My infamy?"

"They're saying you're a devil who stole and ate from the leftover bear meat, and that that's why you're in the jail."

Fighting down nascent rage, Kayu Saitoh breathed heavily through her nose.

"Calm down," the voice said soothingly. "I don't believe that you would've done something like that. So what *did* you do?"

Kayu Saitoh put her hand over her nose and said, "And I'm supposed to just tell you that?"

"I'm getting the feeling that you don't trust me."

"You could be some secret informant who's come to see how much I know."

The woman quietly laughed. "A secret informant, huh?"

Recognizing sincerity in the laugh, Kayu Saitoh decided that even if she didn't trust the woman, she could at least report the truth. She offered a highly condensed summary of what had happened: how she found the bone with the unnatural crack, how Mei Mitsuya and the others had reacted, and how she had been locked up as a result. As she talked, her mysterious would-be confidant remained so silent that she began to feel like she was talking to a figment of some foolish hallucination. But when she finished, the voice remarked, "I thought that might be the case."

"So you know then," Kayu Saitoh said. "You know who those bones belonged to, and you know what the crack means."

"No," the woman said, then paused. "I came to the Mountain after the Incident had happened. But I heard rumors, and I even asked Mei Mitsuya about it."

"What did she say?"

"I got a similar reaction to what you got. 'It's not true,' she said, 'and even if it was, forget it, and it won't have happened.'"

"Didn't you investigate any further?" Kayu Saitoh asked.

"Please don't assume everyone is like yourself, Kayu Saitoh. I'm not you. I obeyed Mei Mitsuya's suggestion, and I decided to forget about the matter. I know it was a dishonest thing to do, but I didn't want life to become any more difficult."

"Please tell me what you heard. I don't care if it was only a rumor. What was this Incident?"

"Sixteen years ago," the woman whispered, "a woman was killed."

"Sixteen years ago..."

Despite the darkness, Kayu Saitoh squinted her eyes in thought as she performed the calculation. Any woman older than eighty-six would know what had happened. Of those who had survived, that was Mei Mitsuya, Itsuru Obuchi, Masari Shiina, Makura Katsuragawa, Naki Sokabe, Nokobi Hidaka, Shigi Yamamoto, Kyu Hoshina, Hotori Oze, Ire Tachibana, Kushi Tachibana, and Hono Ishizuka. Setting Shigi Yamamoto aside, due to her mental state, and Kyu Hoshina, who hadn't arrived in Dendera until fourteen years ago, that still left ten who had either witnessed or taken part in the Incident.

Kayu Saitoh cursed. "Something really did happen, didn't it? And they hid it from me, those half-baked bastards."

"You're getting loud again," the woman cautioned. "It seems like all talk of the Incident was made taboo. Most of the women don't know a thing about it. I have to admit I understand why the older ones don't want talk of it to spread."

"Well, I admit no such thing," Kayu Saitoh remarked.

"You know, you haven't even been here one month. How did you come across this knowledge so quickly?"

"I found the ribcage in the burial grounds. One of the bones had been gouged by a knife."

"That's solid proof," the voice said.

"Those thugs have probably crushed the bones into powder by now."

"I wish I could have seen the bones first."

"Huh?"

"I'm going to help you, Kayu Saitoh," came the voice in the darkness. "I'm going to look into what happened sixteen years ago."

"If you do that," Kayu Saitoh replied, "you'll get tossed in here with me."

"Dendera won't be around much longer. With the bear gone, Mei Mitsuya will raid the Village soon. Win or lose, the Village will learn of Dendera's existence."

"Are you... a Dove?"

"I'm a Hawk. I'm not doing this because I want to stir up trouble."

"If not that, then why? You forgot about the matter once already."

After a brief silence, the darkness spoke. "The woman who was killed sixteen years ago... was my sister."

Kayu Saitoh's first thought was of the twins, Ire Tachibana and Kushi Tachibana. Over many years, Kayu Saitoh had taken care of her younger brother, and she understood all too easily what it would be like for a close relative to be killed not by beast but by another human being. Amid an upswell of sympathy, she tried to think of who in Dendera would have had an older sister. But she hadn't been close to many in the Village, and no one came to mind.

The voice spoke again. "I bear no grudges against my sister's killers, not after so much time. I just want to know what happened. I want to know what happened sixteen years ago and why my sister was killed."

"And yet you gave in to your fears and pretended to forget about it all this while."

"That won't happen again. Kayu Saitoh, I couldn't ignore what they're doing to you. That proves that I still care deeply about my sister—and the Incident."

"All right. So what?"

"You've given me another chance to take a stand. I won't let you die."

Kayu Saitoh didn't completely trust the voice in the shadows, but neither did she detect in it any hint of dishonesty, but rather a deep-rooted desire to reclaim lost honor.

"I understand," Kayu Saitoh said, nodding. "I can appreciate your way of thinking. I generally wouldn't fancy anyone who's too afraid to show herself, but since you have honor, I'll make an exception."

"Good." The woman sighed with what sounded like relief. "Thank you."

"May I ask you one thing?" Kayu Saitoh said.

"What?"

"Why do you keep on living?"

"Why I keep on living?" the voice repeated. "I'd have to say...to strike a blow."

"Against whom?" Kayu Saitoh asked.

"Against one and all," the voice said, adding that she would return when she knew something. The shadowy presence went away.

Kayu Saitoh ruminated on this new thought—to strike a blow. The idea wasn't a perfect match for her current outlook or emotional state, but it permeated her thoughts with no particular sense of incongruity. Free from depression, Kayu Saitoh was able to find sleep.

The next morning, Hono Ishizuka and Makura Katsuragawa came with water and a potato, which Kayu Saitoh received without giving resistance. She ate the potato with only her saliva to soften it. Apparently finding her obedience suspect, Hono Ishizuka asked what was with her, but Kayu Saitoh ignored the comment and continued eating her potato. In doing so, she learned that silence could make a more efficient and effective statement than words.

Nothing happened that night or the night after, but late the following one, the mysterious presence returned. Kayu Saitoh peered into the darkness but still couldn't perceive even a silhouette.

"It took you a while," Kayu Saitoh said gruffly, feeling peevish even if she didn't know why. "I was wondering if you'd been caught and killed."

"I wouldn't be so careless as that," the voice said. "So how's life in jail?"

"I'm here, as if I have any other choice."

"Keep your voice down."

"As if I have any other choice," Kayu Saitoh repeated in a whisper. "Nothing changes. Only my thoughts are free to roam."

"And have you thought of anything?"

"I think I want something to believe in—a creed."

"A creed, huh?" the voice said, but didn't inquire any further. "Mei Mitsuya made an announcement this morning. The raid against the Village will take place the day after tomorrow."

"The day after tomorrow? Foolishness." Kayu Saitoh regarded it too much of a rush, even for them. "They have no chance of winning."

"The Hawks would disagree with you. They're full of confidence, having chased off the bear. And they have new weapons too."

"What weapons?"

"The cub's bones," the voice replied. "They're sharpening the bones into daggers and spearheads."

"That seems crude, but I suppose it's a fair bit better than wooden spears alone." Kayu Saitoh snorted. "What about Hono Ishizuka and Masari Shiina? Have the Doves lost their power?"

"With the Hawks full of confidence, the Doves are incapable of stopping them now."

"Then what good are they?" Kayu Saitoh sneered. She changed the subject. "What about our main concern? What about the Incident sixteen years back?"

"I can't do anything that would draw attention, so I haven't been able to come up with much. But I was able to make contact with someone who's still bothered about the Incident—though she's the one who told me about it in the first place."

"Who is it?"

"I can't tell you that, but have no fear. She can be trusted. And I was able to get new information out of her. It turns out that my sister wasn't the only one who died."

"Was it a mass killing?" Kayu Saitoh asked.

"I don't know," the voice replied.

Kayu Saitoh was getting frustrated. "Damn it, come back when you have the rest of the story."

"Do you think it was easy for me to find out that much?"

"We don't have enough even to speculate what happened sixteen years ago." Kayu Saitoh folded her arms in the dark. "Wait a minute, do you think it could have been a struggle between the Hawks and the Doves?"

"If that were the case, then Masari Shiina and Hono Ishizuka would be proclaiming themselves victims. Besides, there's no evidence of any internal struggle."

"Go find the evidence."

"If I do anything more, I'll be noticed for sure."

Feeling irritation at being stuck in the jail, Kayu Saitoh said, "If Dendera will come to its end in two days, you can act freely. That's what I'd be doing."

"Not everyone can do what you can," the woman said. "Anyway, I have my own plan."

"What's your plan?"

"I'm going to use the raid. During the confusion of battle, someone might talk."

Disappointed, Kayu Saitoh said, "That's too hopeful."

"Too hopeful? No, I just haven't abandoned all hope yet."

Something clattered against the cage's floor. The other woman had tossed in something solid. Kayu Saitoh groped about for the object, and her fingers touched something cold. "What is this?" she asked.

"It's a sign of my appreciation. A spoon, actually. It's made from the cub's bones, so it's large and durable."

"A spoon?"

"Kayu Saitoh, there's something I need to tell you before I go." The woman's already serious tone became solemn. "It seems that Dendera has decided to leave you in that cage."

"And abandon me to die?"

"Seems so."

Words of disgust came from deep in her throat. "Those bastards will do anything, no matter how shameful, as long as it'll keep me quiet."

"For now," the voice said, "use what I gave you to free yourself. What'll happen next is up to you. You have your own way of living; do as you will."

Instead of responding, Kayu Saitoh bit her lower lip as she gripped the spoon.

"What's wrong?" said the voice on the other side of the bars. "Why so quiet all of a sudden? You can leave Dendera and go on to reach the Paradise you so desire. You can confront the women here. You can do whatever you like. You're completely free now. Goodbye. May we meet again if circumstances allow."

"Wait," Kayu Saitoh called out.

"I thought I told you to keep your voice down. What's wrong? Are you frightened now that you're suddenly free?"

"Who are you? Tell me already. It's not fair to put me in your debt and then disappear."

"Not fair? Don't try to trick me into telling you."

"Just tell me already."

The voice replied without hesitation. "I'm your supporter. I want you to live. When you get out of here, I don't want you to Climb the Mountain. I want you to go on living. Goodbye—I mean it this time. If we both live, I hope we can meet again. I'm grateful to you, Kayu Saitoh."

The unseen presence moved, melting into the darkness, and then was gone.

As Kayu Saitoh considered what she should do next, a part of her knew that she mustn't betray her supporter's entreaty, even if she didn't understand exactly what that meant. She stuck her spoon into the dirt floor. The utensil made less noise and moved the earth more easily than she had expected. She chipped away at the dirt ceiling too, then grabbed one of the wooden bars and gave it a solid yank. It came out with ease. Having gained her freedom, Kayu Saitoh wrapped the fur around her shoulders, gripped her spoon, and slipped from the cage.

3

Joints long idle now protested her movement, but Kayu Saitoh ignored the pain as she emerged from the manor's ground level. Shadows loomed over Dendera, yet the outside was far brighter than underground, and Kayu Saitoh's eyes took in the scene with ease. Several fire baskets had been lit; even though the bear hadn't returned, the women were without proof of its death and remained on the lookout. Kayu Saitoh scurried from the doorway and leaned herself against the manor's outer wall as she considered her next course of action. *Run. Fight. Hide.* Several options presented themselves in her thoughts, but none stood above the rest. She surveyed her surroundings. The moonlight reflected on snowy ground, which joined into the Mountain looming in the distance.

She could go anywhere.

The notion granted her courage. Vitality filled her to overflowing, her mind was refreshed, and warmth coursed through her body. Her thoughts lagged behind this impulsive notion, but mindful of the white robe cloth wrapped around her head, she took in a deep breath and made her decision. She would go as far as she could go. If forced to strike down anything that came to stand in her path, she could do so with the bear-bone spoon. This was her decision.

Kayu Saitoh took her first step with this new resolve at almost exactly the same time she heard the scream. A small group of women appeared in the far-off firelight at the edge of the settlement. Squinting, she could see five women: Mei Mitsuya, Nokobi Hidaka, Tsugu Ohi, Kan

Tominaga, and Tsusa Hiiragi. They seemed to be chasing something.

Kayu Saitoh recognized the feeble screams and concluded that the women must be chasing Makura Katsuragawa.

Quickly surrounded, Makura Katsuragawa dropped to the ground. Cautiously, Kayu Saitoh approached the group. The circle of five trained their spears on the blubbering woman. With their focus entirely upon Makura Katsuragawa, Kayu Saitoh was able to approach the small group until she was almost upon them.

The moon's light sent a pale cast over Makura Katsuragawa's already pale features. "Please don't, please don't," she begged again and again. Her frail voice seemed to disappear as soon as it passed her lips. The circled women offered no response to her cries, instead talking among themselves as they kept their speartips aimed at the woman.

Then Mei Mitsuya stepped forward and said, "Makura Katsuragawa, listen to what I have to say. You'll be all right. I can help you."

"You can help me?" Makura Katsuragawa said, her voice still feeble. "You're lying. You can't help—"

Her words cut off mid-sentence as she began to cough fiercely. She spasmed and writhed in the snow, as the women who surrounded her began to panic. Tsusa Hiiragi whispered, horror in her voice, "What is this?"

Only the chief remained unperturbed. "Makura Katsuragawa, return to Dendera," she said. "There's nowhere else for you to go."

"I—I," Makura Katsuragawa said, having to squeeze out each word. "I want to go to the Mountain. I want to finish my Climb. I want to go to Paradise."

As she spoke, her voice gradually weakened, until she suddenly made a strange retching sound, and her back shook with violent, periodic jolts. Kayu Saitoh cried out by reflex, but no one noticed, as her sound had been swallowed by the far louder cries of the ring of women as they leaped backward.

Makura Katsuragawa was vomiting blood.

Each time her back shook, she brought up a large amount of the stuff, painting the snow around her in red. The blood gave off a stench unnatural and foul, fetid and meaty, as if her guts had rotted and melted into blood.

"Help—help me..."

Even as she continued to empty herself of blood, Makura Katsuragawa stood and tried to approach the other women, who tossed down their spears and fled in panic.

"Remain calm," the chief ordered. "Hurry up and capture her."

But the elder's commands didn't reach the others as they scattered in flight, trying to distance themselves from the vomiting woman. The little group was a group no more, the women making a disgraceful display, bounding about like crippled rabbits.

Only Tsugu Ohi hadn't moved.

Still gripping her wooden spear, she hadn't moved.

Suddenly, she dropped her spear, then keeled over on the spot and vomited massive quantities of blood. The foul smell thickened. Each of the panicking women, and even Makura Katsuragawa, saw her and stopped where they were. All remained unnaturally still and quiet—so quiet that Kayu Saitoh could hear the clouds drifting through the sky.

"A plague!" Makura Katsuragawa's scream shattered the silence. "It's a plague! I'm going to die! I'm going to die!"

The woman ran about far faster than could be expected from someone who had just sprayed blood from her mouth and her notched-out nose.

"Quiet. Quiet," Mei Mitsuya shouted. "Somebody stop her!"

But again the chief's orders went unheard, and the utterly disordered group resumed their chaotic flight. They shrieked in mindless panic, shouting, *A plague, a plague.*

Plague, as a word, was itself a kind of plague that quickly propagated through Dendera as women, awoken from slumber, emerged from their huts. Makura Katsuragawa screamed and ran about. Tsugu Ohi was completely motionless. Blood had splattered across the snow. As each woman saw this scene, she too joined in the maelstrom, shouting, "A plague, a plague."

Amid the frenzy, Makura Katsuragawa saw Kayu Saitoh. The woman's taut, contorted expression softened, and she ran over. "Kayu, please help me," she said, reaching her hand to Kayu Saitoh's shoulder. "I don't want this. I don't want this. I don't want to die from a plague."

Steadying the perilously shaking woman, Kayu Saitoh asked, "What is this plague?"

"It's a plague. A *plague*. I'm going to die. They're going to kill me."

"They're going to kill you?"

Then someone said, "You, what are you doing here?"

Kayu Saitoh turned to find Mei Mitsuya staring her down.

"I don't want this!" Makura Katsuragawa shrieked, fearfully ducking behind Kayu Saitoh to hide from the chief. "Don't come near. Don't come near, m-m-murderer."

Reacting immediately, Kayu Saitoh asked, "What do you mean, murderer?"

"Mei," Makura Katsuragawa moaned. "Mei Mitsuya...when the plague spread through Dendera, she killed the ones who were sick. She stabbed them in the chest. She'll kill me too! She'll do it where everyone can see. It's a plague. The plague has come."

Chapter 6

Amidst the Carnage

The cage was mended from Kayu Saitoh's breakout, Makura Katsuragawa confined inside it, Tsugu Ohi's body delivered to rest in the burial ground, the blood spatters concealed in snow, and the witnesses ordered to silence; then Mei Mitsuya led Kayu Saitoh up to the second floor and revealed what had happened sixteen years before—the truth behind the Incident.

Midsummer, sixteen years earlier, one of the women retched up blood. At first, the others presumed her ill and cared for her, but when the same symptom manifested in several of her caretakers, it became clear that this was a plague. Soon the victims grew in number, and of the twenty-nine women who then resided in Dendera, thirteen died. One of two things happened to all who came down with the plague: either she vomited foul-smelling blood and died suddenly, or she vomited foul-smelling blood for several weeks and then died. The remaining women fell into a panic, then ultimately settled on one conclusion:

kill the infected. It was a decision made not by Mei Mitsuya, but Dendera itself. All agreed, whether Doves or Hawks. Masari Shiina, the head of the Doves, as well as Hono Ishizuka, who had arrived in Dendera that same year, both consented to the killing of the infected. Once resolved to carry out the killings, Mei Mitsuya chose a method inspired by the Village's numerous punishments. She gathered the women in the clearing, presented to the group a single unsharpened stone dagger, and ordered them all to fashion its edge into a sharp blade. Drenched in sweat under the blazing sun, the gathered women hewed the dagger. When each had sharpened it all she could, another replaced her, and another, and so on, and when the sun set, the dagger was finished.

Three women were displaying symptoms of the plague, and Mei Mitsuya had them laid out beside her atop the balcony. Standing there, feeling the collective gaze of all of Dendera upon her, she killed the infected women. Their bodies were interred in the burial ground, and the plague disappeared. When autumn came, it was as if the time of the plague had never happened.

That was all Mei Mitsuya had to say, but Kayu Saitoh didn't consider the discussion finished. The chief had mentioned the three slain women by name, and one of their family names was familiar: Kiriyama. She tried to match Soh Kiriyama's voice to that of her mysterious benefactor, only to realize she'd never heard the woman speak.

But when Kayu Saitoh spoke, she instead started with the question she wanted to ask more than any other.

"Why did you hide what you did?"

"It's not the kind of thing you go around telling everyone, now is it? Nothing is more terrifying than an unstoppable disease."

"Shouldn't we at least tell Soh Kiriyama?"

"Leave her be." Mei Mitsuya stood, stepped out to the windy balcony, and with the strength gone from her voice, she murmured, "The time of the plague has returned."

Unnerved by Mei Mitsuya's display of frailty, Kayu Saitoh attempted to rally herself by asking, "But can't we find a way to stop it? I've heard of medicine that can be made from bear bones or gall bladder."

"Apparently, you have to remove the gall bladder immediately, before it empties into the intestines. It's been five days—according to Hikari Asami, the cub's gall bladder is empty by now." Her back still to Kayu Saitoh, the chief continued, "And was the other one... bones, you said? That's mere superstition."

"You're pathetic. It's only just begun and you've already given up."

"Go and see how Makura Katsuragawa is doing. You'd do well to fully comprehend the horror of the plague."

"Do you... plan on leaving her to die?"

"Leave her to die?" Mei Mitsuya looked over her shoulder, facing Kayu Saitoh with an expressionless look. "I'm not going to leave her to die. I'm going to kill her."

"Killing again, is it?"

"Killing again."

"Someone catches the plague, and we're just going to cast them aside... It's awful."

"Sixteen years ago, Makura Katsuragawa herself did just that. She can hardly object now that it's happening to her. I was the one who did the killing, but we were all of us killers. Makura Katsuragawa may have forced the responsibility upon me alone, but her hands are dirty."

"Why don't you go get medicine?" Kayu Saitoh suggested. "If you mean to attack the Village—that is, if you're going to attack the Village and you mean to win, then go pillage their herb gardens. That's another way to stop it, right?"

Mei Mitsuya's eyes widened in apparent surprise, and she looked at Kayu Saitoh for a long moment. Then her petite lips opened, and a laugh spilled out. Her mouth—and her laughter—slowly grew bigger, until they could have belonged to a demon.

"That's…that's right!" Mei Mitsuya kept laughing as she spoke. "We'll attack the Village, and if we win, everything will belong to Dendera. Their medicine will be Dendera's medicine. All we need to do is seize their herb gardens!"

Her roaring laughter grew louder, soon enveloping not only Kayu Saitoh's eardrums but her entire body. The laughter bore down on her, clinging and oppressive, until Mei Mitsuya abruptly recovered from her fit.

"Our raid will end the plague!" The chief's already red face had flushed to a deeper crimson. "Why didn't I see? I'm a fool! An utter fool!" She punctuated this with another cackle.

"But will anyone take part in the raid?" Kayu Saitoh hadn't yet shaken her doubts. "Dendera is in a terrible state. The bear killed so many, and now the plague is spreading."

"Remember these words, Kayu Saitoh. When dark times come,

you don't simply endure in silence—you use it to your advantage." Mei Mitsuya seemed fully back in control of herself. With her laughter restrained, she spoke with solemn gravity. "The people of Dendera tremble like timid dogs. Tell them that by attacking the village, they'll get medicine, and they'll either happily wag their tails or happily bare their fangs. Either way, they'll hearten, and they'll join in the attack. It won't matter if they're Hawks or Doves."

"I understand your reasoning, but the plague is already spreading."

"As the leader, that's something I must overcome," Mei Mitsuya replied. "I may have ordered the witnesses to silence, but by morning, everyone will know of the plague's return. And just like sixteen years ago, a great panic will rule Dendera, and my influence will melt away. Tomorrow, I will be put to the test. If I overcome the test, I will be able to continue on. If I fail, I could die."

"Die? Why would you say such a thing?"

"Don't be so soft." Mei Mitsuya bared her grimy teeth. "If you lose in battle, you die. You should know that!"

As Kayu Saitoh's eyes landed upon each one of the leader's stained teeth, she realized that these words were a creed acquired over a span of one hundred years. Mei Mitsuya had fought for seventy years in the Village and thirty in Dendera. Both were battlegrounds in the truest sense, and defeat was coupled with death. And now Mei Mitsuya was facing a new battle.

Mei Mitsuya continued, "This might be the last time we talk, so I'll teach you something worthwhile." The chief placed a hand to her headscarf. "Hardships, delights, enemies, allies, escape, resolution, and uncertainty—all will become a part of you through victory in battle. It isn't a game. You mustn't let your guard down. If you leave your body to the currents, you will be dragged down with them."

"What are you talking about?"

"It's all right if you don't understand. Just remember my words. If some petty thing stands between you and your desires, think back on what I've told you."

Then she returned to Kayu Saitoh, gently lowered herself to sit in front of her, and added, "I've talked on for quite a while. When we were back in the Village, we never spoke like this."

"Our ages were far apart," Kayu Saitoh said. "You kept all the women in the Village together. I recognized that as a little girl. I knew you were a great woman."

"That dirty Village treated women like something even dirtier. I didn't act out of a particular desire to better our standing, but I wanted to do *something*. That's what it was . . . I wanted to do something."

"Was that another battle to you?"

"I suppose," Mei Mitsuya said with a brief nod. "And next is the raid on the Village."

"What will a raid change? What will victory bring?"

"I wish I could give you a definitive answer, but in truth, I won't know until I try." Mei Mitsuya lifted her face. A century of sunlight had baked her skin dark and red. "And what about you, Kayu Saitoh? Do you still want to Climb the Mountain?"

"I . . . am part of Dendera. Even if I attempt my Climb again, I won't be able to reach Paradise. Look how stained my white robe is."

"You're right. I suppose your robe is no longer suitable for the journey to Paradise."

"I can't go back now, and so I will never talk of the Mountain again."

Kayu Saitoh looked down at the white robes wrapped around her body. The stains of grime and soil and blood were testaments to her survival, but they also transformed the garments into something that could no longer be reasonably called white.

"That's the right attitude," Mei Mitsuya murmured with approval. "Well then, what will you do next now that you've lost the Mountain? You don't have time to deliberate. The plague won't wait to spread. My plans won't wait to be executed. You can fret over your decision, but everything will proceed all the same without you."

"I know," Kayu Saitoh said with sincerity. "That's why I want to make up my mind. I want to break through this, make my decision, and move forward. It doesn't have to be something great. It doesn't have to be what's right. As long as it's something I can believe in, that'll be enough."

Suddenly feeling a chill, she wrapped herself in the fur.

"In that case, Kayu Saitoh, why don't you do something great? Why don't you do something huge, something ridiculous, something that would astonish anyone? Strike down one and all. Conquer one and all. Won't you do that? Won't you move forward? Listen, you need to find a purpose. What do you aspire to? What do you want to do?"

"I..." Kayu Saitoh's lips formed the single word of their own accord, but her sound was so soft that it wasn't even a voice.

Seeing her falter, Mei Mitsuya responded not with ridicule but rather by creasing the corners of her eyes into an accepting smile. "I understand," she murmured, then added, "I have nothing more to say to you." The creases of her eyes returned to their normal place. "Leave."

"Leave . . . ? But what should I do?"

"How should I know? Events are already in motion. Don't delay; go. Don't delay; move forward. Fight to fulfill your aspiration."

Mei Mitsuya's tone of voice impelled Kayu Saitoh to leave. Understanding that this time the conversation was finished, Kayu Saitoh stood and moved toward the ladder leading to the ground floor.

Suddenly, the chief's voice came from behind. "Who released you from the cage?"

Mei Mitsuya didn't respond.

"I don't care who it was, but she's living more purposefully than you."

This time, their conversation was indeed over, and Kayu Saitoh exited the large hut. Now that the plague had returned to Dendera, confessing to her collusion with Soh Kiriyama wouldn't have mattered much, but she kept it to herself anyway. After the coming of one unforeseeable event after another, she wanted to limit her problems to those that already faced her.

Back home, Inui Makabe was busily tending the fire while she talked to Ate Amami about Makura Katsuragawa and Tsugu Ohi's illness. The two talking women didn't give any particular response to Kayu Saitoh's return, while Shigi Yamamoto's lack of response was a given. Trembling and pale-faced, Inui Makabe and Ate Amami appeared to have been unaware of the events sixteen years earlier, not even by rumor. These women were still acting as a family, but Kayu Saitoh supposed, in a passing thought, that come morning the panic would spread, controlling everyone, herself included.

Her prediction proved true.

The old women stirred into motion slightly before the morning light reached into Dendera. They congregated in the clearing without anyone having to suggest it. Their faces obscured by the dark, they frantically exchanged what information they had. Kayu Saitoh was among their number. She hadn't come with a particular purpose, but that didn't mean anything—neither had most of the others who were gathered there with her. If someone were to ask them what action they wanted to take, they likely would not have been able to provide an answer.

As Kayu Saitoh listened to the volleying jumble of words, one rumor caught her attention: the origin of this outbreak was the bear cub's meat. The cub had rampaged through the burial ground and had likely eaten of the bones of the plague victims from sixteen years ago. The women had eaten the cub's meat, the reasoning went, and couldn't that be the cause of the plague's return? Kayu Saitoh didn't know who said this first, but the conjecture was uncannily persuasive and before long became a commonly held belief among the women. Kayu Saitoh recalled the feast. Hono Ishizuka, Naki Sokabe, Masari Shiina, Hotori Oze, Ire Tachibana, and Kushi Tachibana hadn't lined up for the bear stew. At the time, Kayu Saitoh, overcome by hunger, hadn't thought anything of their abstinence. Now she put her mind to work, trying to form some kind of hypothesis. But when the idea came to her, it came not as some uncertain hypothesis, but a singular, absolute conclusion.

Someone shouted, "It was the bear meat!"

If only for an instant, Kayu Saitoh thought her own thoughts had taken form and burst out—that was how closely the shout mirrored them. Evidently, she wasn't the only one thinking along those lines, as a good many other women looked up with surprised or, for some, embarrassed expressions, their eyes searching for the source of the outburst.

The speaker was Naki Sokabe.

"I didn't eat the bear! I had a bad feeling about it," she cried, her voice a rasping assault. "Right? That cub rampaged through the burial ground. How could we eat it and expect to be unharmed?"

This proclamation equated to a death sentence for those who had eaten the meat—which was the majority of the women. From here and there came sobs, almost shrieks, which soon unified and transformed into anger. Kayu Saitoh realized that she too was getting angry, and that this anger was without reason, but yet she submitted to it, letting her outrage unfold. Her muscles throbbed, she lost control of her mind, and nearly unaware of her own actions, she spread her arms and cried, "The bear meat was bad!"

The simplicity of the collective rage felt good. Other women cried out as she had, and the conjecture became belief. None of them had a plan, but events proceeded with or without one. No one needed to take the lead. The old women shouted, radiating heat, and the snow in the clearing turned to a slushy mess. The crowd's heat rose, and the sound of trampling, excited footsteps was explosive, and the rage and fever made them want to strike someone. They wanted to find an enemy. It felt incredibly natural for the crowd to turn these feelings toward the manor at the front of the clearing, and to the manor's owner. Mei Mitsuya was the source of all wrong. Even Kayu Saitoh felt the same way, though assuming the plague had been lurking in the bear meat, Mei Mitsuya couldn't possibly have divined the fact. But the hostile shouts continued to spread. The other women were shouting Mei Mitsuya's name in contempt, so Kayu Saitoh tried it as well. When she did, relief and the pleasure of conformity ran loose within her, jumbling with the fever and the fury and the exhilaration, and she no longer understood why she was so sweaty, or why she was shouting so loudly, or what thoughts were in her mind—or why she should ever need to understand such things at all. Her awareness was an unsteady haze from which only the feeling of rage emerged clear. In this state, the old women—and Kayu Saitoh—succeeded in convincing themselves that Mei Mitsuya was the instigator of the plague's outbreak. They succeeded in holding that conviction while being blind to any counterarguments and the frailty of their evidence. Their radiant heat and odors swirled and rose, crashing against the manor.

Mei Mitsuya appeared on the balcony. "Quiet, all of you! Silence! You all go stampeding down the same wrong path, and then what? A happy march straight to hell? Is that what you want?"

Kayu Saitoh heard the chief's words but remained unable to come to her senses; instead, she could only thrust her hands high and bellow Mei Mitsuya's name. The other old women too hurled angry cries at the chief.

"Don't conflate the bear meat with the plague! If we had eaten meat infected with the plague, that would be one thing, but it was only a bear cub." Mei Mitsuya didn't shy away from the outcries, but rather confronted them head on. "What really matters is what fool set off all this panic. *She's* the true plague! Reveal yourself, you plague, and I will show you no mercy."

Rather than trying to nullify the panic, the chief and overlord of Dendera added a threat and a new offense, which she attempted to pin on someone else. As far as ploys went, this was an effective one—all the more so with the old women's propensity for taking direction from anyone with a loud enough voice—and most times, under ordinary circumstances, this method would likely have played out as Mei Mitsuya anticipated, even though it wouldn't solve the underlying issues.

But this wasn't an ordinary time.

Without the slightest forewarning, several screams came from somewhere behind Kayu Saitoh. The shrieks were shrill and girlish, made by old women forgetting that they were old women.

Kayu Saitoh looked over her shoulder, and from the corner of her eyes she saw something red. She recognized it immediately as blood, and Somo Izumi had expelled it. The woman was coughing blood that splashed onto those around her. Her neck and arms twisted in impossible directions, and she convulsed and coughed blood again and again, and then she fell. No one came to her aid; rather, the entirely opposite idea spread through the crowd.

"We-we have to kill her," someone whispered.

That was the mob's conclusion.

Once employed as a solution, killing became the natural course. After the first woman began kicking the fallen Somo Izumi in the stomach, violence sparked into existence and spread in a wave not only through those near Somo Izumi but others farther away. The women moved as one, and Kayu Saitoh found herself separated from the crowd. On her own now, she regained some measure of composure and realized she had been caught up in the frenzy, but it was too late. The women wouldn't stop. Mei Mitsuya wouldn't be heard. What Kayu Saitoh had done wouldn't be taken back. Amid the clamor, Somo Izumi was being killed.

"I accept your decision!" Mei Mitsuya shouted. "All right, I'll kill them. Not just Somo Izumi, but also Makura Katsuragawa. Just like sixteen years ago!"

Her voice finally reached the crowd.

The women looked up at the balcony and raised a great cheer. Just then, a single ray of morning sunlight pierced through the clouds and reached the clearing. Another bright and pure dawn was coming, its light falling upon women wanting to kill one of their own.

Mei Mitsuya's eyes were bloodshot, distressed by events having not gone according to plan and keenly aware that when the curtain rose on her day of reckoning, she had failed immediately. Mei Mitsuya lowered her head, steadied her breathing, then tossed down an unsharpened knife—though for now, it was less a knife than it was a piece of stone.

"Put Somo Izumi in the cage until your work is done."

With no further word, Mei Mitsuya stepped back from the balcony and out of sight.

This was to be a repeat of sixteen years ago.

With that, tensions calmed.

The women went into a flurry of activity. Some hauled the bloodied and battered Somo Izumi to the cage, while others returned to their homes to fetch their sharpening stones, which they compared to see whose would be able to fashion the sharpest edge. The women seemed unified in their desire to carry out their unadulterated intent to kill. Meanwhile, Kayu Saitoh felt without a place, unsure of what to do. Despising her own inaction, she smacked her fist against the gash on her head as hard as she could. The intense pain brought her momentary satisfaction.

But then she realized Hotori Oze had been watching her, and her spirits fell. Hotori Oze's eyes seemed to be following the other women, observing them as they moved about.

"What are you looking at?" Kayu Saitoh snapped.

"The way things are going, Mei Mitsuya will lose her authority. And I can't say prospects for the assault on the Village are good."

"That's too bad for you, Hawk."

"I might also deem the thwarting of her premature raid to be a positive outcome. The attack Mei Mitsuya envisions is a bit different than what I would consider ideal."

"And what's your ideal?"

"I want to burn the Village to the ground. Mere death and destruction won't satisfy me. I want to thoroughly crush it, shred it to pieces, and leave no trace behind. I think fire presents the best option—set every person, every building, every single thing ablaze. Take it out by the roots." Despite the brutality of her words, her expression remained placid. "I never sensed that level of conviction in Mei Mitsuya's plans. She was angry, but she still held sentiment for the Village."

"And did Mei Mitsuya ever tell you that?"

"No, not at all. It's just my personal doubts."

Hotori Oze's opinion was new to Kayu Saitoh. Whether or not the woman was right, finding homesickness and affection for the Village in the chief's demeanor was a feat of which Kayu Saitoh was incapable.

Hotori Oze continued, "Mei Mitsuya ate the bear meat and gave it to the Hawks. That's why I have my doubts. All I care about is bringing an overwhelming assault against the Village. I'm not interested in bears, and I don't want to eat bear meat of dubious quality. Regardless of the source of the plague, Mei Mitsuya's half-hearted approach got us into this squabble over the bear meat, and now she has to stage this chicanery. In the final moments before our attack, she got careless. A person like that wouldn't—and *couldn't*—burn the Village roots and all."

"What could have made you start thinking this way—to talk about burning the Village roots and all?"

"Don't you understand?" Hotori Oze arched an eyebrow. "I hate it. I hate that Village so much I can't stand it. It makes me feel sick. It offends me. It disgusts me. The place I used to live wasn't like that nasty Village; it was beautiful and pure. Your Village doesn't hold a shred of anything of beauty; where I grew up was filled with nothing else."

"Shut up. I've heard enough."

"What's wrong, Kayu Saitoh? You sound angry. What, do you love that nasty Village?"

"Stop it. Stop babbling like a little girl." Kayu Saitoh's hand reflexively balled into a fist. Hotori Oze regarded her with a cool gaze, not making any attempt to retreat or smooth over what she'd said. Kayu

Saitoh could no longer decide what to do with her fist, so she walked away instead.

Nineteen women—Naki Sokabe, Itsuru Obuchi, Hono Ishizuka, Kotei Hoshii, Maka Kikuchi, Ate Amami, Chinu Nitta, Inui Makabe, Tai Komaki, Koto Onodera, Tahi Kitajima, Ume Itano, Kan Tominaga, Usuma Tsutsumi, Tema Tsukamoto, Tamishi Minamide, Tsusa Hiiragi, Ire Tachibana, and Kushi Tachibana—were in the clearing. In solemn silence, they dutifully sharpened the knife that was to kill Makura Katsuragawa and Somo Izumi. Each woman hammered the blunt stone knife with the sharpening stone a few times, then was relieved by the woman next in line behind her, who would hammer the knife a few more times, then be relieved by the woman next in line, and so on. The women would repeat this process until the knife was sharp. This act of mutual complicity disturbed Kayu Saitoh. The women put on a display of being willing to get their hands dirty, but Kayu Saitoh saw through the transparent ruse—their actions were in fact diluting the crime—and she found it reprehensible.

While Dendera headed down its new course, Kayu Saitoh went on a solitary walk.

She didn't have any destination. Without the strength to return home and choose indifference alongside Shigi Yamamoto, without the courage to cut through the crowd and enter the manor, and without the resolve to visit Makura Katsuragawa and Somo Izumi's prison, she simply wandered. The heavy snow that blanketed Dendera glittered in the morning sunlight. Only after she'd already walked part of the way did Kayu Saitoh realize her legs were taking her to the burial ground. When it came into view, she saw the area had been put back into order, perhaps through the employment of mass graves. The burial stones had been returned to their proper places, the wooden grave markers had been exchanged for new ones, and the scattered bones had been reburied.

Someone was standing there, facing the graveyard.

Kayu Saitoh was still some distance away, but somehow she knew the woman was Soh Kiriyama. She calmly approached and called her name. When the woman turned, it was indeed her.

A gentle look came to Soh Kiriyama's grimy, unwashed face. She said, "It seems you couldn't stand it either," and returned her gaze to the graveyard.

Realization of the truth in Soh Kiriyama's words brought some small measure of order to Kayu Saitoh's emotions.

"What you did ended up being all for nothing," Kayu Saitoh said, standing beside the woman. Both of them stared into the graveyard. "You know, don't you? Your sister was killed to pacify those who were terrified of the plague."

"There's something I want to tell you, Kayu Saitoh."

"What's that?"

"Yesterday, I vomited blood."

"What?" Kayu Saitoh blurted.

"Keep your voice down," Soh Kiriyama said with a smile. "My bones might be getting that same crack my sister's have."

After a pause, Kayu Saitoh said, "Don't tell anyone."

"Either way, I'll soon be found out. It's only a matter of time."

Kayu Saitoh cursed, then gritted her teeth as if she could grind away the senselessness of their situation. "Why is this happening? Why are we all dying? After the bear, next comes the plague?"

"This time, people will be killing people."

Soh Kiriyama stared at the burial grounds and the graves in which now rested the women who had lived in Dendera and died in Dendera.

Nothing could be done for those who had already perished. They knew nothing and could do nothing as their flesh and bones disintegrated into the burial dirt. Kayu Saitoh glanced at her right arm. Emaciated with age to skin and bone, it wasn't all that different from those of the dead, but she was alive, and she felt an urge to move it. She sensed a similar urge for action within Soh Kiriyama. Even while her disease could kill her at any moment, she emanated a will for action; a resolve to do something before she became no more useful than those who rested in the graveyard.

Without turning to look at the woman, Kayu Saitoh asked, "You've gone quiet. What are you thinking?"

"I'm thinking about my sister, myself, the plague . . . and, well, a lot of things."

"Have you come to a conclusion?"

"I'll have a hard time letting them kill me without a fight. I suppose that counts as a conclusion. What about you, Kayu Saitoh? Aren't you going to leave Dendera and find your death?"

"Aren't you the one who told me to live?"

"When I said that, I didn't know I had the plague."

"I don't see how your having the plague has anything at all to do with my staying in Dendera."

Softly, Soh Kiriyama said, "You're right, it doesn't."

Kayu Saitoh listened without looking at the woman, whose voice was, as she had suspected, the same as the one Kayu Saitoh had heard in the darkness of her prison. As she listened, an unguarded feeling of security enveloped her.

But Kayu Saitoh squashed this feeling and probed Soh Kiriyama with another question.

"Just now, you said…you'd have a hard time letting them kill you without a fight. Do you mean to resist them?"

Silence fell over them. This wasn't a refusal to answer, but Soh Kiriyama required time to sort through her emotions.

"Kayu Saitoh," she said after a time, "I might end up causing you trouble. I'm sorry for that. We were able to become so close in that darkness. I'll never forget our talks."

"Neither will I," Kayu Saitoh said with a nod. "I won't forget."

"And a little bit ago, you told me that what I had done was for nothing."

"You were determined to uncover what had happened in the past, but look how everybody ended up finding out. So it was all for nothing, wasn't it?"

"It wasn't for nothing." Soh Kiriyama shook her head. "I learned how to be brave."

"What are you talking about?"

"You'll soon see."

Soh Kiriyama turned and departed the burial grounds.

If Kayu Saitoh had thought to follow, she could have, but instead she kept staring at the graves. She didn't exactly know what Soh Kiriyama intended, but the woman's options were limited, and Kayu Saitoh would not be able to aid or oppose her in any of them.

The sun climbed to its apex, and the dazzling, flickering sunlight announced that the day was half gone. Kayu Saitoh returned to the clearing where the fanatical women were gathered.

Their work finished, the women inspected and re-inspected the sharpened knife as they passed through that uncertain period before the next development. Kayu Saitoh sensed something vaguely unnatural about Ate Amami's presence there, but that was merely based on Kayu Saitoh's self-imposed preconceptions of the woman; after all, Ate Amami could have been seized by the fear of the plague. Nothing would have been odd about that. But this observation drew Kayu Saitoh's attention to Hono Ishizuka's inexplicable involvement in the sharpening of the knife. Even when the bear appeared, that woman had remained cool-headed. No matter how Kayu Saitoh looked at it, her participation in the likely-meaningless ritual slayings was bizarre.

Kayu Saitoh wondered if Hono Ishizuka knew something about the plague, or if the two women were participating with an ulterior motive. The seed of suspicion grew unabated inside her.

"It begins," came Mei Mitsuya's voice. She appeared on the balcony.

A black excitement spread through the clearing.

Tahi Kitajima and Maka Kikuchi entered the manor and returned with Makura Katsuragawa and Somo Izumi. Makura Katsuragawa's eyes quivered, puffy from crying, as she shouted, "Help me, help me!"

Somo Izumi had regained consciousness, and she lifted her face, reddened by the crowd's beatings and her vomited blood, and cursed the crowd with her withering glare.

Kayu Saitoh heard footsteps crunching on snow. She looked to the direction of the sound and saw Soh Kiriyama gripping a wooden spear. The woman walked past Kayu Saitoh without sparing her even a glance. Again Kayu Saitoh could sense the woman's desire to take action—a vortex of will within her that the other women failed to detect—as they amiably regarded her as a comrade, saying things like, "Where have you been?"

Without a word, Soh Kiriyama stood beside Tahi Kitajima and Maka Kikuchi, who were holding the infected women in place, and she thrust out her spear. The wooden tip pierced through Tahi Kitajima's neck and kept going until it had jabbed into Maka Kikuchi's neck.

With their guards dead, Makura Katsuragawa and Somo Izumi took off running, and Soh Kiriyama ran after, as if in chase.

Mei Mitsuya's booming voice echoed from the balcony above. "After them! Kill them!"

The seventeen women standing stunned in the clearing snapped back to their senses. With tearful expressions and bewildered by the sudden violence, they began searching for the three plague carriers. Kayu Saitoh, to whom these events hadn't been unforeseen, was nevertheless interested in seeing how they played out, and so she took part in the search. The women instinctively broke apart into several groups. Kayu Saitoh, Mei Mitsuya, Usuma Tsutsumi, and Kan Tominaga entered the hut where Kura Kuroi and the others had been brutally slain. The corpses and viscera had been cleaned up, but the walls hadn't been repaired, and snow had blown inside. The search party remained alert for any sudden attacks, but they found no one, not even a trace.

Usuma Tsutsumi whispered, "You don't suppose they went to the Mountain, do you?"

"The Mountain?" Kan Tominaga said. "Why would they go there?"

"Maybe they realized they had no hope, and gave up and Climbed the Mountain. Or . . ."

"Or?"

"Maybe they went back to the Village."

Some time passed under heavy silence.

Usuma Tsutsumi's speculation troubled them all. If the three plague-bearing women returned to the Village, they would likely reveal Dendera's existence. Kayu Saitoh couldn't predict what the Village would do once they learned about Dendera, but she recognized that the women's surprise attack would no longer be possible, and the Village might attack Dendera instead. At the very least, this would nullify the women's largest advantage: the Village was ignorant of Dendera, while Dendera knew about the Village.

"Don't worry. They won't go back to the Village," Mei Mitsuya said. "What would happen if they did? They'd be killed, of course. They've witnessed it themselves. No, they have to be nearby. Shut up and search."

Her words held some truth, and the women calmed down and resumed their search amid the oppressive, clinging stench of blood. But they remained unable to find the three women. Then, just as one of them suggested moving their search to another hut, Koto Onodera burst into the room.

"What is it?" Mei Mitsuya asked. "Did you find them?"

"Th-they," Koto Onodera gasped, heaving her shoulders, "they've shut themselves in the storehouse. It's a siege."

"Bastards!" Mei Mitsuya screamed, teeth bared, spittle bubbling. She ran outside through the wall the bear had destroyed.

Kayu Saitoh followed after, but the storehouse was a good distance away, and along the way she tired and tripped in the snow. She didn't feel the coldness or pain. Such sensations were superseded by an unidentifiable fear that made her legs shake. She forced herself to stand, and she ran nearly oblivious to anything else. *A siege at the storehouse.* The thought filled her awareness. That alone was enough to make her certain that Soh Kiriyama's group truly meant to fight Dendera.

By the time Kayu Saitoh arrived at the storehouse, the other women had already surrounded the building.

But nobody was doing anything.

"What are you doing?" Kayu Saitoh asked Nokobi Hidaka, who was glaring at the storehouse door. "Open the door already."

"I can't tell if they are pushing against it or if they've barred it, but the door won't open."

"Bust it down then."

"We built it sturdy so it would withstand such attempts. Our spears are useless."

The storehouse, built differently than the other structures in Dendera, appeared impenetrable to most lines of attack. Kayu Saitoh snatched Nokobi Hidaka's wooden spear and struck the door with it. At the first blow, the spear snapped like a twig.

"Let's set it on fire!" Tai Komaki suggested. "We'll burn it down. We can burn down the storehouse and the plague inside it."

"Our food is inside," Hono Ishizuka pointed out. "If we do that, we'll starve to death. We won't have a single potato to eat. We'll die."

"If we don't do anything, we'll die of the plague. The plague will kill us before the starvation will."

"Well, the plague is terrifying, but starvation even more so. Do you really want to go through such suffering?"

"Shut up!" Tai Komaki said, her eyes defiant. "Do you want to get the plague? Do you want to retch putrid blood before you die?"

"If we'd stored up more food, we wouldn't be having this problem. We could've set the storehouse on fire." Hono Ishizuka didn't attempt to hide her anger. "This is all because you Hawks idled about with your training instead of helping us gather food. You Hawks do nothing but cause Dendera trouble."

"What did you say?"

"It was only thanks to the Doves' stockpiles that we made it through the famine ten years ago with minimal losses."

Mei Mitsuya muttered, "Would you stop that? What good does talking like that do us?"

The two women realized their argument was pointless, and their conflict dissipated, leaving only silence. The group of women got back to taking up their positions around the storehouse, itself silent as well.

But when Kayu Saitoh realized what role she could play, she went to stand in front of the storehouse.

"Soh Kiriyama, can you hear me?" she shouted. "I understand that you're serious. I won't disrespect you by asking you to open the door. But let me tell you this one thing: you're wrong. You're so very wrong. If you resist this way, you'll only die. Those of you inside that storehouse, and those of us outside—we'll all die in this confusion and ignorance. This isn't a victory. You're not making a point. Hey, what's wrong with you? Answer me. Answer me!"

No reply came.

Kayu Saitoh recalled what Soh Kiriyama had said: "I'll have a hard time letting them kill me without a fight." She realized that this conviction was shared by all the women who escaped the Mountain to live in Dendera. The difference between the three fugitives and the women of Dendera was the circumstances of their resistance. With this realization, Kayu Saitoh stared at the storehouse and saw danger in failing to take the three women seriously. They weren't simply clinging to their lives; they were making their last, desperate stand.

2

Night came, but nothing had changed. Several fire baskets cast light upon the storehouse, while the surrounding armed women, beset by a mixture of hunger and coldness and irritation, expectantly awaited a new sign of movement from within. But all in the storehouse remained still; its occupants issued not a single demand and made not a single noise. The women on the outside weren't merely idle. Hono

Ishizuka and several of the others had made several attempts to open negotiations. Eight of the women, headed by Mei Mitsuya, went up the Mountain to chop down a fir tree. They planned on using a log to batter down the door. These two separate approaches—negotiation and attack—proceeded concurrently. All had agreed to leave fire as only the last resort. They absolutely couldn't lose the precious provisions stored inside.

With Soh Kiriyama and the others holed up inside the storehouse, the rest of the women hadn't been able to eat. The women of Dendera were chronically malnourished and accustomed to hunger, but robbed of the knowledge of when their next meal would come, the hunger wasn't so easily endured. The fire baskets illuminated their haggard faces and anxious expressions. On the inside, their empty, aching stomachs churned, sapping their spirits before their physical strength had a chance to wane. Too exhausted to move, the women were half-heartedly watching the motionless storehouse when Hono Ishizuka came to stand in front of Kayu Saitoh. The woman's face too showed exhaustion.

"Hey, Kayu. You don't have to keep standing there. Move where some of the fire can reach you. It'll make you feel a little bit better."

"Please leave me alone. I'll move when I want to."

"I know everyone's on edge, between the plague and the hunger, but you seem upset about something else. What's gotten you in such a foul mood?"

"I'm not in a foul mood. I just have the feeling there's a better way to go about this."

"A better way...I certainly can't think of one." Hono Ishizuka glanced over her shoulder at the storehouse. "They've got all of our food. *We're* the ones who are imprisoned out here. If this goes on for days, we'll have to go foraging in the Mountain."

"What about water? No matter how much food they have, they can't survive without water."

"The storehouse holds water reserves for times of emergency. If they're careful, they can make it last for several days. No matter what else, those three won't be dying from hunger or thirst."

Kayu Saitoh thought of something that had been bothering her. "I heard someone saying that the Doves had saved the Hawks during some big famine. What was that about?"

"Oh, that's nothing important. What you said covers it. We were hit by a famine ten years ago, Dendera ran out of provisions, and five of us died. The Doves shared their food reserves with the Hawks."

"And I'm sure you got something out of it."

"Actually, we did." Hono Ishizuka gave her a quick nod. "After that, the Hawks lost some of their power, and more women joined us Doves. Before then, it had just been Masari and me."

"Come to think of it, what's Masari Shiina doing? If Dendera is so important to her, where is she now?"

Kayu Saitoh searched the firelit faces for the woman but didn't find her.

Hono Ishizuka said, "This rough stuff is the duty of the young—and to be blunt, the Hawks."

"Listen, Hono Ishizuka," Kayu Saitoh said, trying to appeal to the woman with her tone. "You know something about the plague, don't you?"

Her expression completely unchanged, Hono Ishizuka replied with a question. "Why would you think that?"

"No reason. The thought just came to me. That's all."

"Since you were kind enough not to hide your suspicions about me, I'll give you a straight answer. I honestly don't know anything about the plague."

"But you didn't have any of the bear stew."

"I lived through the events sixteen years ago, so I was being cautious. Nothing more. Didn't Naki say it this morning? She had an objection to eating the meat of the cub that rampaged through the plague victims' graves."

"Do you really believe that? Do you believe that the bear's meat has caused the plague to spread again?"

"I don't know." Hono Ishizuka shook hear head wearily. "We can never know what the cause is—we just live here in Dendera. That's why I took a precaution. I don't think there's anything unusual about that. If I had known that the meat would cause the plague, at the very least I wouldn't have allowed the Doves to eat any of it."

Having said that, Hono Ishizuka walked around to the opposite side of the storehouse and disappeared into the shadows. For a moment, Kayu Saitoh watched the woman go, but then she realized that wasn't her role, and she joined the others finding warmth around one of the fire baskets.

The storehouse remained ever still.

As Kayu Saitoh puzzled over what the three women were doing

inside, her hand began to itch from the fire's heat, and she scratched at it like a filthy monkey.

Eventually, a voice called out from the darkness. The eight women had returned from the Mountain carrying a log. From the looks of the log, Kayu Saitoh thought that no matter how well barricaded, the door wouldn't stand a chance.

The eight women's spirited expressions conveyed their confidence in the success of their plan. They laid the log to rest on the ground and brought their frozen bodies to the heat of the fires. Mei Mitsuya warmed herself as she explained her plan. As far as plans went, hers was simple. If the further attempts at negotiation were ignored, they would use the log to break open the door, and then they would butcher the three plague-bearers inside. Smiles of relief and optimism spread on the faces of the listening women, who then began a growling chant, saying, "Kill the plague, kill the plague." Kayu Saitoh didn't join in, but neither did she object to the butchering of the three women cloistered inside. She didn't even think it was the wrong thing to do. She still had a thought or two for Soh Kiriyama, Makura Katsuragawa, and Somo Izumi, but she wasn't in a position to give them any serious amount of consideration.

"All right, let's begin!" Mei Mitsuya shouted and ran to the log. The others in her group followed, took their positions, four on each side, and heaved up the log. From the point of view of the storehouse, Mei Mitsuya, Inui Makabe, Kyu Hoshina, and Ume Itano held the right side, while Chinu Nitta, Tai Komaki, Guri Togawa, and Naki Sokabe took the left, and they all stood at the ready. Hono Ishizuka hadn't returned, so Hotori Oze attempted the negotiations, but no matter what she said, no response came. Mei Mitsuya held up her hand, and the rest of the women divided into two groups and moved to each side of the doorway, ready to attack as soon as the door was broken open. Kayu Saitoh had joined with the group on the left, looking from the storehouse.

When all were ready, Mei Mitsuya let loose a bestial roar. Her voice lit a fire within the others. The sensations of battle filled Kayu Saitoh; her breaths came heavily and she clutched her wooden spear, no longer capable of reconsidering what—or whom—that weapon would be killing.

The women holding the log charged ahead with ferocious force. When the storehouse door suddenly opened, they were unable to halt that force, and the eight women and the log went all the way inside. Mei Mitsuya, Kyu Hoshina, and Ume Itano scrambled back out, but in the next instant, the door was closed again. None of them knew what had happened; none of them realized what had been done to them.

What brought them to understand were the screams coming from within the building. When Kayu Saitoh heard them, she finally realized that their plan had been countered. The three women inside had predicted the others would try to ram through the door and came up with an effective countermeasure. In secret, they unbarred the door, and just as the charge came, they opened the entrance on their assailants and locked them inside. Mei Mitsuya, Kyu Hoshina, and Ume Itano had barely escaped, but the other five—Inui Makabe, Chinu Nitta, Tai Komaki, Guri Togawa, and Naki Sokabe were trapped inside. And now came the screams. The door sprang open again, one of the old women was tossed out, and the door immediately closed. It was Inui Makabe. Her stomach was punctured in several places. Kayu Saitoh could see her chest rising and falling, so she thought the woman was still alive. But this was a simple misunderstanding; the motion was nothing more than the muscle spasms of the freshly deceased.

After Inui Makabe's corpse had been tossed out, the storehouse returned to silence. The door didn't open, and no more screams could be heard. The women outside could only stare at the closed door. Kayu Saitoh thrust her spear into the ground and hastily left the scene. She had made a grave error. She had bungled a crucial judgment. These thoughts occupied her head as rage against Soh Kiriyama bubbled up inside her, while the same anger spread through the crowd surrounding the storehouse. Infuriated, Kayu Saitoh walked through the night. Most of the women were gathered at the storehouse, and a deep stillness filled the rest of Dendera, with little separating the settlement from the Mountain itself.

She heard something, possibly a voice. She stopped and listened, and this time she could make out the voice as what it was: a moan. It was the moan of unceasing pain and fear wanting to be released, if only by some small measure. It seemed to come from within a nearby hut, and Kayu Saitoh peered inside. There, Ire Tachibana and Kushi Tachibana had collapsed in front of the hearth. A stone pot rested beside them. From the stench of the blood, Kayu Saitoh realized what had happened and quickly backed away from the hut. Breathing in and out through her nose, as if the night air would cleanse away the lingering smell, she tried to think of where Hono Ishizuka and Masari Shiina were and what they were doing.

"Kayu."

As if Kayu Saitoh's thoughts had taken form, Hono Ishizuka appeared behind her.

Kayu Saitoh shoved Hono Ishizuka against the wall of the hut. "The plague and the bear meat are completely unrelated! Ire Tachibana and Kushi Tachibana didn't eat the stew. But they're vomiting foul blood."

"Kayu," Hono Ishizuka repeated, her expression solemn. "Not a word of what you've seen to anyone."

"The plague is spreading. It's spreading, and it has nothing to do with the bear meat. How can I not tell the others?"

"Telling them the bear meat didn't cause it won't change anything. It'll only add to the chaos, and everyone might start killing each other. We need to let them go on thinking the bear meat was the source."

"Hono Ishizuka... You *do* know something about the plague."

"If I knew, I'd be doing something to stop it. Kayu, I'm a Dove, not a monster." Her eyes glistened with indignant anger. "After we spoke in front of the storehouse, I thought that the situation would remain unchanged for a time, and I was going to go into the Mountain to look for food. But then..."

"You found these two vomiting blood, is that it?"

"I don't think anyone but us knows."

"This isn't something that can remain hidden forever."

"I'll handle it."

"That's a fool's talk."

"It's no such thing," Hono Ishizuka said heatedly. "I will protect Dendera no matter what. I won't let something like this end us."

"Where do you find such spirit?" Kayu Saitoh said, but overpowered by Hono Ishizuka's palpable determination, she released the woman.

"Kayu, you have it too. The people who live in Dendera have only Dendera." Hono Ishizuka felt at her shoulder where Kayu Saitoh's grip had been. "Climbing the Mountain is forever closed to us, and we have no hope of defeating the Village. All we have left is Dendera. To protect its continued existence, I would perform any deception, and I would tell any lie."

"I won't lie," Kayu Saitoh said without hesitation.

"That means telling everyone about Ire and Kushi. If you do that, there'll be slaughter. You'll be the villain of Dendera."

"Nonsense. I'll only be telling the truth. And you mean to tell me to keep it to myself? That won't make the plague go away."

"It went away sixteen years ago," Hono Ishizuka said. "We killed the ones with the symptoms, and the plague went away. We don't have any proof connecting the two, but... No, *because* we don't have any proof, we have to do the same thing this time."

"You want to kill Ire Tachibana and Kushi Tachibana? They're still breathing."

"What if I did? Would that make me the villain?"

"I'm going to follow my beliefs. You can follow yours."

"Then I will. I'll let the rest of you take care of the three in the storehouse."

Kayu Saitoh returned to the storehouse, but she decided to keep quiet about the new victims. Beside one of the fire baskets, she joined Hyoh Hamamura, who told her that nothing new had transpired. No further reaction had come from the storehouse, and the safety of the four women who'd been trapped inside remained unknown. If there had been anything that could be called progress, it was that Inui Makabe's body had been moved aside.

Meanwhile, Mei Mitsuya had collected herself and was holding a discussion, this time speaking quietly so as not to be overheard by their enemies. The topic was what to do with the women trapped inside—Chinu Nitta, Tai Komaki, Guri Togawa, and Naki Sokabe—assuming they still lived. Two possibilities were discussed: either they were allies to be rescued, or they were potentially dangerous plague-carriers to be cast aside. In short order, the women unanimously picked the latter. They were exhausted, and nothing remained in their thoughts aside from self-preservation. Like that, the night passed, and none of them had slept when the new dawn came.

3

Even when daylight shone upon Dendera, the situation remained unchanged. Wearied, the old women waited with listless anger and frustration. Kayu Saitoh gave one displeased yawn after another, each leaving her with the dreadful, bitter taste of quiescence; the dreadful, bitter taste of unending starvation, without battle—even defeat—in sight. Of the women, only Mei Mitsuya maintained her zeal.

She commanded the women to go with her to chop down another fir tree, but none gave even the hint of a response.

"One single failure, and this is how you become? Fine. I'll do it myself!"

Mei Mitsuya gave them a look of unbridled contempt, then disappeared off somewhere. The other women again paid her no attention and went on doing nothing aside from placing wood in the fire baskets.

Kayu Saitoh didn't react either. She kept turning thoughts over in her mind—Soh Kiriyama's decision; Ire Tachibana and Kushi Tachibana's undisclosed contagion; her discussion with Hono Ishizuka; herself, as a villain—but she couldn't transfer any of it into concrete actions. All she could do was cling to the bear cub pelt around her neck. She opened her hand and looked down at her fingers. In the glare of the morning light, her fingers appeared mere twigs.

In this stasis, only time marched diligently ahead, and at some point, the sun had moved, shining down on them from directly overhead. But the women didn't move from the fires. Starvation coursed through their bodies, draining them of the strength needed to make any judgments, let alone to take any action that might create progress. Kayu Saitoh noticed a close similarity between this experience and the Climb. But this wasn't the Mountain; this was Dendera. This wasn't the Mountain, which existed for death; this was Dendera, which existed for life. For this reason, death in Dendera wouldn't lead to Paradise. Kayu Saitoh clutched her empty stomach and let out a pitiful moan as far removed from pride and passion as could be, while the other women trembled by the fire baskets, their expressions stripped of all dignity.

But not everyone could remain idle forever. The world wasn't shaped by only those who stagnate and surrender. Some held on to dignity and pride, and through their actions do events advance.

In Dendera, this was the three women inside the storehouse.

Kayu Saitoh felt a surge of heat. She looked up, stretching the wrinkled sags of her neck. The fire baskets were burning the same as they had been. But Kayu Saitoh felt a crackling warmth spread across the front of her body. Someone shouted. The storehouse had ignited. Distinctly visible even in the midday sun, thick, lapping flames crossed the rooftop. By the time Kayu Saitoh saw the fire, more than half of the roof was ablaze. Black smoke arose belatedly and climbed into the sky. The walls creaked and squealed as the fire evaporated the moisture within them. The flames embracing the outer walls were nearly transparent, their intensity imparted by the savage heat.

The silent storehouse's sudden and violent proclamation sent the women into chaos. None of them, Kayu Saitoh included, had seen the first moment of ignition.

"Fire! There's a fire!" Hyoh Hamamura shouted, her expression stiff. "Who did it? Who started it? Who acted too soon?"

"No one did it," Kotei Hoshii said. "None of us would do such a—Oh!" the woman exclaimed. "They started the fire themselves!"

Heedless of the panicking women, the flames strengthened and blazed. The black smoke expanded with impossible speed, completely blocking any view of the storehouse.

Suddenly, a mass of flames erupted.

The flames crashed into Hyoh Hamamura. She caught fire, and

screaming she fell to the ground and into the black, billowing smoke. She struggled in anguish, but soon her movements turned clumsy, and then stopped, and then she just burned. Kayu Saitoh peered into the smoke and the fire. Her eyes found the mass of flames that had incinerated Hyoh Hamamura. It had a face, smoldering, and it belonged to Tai Komaki. Kayu Saitoh realized what was happening.

"Run!" she shouted reflexively.

But just then, more masses of flame burst out from the blaze one after another. They were Chinu Nitta, Guri Togawa, and Naki Sokabe, alive and enveloped in flames. Due in part to Kayu Saitoh's warning, the other women managed to dodge the fiery masses. But the next one out proved more trouble. The burning woman pursued them relentlessly, screaming incoherently. She crashed into Koto Onodera from behind. The woman's body erupted in flames, and she rolled to the ground. The stench of burning flesh spread in the air. The mass of flame chose Kayu Saitoh for her next target and charged, pushing through the smoke. And then, suddenly, she was sent tumbling in a different direction. Holding a spear, Itsuru Obuchi emerged from the smoke.

"Are you all right?" Itsuru Obuchi asked, her lips trembling. "What the hell is happening?"

The mass of flames writhed about on the ground, then went lifeless. Kayu Saitoh kicked snow to put out the remaining flames, and could finally—and barely—tell it had been Somo Izumi. Where her face used to be, red flesh popped and hissed between the cracks in her charred skin, and blood, expanding from the heat, oozed out.

"They set themselves on fire and charged us," Kayu Saitoh said, heaving her shoulders. "This is their last stand!"

"They've gone mad," Itsuru Obuchi said, gazing down at Somo Izumi's blackened corpse. "They got the plague, they were going to be killed by their friends, and they went mad."

Mei Mitsuya's voice boomed, "Don't let your guards down!" The chief had returned. "This isn't over yet. Pick up your weapons."

Her call didn't impel the women's spirits into battle but rather gave their defensive natures a push. They began searching the smoke-covered ground for their weapons. Many of them seemed lost in confusion.

Right away, Itsuru Obuchi asked, "Mei, where were you?"

"I was looking for Hono Ishizuka." Mei Mitsuya bared her teeth. "It's over. Dendera is finished."

Kayu Saitoh wondered if Mei Mitsuya had found out about Ire Tachibana and Kushi Tachibana's acquisition of the plague, but she couldn't find out. Two more masses of flames leaped from the burning storehouse. The fires enveloping them prevented Kayu Saitoh from being able to discern which was which, but they had to have been Soh Kiriyama and Makura Katsuragawa. As the fireballs came in chase, the women tossed aside the weapons they'd only just now found and ran around in search of escape. In truth, they wouldn't have been able to do anything even had they held on to their weapons. Their opponents were bathed in flames; to be touched by them was to die, and taking them out meant letting them get into close range, which in turn meant risking death. Red-faced, Mei Mitsuya howled, "Fight!" but no one listened. As panic heaped upon panic, the women made a frantic attempt to flee a scene that had lost all reason and sense.

One fiery mass clung to Kan Tominaga's back. The woman's face contorted, her eyeballs nearly popping out of their sockets, and she screamed, "Let me go let me go!" But quickly the flames covered her. The burning heat made her lose her senses, and she ran about uncontrollably, weaving toward Kayu Saitoh, Itsuru Obuchi, and Mei Mitsuya. Mei Mitsuya shouted, "You fool!" and planted her spear into the flaming mass that was Kan Tominaga. But then the fiery mass that had first set Kan Tominaga alight screamed, "Help me, help me!" and rushed toward Kayu Saitoh. The voice belonged to Makura Katsuragawa, and it slowed Kayu Saitoh's reaction. She assessed the threat a second late and took too long before she started running. Makura Katsuragawa's flaming arms reached for her, igniting the fur around her neck and the cloth bandage over her head. Kayu Saitoh discarded both just as Mei Mitsuya stabbed Makura Katsuragawa with her spear.

"You're another fool!" Mei Mitsuya screamed. "Fools! Fools! Fools! Fools fools fools fools!"

Makura Katsuragawa had fallen, but she grasped the spear protruding from her stomach and again shrieked, "Help me!"

Despite the flames spreading to the wooden spear, Mei Mitsuya drove it farther into Makura Katsuragawa's stomach. Makura Katsuragawa died, but the flames of course didn't. The fire climbed the spear and ignited the chief's white robes. With a *bwoom* sound, Mei Mitsuya's body was swallowed by bright red flames.

She flailed in agony, and Kayu Saitoh hurriedly flung snow to put out her fire, but another mass of flames appeared and dove on top of the chief. For a split second Kayu Saitoh saw Soh Kiriyama's burned and blistered face through the flames. Soh Kiriyama went limp, becoming one with Mei Mitsuya's burning body. Kayu Saitoh kept on hurling as much snow onto them as she could, but the fire blazed unabated.

"Mei Mitsuya!" Kayu Saitoh shouted at the fire, within which nothing moved, not even a twitch. "Come on, what are you doing? You can't die like this. Not as pointlessly as this!"

She started to reach for the chief, but Itsuru Obuchi grabbed Kayu Saitoh under her arms and restrained her.

"What are you doing?" Itsuru Obuchi said. "Stop it! It's finished... It's finished."

Her words rang true. Though the fire and smoke continued to rule over the area, the incident had come to a complete end. Nothing was left but for the numerous charred bodies to release their embers. The survivors, their expressions vacant, had sunk to the smoke-covered ground.

Kayu Saitoh gnashed her teeth and muttered, "We're finished."

Just then, the storehouse rumbled and collapsed. The rush of hot air dispersed the surrounding black smoke and, aside from the numerous charred corpses and the burned-out ruin of the storehouse, the view of Dendera remained mostly unchanged from its earlier state.

Kayu Saitoh heard two pairs of footsteps approaching.

One was an old woman whose white hair covered the left half of her face. A gust of wind tossed her bangs to the side and revealed a pool of darkness inhabiting the place where her left eye should have been.

It was Masari Shiina.

Hono Ishizuka walked behind her.

Masari Shiina stood with dignity before the women. Her right eye's commanding gaze swept across them.

She opened by announcing, "The plague has been completely consumed by the fire." Then she added, "However, so has our storehouse—and our food. But be at ease. The Doves have a food reserve. We'll distribute it to you all. First, fill your stomachs. Eat something warm."

Her right eye swept over them again. "The plague has been consumed by the fire, but the cost was great. First, we survivors must rebuild Dendera. For that reason, as of today, the Hawks are disbanded. Mei Mitsuya is dead. Dendera's leader is dead. The head of the Hawks is dead. And many others are dead. In these circumstances, attacking the Village is impossible. We must live on. We will rebuild Dendera. We Doves will command this work. The plague is no more. Safety has returned. But strengthening our safety is a necessity. And the Doves' efforts are a necessity. I—the Doves—have food. Eat as much as you wish. We will accept you. We don't want to be your enemy. All we want is to live with a single, shared sentiment. I understand your ill will toward the Village, but now isn't the time for such things. Warring against the Village is not everything. For now, you don't have to understand what I'm saying. Today, you all fought, you toiled, and you triumphed. You've won the right to take rest; you've earned the right to take nourishment. And those things I can provide you. We accept you."

Listening to Masari Shiina's speech, Kayu Saitoh felt hunger and exhaustion coursing through her body. At the same time, some part of her, proper and shining in gold, cried out in earnest, *This woman is lying. This woman, Masari Shiina, the Dove, is lying. The plague isn't over. The bear meat wasn't responsible for the plague. I saw Ire Tachibana and Kushi Tachibana dying, and they hadn't eaten the stew. Masari Shiina and Hono Ishizuka know this. But now they conceal the truth and spin honeyed words to sway women weary from starvation, exhaustion, and fear. They're trying to make you submit. They're trying to make you theirs. They're trying to make you forget Mei Mitsuya. Well, I won't accept it. I will not accept their plan. Rejection, denial, and rebellion are a flame inside me that won't be extinguished. This has nothing to do with the Village and Dendera, or the Hawks and the Doves—I will not accept this shameful scheme. I will never permit it.*

The shining, golden part of her shouted for all to hear, but as Kayu Saitoh savored thoughts of sleeping with a full stomach, her throat produced only an empty vibration.

Part 2

Chapter 7

On the Brink

Winter went on as it had before; though the season had seen many events begin and end, in terms of stage and scene—to put it in somewhat grandiose terms—one fact stood out in sharp relief: not a single thing had changed.

Thirty years had passed since Dendera was founded, and thirty days had passed since Kayu Saitoh came to Dendera. Dendera remained in existence and so did Kayu Saitoh.

Kayu Saitoh was sifting through the burned-out remains of the storehouse in search of useable charcoal. The sun was glaring, the morning blinding, while a chilling wind blew down from the Mountain, and a head cold burned in her throat, which twitched like that of a cat trying not to regurgitate, but despite all this, she remained focused on her work. She did so not out of a desire to make herself forget anything but rather to hew to reality. The season marched on, and the coldness had grown more bitter over the past few days. More charcoal was necessary.

In air so cold it seemed to freeze each breath as soon as she exhaled it, Kayu Saitoh continued her work. Charcoal was smeared across her entire body, including her scraped-up hand and the scar of her mostly healed head wound, while her white robes, caked with soot and dirt and dried blood, couldn't have been more filthy. Anyone looking at her would have seen not a woman but a black mass. And this black mass was thinking of the fiery masses that had appeared nine days before, and of the women who had perished to them, but her hands didn't rest from their work.

2

Though neither the stage nor scene had changed, the events had greatly reduced Dendera's population from fifty to nineteen. Two of the huts and the two storehouses were no longer fit to be used; all food aside from the Doves' stockpile had been incinerated; Mei Mitsuya had died to the flames; the Hawks had lost their authority along with many of their number, while the Doves had lost many but gained influence and absorbed the Hawks; and Masari Shiina was now the chief of Dendera.

The new chief's first move was to offer the women ample food and rest. Next, she ordered several projects intended to redirect the women away from their desire to attack the Village and toward Dendera's recovery. Within days, Dendera was back on a solid foundation, and after the incident at the storehouse, the plague hadn't returned. The women regained a peaceful existence. Yet food was scarce, and all were fatigued from the continuous work. Moreover, with their numbers reduced to only nineteen, each woman's statements and convictions now stood out. But Masari Shiina maintained her command with enticements of food, and the women devoted their efforts to Dendera's reconstruction.

Such was the current situation.

On her way home after having finished her work, Kayu Saitoh saw several figures gathered behind the manor, formerly home to Mei Mitsuya, currently occupied by Masari Shiina. Three women were having a discussion. Each had Climbed the Mountain five years before: Hogi Takamiya, Shijira Iikubo, and Maru Kusachi. Kayu Saitoh didn't know them well, and she didn't think well of them. Even when Mei Mitsuya lived, they had hardly helped with any of the work, idling by without enthusiasm either for attacking the Village or for sustaining Dendera. Their behavior had been similar back when they lived in the Village.

Noticing Kayu Saitoh, Hogi Takamiya said, "Well look at you—you're completely black. How terribly filthy you are. And you did that to yourself all for the sake of others."

"Are you mocking me?" Kayu Saitoh replied, ready for a fight.

"Not at all, not at all," Hogi Takamiya needlessly repeated. "I only wanted to say how *noble* it is for you to work yourself until you're completely black."

"And what are you three doing? We're supposed to be building a new storehouse and constructing the trap."

"We finished our tasks."

"Then help with another."

Hogi Takamiya smirked. "We're not interested in slaving away over some trap for the bear to destroy."

Masari Shiina believed that the bear, still alive, would again attack Dendera. Despite the efforts required to rebuild Dendera, the new chief had set half of the women to work constructing a trap to kill the creature. The so-called trap was really only a small hut, but Masari Shiina, inspired by Soh Kiriyama's rebellion nine days prior, intended to incorporate powerful fire into the trap. Her idea was to shut the bear inside and burn it alive. Having experienced the mayhem firsthand, the other women thought it an effective plan, and Kayu Saitoh agreed. When she heard the plan, she touched at the scar running across her head and reasoned that charging the bear with a single flimsy weapon—one that might or might not even pierce one of its beady eyes—wouldn't yield a result that was worth the risk.

Facing down Hogi Takamiya, Kayu Saitoh insisted, "The bear isn't going to destroy the trap, *we* are—with the bear inside it."

"Assuming the bear abides by the plan," Hogi Takamiya said, sounding bored. "When I look at you all, I only see little children playing at digging holes for wild rabbits to fall into."

"That's because you've expected to lose from the beginning."

"Then you who expect to win can give it your best," Hogi Takamiya said, and beside her, Shijira Iikubo responded with a laugh that shook the withered lips of her toothless mouth. Maru Kusachi, whose stooped back made her small frame appear even smaller, didn't display a particular response aside from placing her hands on her hips. Kayu Saitoh surreptitiously sniffed herself, catching a whiff of charcoal mixed with her own body odor. Producing a disapproving grunt from her sore throat, she thought, *They're nothing more than feckless, spoiled children. A wild rabbit facing death at the bottom of a pit has far greater beauty than they.*

3

Amid Dendera's reconstruction, Masari Shiina reorganized the nineteen survivors' living arrangements. She emptied the four western huts, including the two that had been destroyed by the bears' ferocious incursion, and redistributed the women among the five huts to the east. In the easternmost were Kayu Saitoh, Shigi Yamamoto, and Nokobi Hidaka; next door were Hotori Oze, Usuma Tsutsumi, and Itsuru Obuchi; followed by Hogi Takamiya, Ume Itano, and Tsusa Hiiragi; next were Ate Amami, Hikari Asami, and Shijira Iikubo; next were Kotei Hoshii, Tamishi Minamide, and Tema Tsukamoto; and in the manor were Masari Shiina, Hono Ishizuka, Kyu Hoshina, and Maru Kusachi. Kayu Saitoh saw one ulterior motive to the reorganization. Seven of the women—Ate Amami, Kotei Hoshii, Hotori Oze, Hikari Asami, Ume Itano, Kyu Hoshina, and Nokobi Hidaka—had belonged to the Hawk faction, and Kayu Saitoh suspected that Masari Shiina, wanting to quell any potential problems, had divided the Hawks to prevent them from forming an alliance.

When Kayu Saitoh returned to the hut assigned to her by the calculating chief, Shigi Yamamoto and Nokobi Hidaka were huddled around the sunken hearth. Kayu Saitoh sat facing Nokobi Hidaka and extracted a potato from the hearth's ash. The vegetable had cooked through, and she broke it in two and stuffed the pieces into her cheeks. Coldness had permeated her body, and her gums protested the potato's scalding heat more than they should have, but she chewed anyway. The Doves' food reserves were a fair bit more plentiful than Kayu Saitoh had supposed, and the women were rationed several potatoes daily. When she stirred the ashes in search of a second potato, Nokobi Hidaka found it first and handed it to her.

"You found it," Kayu Saitoh said, "so you eat it."

"This isn't my potato," Nokobi Hidaka grumbled. "It's the Doves' potato. It's table scraps, courtesy of the Doves."

"If you let things like that bother you, you won't be able to keep alive."

"But Kayu, you must be thinking the same thing as you eat those potatoes."

"Hawkish talk is dangerous in Dendera now—and futile." To communicate her point, she snatched the potato from the woman's hand.

"If things go on like this, the raid will be nothing more than a lost dream." Nokobi Hidaka looked at the ashes that clung to her empty hand. "Mei must be so sad now."

"Quit that talk."

Masari Shiina had forbidden any discussion of not only the plague but of the former chief and the mutineers. Just like what was done sixteen years ago, she was trying to make the events be forgotten.

"Quit it, huh?" Nokobi Hidaka snorted. "You can only say that because you haven't been in Dendera long. I think I've told you this before, but I've lived here for eighteen years now. I'm eighty-eight. That's a long time. So I knew Mei well. As I do Masari."

Kayu Saitoh lowered her voice. "Do you think Masari Shiina was waiting a long time for this to happen?"

"She hated Mei. When the Mountain-Barring happened, Mei was the one who incited the women of the Village to a frenzy." Nokobi Hidaka scratched the splotchy skin of her neck. "Relations were stormy between them even back in the Village."

"I didn't know that," Kayu Saitoh whispered. Being much younger than the two women, she hadn't been aware of their animosity in the Village.

"Apart from that, they were the heads of the Hawk and Dove factions. For Masari, the bear's coming might not have been that unwelcome. But the saddest part is that without Mei, the raid will never happen. Even Itsuru grieved her passing deeply. I...wonder if that woman is all right."

"Living long doesn't seem to be that easy."

"You got that right. I wanted to attack the Village."

"Then do it alone—if you're brave enough," Kayu Saitoh replied, peeling the skin from her potato. But then she realized she sounded as if she had completely submitted to Masari Shiina. "Of course I have my own thoughts sometimes," she added. "No matter who the chief is, I don't see any purpose to living in Dendera."

"So what are you going to do then, Climb the Mountain?"

"I don't want to. There's even less purpose to that. I can't go to

Paradise. I can only live. So I have to do something that only a person who's alive can do. That's how I've come to think. That's the only way I can think now."

"A raid is something only someone who's alive can do."

"No, that would be a small thing. Sure, the act itself might be big, but it wouldn't resolve anything. At the very least, it wouldn't fulfill me or even change how I feel."

"What do you want to do, Kayu?"

"I want an aspiration," Kayu Saitoh said, thinking back to her final conversation with Mei Mitsuya. "I don't need anyone else's approval. The act itself could even be something insignificant. But I want an aspiration—something to believe in."

"And you're saying it would have nothing to do with the Hawks or the Doves? I'm not sure I understand." Nokobi Hidaka tiled her head to the side. "And working for the Doves, in this Dendera they've taken over—that's how you'll find your bigger purpose?"

"Before I can do anything else, I need to eat, and I need to live."

Kayu Saitoh put the potato in her mouth and looked to Shigi Yamamoto. She couldn't tell whether the woman was listening to their conversation or not.

Even as Dendera changed, Shigi Yamamoto's behavior remained constant. Now, as before, she muttered words that no one but she could understand.

Kayu Saitoh chewed her potato, wondering if Shigi Yamamoto had found her own aspiration. No one else would share it, or even know what it was, but possibly she had found something that could bring her true fulfillment, and possibly, at this very moment, she might be devoted to doing everything she could to achieve it.

4

Patting her starch-filled stomach, Kayu Saitoh headed for the edge of the clearing, where she saw and entered a circle of women with Hono Ishizuka at the center. The hut that was to be a bear trap needed to be sturdy enough to contain the beast, and its construction required a great many materials and laborers. Like the other huts, the vertical posts would consist of wooden logs plunged into a foundation of leveled dirt. In this case, however, logs would also take the place of the straw walls.

Hono Ishizuka cheerfully directed the project. The woman's high spirits quickly sapped Kayu Saitoh's desire to work. Hono Ishizuka probably didn't see anything inappropriate about giving orders with that smirk on her face—after all, no one remained to oppose her viewpoint—but her manner came across to Kayu Saitoh as something unforgivable. But Dendera's currents had shifted course, and Kayu Saitoh was merely engulfed in them—opposing the new order while keeping herself alive wouldn't be easy. Instead, she hid her feelings and joined in. But in this state of mind, her efforts went as poorly as would be expected, and she accidentally stubbed her toes on the wood quite a few times. Hono Ishizuka regarded her with scorn and asked her if she wouldn't please try taking the work seriously. Kayu Saitoh's anger came to a boil. She tossed down the wood she'd been carrying on her shoulder and asserted how much she'd done for Dendera, but her protests found no sympathy; all her self-justifications, founded upon little more than pride and privilege, didn't change the fact that she couldn't work worth a damn.

Without interrupting her duties, Ate Amami advised, "If you can't help, you should go home."

"You're talking like you're one of them." A new anger bubbled up inside Kayu Saitoh. "Weren't you a Hawk, Ate Amami? I seem to remember you babbling about attacking the Village."

"We don't know when the bear will come back, that's all."

Even Kyu Hoshina joined in, saying, "She's right, Kayu. Nobody's talking about Hawks or Doves here."

Disappointed, Kayu Saitoh said, "Disgraceful. Go ahead, build your trap for all I care. Just drop that unseemly attitude."

"Kayu, we're all doing what we can to survive," Kyu Hoshina said. "If you're going to get in the way, then just go home. Even when things change in Dendera, you still complain. You should be ashamed."

"Your submission is more shameful."

"If you keep trying to stir up trouble, we'll use you as bear bait," Kyu Hoshina said. Derisive laughter spread among the women.

Kayu Saitoh couldn't forgive Ate Amami and Kyu Hoshina, who had supposedly been in the top ranks of the Hawks, for letting themselves be used by Hono Ishizuka, and worse still, for working without carrying any anger or a sense that anything was wrong. Though Kayu Saitoh hadn't backed either the Doves or the Hawks, feelings of condemnation and betrayal overwhelmed her, and she left the area. She recognized that the work of building the bear trap belonged to others, and then she realized that she had nowhere she needed to go, and no one she needed to meet, and her footsteps faltered. If she had decided to get sentimental, she could have, but upon reflection, she judged it a disrespect to think of those who had departed only now that they were gone. She decided that if she was going to walk her solitary path, she should at least do so with a steady step.

Kayu Saitoh's feet had taken her toward the burial ground.

After the outbreak, the graveyard had come to be seen as a taboo place. With no visitors, the grounds had become half-buried in mounds of snow. The accumulations of snow on the gravestones seemed to swell like the hunched shoulders of beasts, and an imposing stillness inhabited the burial ground. Kayu Saitoh tried to block out any thoughts for the dead, but she couldn't help thinking of Kura Kuroi, Mei Mitsuya, Soh Kiriyama, and the others.

As she tried to rein in her reminiscences, she heard the crunch of footsteps in snow. Behind the graveyard—at what could be called the boundary between Dendera and the Mountain—something moved. Kayu Saitoh sought cover behind a group of trees. From her new position, she could see several footstep trails leading away from Dendera. She followed them and found that group of three women—Hogi Takamiya, Shijira Iikubo, and Maru Kusachi. The three were talking as they amused themselves by trampling on the snow and the bamboo grass. Crouching, Kayu Saitoh moved close enough to hear what they were saying. Careful not to make any noise, she hid herself in a patch of bamboo grass and focused on listening.

Only barely could she make out what Hogi Takamiya was saying.

"They're building a storehouse and a trap and all that. And they're making them so good and strong. Such diligence. And yet they're blind to what's far more serious."

"Utterly blind." This voice belonged to Shijira Iikubo. "If I may be so pompous, we control whether or not Dendera lives or dies. That's being pompous, of course."

"But it doesn't matter if we can't figure out what exactly *it* is. Should we make her talk? We could beat it out of her."

"It would be dangerous to do anything that would make us stand out. There's only nineteen women left in Dendera. If we make a move, we'll attract attention. And that Masari Shiina's got sharp eyes. She's not like Mei Mitsuya."

"If it were up to me, I'd rather do everything at once instead of sneaking about."

"That's because you make up your mind before you think," Shijira Iikubo snapped.

"That's being harsh," Hogi Takamiya said, but then laughed cheerfully. "Anyway, what about you? What do you think?"

"Well," a soft voice said. It was Maru Kusachi. "We should keep observing a little while longer. Being put into different huts is a hindrance, but we'll figure something out."

"Observe, huh?" Hogi Takamiya muttered. "But if someone else gets killed in the meantime, what then?"

"If that happens, maybe it won't matter anymore."

Their conversation had apparently ended. Kayu Saitoh heard the three pairs of footsteps approaching, but the three returned to Dendera without noticing her. She'd only caught a fragment of their conversation, not even enough for her to speculate what they were talking about, but whatever it was, it didn't seem good for Dendera. But, unsure of her place in Dendera, Kayu Saitoh didn't know whom she should tell—or shouldn't tell—the things she'd overheard. Her discovery of this group of women with their own ideas was utterly vexing. Nevertheless, she was getting back on her feet, beginning to return to Dendera, when she felt something cold touch the scar on her head. She looked up and saw several droplets falling.

It was raining.

Rain was unusual this time of year and at this temperature. Being bathed in this rain from another place and time had an inexplicably therapeutic effect on her mood. The rain came at first in a weak drizzle but soon gained in force and volume until it came in a pattering torrent. The snow absorbed the raindrops at first, but soon gave way, turning clear and wet. Kayu Saitoh walked through the rain, and the moisture quickly ate through her straw coat and straw sandals. Her body, mostly skin and bones, immediately froze. She looked up again and saw a mass of rainclouds that had appeared where the blue sky had once been. In the Village, unseasonal winter rains such as this were abhorred as signs of coming famine. If such a rain continued, the young women were forced to perform a Rain-Stopping. Since fiery disasters were said to visit the hut of any woman who entered the Mountain, the Rain-Stopping turned that punishment to the Village's benefit. When the unseasonal rain came, multiple women lined up in clear view at the Mountain's base and simply waited for the storm to lift. Sometimes, some of the women died from lung infections, but the custom persisted to this day. Kayu Saitoh walked through the rain and contemplated that somewhere down the Mountain, women from the Village would be standing there, trembling. Kayu Saitoh returned to her home, where Shigi Yamamoto was sitting in front of the sunken hearth. As Kayu Saitoh removed her dripping-wet white robes and her straw sandals, Shigi Yamamoto stared into the hearth, incognizant of her arrival and indifferent to the sound of the falling rain.

5

Night came, but the rain didn't stop, soon making its way through the flimsy roof and into the room. Kayu Saitoh and Nokobi Hidaka tried stuffing more straw into the ceiling, but their efforts proved ineffectual, and they gave up, instead placing an empty stone pot on the floor beneath the leak. The stone bowl filled quickly, and they had to keep tossing the rainwater outside. With no expectation of receiving any help from Shigi Yamamoto whatsoever, Kayu Saitoh and Nokobi Hidaka had to take turns dumping the water themselves.

"What an awful downpour," Nokobi Hidaka said as she put more wood into the hearth. "I hope the trap isn't destroyed. We just finished it."

Kayu Saitoh draped her damp white robes over shoulders and said sourly, "If rain like this could destroy it, that bear would blow it down with a single breath."

"I was only saying. The trap is fine. We can be at ease now."

"There'll be no ease until we store up more food."

"The trap and the storehouse are both finished. From tomorrow on, we'll spend the days foraging. Also, we're due for another Climb, and we need to hurry and find whoever got sent into the Mountain. We have so much to do."

Only upon hearing Nokobi Hidaka's words did Kayu Saitoh realize the obvious truth: Others besides herself would turn seventy this year; she would not be the only one to Climb the Mountain.

"I get the feeling it would be a better kindness to let her die in the Mountain," Kayu Saitoh muttered. "Life in Dendera isn't easy. Rather than drag her feeble body in search of food, and live trembling from the snow and the rain and the bear, she might be better off dying in the Mountain thinking thoughts of Paradise."

"Dying alone in the darkness of the Mountain is certainly not better. Besides, the more we can increase our numbers, the better our chances of attacking the Village become."

"Nokobi Hidaka... you're still thinking about that?"

"Won't you attack with me, Kayu?"

"Huh?"

"I can trust you, so I'll tell you this." Nokobi Hidaka leaned forward. "Today, when we were building the trap, I was able to have a little talk with Hotori Oze without anyone noticing. She hasn't given up on the attack."

The log crackled in the hearth.

After a moment, Kayu Saitoh spoke, her voice automatically dropping to a whisper. "That was a dangerous thing to do."

"I said that no one noticed. I was careful."

"And the two of you intend to attack by yourselves?"

"Weren't you the one who told me to do it alone if I was brave enough?"

"I was just talking."

"I should hope so." Nokobi Hidaka chuckled. "I won't do anything rash. I won't move until the time is right."

As she listened to the rain fall into the stone pot, Kayu Saitoh said, "Masari Shiina and Hono Ishizuka might already be aware of how you feel. They've split up the Hawks into different huts, haven't they? That's proof that they're taking precautions."

"Even if the Hawks are split up, even if Mei is dead, my hate for the Village won't go away." Nokobi Hidaka touched a hand to her wrinkled cheek. "Even the Doves have to feel some resentment or something toward the Village. As long as those feelings exist among those of Dendera, there will always be Hawks." She looked Kayu Saitoh straight on. "What I think, Kayu, is that you need to attack the Village. I don't know your true feelings, but I can see that you don't know them either."

"Don't talk like you know."

"But if you attack the Village, couldn't it be that you'll find this aspiration you so desire?"

Filled with discontent, Kayu Saitoh repeated, "Don't talk like you know."

"Look, I don't care for Dendera either," Nokobi Hidaka said, giving weight to her words. "And I don't mean that just because our leader changed from Mei to Masari. I've felt that way for a long time. By hiding the plague and the killings, we act just the same as the Village. We weren't born in Dendera. We were born in the Village and raised in the Village. All of our deeds and all of our relationships are rooted in the Village."

"But you want to attack the Village. You want to kill everyone."

"I wanted to be born somewhere else... That's all," Nokobi Hidaka said softly. "If only I had, then I wouldn't have been forced to Climb the Mountain. I could have lived my whole life in prosperity. I could have lived my whole life in happiness. I could have died still treasuring my birth, my growth, my deeds, and my relationships. But that's impossible here. The Village exists through violence, and Dendera exists through deception. And yet only our relationships are true. It's enough to drive you mad."

"And that's why you want to attack them—because it pains you to see people working their whole lives when they can't even get along with each other?"

"That's right," Nokobi Hidaka said.

"Ridiculous. It's too extreme. Is that line of thinking enough to make you truly able to carry out an attack? Can you really kill all of them? Can you really butcher your family and your acquaintances? The way I see it, you're just trying to destroy everything they've done."

"That's right."

"Will destroying everything bring you satisfaction?"

"If that means their deeds and relationships will cease to be," Nokobi Hidaka said. "I never wanted to live long enough to tell a lie. When we captured Makura in secret after she developed the symptoms, and when

I hid the plague from sixteen years ago from you, I felt it was wrong... but I can't take back what I did."

Struck by an intuition, Kayu Saitoh said, "Nokobi Hidaka, were you the one who told Soh Kiriyama?"

Without any sign of surprise, Nokobi Hidaka nodded and explained that she had been friends with Soh Kiriyama's older sister. She and the sister had been close in age, and consequently she knew Soh Kiriyama as more than an acquaintance. Kayu Saitoh crossed her arms and watched a bead of water prepare to fall from the edge of the ceiling beam. As she thought about how so many different ways of thinking had led to the same idea of raiding the Village, her face took on a look not far from fatigue.

"Everyone has their own reason to attack the Village," Kayu Saitoh said. "Why you're attacking the Village, why Hotori Oze is attacking the Village, and why Mei Mitsuya wanted to attack the Village—they're all different."

"Ate Amami, Hikari Asami, and the other Hawks might still want to, but they too likely have their own separate reasons. Other people are different from me."

Finished with this conversation, Kayu Saitoh said, "If you understand that, then quit trying to lure me into the Hawks. I'm not interested in your ideology."

Nokobi Hidaka stood, then picked up the water pot and carried it outside. Her manner wasn't that of giving up on Kayu Saitoh, but rather that she was simply giving the woman time to think, and moreover, she wasn't trying to hide it. Kayu Saitoh responded with a snort.

On the other hand, she envied Nokobi Hidaka for holding on to her thoughts of attack despite the current situation. She stretched her neck, then searched her thoughts for what her own aspiration should be if she wasn't attached to Dendera, was skeptical about the assault on the Village, and could no longer Climb the Mountain. During her seventy years in the Village, she had gotten by without giving particular thought to anything, and she wasn't used to doing it now. In her lack of experience, a part of her naively believed that if she kept on thinking and thinking enough the answer must come to her. She hadn't learned that some problems could never, ever be solved, no matter how hard she puzzled over them, and no matter how much advice she was given. This was a limitation Kayu Saitoh faced at this moment.

Nokobi Hidaka returned carrying the empty stone pot. In the Village, she had been an entirely average woman. She held no convictions or anything else that made her stand out. Like any woman, she married into a house and made that house her life. Kayu Saitoh didn't know what experiences and resentments the woman had accumulated during that ordinary life that informed who she was now.

As Kayu Saitoh thought upon these things, she suddenly realized that Masari Shiina might hate the Village more than anyone else. She had lost her eye in the Mountain-Barring to which she had had only a tangential connection. Taking that into account, Masari Shiina had earned the right to attack the Village more than any other, yet as the chief of Dendera and the head of the Doves, why she focused her efforts on Dendera's reconstruction was a mystery to Kayu Saitoh. Trying to imagine the new chief's feelings toward the Village only made her a little confused.

Before she knew it, she was asking the question aloud.

"Why do you think Masari Shiina won't attack the Village?"

Warming herself in the heat of the hearth, Nokobi Hidaka replied, "How should I know? Like I said, other people are different from me."

"So Masari Shiina has her own personal motivations. I wonder what Hono Ishizuka thinks about that."

"Again, only she knows. But Hawk or Dove, hate for the Village is the one thing we all share equally. All that differs is the path of the revenge; the direction of the fury. Listen, Kayu, that aspiration or whatever it is you're looking for—it might be in revenge or fury after all."

Kayu Saitoh turned her gaze to the silent, sitting Shigi Yamamoto and thought, *If that's the case, then even this one has an aspiration.* But the woman remained unresponsive.

Exhausted from all her thinking, Kayu Saitoh sighed. "I had no idea finding my own aspiration—finding my own way of thinking—would take so much effort...even after seventy years of living."

"I know what you're saying. Everyone else acts as they please, and you act as you please too. It can be a shock."

"A shock... You're right. I've been in constant shock since I came to Dendera."

"You learned you're not some tree or some rock. That would unsettle anyone. Now, how about we put some more wood in that fire. We're not trees or rocks—if we don't keep warm, we'll die."

Nokobi Hidaka went to fetch some firewood from the pile on the dirt floor at the hut's entrance.

As Kayu Saitoh listened to the raindrops hitting the roof, a penitent resolve came to her, albeit indistinctly. If she had to force this feeling into words, it would have been this: for each individual to fulfill her personal aspiration, she either needed to draw in others to her cause or go it alone. In addition, under Masari Shiina's leadership, Dendera's currents had strengthened even further. Instead of constantly raising her objections to each and every constraint placed upon her—including the larger constraint that was Dendera, and the smaller ones that were the other women—Kayu Saitoh needed to establish her own aspiration. For the first time, she saw objectively the distance between herself and Dendera, and herself and the other women. This of course didn't immediately change anything, but she was content in feeling that she had progressed beyond pouring all her energy into negativity.

6

That sort of resolve—or any kind of newfound direction in life—meant nothing to Redback, being a creature of the wild. She kicked at the earth with her four legs, propelling her giant body forward. But if she was to continue on, she needed meat, and for that, she returned to land where the Two-Legs dwelled.

7

"You've come," Masari Shiina said, her voice unperturbed. "You've come, you damn bear."

Because Masari Shiina assumed the brown bear would attack again and had assigned women to watch duty, she had been able to respond even when the attack came at night. When the word came from Usuma Tsutsumi, who was one of the lookouts, the chief promptly assembled all of the women inside the manor. Kayu Saitoh and Nokobi Hidaka had even brought Shigi Yamamoto inside. The nervous women filled the space of the ground floor room and, amid their own collective stench, awaited Masari Shiina's next announcement. As the scar on her head throbbed, Kayu Saitoh tried to detect the presence of the bear she knew must be near, but the sound of the pouring rain blotted out all else.

Masari Shiina stood before the women, affixing them in place with the stare of her single eye. She spoke.

"According to a report from one of our watch, the bear has entered Dendera and is roaming near the burial grounds. But you have no need to fear. This is not the Dendera of Mei Mitsuya's time. We have a trap. Unfortunately, in this rain, we can't cage the bear inside and burn it alive, but we have more than one way of using the trap. We will barricade ourselves inside, and it will be our impregnable fortress. Do not worry. Do not fear. Do not be ruled by panic, for it is panic that invites death. If we keep our nerve, victory will be ours. No one else will die. That is all."

The women began to move.

Kayu Saitoh and Nokobi Hidaka pulled Shigi Yamamoto outside

with them. With the moon shrouded behind heavy clouds, the fire baskets extinguished by the rain, and the women's torches kept unlit lest the bear see them, the outside was in near total darkness. Kayu Saitoh strained her eyes to see, but she could hardly catch sight of her own body, let alone the bear. What she couldn't see, she imagined, and several seeds of doubt began to sprout inside her. She wasn't the only one to be stricken by this affliction, and she heard one of the women let out a terrified moan. Kayu Saitoh responded to the sound with immediate disgust and tasted shame at knowing it had almost been her. She and Nokobi Hidaka were carrying Shigi Yamamoto by the arms, and she firmly pulled Shigi Yamamoto closer. Kayu Saitoh thought that if she gave in to foolish hysteria, she would cause Shigi Yamamoto trouble—possibly even to a fatal degree—so she turned the panic into courage. Even so, with the darkness remaining ever so dark, and the bear's location remaining a mystery, the women took a considerably long time to reach the trap at the clearing's edge. But the rain concealed their scent and sound, and they arrived unnoticed by the bear. As the raindrops pelted her, Kayu Saitoh reached out into the darkness with one hand. She felt the wall. She hadn't seen the completed structure, but she had heard Hono Ishizuka's description of the plan and was relieved to find that the sturdiness of the wall attested to the women's capable construction. The door took several women to open and let out a leaden groan as it did.

Once the women were through the doorway and had confirmed by roll call that all had made it inside, Hikari Asami and Ate Amami closed the door with considerable effort. Kayu Saitoh sat Shigi Yamamoto down and, relying on the faint light of the crude hearth set into the center of the space, surveyed the interior. From the walls to the ceiling, layered stacks of logs surrounded the women. Several fist-sized holes had been opened in intervals along the walls, and in each corner was a more-than-ample supply of wooden spears. The nineteen women filled this space, waiting, their shoulders jostling, even their breaths battering against one another. Even under normal conditions, the room would have been hot and stuffy from their body heat alone, but the women were feverish with fright, and a thick, nauseating stench hung in the air. Kayu Saitoh's throat twitched, sticky, and she felt suffocated.

Soon, she heard the sound of something large stepping in the muddy earth. The noise continued, growing louder than the rain. Kayu Saitoh felt as though her insides were fervently leaping about. She pressed firmly against her stomach, battling the sensation, and listened. The stomping footsteps approached. *The bear.* That sole thought occupied Kayu Saitoh's mind. *The bear. The bear. The bear. The bear.* She strained her ears to listen, but something soon provided more confirmation than the sound.

She saw something bright red through one of the holes in the wall.

The color stood out even in the gloom, and she knew exactly what it was: the thick red fur that grew from the rear of the bear's head down its back. Kayu Saitoh's body went as stiff as a dried-out twig. As blood rushed to her eyes, she looked out through the hole. The red fur, as gorgeous as it was wet, glistened brazenly in the darkness. At the sight of the bear, the women began to drip sweat from their foreheads and under their arms, but one stood watch in steadfast confidence of their victory, and that was Masari Shiina. The chief positioned herself at the wall closest to the bear, opened her right eye wide, looked through the hole, then quietly raised her arm. She was signaling the women to prepare to attack. Kayu Saitoh tilted her head slightly to see the women nearest the chief—Hono Ishizuka, Ate Amami, Hikari Asami, Itsuru Obuchi, Ume Itano, and Tsusa Hiiragi—pick up wooden spears from the pile without making a sound.

Masari Shiina swept her hand down.

The six women thrust their spears through the fist-size holes.

The next instant came a bellowing roar of surprise and pain from the sudden attack. Then a fierce impact and noise assailed the trap and startled the women inside. Hono Ishizuka, Ate Amami, and Ume Itano recoiled, while Hikari Asami, Itsuru Obuchi, and Tsusa Hiiragi's spears shattered. Outside, the bear raged, battering the walls again and again. A snapping log sent the women's fear to a new level. The women packed inside the narrow confines clashed shoulders and buttocks and legs as they began to panic.

"Only one log broke," Masari Shiina said as if nothing had happened. "Keep attacking."

"Aye, aye!" replied Tsusa Hiiragi, who seemed to have found her bravery. The woman lifted another spear and jabbed it through one of the holes. The bear roared again. Pushing past anyone in her way, Kayu Saitoh ran to the wall. From directly on the other side came the sound and shocks of the beast's powerful forelegs trying to break through, but no matter how giant the creature, destroying a log wall wouldn't be easy.

Kayu Saitoh picked up a spear and thrust it through one of the holes. It didn't go very deep, but she felt the wooden tip dig into something.

She pulled back her spear and thrust it again. This time, she felt more of an effect, and exhilaration overcame her.

"I've pierced it!" Kayu Saitoh shouted. "I've pierced it! Damn, we can kill this thing!"

Her words ignited the women's fighting spirit, and Ate Amami, Hikari Asami, and Itsuru Obuchi readied their spears and plunged them through the holes. Their attacks were met with more howls and cries.

Then, suddenly, Kayu Saitoh felt nothing on the other end of her spear.

Gone were the cries, and gone was the sound of walls being battered.

She pulled back her spear and looked through the hole, but the outside was completely still. All she heard was the sound of the rain, and all she saw was darkness.

Tsusa Hiiragi snorted and looked out through one of the holes. "The bear ran away, did it?"

"Don't go outside," Masari Shiina commanded.

Time crawled. The women had looked outside all four of the walls and saw no bear, but with the rain and the darkness, they might have only missed it, and there was the possibility that the creature had only feigned its escape and was hiding somewhere nearby. From inside, the women had no way of finding out. All they could do was wait, quiet and still, until they could be sure. The wait was stifling. The women were more nervous now than before the bear had come, but more lifeless at the same time. All they did was wait. Kayu Saitoh wiped sweat from her face and watched through the hole as if she were a part of the wall itself, but she learned nothing save for the smell of the rain. She put her ear to the wall, but the downpour blocked out any other sound. Soon, some women gave in to fatigue and stale air and slumped down, miserable. When the hearth's fire died out, darkness and cold added to their suffering. Kayu Saitoh was not exempt, and when she stared out through the hole in the wall and saw nothing, she could no longer tell if it was because of the darkness or if she had gone blind. She put her hand to the wall to steady her wavering body. She needed to breathe deeply of the outside air or she would throw up all of the unpleasantness inside her.

But she withstood this intense urge, and at some point, she noticed that light was coming to the outside. The rain hadn't stopped, but the bear was nowhere in sight. Women at other holes announced that they didn't see the bear either. After looking out every hole, Masari Shiina finally allowed them out. They opened the door, and refreshing, cold air blew in, but the women remained cautious and carefully stuck out their necks. Once they were sure the bear was gone, they tumbled outside like a shabby avalanche. Tsusa Hiiragi vomited the moment she leaped out the door. As Kayu Saitoh staggered outside, she turned back to look at the trap. Several cracks ran through the logs. Hikari Asami ran a hand along one of the cracks and whispered, as if to herself, that the walls needed reinforcing.

To Masari Shiina, Kotei Hoshii said amicably, "Incredible. You're incredible. The bear gave up and retreated."

"Yeah, that's right," Hono Ishizuka agreed. "It's marvelous. Masari really is our chief. A real tactician."

"We didn't kill it," Masari Shiina said, her demeanor and expression unchanged. She turned to face the other women, who were savoring the lingering taste of victory. "The bear left, but it's only temporary. It will attack Dendera again, and soon. The only place we can survive is in Dendera. We must defend it with our lives. Next time, we must destroy the creature by fire. We mustn't let down our guards. We mustn't be careless. Those of you who have been assigned guard duty, return to your posts at once. That is all."

Her orders were harsh, but the women felt satisfied after their great achievement. For the first time, they sensed victory over the bear was possible, and the feeling was intoxicating. Kayu Saitoh smiled, and the rain washed away her oily sweat.

They could win.

They could conquer.

The women's body heat and good spirits rose into the air and melded into the delicate predawn fog that enveloped Dendera.

8

When the fog came and blocked her view, Redback turned from watching the Two-Legs from the base of the mountain. Stab wounds covered her front legs and chest, but with her giant body, they were merely tiny things.

Still, Redback snorted.

The Two-Legs acted differently than they ever had before, and this frightened her.

In a contest of simple physical strength, she knew she was far more powerful. But she understood that when the Two-Legs used those strange sticks that spat fire, or when they presented her with a situation beyond her comprehension, her prospects of victory diminished. This time, Redback had been utterly confounded, and she didn't get in a single attack on the Two-Legs. The defeat, a savage blow to Redback's pride, brought back the fear she'd once held toward the Two-Legs. Raindrops penetrated Redback's wounds and produced tingling pain. To relieve her stress, Redback pounded a fir tree, but the trunk developed only a single, paltry crack. Redback realized that she was beginning to weaken from starvation. After her right eye had been crushed, all she'd been able to put into her stomach was the inner bark of some fir trees and water. Malnutrition blurred the vision of her single remaining eye.

Redback was headed toward death.

Having failed to obtain any meat, Redback pondered whether she should relinquish the mountain. She had nowhere else to go, but she could no longer stretch out the meager offerings of this blighted land, and she couldn't predict the Two-Legs' next move. It was getting harder to stay alive here.

Weary, Redback slumped over. This was an unpardonable posture for one who was sovereign over her surroundings, but the simple act of walking fatigued her. She sniffed with her chestnut nose, but her sense of smell had dulled, unable to register anything but the scent of the rain. Her dark, reddish-brown fur, malnourished, failed to repel the rain, and her body was losing its warmth. She forced strength into her four legs and managed to raise herself. Instinct alerted her that if she lay down now, she would freeze to death before she could starve. Her feral essence suddenly swelled, latching on to the rage she held toward the Two-Legs. Her strength had hit rock-bottom, but her rage was inexhaustible. She turned this rage into power and stood firm on her back legs, lifting herself upright, and she struck at the cracked fir tree. It snapped in half.

She learned that anger could fuel her body.

As if testing this new knowledge, she focused strength into her front legs, and even her mind returned to that vivid thought: *Kill and devour.* This mountain did not belong to the Two-Legs. Through her rage, Redback vowed: as long as they strode about reeking of arrogance, as long as she, who killed and devoured all, lived, she would never back down. This was her creed, singular and absolute. Her family had been living in the mountain long, long before the Two-Legs came. Redback's family lived in the mountain and ruled the mountain. Her rage against these invaders was only proper. Repelling trespassers from their territory was what the creatures of the wild did. But this time, Redback had yielded in retreat, because the Two-Legs had changed their tactics. Now, she thought, she needed to change *her* tactics too.

Chapter 8

Over the Edge

When morning came, the rain turned abruptly to snow and again colored the Mountain in pure white. The downpour had furrowed the earth, making pathways for red-ochre-colored rivulets of thawed snow, but these were quickly covered over anew. The rain and fog had lifted, and the snow finished falling, and under a clear sky, five women—Kayu Saitoh, Kyu Hoshina, Tema Tsukamoto, Tsusa Hiiragi, and Itsuru Obuchi—ascended the Mountain using wooden spears as walking sticks. They had two goals: find the latest Climber and procure food along the way. Though Dendera's leadership had changed, those two duties remained a constant. Kayu Saitoh felt somewhat excited to be joining the search party for the first time. Her attention was unfocused, and her gaze flitted here and there. Gone from her mind were any thoughts of the bear's attack the night before or even of the party's primary mission to gather food.

A smile spread on Kyu Hoshina's darkly tanned face, and she said, "Kayu, nobody's going to be over that way. Those are just rocks."

Trying to conceal her cheerful mood, Kayu Saitoh spoke softly and said, "I know that much."

"Well, today is really about gathering food. The search is only incidental."

"Why? If we don't find her quickly, she'll die. Not everyone can survive on the Mountain like you."

"Of course I want to find her, but if we run into her escort, it'll be huge trouble."

Kyu Hoshina kept a quick pace, as if she were trying to outrun the dazzling light of the midday sun.

The Climbs were performed between afternoon and evening. The reason for this was simple: to allow safe descent for the person who carried their elder up the Mountain. This consequently afforded the abandoned elders the chance to descend as well, but no matter what their circumstances—how familiar they were with animal trails, for example—the journey was not something seniors clad only in a single white robe could surmount alone. That said, some did return. Their stories had been told repeatedly to Kayu Saitoh as shameful things, and she had seen it happen once herself.

It was a woman who had been married into a charcoal-maker's house and had returned, crying and looking monstrous, to the Village. The townspeople captured her immediately and took days killing her, in a process much like torture, as if in emphasis that they would not under any circumstances permit her to go to Paradise. Her corpse was broken into pieces and put in with the night soil. Witnessing this as a young woman, Kayu Saitoh thought how disgraceful it was to end up not in Paradise but in night soil, and she vowed deeply that once she had Climbed the Mountain, she would die with purity. And when she turned seventy, she was carried to the Mountain. As was the case in most families, her own son took her. That was a son's duty. When his parents turned seventy, he carried them to the Mountain. When he turned seventy, he would be carried by his son, and that son would be carried by the next. Through this process, the Village's population and food supply remained stable.

When it came to Climbing the Mountain, love was immaterial.

The people of the Village felt affection and attachment toward their parents—after all, they were human—but Climbing the Mountain was sacrosanct. Refusal only meant the ruination of their houses; there was no option but to do it. Consequently, the people of the Village excelled in blocking out any and all thoughts relating to Climbing the Mountain. Some cried as they carried their parents to the Mountain, but none showed mercy, and their legs never, ever stopped moving into the heart of the Mountain. Kayu Saitoh's son hadn't cried, but she could feel his back trembling underneath her. This display of emotion hadn't particularly bothered her, but she did think that he had no reason to be sad, as she would be arriving in Paradise only a little earlier than he.

But Kayu Saitoh was still alive and feeling eager in her search for another woman who had been carried to the Mountain as she had. She wondered what would be the creed of the woman they would rescue and bring back to Dendera. Would she rejoice as most women did, would she rage like Kayu Saitoh had, or would she react in some different way?

Now that establishing an aspiration was Kayu Saitoh's foremost priority, she hoped to hear something new. Of course, that something new might not necessarily complement her current state of mind, but she couldn't help but hope regardless. As she walked through the Mountain, she tried to picture the faces of the other women who had approached seventy alongside her, but among the people of the Village, she had only been close to Kura Kuroi, and her mind came up empty. Still, her hopeful feeling persisted.

Kayu Saitoh kept walking. Her feet were steady on the snowy path, due only in part to experience. The sureness of her step was testament to her immersion in Dendera.

In time, the animal trail merged into the incline of a ravine.

The ravine's base lay fairly low to the right, and to the left was a steep rise nearly as tall as a fir tree. The five women proceeded single file along the treacherous path—if it could even be called a path. Kyu Hoshina led, followed by Itsuru Obuchi, Kayu Saitoh, Tsusa Hiiragi, and Tema Tsukamoto in that order. Kayu Saitoh looked down the ravine where the expanse of snow-covered firs made a white forest.

Then she said, "I just thought of something... something I've been meaning to ask." She stared into the back of Itsuru Obuchi's straw coat. "Say we find someone Climbing the Mountain. What if it's a man? Do we kill him?"

"That would be too dangerous," Itsuru Obuchi said. The woman was trembling, perhaps struggling to stay on the narrow trail. "We won't do anything like that. We just quietly leave so that we're not noticed. We forget about him."

"Men can eat shit," Tema Tsukamoto said menacingly from the rear. "It's men who forced us here. Like we'd ever let them into Dendera."

"But both men and women Climb the Mountain all the same," Kayu Saitoh said.

With surprise in her voice, Tema Tsukamoto said, "Don't tell me you're considering rescuing the men too."

"They might be good in a fight," Kayu offered. "After all, there's only nineteen of us left in Dendera."

"We have our trap," Kyu Hoshina said from the front. "We'd need a better reason than that to include men in Dendera. After all, we drove off the bear—next time, we'll burn the beast alive. It'll be brutal."

None of the women rebuked her words as being too optimistic, and Kayu Saitoh for one held the firm belief that the bear could be defeated. With the women's newfound confidence after the previous night's events, the notion of accepting men for their combat strength had no room to propagate. Besides, Kayu Saitoh's feelings toward men were ambivalent. If someone else had proposed the same idea to her, she might have rejected it based on emotion rather than logic.

Thinking of the Village inevitably—if not immediately—caused her feelings toward the men to surface. The men occupied the core of the Village; everything was decided by them, and everything proceeded according to them. Kayu Saitoh hadn't the perspective to find anything unusual in that arrangement, and it didn't bother her that the men were in charge. Yet there were more than a few rules made solely at the whim of the males, and she disapproved of how they treated the women (the use of monthly huts, for one). But as a woman, she was unable to raise her grievances. For one matter, talk would change nothing, and in many ways, the women relied on the men to keep alive. Kayu Saitoh had difficulty turning her feelings toward the men into hate. She understood, intuitively, why the men couldn't be allowed into Dendera, but it was difficult to apply that notion, that feeling, directly upon the men who lived in the Village. She had for a fact lived under their protection. She had experienced being a woman; in her younger years, they were kind to her, and she had come to know several of them. In all these things, she had been happy. The other women shouldn't have been much different. Of the Village women, Mei Mitsuya alone had taken offense, and she stirred up the others to demand an improvement in their lives. But after she was taken to the Mountain, the commotion was settled in a perfunctory manner. Such was the level of concern among the men and women alike. Moreover, under the reality that Climbing the Mountain affected both genders equally, no turmoil broke out.

Seeking to identify the feeling that filled her, Kayu Saitoh asked, "Would you just quietly leave if you found your husband abandoned on the Mountain?"

"My husband?" Itsuru Obuchi said wistfully. "My husband Climbed the Mountain long ago."

"What if he hadn't Climbed the Mountain, and he was still alive?"

"What would you do, Kayu?"

"I…" Kayu Saitoh tried to think of her husband, whose Climb was four years ago, but the answer was not one she could find in an instant. "I…think I would want to save him. Of course."

Behind Kayu Saitoh, Tsusa Hiiragi said, "If it was one of the younger men, I would."

Tema Tsukamoto scoffed. "Hah, like they'd do anything with an old woman like you. You can talk like that when you've dusted off the cobwebs."

The women, Kayu Saitoh excluded, shared a vulgar cackle. They seemed to hope ribald comments would let them sidestep the question at hand, but that kind of ruse wouldn't last forever. Soon their laughter abated, and they walked the trail in silence. It was an uncomfortable silence. The irregular crunch of ice under straw sandals, snow falling from tree branches, the blowing wind; these were the only sounds around them. Worse, the women were empty-handed. They found no wild rabbits, no birds, no abandoned elder of either sex. Giving up, the five dragged their weary bodies back down the trail. It was a homecoming laden with the weight of their failure.

Leading the return, a bewildered Kyu Hoshina said, "What's going on? This hasn't happened before. I've never seen the Mountain like this—and I lived up here for three years. Even in the great famine ten years ago, there were still rabbits."

From behind, Tsusa Hiiragi said, "I know we're in the middle of winter, but it really is unusual to be unable to find a single rabbit. Did they all die off?"

Kayu Saitoh shared their unease. With the absence of even the birds' chirping, she wondered if the Mountain's bounty had exhausted, leading to the starvation of all its many creatures.

"We had that big unseasonal storm yesterday," Itsuru Obuchi muttered. "Another great famine might be coming."

The women's displeasure at least made their descent more lively as they all complained together. They were all hungry. They daydreamed of sweet, fatty meat. Their displeasure broadened to include talk of attacking the Village. As Kyu Hoshina followed the trail, she jokingly suggested that they should assault the Village themselves. Itsuru Obuchi shook her head slightly and warned her to be quiet.

"Kyu, you mustn't say that sort of thing in Dendera. We'll overlook it here, but just see what happens if you let Masari catch wind of it. Who knows what your punishment would be."

"Oh, that's right, most of you lot are long-time Doves," Kyu Hoshina said, sounding displeased. "With Mei dead and Masari the new leader, the Doves have it pretty easy now, don't they?"

"Don't you use Mei's name like that, *little girl,*" Itsuru Obuchi said.

Kyu Hoshina stopped in place and remarked that age was irrelevant here, and the four women lined up behind her had to stop as well.

"Irrelevant? Nonsense!" Itsuru Obuchi was shaking slightly. "Of anyone alive in Dendera today, I arrived the soonest after Mei. That's how long we were together. Yes, I'm a Dove, but I won't let you mock her name."

"Mei is dead," Kyu Hoshina said without turning. "You need to let go sometime. It's getting pathetic."

But Kayu Saitoh was the one to respond. "Stop it. You don't have the right to talk like that."

"Kayu," Kyu Hoshina said, still facing forward, "whatever do you mean by 'right'? Perhaps you can enlighten me."

"You've been completely taken in by Masari Shiina. Itsuru Obuchi has been a Dove for a long time, yet you were a Hawk, through and through. But now you've reversed your attitude and are working on the Doves' behalf. Kyu Hoshina, *you're* the one who's pathetic."

Immediately Kyu Hoshina responded, "I'm not working on the Doves' behalf. I'm helping to kill the bear. That's different than working for the Doves. And can't the same be said for you? Wouldn't you say this foraging expedition is on the Doves' behalf?"

"I'm talking about attitude. There's not a shred of beauty in you, standing there saying hurtful things. It's a shame; when we were looking for Sasaka Yagi's body and you stared down that bear, you were so beautiful."

"Drop it," Tsusa Hiiragi cut in.

Without a word, Kyu Hoshina began to walk. Kayu Saitoh couldn't tell if her words had given the woman something to think about, or if she was simply thinking about Sasaka Yagi.

Again silence ruled over their group. Whether Hawk or Dove, each woman had her own opinion about Masari Shiina taking over after Mei Mitsuya and the Doves gaining dominance over the Hawks. Being neither Hawk nor Dove, Kayu Saitoh's situation was a little different, but her mood sank, and a fermentative warmth spread in her empty stomach, accompanied by sharp, acidic pangs.

Tsusa Hiiragi shouted, "Wait! Hold on," breaking the silence that she herself had solicited.

The two in front halted, and Kayu Saitoh made her legs stop walking. With some effort, she turned around on the narrow path. Tsusa Hiiragi's face was the color of white seen only on those who had witnessed something terrible—and who knew that that terrible thing was getting even worse. Kayu Saitoh had been about to ask what was wrong, but she didn't need to; the reality was so obvious that she recognized it at a glance.

Tema Tsukamoto, who should have been walking at the rear, was gone.

Immediately Kayu Saitoh asked, "When?"

"I don't know," Tsusa Hiiragi mumbled. "She…was quiet for so long, and I thought that was odd, so I looked over my shoulder. But she was already gone."

Itsuru Obuchi said, "She probably fell into the ravine," but her expression looked like she was having trouble believing the idea.

Kayu Saitoh squashed the possibility, saying, "If so, she would have screamed."

"She was with us on the way up," Kyu Hoshina said. "It must have happened on the return. Let's go back."

The four old women went back the way they had come. Because they had to reverse course on the narrow path, Tsusa Hiiragi now took the lead. Holding out her wooden spear ahead of her, she walked on unsteady legs. Itsuru Obuchi told her to hurry up, but the woman had been overcome by fear and walked no faster. Soon, the four women found a pool of red on the trail. By now, this was no unfamiliar sight to them, and before they could react with surprise at the bloodstain, they had already gone on the alert. The blood ran up the side of the ravine.

"An ambush," Itsuru Obuchi said, glaring up the steep slope. "That damned bear has changed tactics. It must have recognized that it couldn't win by acting as it had before."

Itsuru Obuchi's conjecture was both astonishing and clear.

Up until now, the bear had attacked them head on, while cunning stratagems had always been the domain of the women. But this time, it was the women who had been outwitted. And their situation was grim: the four were in the Mountain—the bear's stronghold—and worse yet, they were caught standing on this narrow trail.

The bear would use its head when it attacked.

Kayu Saitoh realized that her hand, holding the spear, was trembling.

Tsusa Hiiragi shrieked, "What do we do?"

"Keep quiet," Kyu Hoshina warned. "We have to run. We have to keep quiet and run."

"But Tema Tsukamoto..."

"We leave her."

For a moment, the women seemed about to say something against Kyu Hoshina's decision, but then they quickly turned on their heels and ran. On the narrow animal trail, they couldn't work up too much speed; one misstep would mean a tumble down the ravine. Kayu Saitoh moved with little grace. Then she smelled a familiar, pungent odor, and she heard something plowing through the snow, but she ignored these things and ran. From behind her, Tsusa Hiiragi screamed, and when the blood rained down, Kayu Saitoh couldn't help looking over her shoulder. The bear had pierced its claws through Tsusa Hiiragi's back and lifted her off the ground. As she was being dragged up the wall of the ravine, she looked down in shock at the tips of the claws poking out through her stomach. Unable to spare the time to watch her go, the three remaining women ran as hard as they could.

The ground rumbled, and the bear's head appeared above them.

The next instant, its front paws swung down, the old women ducking by reflex. Claws swished through Kayu Saitoh's hair. Like a cat trying to catch a barely escaping rat, the bear tenaciously stretched out its front legs. Keeping low, the women scurried forward, but then, at the front of the line, Itsuru Obuchi screamed as her right hand sailed off into the air.

"Jump down!" Kyu Hoshina shouted.

Without pausing to ready themselves, the women jumped down into the ravine. Unable to perceive any sights or sounds, Kayu Saitoh tumbled down, striking against one small, hard object after another, and the next thing she knew, she was landing hard. Her breath stopped, she was numb from the inside out, and flashes of yellows and greens and violets came to the edges of her vision. She coughed away the pain in her back and somehow managed to stand. She was inside the woods. She looked down at herself, saw that her straw coat had disintegrated and that countless scratches ran along her arms and legs, and realized that the branches of a fir tree had softened her landing. Kyu Hoshina and Itsuru Obuchi had also lost their straw coats and were covered in similar scratches, but they too were able to stand.

The trees blocked their view of the bear higher up the ravine, but the three women shared the same thought: the bear wouldn't likely hesitate to give chase. They didn't have much time.

"Are . . . you all right?" Kayu Saitoh said, seeing that Itsuru Obuchi's right hand was gone. "It's come off."

"That's not as much trouble as these woods are," Itsuru Obuchi said, seeming to give no mind to her wrist. Instead the woman looked around at the expanse of fir trees surrounding them. "Can we get back to Dendera from here?"

"We can," Kyu Hoshina said. "I lived on the Mountain for three years. Most of these lands are stored in my head. We can get back to Dendera—that's if we can outrun the bear, of course."

"We have to let them know what happened. We have to tell Dendera that the bear has changed tactics. If we don't, they'll be massacred as they go heedlessly into the Mountain."

Itsuru Obuchi finally looked at the horrific state of her wrist, but quickly looked back up.

The bear had roared.

The roar echoed and echoed, and snow fluttered from the branches of the fir trees.

The next instant, a pungent wind shook through the trees, and the bear crashed down to the bottom of the ravine. Trees violently cracked and snapped, the ground sounded like it had been ripped asunder, and a spreading rumble shook snow from the branches, sending snowflakes showering down on the three women.

The snow settled and revealed the bear's massive bulk.

Terrifyingly thick legs, aggressively swelling shoulders, an underside with its needlelike fur, honey-colored claws, an exceptionally large head, intimidating fangs glistening, red fur standing up on its back, and its one remaining eye: the sum of these parts, this gigantic brown bear, stood upright before the three women; an already oppressive figure whose stance made it all the larger. Tsusa Hiiragi's guts dangled from its claws.

The bear moved its left eye.

Absent in that beady orb was any tinge of pastoral kinship, not that such a thing was to be expected. Instead, the eye glittered with unmitigated rage. The beast opened its scarlet maw, sending out its sweet, acrid breath, and advanced one step. The women retreated one step. But the strides of bear and man were insurmountably different, and the only consequence was that they had allowed the bear to get closer.

Glaring at the bear, Itsuru Obuchi said, "Run, you two."

"What are doing?" Kyu Hoshina asked, "sacrificing yourself? That won't save any of us."

"This is my punishment for living too long."

Itsuru Obuchi clenched her remaining hand and charged at the bear. Urged on by her intensity, Kayu Saitoh and Kyu Hoshina ran the other way. Kayu Saitoh knew that they needed to build up as much distance as possible, and yet she felt that she needed to bear witness to Itsuru Obuchi, so as she ran, she watched over her shoulder. Itsuru Obuchi was clinging to the bear's thigh by only her teeth and her left hand. The bear had tenacious legs and claws, but to wield them, the beast had developed a bulky frame. And in that bulk, Itsuru Obuchi had planted herself in a place where the bear's attacks couldn't easily reach. But that was merely a single surprise attack for which she had prepared no follow-up. The fight was over the moment the beast had regained its composure. The bear reached its front right paw to its thigh and pried her away. She struggled, but against the bear, her efforts hadn't the slightest effect.

Something struck Kayu Saitoh's shoulder. It was Kyu Hoshina, running beside her. Immediately understanding the message communicated by the jolt of pain, Kayu Saitoh looked ahead. Itsuru Obuchi did what she had done so that they could inform Dendera of this new threat. It wasn't necessary for Kayu Saitoh to watch the brutal death that came at bravery's end; neither had she earned the right to witness it. All she could do was run.

2

It had been too long since Redback had lost herself in the devouring of flesh. The meat worked its way into her weakened and malnourished body and swept away her fatigue, the blurriness in her vision, and her feelings of starvation. Redback licked the blood from inside her maw with her rough tongue, and for now was satisfied. But her hunger wasn't. And yet she believed that she would not be able to repeat her most current tactic. The Two-Legs had seen what she had done and would again change their tactics, or at the very least, they would not twice enter the Mountain unprepared. When she compared herself with the Two-Legs, she found herself lacking in wit. It irritated her to be aware that even if she could read their next move, she lacked the capacity to know how to deal with it.

Despite this, Redback went to sleep. Her large body needed rest. As she dozed, she thought of the spring that would come after this season had passed.

3

With contempt in her voice, Hono Ishizuka said, "So instead of coming to Dendera, the bear is waiting for us to come to the Mountain. At least that's what those women believe, but where's the proof? Did the bear tell them? Don't sow disorder in Dendera with your wild rumors."

"I'll kill you!" Kyu Hoshina said. She reached out to strangle the woman, but Kayu Saitoh stopped her.

"Don't," Kayu Saitoh said with great, weary patience. "They have no pride. They don't understand."

"Pride?" Hono Ishizuka said. "Dressing up your words won't change anything. Perhaps that word would carry more weight had you not fled and abandoned your companions."

"I'll kill you!" Kyu Hoshina barked. "You don't know anything! You don't know how brave Itsuru was!"

When Kayu Saitoh and Kyu Hoshina had managed to make it back to Dendera, they ran straight for the manor, where Hono Ishizuka, Masari Shiina, and Maru Kusachi were sharpening sticks into wooden spears. They told the three everything that had happened and everything they had felt, but received only Hono Ishizuka's cold indifference.

With a single-minded resolve, Hono Ishizuka announced, "We keep foraging."

"Do you mean to make Itsuru's death in vain? I should have known you were hopeless." Flecks of dirt fell from Kyu Hoshina's trembling neck. "The Doves are a motley crew indeed."

"Our food reserves aren't limitless. If we don't go into the Mountain and find food, we'll starve to death."

"If we end up killed—killed on the Mountain and not in Dendera—I suppose you'll be taking the blame—just like with the Finger-Cutting."

In the Village, the husbands came up with the new ideas, from changing breeds of rice seed to devising preservation methods for the potatoes. If one of the ideas ended up being a significant mistake, the man who had made the decision could receive a punishment called Finger-Cutting, in which, much as the name indicated, his finger was severed by a hatchet. Anyone, no matter how powerful, who hindered the operation of the Village became the target of hate. If his failure led to the loss of *food,* that hate could very well develop into thoughts of murder. The Finger-Cutting sacrificed a single finger to prevent such sentiments from erupting into acts.

"I'm prepared for that," Hono Ishizuka said with a nod. "I can even bite off my finger with my teeth."

"Your *finger*? Don't be so soft." Kyu Hoshina snorted. "If anyone dies because of your bad judgment, the women of Dendera won't be satisfied by a single finger. I think it'll be your neck."

"In that case, Kyu, I'll assume you're prepared to have your throat cut too. Let's say we trust what you're telling us, and we stop searching for food. If anyone starves to death, we won't hesitate to cut your throat."

Kayu Saitoh let go of Kyu Hoshina's hand and said, "Hono Ishizuka, do you think that's how you're getting out of this? What you just said is a coward's view. You're equating entirely different levels of resolve."

Hono Ishizuka glared at Kayu Saitoh. "But if we don't go into the Mountain and find food, we will certainly starve, and the bear is certainly in the Mountain. Someone too afraid of both to do anything is the greater coward."

An intense, interminable silence fell. The three women glowered at each other until Hono Ishizuka looked to Masari Shiina and asked the leader what her opinion was. Masari Shiina placidly parted her lips and said that Hono Ishizuka's opinion was more correct.

"But," the chief continued, "we mustn't ignore the views of those who suffered the bear's surprise attack. There's nothing particularly hard to believe about the notion that the bear, having been soundly walloped, is wary of Dendera and has devised some ploy in response." Masari Shiina turned her one eye on Kyu Hoshina. "Listen to me. I am fully prepared to stake my life upon my orders. I place importance on Dendera's preservation and improvement, but between the two, preservation is more important. Without preservation of what we have, there can be no improvement. As far as that is concerned, I support your judgment. Together, we built a trap to kill the bear. It was a little fortress. But if we were able to do that, we can make a bigger fortress too."

Hono Ishizuka said, "A bigger fortress... What do you mean?"

"Dendera itself will be our fortress. We'll make the whole of Dendera our trap. For now, we suspend our searches for food and women. We'll wait for the bear to get so hungry that it'll have to come to us. We'll see which of us can endure longer. The duration of our encirclement will be determined by our remaining reserves. I'll report when I've made the calculation. That is all."

"Masari, that's too risky," Hono Ishizuka protested. "We'll starve to death."

"To fight the bear inside the Mountain would be the height of stupidity. We'd be fools if we got ourselves killed going out in search of food. If we're to face that beast, we have to make use of Dendera. We have no other possible strategy but to wait for the bear to come to us."

"But our food reserves really are—"

"That is all." Masari Shiina turned away, not to put an end to the conversation, but because it was already over. She put her hand on the ladder that led to the second floor.

"Wait, please," Kayu Saitoh said. "Have you not thought about abandoning Dendera?"

As the words came from her mouth, Kayu Saitoh knew the chief had considered no such thing—she just wanted to say it herself.

"Abandon it?" Masari Shiina said, stopping with her back turned. "Abandon it and go where?"

"I don't know... but there are many lands. We don't have to stay here. We can move far enough away that the bear won't follow, and we can build a new Dendera... as long as we have the resolve."

"So, those abandoned by the Village will abandon Dendera, is that it? And we'll live in some other land? Absurd."

"Why is it absurd?" At some point, the words had started to come naturally to Kayu Saitoh. When she spoke, her words no longer rang as artificial. "Why do you cling to Dendera so? We could just live somewhere else, couldn't we? Couldn't you be happy that way?"

"I won't flee Dendera. I will live here, and I will keep this place alive."

"You damn pig-headed woman. I don't understand you."

"You don't understand because you were always just a mess—in the Village and in Dendera."

Masari Shiina disappeared upstairs, and the conversation really had ended. Kayu Saitoh felt unsure over many things at once, Kyu Hoshina shook with anger, and Hono Ishizuka left the manor without showing any particular emotion. Maru Kusachi hadn't spoken a word the entire time, and she remained silent as she continued fashioning the wooden spears.

4

That night, Hono Ishizuka came to each hut to convey Masari Shiina's orders: they would seal themselves in for twelve days beginning in the morning, watch duties would continue for the duration, and they would be given an allotment of only so much food. An air of stagnation returned to the settlement that had become lively with the confidence of victory, and the women were fatigued before anything even started.

When Hono Ishizuka delivered the instructions to Kayu Saitoh's hut, the woman remarked in a parting shot that she didn't agree with Kayu Saitoh's opinion.

"Don't mind her," Nokobi Hidaka said as she stirred her bowl of soup—broth with a few floating kernels of corn. "You're not wrong. Itsuru gave her life so we could have that knowledge. You're not wrong."

"Yeah," Kayu Saitoh said, but her thoughts were somewhere completely different, on the idea that had spontaneously come to her while she was talking with Masari Shiina: abandon Dendera and move to a different land. She asked herself why she had let her mouth run like that and why the idea persisted in her mind. She began to get the feeling that this could be the profound change that she was seeking—her aspiration. She didn't sense anything unnatural, or fleeting and arbitrary in the notion, nor did she find, as she had feared she might, any feelings of self-condemnation. For now, at least, she felt reassured that she wasn't deceiving herself.

But even if this mass relocation were to happen, by definition it wasn't something a single person could or would do alone. To relocate alone was merely a retreat, but *en masse*, it became a creed; it became strength; and it became a profound change. The truth in this made Kayu Saitoh feel deeply satisfied. A gloom had taken hold in Dendera, but Kayu Saitoh felt exuberant. The more dreary and gloomy Dendera became, the more vivid was the idea of profound change.

The twelve days of stagnation and starvation began.

With more free time than they knew how to fill, the women tried to find work within Dendera, but aside from whittling spears in their huts, or cutting firewood outside, there was nothing that needed to be done. Some even began speaking enviously of the women on guard duty, a task normally regarded as a chore. Amid frequent yawns, Kayu Saitoh wandered aimlessly outside. She looked to the white-covered Mountain and thought of Itsuru Obuchi. Her mind turned to the irrational hope that the woman had escaped the bear's savage attacks and was still alive somewhere on the Mountain. The hope took an unexpectedly tenacious hold in her thoughts. Kayu Saitoh looked away from the Mountain and down at the ground. She cursed the snow for preventing the women from planting crops, when a single word came to her.

Spring.

Now was the coldest time of the year, but spring would eventually come. Kayu Saitoh hadn't experienced spring in Dendera, but she thought it must be a little easier. Realizing that fantasizing of spring in this season was a form of escapism, she instead made herself think about the far more real matter of the migration as she continued walking.

She heard several voices. Four Hawks—Ate Amami, Kotei Hoshii, Hotori Oze, and Ume Itano—were dismantling, as if gutting a giant fish, the walls of a hut abandoned after the bear had destroyed it.

Kayu Saitoh approached the women and asked what they were doing.

Kicking at some ice to break it free from the wall, Ate Amami replied, "We're building a watchtower. It'll be a lot better than just lolling about on guard."

"I'm no fool about to be killed by the bear," Hotori Oze said, nodding. "Although starving to death is even more foolish."

"A watchtower is a great idea. Is it on Masari Shiina's orders?"

"Don't be daft. It's our idea," Hotori Oze said. With irritation in her voice, she added, "The Doves won't listen to anyone else's ideas."

The current directive, this bigger fortress, was not an active approach. By being ordered to simply wait for the bear's assault, the women had been given free time, which they seemed to be using to revive their personal ideologies. Kayu Saitoh realized that people needed to be given work or they would do as they pleased.

"What do you think?" Ate Amami said. "How about helping us?"

With nothing else to do and no reason to decline, Kayu Saitoh helped the women with their tower. It was a simple task—upending several logs and building a platform large enough for people to stand upon—but Dendera lacked in both materials and tools, and building a proper tower was out of the question. The women removed what lumber was still usable from the empty house, and with all the holes they left in it, the abandoned building looked like it could have been home to a particularly industrious mouse. Unlike the storehouses or the trap, the house was of simple construction and was easily dismantled. As she worked, her hands freezing, Kayu Saitoh understood how the bear had been able to tear through the structure in a single strike.

The women gathered the necessary materials quickly, but driving the logs into the earth was difficult work—or, to be more precise, digging the holes in the earth to drive the logs into was difficult work. With the dirt frozen solid, and the tools at their disposal limited, the old women spent a long time digging. Then, working together, they lifted the logs and placed them in the holes. Kotei Hoshii threw her body at the standing logs, and the wood gave only a tremble. Satisfied at the structure's sturdiness, the women arranged pieces of wood into a simple platform to go on top of the logs. The tower may not have stood perfectly vertical, but it was complete.

"All right, let's climb up top," Ate Amami said, her voice spirited. "We've earned the right to be the first to climb the tower."

The women began their careful ascent. Kayu Saitoh too was cautious and gripped the logs tightly with both arms. It was tough work for her fatigued body, but she managed to climb to the top. Standing beside the other women on the creaking, rickety floor, she took in the view. The sun was setting, the Mountain beautiful in twilight, the persimmon-colored sky seeming to glow of its own accord. Kayu Saitoh gazed in such rapt attention that she didn't even let slip a sound of her wonder. The tower stood only as tall as two women, and yet the change in perspective transformed the familiar view into something fresh.

Transfixed by the sight of the Mountain, Ate Amami said, as if in a dream, "On the other side is the Village."

Hotori Oze, her voice and demeanor unchanged, said, "And here we live in Dendera on the opposite side. And because of that bear, we can't attack them."

"It's so frustrating."

"I think we'd have to attack them before spring—if we could, that is."

Kayu Saitoh found it surprising to hear Hotori Oze mention the season of rebirth in the context of killing. She asked the woman why she thought it necessary to attack in the winter.

"It's simple," Hotori Oze answered. "The gap between our fighting strengths will widen. In the winter, both the Village and Dendera are weary. We'll be able to find an opening for our incursion."

"Hotori Oze, you really do think of nothing but attacking."

"It's only obvious that I should hate that foul Village. Do you not, Kayu Saitoh?"

Kayu Saitoh decided to ignore her, and soon the panorama subtly shifted her inner thoughts toward the desire for resettlement. Remaining unaware of this shift, Kayu Saitoh basked in her simple sense of fulfillment as she returned to her hut.

But when night arrived, it came with hunger that brought her back to her senses. With the return of her long-absent hunger, her stomach growled greedily, churning with the empty sounds of digestion. Having grown accustomed to potatoes and dried fish, her stomach hadn't been satisfied by her meal—if it could even be called that—of broth with a scant few kernels of corn. Nokobi Hidaka jabbed firewood into the hearth and made a pitiful search for potatoes that wouldn't be there. Shigi Yamamoto remained as she always was, whether her stomach was empty or not, and continued her unintelligible mumbling. Kayu Saitoh realized she was slipping into torpor, and disappointed in herself, she forced her legs to stand. She had been chosen for that night's watch duty. She stepped out into Dendera at night and began her rounds. But even if the giant bear were to be walking about in the open, the beast would have been hard to spot; beyond the light of the fire baskets was only darkness. With only a torch to aid her, she tamed the desire to sleep that lodged in her frozen body, and she kept watch over Dendera until the next day had come in full.

Stagnation. Starvation. Languor. The women suffered these in a daily repetition. With no duties aside from keeping watch, with no food aside from meager broth, the women's exhaustion reached its limits.

By the seventh day of their besiegement, even moving required resolve, but Kayu Saitoh nevertheless forced herself to remain active. Nokobi Hidaka stretched out on the floor, yawning repeatedly and muttering about how hungry she was, but Kayu Saitoh regarded the woman's continued laxity as vulgar and shameful. There had been people like her in the Village. They liked it when others were made targets of a Mountain-Barring or a Finger-Cutting, and they liked to watch the punishments too; they blabbed other people's secrets and watched in amusement as their victims were meted out punishments. When those sorts of people weren't looking down on others, they were either sleeping idly or flushing from the fear that their own dirty secrets would be revealed. Kayu Saitoh worried that if she gave in to her hunger and lay down even once, she would become like them, and such would begin her degeneration. And so she kept moving about, even if she had to compel herself to do so. In truth, Nokobi Hidaka had degenerated and fallen into depression. The moment the woman finished her meager meals, she immediately lay back down, sucked in a bereft breath, and moaned about how hungry she was. Rather than sympathize with the woman, Kayu Saitoh felt disappointed by her. She tried to think of those who had died, but she realized that thinking of the dead only because the behavior of the living seemed dull was a form of escapism, and escapism was a vulgar and shameful act. This only heightened her disappointment in herself.

Two more days passed, but the bear still showed no sign of coming. The food supply had at last run out, and the women began to eat straw, grinding it and kneading it with water in a stone pot. The mixture was harsh and astringent, and took effort to swallow, but it was all they had to keep starvation at bay. The very same day the Doves' stockpile had emptied, their authority was diminished. Few listened to Masari Shiina and Hono Ishizuka's commands, but the watch duty continued voluntarily.

The evening came with no hope of a meal. Kayu Saitoh was sitting in front of the hearth. Shigi Yamamoto was sitting in the same manner, but that was what she always did. Nokobi Hidaka was lying beside the hearth, staring forlornly into the empty stone pot.

"I'm starving," Nokobi Hidaka said, putting a hand to her hollow cheek. "I've never been so miserable. I don't care if that bear comes out—I want to go into the Mountain and find food."

"You can't," Kayu Saitoh said. Malnutrition had left her mouth dry and turned her voice into gravel. "We've made it this far, but if you do that, everything we've suffered will have been for nothing. The bear is starving too. It'll come to Dendera soon. Until then, we endure."

"What are we living for?"

"Huh?"

"I don't even know anymore." Nokobi Hidaka reached for a piece of straw and put it directly into her mouth. "We fear the plague, we fear the bear, and in the end, we starve. For what reason . . . are we still living?"

"You're thinking crazy things."

"Kayu, you were right. We should have Climbed the Mountain as we were told. Lately, I've been thinking . . . I was wrong."

"About what?"

"About the attack. It was arrogance. Who did I think I was?" Nokobi Hidaka wearily spat out the straw and whispered, "I should have stayed in the Mountain." The woman's sunken eyes quivered. "If I had finished the Climb, I would be in Paradise now. I'd be stuffing myself with meats and pastries."

"Don't talk like that. It's depressing."

"I'm already depressed. I'm starving. I want to die."

"Wait three more days," Kayu Saitoh urged. "In three more days, we'll be at the end of this. If the bear hasn't come by then, Masari Shiina will change her mind."

"Three days!" Nokobi Hidaka shouted, her voice startlingly loud. "As if I can wait that long!"

"Yelling will only make you hungrier."

"Not that it matters," Nokobi Hidaka said, sitting up. "The rabbits are dead. The Mountain has nothing for us."

"If that's true, Nokobi Hidaka, then won't you leave Dendera with me?"

Kayu Saitoh hadn't planned on revealing her idea to the woman, but the words had come out on their own.

She didn't know if this was the appropriate time, or if Nokobi Hidaka was the woman she should tell first, or for that matter how serious about the idea she was herself, but she knew that once she started to say it, she had to finish. Kayu Saitoh was deeply conflicted, but she hadn't been able to stop mid-sentence, and she couldn't pass it off as a joke. She had to say it all.

"Leave...Dendera?" Nokobi Hidaka said with a mystified expression. "What are you saying?"

"Couldn't we leave Dendera and begin a new life somewhere else?" She found herself believing in each word as she said it, and she pressed on. "Let's resettle."

Slowly, Nokobi Hidaka said, "Resettle," her mouth working as if she were eating the word itself.

"There's no point in waiting in a place like this for the bear to come. If the bear comes, or if we starve first, either way we die. And if we're going to die anyway, why don't we take ourselves somewhere else, to another land? Spring will soon come. The cold will fade. The snow will melt. Come, live with me someplace new."

"But where would we go?"

"How should I know?"

"Can you guarantee we could find a land more favorable than here?"

"How should I know?" Kayu Saitoh repeated. "I have no idea, but we have to try. It's better than dying to some bear or starvation." Stirred by her own words, she stood, if unsteadily. "Tomorrow, I think I'll tell this to the people of Dendera. If we don't hurry, someone will die first. Even if our current plan goes off as intended, I question what some starving old women could do when the bear comes. We might lose. So I want to talk about it first—even though I don't know how many will see things my way."

"Kayu, you're the first person I've heard suggest that."

"Dendera has never been in this much peril before. This place is already over. So can't we abandon it? Can't we escape? There's nothing here we need to hold on to."

"All right, I'll do it."

"That's a big help," Kayu Saitoh said, meaning it. "That's a big help."

"The first question is how many will come with us."

"I think Kyu Hoshina will." Kayu Saitoh looked to Shigi Yamamoto, who moved not a bit. "We'll carry this one with us."

Now that she had put her new vision into words—even if it had happened on impulse—Kayu Saitoh once again felt fulfilled. As an immense cloud of fear hung over Dendera, her words shone like nothing else. She felt like she might be able to bring about profound and fundamental change. Her plan to resettle could potentially leave all of their problems behind. All their problems were what they'd be leaving. Lost in a contented reverie, a gentle but unyielding need to sleep overcame her. Untroubled by her hunger, she began to sink into a saccharine slumber. She was vaguely aware of the sound of Nokobi Hidaka leaving the hut to go on watch duty, and then, as if abruptly cut off from consciousness, she was asleep.

The next morning, when Kayu Saitoh opened her eyes, the first thing she saw was Nokobi Hidaka vomiting great amounts of blood into the stone pot.

5

Nokobi Hidaka collapsed where she was. Kayu Saitoh rushed to her and held her up, but the woman didn't respond. Kayu Saitoh ran outside, scooped up some snow, and threw it on Nokobi Hidaka's face. The woman cracked open her eyes and moved her red-stained lips, mumbling something. A foul stench rose from her mouth.

Unmistakably, the plague had returned.

And unmistakably, Nokobi Hidaka had it.

Kayu Saitoh's thoughts flashed back to the past, and in her mind's eye she was back in the slaughter and the blaze that the plague had brought about.

"It's hopeless," Kayu Saitoh whispered without thought.

It's hopeless, she knew. *If that madness swallows us again, Dendera will really be finished this time. It's hopeless.* She called out Nokobi Hidaka's name again and again. The woman continued to mutter, her blank eyes moving weakly about. Suddenly, the life came back to her eyes and she sprang up like a seedling and moved away from Kayu Saitoh.

"No!" she shouted. "W-why...why is this happening to me? No. This isn't the plague. I just wasn't feeling well. That's all. Of course, that's all. Of course..."

She didn't say anything after that. Vomiting blood again, she curled up in pain. The torrent of blood pooled and spread, and stained the white robes of Shigi Yamamoto, who remained seated and unresponsive.

"Don't move," Kayu Saitoh said, rubbing Nokobi Hidaka's back. "Just lie down. You need to rest."

Nokobi Hidaka didn't stop spewing blood. Her neck muscles spasmed, her back trembled, and the vital fluid seemed like it would keep coming until she had none left inside. Kayu Saitoh didn't know what she should do aside from rubbing Nokobi Hidaka's back, and the frustration of it was overwhelming. She looked to Shigi Yamamoto for help, but the woman didn't move a muscle, even with the blood soiling her, instead sitting still beside the hearth.

At some point Nokobi Hidaka ceased to vomit, and she placed her hands on the floor in a pool of her own blood. Then, with a quivering hand, she wiped her mouth.

Her voice uncannily clear, Nokobi Hidaka said, "No, this is the plague. The plague has... has done me in. Isn't that so, Kayu? Am I wrong?"

"You're not wrong."

"Hadn't we wiped it out? Hadn't it gone away? This must be because I ate that bear meat."

"No. The meat wasn't the source of the plague. Nokobi Hidaka, you did nothing wrong."

"I did. I did." Nokobi Hidaka spat out the blood that lingered in her mouth. "I killed the women with the plague sixteen years ago, and I killed them again this time."

"You're not a bad person. You don't need to talk like that."

"I won't be able to resettle with you." Tears welled in her eyes. "I beg you. Don't tell anyone about this. I don't want to be killed. I don't want to be butchered. I don't want to be set on fire."

"Don't worry. I won't let anyone do that to you," Kayu Saitoh said. "But I have to tell them about the plague."

"I don't want to be butchered. I don't!"

Nokobi Hidaka sat up and reached out her red-stained palms to Kayu Saitoh.

"Calm down," Kayu Saitoh said, pressing against her hands. "I won't let them kill you. I promise I won't."

"It's the plague! They'll kill me!"

"I told you I promised, didn't I? Killing doesn't stop the plague. I know it doesn't, so I won't let them."

Kayu Saitoh had proclaimed her resolve, but all she could do for Nokobi Hidaka at the moment was to lay her down and rinse the blood from her body. Then she mopped up the floor with snow and laid the woman to rest, but she did not do so while keeping calm. Inside her, turmoil built upon turmoil. She even started to let out guttural moans. She was a mindless beast, her arms and legs working briskly, but almost entirely of their own accord. As if in confirmation, her mind began to turn off. She felt herself wanting to take out her frustrations on the motionless Shigi Yamamoto, and she hated herself for it. She looked down at Nokobi Hidaka. Wrapped up in bloodstained robes, the woman was breathing raggedly, but soon she reached sleep. Her breathing steadied, but her face was ashen and the corners of her eyes developed an indeterminate twitch.

Kayu Saitoh left the hut and walked through the forlorn morning. Masari Shiina's manor was her destination. She couldn't predict the reaction she'd receive, but she felt obligated to inform the chief of the plague's reemergence. Kayu Saitoh's thoughts were still in turmoil, but as she stepped across the snow, she vowed to oppose the death sentence should one come from Masari Shiina's lips. If Kayu Saitoh could do nothing else, she would at least prevent Nokobi Hidaka from becoming a sacrifice. As she swore this to herself, she also felt a duty to talk about the resettlement. Though unsure of the reception any of her words would receive, Kayu Saitoh nevertheless stepped into the manor.

And there she saw that further events had already developed.

Someone had come to the manor ahead of her, and it was Hotori Oze.

The woman's white robes were stained red and exuded a foul odor.

"What the hell is this?" Hotori Oze was yelling. Kayu Saitoh had never heard her in such a rage. "I'm serious. I don't want to die to some plague. Listen, Doves, what the hell is this? I didn't eat the bear meat. We killed the ones who did. So why do I have the plague?"

Hotori Oze directed her hostile gaze on Masari Shiina and Hono Ishizuka. Her eyes were wild, seething in surrender to the heat of hatred. Kayu Saitoh had never seen her like this either.

Masari Shiina and Hono Ishizuka faced the crazed woman head on. They were determined to overpower her with their knowledge and their pride, and without retreat, denial, or deception. Maru Kusachi, on the other hand, was looking anywhere else, uninvolved.

"Well, even if you ask us like that," Hono Ishizuka said, "we still won't have an answer for you." Her expression remained composed, but a twitch in her cheek revealed the effort that took. "Hotori, would you please calm down? We don't know the source of the plague either."

"I don't want to die this way. I need to destroy the Village. Why the plague?"

Trying to placate her, Hono Ishizuka said, "Going forward, I'd like to reinvestigate this plague."

"Reinvestigate? Nonsense. Utter nonsense. I've had enough of your mockery!"

"Wait a minute, Hotori. Why are you yelling at me?"

"Don't look at me like that! I'll give *you* this damn plague."

Hotori Oze lurched for Hono Ishizuka, but Kayu Saitoh restrained her. Hotori Oze flailed about, yelling, "Let me go!" but Kayu Saitoh wrapped her arms around the woman's. It was only then that the women noticed Kayu Saitoh's presence.

"Kayu," Hono Ishizuka asked, "what are you doing over there?"

The woman's eyes went to Kayu Saitoh's face, dropped to her blood-stained robes, and then went wide.

"It's not me," Kayu Saitoh explained reflexively. "Nokobi Hidaka caught the plague. It happened this morning."

"Nokobi Hidaka, huh?" Hotori Oze said, putting on an expression not far from a smile. "So it's not just me, then. Hah, well, well, so the plague attacks Dendera once more. That's the end now, isn't it?"

Kayu Saitoh asked, "When did you start showing the symptoms, Hotori?"

"Just a moment ago. I threw up blood," she replied brusquely. "I didn't eat the bear, but I still threw up blood. Foul-smelling blood, and a lot of it too."

"Well, Hono Ishizuka, how are you going to explain this to the rest of Dendera?" Kayu Saitoh glared at Hono Ishizuka, with the thought of Ire Tachibana and Kushi Tachibana on her mind. "Anyone can see that the plague had nothing to do with the bear meat. It's out in the open now."

"Again, you can ask us that sort of thing all you like, and we still won't have an answer. We know next to nothing about the plague, and that's that."

"You don't know what this plague is. Your food reserves have dried up. The Doves' reputation is plummeting."

"Kayu, this is hardly the time to be talking like—"

Hotori Oze shook free of Kayu Saitoh's arms. "What are you going to do? Tell me, Dove. What are you going to do? What are you going to do with me? What are you going to do about the plague? Shall I spread it for you?"

Whether or not the decision was beyond Hono Ishizuka's capacity, Masari Shiina stepped forward. She swept her single eye across them. Kayu Saitoh couldn't detect any trace of frustration in the leader's gaze.

"I commend you for not hiding your condition," Masari Shiina said, looking to Hotori Oze. "I do not believe that killing you will bring any peace of mind to the women of Dendera. Instead, we would prefer to work toward the discovery of the plague's cause."

"Work toward the—" Hotori Oze sputtered. "That's the best you can say? Well, what are you going to do with me?"

"I'd like you to tell me your actions over the past several days. We've been in this besiegement for twelve days. We know the plague couldn't have come from outside. Therefore, the source must be somewhere within Dendera."

The leader next looked to Kayu Saitoh. "Bring Nokobi Hidaka here as quickly as you can. I want to hear her story. The plague's source could be hidden in something both of these women have done."

Kayu Saitoh hesitated, then looked Masari Shiina straight on and said, "Instead of that, won't you consider leaving Dendera? It's not too late. Let's resettle. Abandon Dendera. Right now."

"You're still talking about that?"

"This has happened because you forever persist in clinging to Dendera. Why won't you even try looking for a new place where there's no bear and no plague?"

In a menacing tone, Hotori Oze said, "Listen, Kayu Saitoh, you're only able to talk like that because you don't have the plague. You think you can start some new life, but it's only a fantasy that has enthralled you."

Masari Shiina said, "I won't abandon Dendera. And I won't run from the plague. Quit this foolishness and quickly bring Nokobi Hidaka here. And don't stir up a fuss about it."

"Shit! How obstinate can you ladies be?" Kayu Saitoh retorted, but it amounted to nothing more than a parting shot. She had said what she needed to say, had behaved how she needed to behave, and had done all she could do, and she recognized that what she now needed to do was listen to Nokobi Hidaka's story.

Kayu Saitoh turned in anger and left the manor. She was on her way back to the hut when she noticed Maru Kusachi moving ahead of her. What Kayu Saitoh immediately felt was nothing more than a hunch, but she sensed that Maru Kusachi was trying to escape to somewhere far away. She tackled the woman from behind and pressed the back of her head into the snow.

"Don't try to escape," Kayu Saitoh said. "Where do you think you're going?"

"Would you let me go?" Maru Kusachi said through the snow in her mouth. "You're hurting me, and I'm cold."

"If you're straight with me, I'll let you go. Where are you—you three—going? Try to deny it and I'll kill you right here."

"Go ahead."

"Damn you."

Kayu Saitoh clicked her tongue and removed herself from the woman.

Maru Kusachi stood up, projecting an aloof air, then brushed the snow off her face and white robes and looked at Kayu Saitoh with an entirely unperturbed expression. That was when Kayu Saitoh realized that this woman wouldn't bow to any manner of threat. There had been people like her—though not many—back in the Village. Nothing unsettled them, and nothing got to them. And Kayu Saitoh didn't know how to deal with people like that.

And so she decided to be blunt. "I hate your kind most of all."

"You can say that to me, coming out of nowhere?" Maru Kusachi was blunt as well. "I don't believe I've ever done anything to bother you."

"No?"

"If I—just for example—were to destroy Dendera, would that bother you?"

"I don't know. I don't know what you're talking about. But it would bother me if any more people died. Isn't that what you three are planning? Aren't you three planning on going somewhere?"

"But where would we go?"

"How the hell should I know? It's just a thought I had. I got the feeling that you, Hogi Takamiya, and Shijira Iikubo might be going somewhere."

Immediately Maru Kusachi replied, "And here I thought *you* were the one going away. Aren't you about to go resettle somewhere? Aren't you going to move to where there's no bear and no plague? Tell me now, where is such a place?"

"I think you three know that better than any of the rest of us."

"Aren't you something," Maru Kusachi said with an approving nod. "You have quite the knack for grasping the situation, even if you don't have much practice at it."

"What are you going on about?"

"And such superb intuition," Maru Kusachi continued. "You just might have been able to hold Dendera together—if only you were more experienced. It's a shame, really."

"Enough of that. Just answer me." Kayu Saitoh raised her voice in impatience. "You, Hogi Takamiya, and Shijira Iikubo. What are you plotting? You're not Hawks, and you're not Doves."

"Neither are you."

"Don't lump me in with you three."

"That's right. What do you suppose we should call your faction, the Swallows?"

"No, that label better applies to you three—you've already decided where you're flying off to." Kayu Saitoh held her eyes on Maru Kusachi and continued with words founded purely on intuition. "And you'll go there as soon as your plague has destroyed Dendera."

"You're talking as if I'm behind the plague."

"Am I wrong?"

"It's not me."

"It's not *you*?" The woman's reply struck her as odd. "What do you mean by that? Why did you say it that way?"

"I meant what I said." Maru Kusachi didn't break Kayu Saitoh's gaze. "Spreading the plague isn't in my intentions. I...no, *we*—that is Hogi Takamiya, Shijira Iikubo, and I—don't really care. We couldn't care less about the rest of you. But that woman is different."

"Who is different?"

"I wonder if you'll figure it out when you put together Hotori Oze's and Nokobi Hidaka's stories."

"Enough with the secrets. Tell me straight out."

"Maybe later."

"Tell me now."

"The place we're going might actually be somewhere nice. Maybe without a bear. Maybe without a plague. And maybe without starvation."

"Where? Where is it?"

"It's a place you know better than anyone."

At that, Maru Kusachi turned to walk away.

Kayu Saitoh stepped forward, either to catch up to the woman or to pummel her, but then she saw someone running in from a distance.

The swiftly running woman, spear in hand, was Hikari Asami. Seeing the elderly woman sprinting, puffing out white plumes of breath, Kayu Saitoh's intuition announced the worst.

But still, she had to ask. "What is it?"

Hikari Asami clenched her fist around her wooden spear.

"The bear is here."

6

Starvation once again tormented Redback.

As she had predicted, the Two-Legs hadn't again set foot in the mountain. Not wanting to enter the land where they dwelled, she had resisted making an attack, but her resistance had its limit. Redback descended the mountain, moving toward the land where the Two-Legs dwelled. Normally, she moved during the night or the early morning, but hunger overrode her reason, and she set out after dawn. This was against her animal nature, but such rules meant nothing to a creature captive to her craving for meat. Moving quickly, Redback soon reached the ridge overlooking the land of the Two-Legs. Only one thought moved her: *Kill and devour.* Her mind was empty of anything else—save for one other thought. One crucial thought.

Redback was counting on spring.

She had the feeling, a baseless conviction, that if she survived until spring, she would be all right. This thought underpinned her decision to attack and dispelled even her slightest hesitation. Her life depended on this, and her life she would stake upon it. She accepted that death could be the outcome. She had lost any notion of caution or guard. She understood that only by ridding herself of such things would victory be possible. She tensed her powerful front legs, bared her sharp fangs, and charged into the land where the Two-Legs dwelled.

7

Masari Shiina immediately called the women to assemble, but the bear had already begun its charge. By the time the women had sprinted to the manor, the watchtower had been destroyed. They gathered at the manor to the sound of the tower crumbling like paper before the bear's single strike. But not all the women were there; only nine had arrived: Kayu Saitoh, Hono Ishizuka, Ate Amami, Hikari Asami, Kyu Hoshina, Ume Itano, Usuma Tsutsumi, Hotori Oze, and Masari Shiina. Shigi Yamamoto's absence was to be expected, but the other six failed to materialize. Kyu Hoshina clicked her tongue and called them cowards under her breath, but Kayu Saitoh had expected at least four of the six wouldn't show: Maru Kusachi, Hogi Takamiya, and Shijira Iikubo, who had disappeared off somewhere; and Nokobi Hidaka, who had lost all hope to the plague's sudden onset.

Masari Shiina stepped forward.

"We'll burn that bear to ashes," she said. "But first, we need to lure it to the trap. Each of us will be bait to draw the bear. That's how we will win. That's our only path to victory. I am not at all saying any of you will die, but don't think of your lives as precious. Think of those who have lived in Dendera and have died in Dendera, and fight. Think of Dendera itself, and fight. It is with that resolve that I too will face the bear. Aware that I am only bait to draw it into the trap, I will face the bear. That is all."

The women took their positions in the clearing.

As Kayu Saitoh moved into place, she caught sight of the trap at the edge of the clearing. Beside the impressive, reinforced structure, a fire basket blazed. The sight of the building inspired the old women to courage, confidence, and absolute determination.

Even from the distance at which Kayu Saitoh stood, she could see the bear occupied in the further destruction of the tower. She questioned whether the women, no matter how determined, could really lure such a beast into the trap—especially when the bear had already been injured beside it.

The bear seemed to be making a display of its strength, but then the creature suddenly stopped its attack and hunched its shoulders. Kayu Saitoh understood what the bear was about to do.

She shouted, "It's going to charge us!"

Her guess proved true as the bear bore swiftly down on them.

The tremendous charge came with a sound like the earth itself was rumbling. The bear kicked up snow as it ran, quickly closing the distance. As it neared, the savage beast seemed to grow even more giantlike, and the women reacted in fear; with their feet frozen in terror, they weren't capable of leading the creature anywhere. The bear ran faster than seemed possible. It was close enough now that Kayu Saitoh could see every part of it—its thick front legs, wild tangles of fur, fangs thirsting for raw flesh, stout shoulders, the single eye, and the red fur that covered its back. The women didn't move. Kayu Saitoh couldn't even stick her spear out in front of her. Then, just as the women had resolved themselves to die, all the while cursing their rigid legs, the bear changed course. The creature kicked through the debris of the storehouse and vanished off somewhere.

"What was that?" Kyu Hoshina said. Freed from her paralysis, the woman watched the bear go.

"This isn't good," Masari Shiina whispered harshly. "After it. Hurry."

The women swiftly gave chase and soon learned the bear's target. Two of the five eastern huts had been partially destroyed, with pieces of their walls and even roofs torn away. From within came heart-rending shrieks and the sounds of flesh and bone being shredded, in a slow, drawn-out process that went on unbearably long.

"Ah," Usuma Tsutsumi said dispiritedly, "they're being eaten."

Kyu Hoshina gritted her teeth. "They're being eaten because they hid in their hut."

Her low voice almost lost in the horrific sounds of the creature feeding, Hikari Asami said, "The bear must have decided . . . to start with the ones who wouldn't resist."

Tiny shreds of flesh flew out from one of the openings in the wall. Soon after came the rest of what was left of Tamishi Minamide, which was most of her. Kotei Hoshii, who must have seen the terrible sight, came crawling out from the adjacent hut. The bear saw her, smashed through the wall of her hut, and sank its teeth into the flailing woman's skull. Kotei Hoshii wasn't even able to let out a death cry.

The bear held down her twitching body with its front paws and triumphantly began to devour her. The women were too far away to be able to do anything but watch. Gripping their wooden spears, they just observed. As they were watching Kotei Hoshii being eaten, they heard a strange cry and saw one of the women running forward with her hands up, defenseless.

"You bear! Over here! There's meat over here. Plague-diseased meat! This is all your damn fault."

It was Nokobi Hidaka.

The shouting woman was running straight toward the feasting bear. She looked like she was crying, weeping as she wailed, though she was far enough way that Kayu Saitoh couldn't be sure.

"What are you doing?" Kayu Saitoh yelled. "Get back. You'll be eaten!"

But Nokobi Hidaka went up to the bear and smacked it on its big rump. This was to the surprise of all the women, but the bear was surprised most of all. The creature interrupted its meal to swipe at her with its front paw, and she went flying. Her front side was covered in blood. Kayu Saitoh started to run over to the fallen woman, but Kyu Hoshina held her back, so instead, she yelled Nokobi Hidaka's name over and over. As if awakened by Kayu Saitoh's calls, Nokobi Hidaka stood up unsteadily. But when she did, a long strand of her intestines spilled out from the gash in her abdomen. She caught the undulating mass in her arms and kept on running.

In a scratchy whisper, Hotori Oze said, "She's... leading the bear."

Nokobi Hidaka's expression contorted in a fatalistic frenzy, and shouting something, she ran toward the bear. The beast tossed aside Kotei Hoshii's corpse with its paw and turned its single eye upon Nokobi Hidaka, seeming to mark her as its next target. A loop of intestine dangled and flapped at her feet, until she ripped it out of herself and kept on running. The other women stood watching her, but when Masari Shiina yelled for them to get back to the clearing, they snapped out of their astonishment and rushed back to the open area.

"Bear . . . you damned monster," Nokobi Hidaka panted. "Look, I'm over here. I've got the plague. Are you going to eat me, or what? I've got the plague, but you'll eat me." She managed a laugh. "I've got the plague, but you'll eat me!"

She was staggering now and seemed to be having trouble seeing. Instead of heading toward the trap at the edge of the clearing, she was moving toward the manor. At first, the bear kept its distance, observing her from behind, but then, apparently realizing she posed no threat, it charged her. The impact tossed her into the air, where the rest of her intestines spilled out, and she dropped like an empty sack. Not stopping to watch, the bear turned and began to walk back to Tamishi Minamide and Kotei Hoshii's corpses.

The other women, who had regrouped in the clearing, tasted frustration as the bear failed to act as they had expected. But then a wooden spear sailed down from the manor's balcony. It struck the back of the bear's head, and the beast stopped. At first, Kayu Saitoh was convinced that Mei Mitsuya had launched the spear, but then she remembered that Mei Mitsuya was already dead.

Instead, it was Kyu Hoshina standing on the balcony.

"Damn you, bear!" Kyu Hoshina shouted, throwing another spear. "What's wrong, bear? You afraid? Come at me!"

Moving incredibly fast, the bear closed in on the manor. It crashed through the outer mud wall without slowing and slammed into the side of the building. The manor was sturdy and wasn't going to break from a single attack, but cracks formed in the wall, and the entire structure shook unsteadily. Kyu Hoshina held her footing and swung at the bear's head with another spear. The beast stood on its hind legs and pummeled the balcony and the second floor walls. After two, and then three strikes, several logs fell, and floorboards snapped, and the balcony collapsed with a terrible sound.

Hono Ishizuka's lips trembled as she watched the building go down. "Ah, the manor . . . the manor . . ."

The bear threw itself at the manor one more time, and in a cloud of dust and snow, the largest building in Dendera collapsed. Kyu Hoshina crawled out from the wreckage, but pieces of wood had pierced her arms and shoulders, and both her eyes had been crushed. But still, she forced herself to stand and tried to move away, but the bear jabbed its claws through her back.

As Kyu Hoshina died, two other figures moved. They were Hikari Asami and Ate Amami. The two women ran to the destroyed manor, stood in the bear's path as if to block the creature, and readied their spears. The bear let out a loud roar, its foamy spittle a sign that its mind had given way to the call of battle, then charged the two women. Hikari Asami dove to the side, just barely dodging the attack, but Ate Amami was trampled, the beast's four powerful legs crushing most of her body.

Hikari Asami quickly picked herself up, threw her spear at the bear to draw its attention, and ran as fast as she could to the clearing. Foam streamed from the bear's maw as it chased after her.

They all were going to die within moments. Thinking not of the many deaths, and acting almost entirely on reflex, Kayu Saitoh rushed forward. The same seemed true of Ume Itano, whose face was dominated by fear but whose body advanced with courage. In the clearing, the two women stood in Hikari Asami's path. The bear was gaining on her.

"That's enough," Kayu Saitoh shouted. "We'll take it from here."

Whether or not she heard Kayu Saitoh's voice, Hikari Asami dropped to the ground. The bear jumped over her body and barrelled ahead toward Kayu Saitoh and Ume Itano. The bear, kicking up snow as it charged, was right in front of Kayu Saitoh. For an instant, she thought their eyes met. She readied her spear. The weapon hardly inspired confidence that it could stand up to the bear, but it was too late for such thoughts now. She thrust the spear forward. Bested by the force of the beast's charge, the wooden spear shattered into splinters. Something flew past the edge of Kayu Saitoh's vision, and it took her a moment to realize it was Ume Itano.

Suddenly, all sound was gone.

All that existed in the noiseless space was Kayu Saitoh and the bear. Their faces were close enough that they could touch. She could see in detail each and every hair on its face. She saw the bear's little eye, its only eye now, and in it she saw her own reflection. She could smell the bear's odor, the pungent stench of blood and grease and dirt and trees and snow all mixed together and rotting. Kayu Saitoh could feel the bear, and in her thoughts a single image came into view, much like the one she had pictured the third time she had faced the bear. But she ignored the vision even as it unfolded in her mind. She punched with her right fist, hoping to crush the bear's only eye. She couldn't tell if she did or not. Her view suddenly turned crimson, and her hearing came back with a ringing that tore through her entire body. Caught by the bear's charge, she had been flung into the air. She landed hard on the ground, flipping and rolling, scattering snow. When she finally came to a stop, a long distance separated her from where she had been standing. She lifted her head and, disregarding the blood spurting from her nose, she looked for the bear.

She saw the beast, given over to total rage now, charging with breakneck speed toward the trap, and she saw Masari Shiina standing at the open doorway.

The leader's hair and white robes fluttered in a gust of wind from the bear's rush. Her hair lifted, revealing her single right eye, an eye that gazed fixedly at the bear. A smile was on her lips. It was a graceful smile worn only by those who had found victory.

The bear ran straight into the trap, bringing Masari Shiina along with it.

Hono Ishizuka, Usuma Tsutsumi, and Hotori Oze immediately closed the structure's heavy door. Then, and without hesitation, they began trying to push over the fire basket, but it wouldn't tip over. Wood cracked as the bear pummeled the walls from within.

Masari Shiina's desperate shout came from inside. "What are you doing? Burn it down!"

Kayu Saitoh wanted to help tip over the basket, but the strength had left her, and she couldn't even stand up. At first, she was enraged by her helplessness, but when she saw the tears running down Hono Ishizuka's face as she battled with the fire basket, confidence in the woman quelled her temper. The fire basket collapsed in short order, and the blazing heap of firewood fell onto the building's roof. Before long, Kayu Saitoh saw a tiny flame peeking out from the thick smoke, and the next thing she knew, the fire had crawled along the top of the structure, and the trap was up in flames. From within the trap came rumbles and shakings from the bear's attacks and the reverberations of Masari Shiina's raucous laughter. Each time the bear struck, the walls jolted unsteadily. Where she lay in the snow, Kayu Saitoh willed the trap to burn quickly. *Burn quickly,* she prayed, *burn quickly, burn quickly, burn bigger.* The flames covered the roof but hadn't spread throughout the structure. Despite the black smoke climbing into the sky in dramatic plumes, the fire itself failed to spread with any sort of haste. Hono Ishizuka, Usuma Tsutsumi, and Hotori Oze stared into the flames, and from their expressions they too seemed to be praying. Meanwhile, the bear continued to batter at the walls. Kayu Saitoh wished she could move, but she was utterly incapacitated and could do nothing but watch the events unfold while blood streamed from her nose. A tendril of fire reached along the roof and down to one of the walls. In seconds, what had been more hyperbole than fire had now spread across the entire building.

Flames engulfed the trap.

A loud roar came from inside. Kayu Saitoh could no longer hear

Masari Shiina's laughter. The bear's howls and the bear's howls alone rang throughout Dendera. In them, Kayu Saitoh heard confusion, and she knew the beast was scared. Her lips broke into a smile. Gone were the sounds of the bear striking the walls; maybe beating at walls covered in bright red flames was too painful, or maybe the bear had breathed in too much smoke to move. The blaze intensified, now one single massive fire. And the bear was confined inside it. The trap burned and burned, and the heat reached Kayu Saitoh, even at her distance.

"We've won," she muttered, almost delirious, as her face warmed. "We've won. We've won. We've won. We've won. We've won."

The image of the blazing trap seared itself into her memories. But that wasn't enough for her. She was struck by a desire to more fully bask in those flames. Dutiful to this desire, Kayu Saitoh attempted to push herself up with her arms. She didn't move. Or rather, she moved, but part of her didn't—her right arm. Thinking this odd, she looked to the side and saw her elbow bent in an unnatural direction. Running up her palm was a vertical gash, from which various veins protruded. A large chunk of tissue had been gouged out around her elbow, exposing cloudy white fat; bloody pink flesh; tattered, half-translucent muscle; and even bone. And then she couldn't see anything. Darkness abruptly consumed her vision, and then there was nothing.

8

Throughout the day, Kayu Saitoh awoke several times. She couldn't hold her head steady, and everything was red. She couldn't make out anything around her, but from the dullness in her typically sharp hearing and the weariness in her body, she realized she had a fever, and then she lost consciousness again. The next time she came to, she noticed that straw covered her body, but she didn't understand why. She thought she might be dreaming, but in her dreams she was almost always her younger self, so she quickly rejected that notion. She felt as if in a haze in which but one thing was clear and adversarial: pain. Someone lifted up her limp right arm. She didn't know who it was, but she saw white robes and knew it had to be one of the other women. Two others flanked the woman holding her arm. Kayu felt her pain grow. Her right arm felt like it was on fire. But despite this intense pain, she felt nothing beyond her elbow. Amid pain and terror, she tried to scream, but cloth had been stuffed into her mouth, and she couldn't. Her breath came from her nose mixed with streams of snot, and she cried the sticky tears of a fearful child, but these did not amount to a scream. As this went on she battled the severe pain, when suddenly a new type of pain came upon her, mixed with a peculiar coldness. She tried to get a look through her tear-filled eyes and saw enough to realize that the women were placing snow where part of her flesh was missing. The snow quickly melted into red droplets that splattered down to the floor. One of the women muttered that it wasn't working. For some reason, the voice sounded like it was coming from far away, which confused Kayu Saitoh, but she was more interested in finding out what exactly wasn't working. She opened her eyes wider to try to get a better grasp of the situation. When she did, she saw the glitter of a stone dagger. The dagger ate into her flesh and pain shot through her. She howled. But the dagger kept working, and she heard the sound of it cutting wetly through her living tissue. Her vision went red, leaving only her physical senses and the pain to tell her what was happening to her body. Through her anguish, she strained her eyes to see and to free herself from the terror of not knowing. But what happened next triggered her sense of smell more than her sight. One of the other women held something in her hand that gave off the odor of burning wood. Then she saw that it was indeed a piece of wood with a red, smoldering tip. Simultaneous with the stench of charring flesh, her pain burst like a bubble and her teeth clamped down by reflex. The cloth in her mouth prevented her from biting her tongue off, but several of her teeth chipped badly. But in that moment, Kayu Saitoh hadn't the luxury of noticing such details. Each time the woman applied and removed the wood, flesh adhered to it and was ripped away. Kayu Saitoh screamed and cried cloudy tears, but that alone wouldn't empower her to endure the pain. Moreover, she lost the ability to comprehend why she should have to endure it. She tried to raise her left arm to slap away the burning wood, but she couldn't move it. Her legs, her left arm, and her head were all being held down by the women. Kayu Saitoh resisted fiercely. But their grasps were firm, and with most of her strength gone, she couldn't escape. Meanwhile, burning wood scorched her exposed tissue again and again. In time, the pain exhausted her. Before long Kayu Saitoh lost consciousness again, and this time she really did dream. As was to be expected she was now a girl, in a time before her face and neck were wrinkled and her palms and soles were riddled with cracks and her teeth and ears were enfeebled with age, a time when she was beautiful and lived beautifully. In her dream Kayu Saitoh was running through an open field, laughing for the sheer joy of laughing, even though in her actual past there had been precious few scenes like this one, if any. Her actual past had consisted of tilling half-barren fields, sitting in her house sorting the beans, babysitting for her younger brother, and reaching maturity so that she could bear a child. That was how her actual youth had gone. There hadn't been time to run through the fields laughing. Still, Kayu Saitoh never thought of herself as unfortunate.

In the dream, Kayu Saitoh became aware of a mysterious sound. Then she noticed a small vibration accompanying the sound. She craned her supple, unwrinkled neck and looked to the sky. Seeing nothing unusual amid the cloudless blue, she assumed she must have imagined it. She giggled, gently shaking her youthful cheeks. In reality, it was the sound and vibration of the women smashing her protruding bone with a fist-sized rock. With each strike, the bone cracked deeper, and the impact shook ripples through the surrounding flesh, from which dripped a mixture of blood and fatty tissue. Her skull shook with each vibration, and this contributed to her reawakening. That very same moment, the rock came down again, and Kayu Saitoh opened her eyes wide. Her body shook enough to scatter her pooled-up tears into the air. Each time she was struck, she passed out, returning to her smiling youth. But the very same thing brought her back to consciousness. Amid this cycle, her mind whirled, and the already blurry line between dream and reality clouded further. In the end, she experienced both simultaneously: reality, where she gushed sweat and gasped in pain, and the dream, where she giggled and looked up at the sky. Eventually, when the work had been done, with her bone smashed completely, her arm removed, and the protruding end of the bone shaved off, Kayu Saitoh had exhausted all of her senses, and everything was a haze. Thoughts and awareness came only in intermittent fragments. But even in this state, one precious, unwavering part of her held on to a single idea: she didn't want to die. The idea had taken firm root without her noticing. This idea—that she didn't want to die—sustained her as she took deep breaths and slid back into the dream. In the dream, she was, as she almost always was, in the time of her youth. She wore a bright kimono and was filled with happiness just by looking at the world around her, at the birds and the butterflies. With a gentle smile, she walked peacefully through the Village. It was a dream of much beauty. It was a dream of much yearning. She may or may not have experienced it in her real life, but Kayu Saitoh was powerless to deny the beauty of it or how much she yearned for it.

The dream ended, and she opened her eyes.

9

Five women—Hono Ishizuka, Hikari Asami, Ume Itano, Usuma Tsutsumi, and Hotori Oze—were looking down at the freshly awakened Kayu Saitoh.

"How long was I out?"

Her voice sounded like she hadn't spoken in a hundred years, but the women seemed to understand her words. Hono Ishizuka gave her a small nod. With something flickering in the woman's expression, she replied that it had been three days. Kayu Saitoh felt disappointed in herself and rebuked herself for being so useless that she would sleep for three entire days during such a grave time. Though she had just awoken, her thoughts were clear. She had been able to perceive the women's aura of torpidity, and Dendera's air of stagnation. In these she sensed the drifting weariness that came after the end of things. In the women's eyes she immediately spotted the color of the new state of things: the murky blue color of fear.

"What happened to the bear?"

At Kayu Saitoh's question, the murky blue in the women's eyes darkened further, and their heads lowered. These were the eyes of people unable to imagine what the next day would bring. Kayu Saitoh stared at the women in silence, but soon Usuma Tsutsumi answered, her lips trembling as if she were about to cry.

"It escaped."

"It escaped?" Kayu Saitoh couldn't understand. "What are you talking about? It was trapped in all those flames."

"The fire spread too quickly." Usuma Tsutsumi pressed both hands against her own head. "All that burned was the trap itself. The bear broke through the weakened walls... and escaped."

"What, the bear is just fine?"

"It looked burned, but it escaped anyway. The damned thing escaped."

"It's over. It's all over," Hono Ishizuka said, pressing her hands to her head as well. "Masari and all the others—they died for nothing." She groaned. "It was all for nothing. Dendera is finished."

With the woman's words, Kayu Saitoh remembered that the bear had killed Masari Shiina, Kyu Hoshina, and Nokobi Hidaka. Filled with inexpressible rage, she tried to sit herself up.

But the right arm was gone.

She stared for a time at the robe-cloth bandage covering her wound, as if it had nothing to do with her. But when she realized that the throbbing pain she felt was directly connected to what she was looking at, she realized that it was *her* right arm that was gone. Recalling fragments of her dream, she asked the women if they had taken care of her.

"If you could even call it that," Hono Ishizuka said, shaking her head. "We cauterized your wound and crushed your bone. Your arm had been disconnected. I'm ashamed we couldn't do more."

"Don't talk like that. You're making me look ungrateful."

Kayu Saitoh stood. She wavered pitifully, likely because of how much blood she'd lost, and remaining on her feet was a struggle. But Kayu Saitoh was glad to be able to move on her own at all, and she was able to accept the loss of her arm. She had trouble walking unaided, so she picked up a wooden spear and leaned on it like a cane.

"By the way, where is everyone else? It's too dangerous not to stick together. We don't know when the bear will come back."

Kayu Saitoh looked to the other five women, but none responded. They were immersed in deep torpor and existed in a state of total exhaustion. Just as Kayu Saitoh was opening her mouth to ask again, Usuma Tsutsumi suddenly pounded her fist against the floor and half shouted, "That's why we're finished!"

"What do you mean, finished? Tell me in a way I can understand."

"What's not to understand? Whether the bear comes or not, Dendera is finished. We're going to die!" Now she really was shouting. "We're all going to die. We're going to die..."

"If you can move, you should go see for yourself," Hono Ishizuka said lifelessly. "See what Dendera has become. See what happened to it in those three days you were asleep. Go see how it ended."

Kayu Saitoh already intended to do just that. She gripped her spear and dragged herself outside the hut. In an instant, she understood the women's despair.

Dendera truly was finished.

In Dendera—with its watchtower, its manor, and two more huts destroyed by the bear's attack—only stillness pervaded. In Dendera—its bear trap burned down, along with any role the settlement carried in the fight against the beast—no women were there to be seen, nor even their voices to be heard. In Dendera—under a thick blanket of white snow—only destroyed homes and women's corpses remained, and nothing else.

Only ruination remained.

Only finality remained.

As Kayu Saitoh stared into the total destruction that was Dendera, she began to question why everything was so still. The moment the question came to her, she felt chills along her back. Thrusting her spear into the ground, she turned to look at the three remaining undamaged huts. She had just seen that five women were in one of them. She hurried to the adjacent hut and entered it. The cold outside air had eaten its way inside. Filling the absence of the warmth was that familiar foul smell. In front of the unlit hearth lay three women—Hogi Takamiya, Shijira Iikubo, and Maru Kusachi—dead in a large pool of blood. Kayu Saitoh approached them and saw that each of them wore the same galling, smugly satisfied expression. The women showed no signs of having been in pain.

Kayu Saitoh rushed to the third hut. To her annoyance, her body didn't move as well as she expected it to, but she reached the hut. It too radiated cold silence. She practically tumbled inside.

Shigi Yamamoto was seated in front of the hearth as she always was.

Kayu Saitoh stood behind her and tapped her on the shoulder. The woman collapsed to the floor. A trail of blood ran from her mouth down to her stomach. Startled, Kayu Saitoh lost her balance and fell on her rear. She took hold of her spear and tried to forced her body—now trembling for many different reasons—to stand, but her legs had lost their strength. Using her left arm, she dragged herself closer to Shigi Yamamoto. The woman's face was devoid of warmth, and her always mumbling lips were now purple and motionless. She was dead. That particular foul odor lingered on her lips.

In the stone pot were the remnants of a meal.

Kayu Saitoh's mind, which had gone largely unused for seventy years, suddenly began to turn and turn.

This new sensation soon manifested itself as a headache, but with her right arm gone, and her left holding the spear, she had nothing to press against her head. She could only keep on thinking. She would have to know everything.

She poked her spear into the stone pot, breaking the thin layer of ice that had formed on the top, revealing a semi-clear broth in which floated solid shapes—pieces of potato. She tossed aside her spear and fished out one of the potatoes. It was indeed potato, but with a little help from her suspicions, she detected in it that particular odor.

Suddenly, visions of her days in Dendera exploded through her mind. She wasn't thinking, but rather her mind was working of its own accord. Her headache worsened, and she became dizzy. As her head whirled, she saw the other women go about their daily lives, in glimpses she hadn't seen but could now picture. She felt as if the holes in her knowledge were being filled—by the day-to-day experiences of Shigi Yamamoto, and of Maru Kusachi's circle. She recalled Shigi Yamamoto's unvarying behavior. She recalled what Maru Kusachi had said. She made assumptions of them, though the act was selfish and impudent, and closer to fancy than inference, but she was confident in the conclusion that established itself in her mind.

Any desire to resettle now vanished. She knew that the desire had been nothing more than a lie—a deceit practiced upon herself. In truth, Kayu Saitoh had never wanted to resettle. She had never wanted to go to some other land.

What she wanted, her aspiration, had never been to resettle.

From the very beginning, it had been but one thing.

This realization was triggered when she witnessed the many corpses, each with their own clear desire—to go to Paradise.

Theirs was a desire ardent and resolute.

Kayu Saitoh had learned everything. "I was wrong," she whispered through her daze. "It wasn't a plague. They were killed."

Chapter 9

TOWARD NOBLE DEATH

Hono Ishizuka was the first to speak. "It wasn't a plague? I don't understand. Kayu . . . what are you saying?"

"I'm saying what happened." Kayu Saitoh sat in front of the hearth and looked at the five confused-looking women. "There was never a plague in Dendera. Not once. Not sixteen years ago, and not this time. There is no plague."

Not backing down, Hono Ishizuka said, "But all those people threw up blood and died. That's what happened. It was obviously a plague. If not, then what was it?"

"Poisoned food."

"Poisoned food?" The fight left Hono Ishizuka's voice, and her perplexed expression became even more so. "What's that, some kind of joke?"

"I don't see why I'd be joking."

"So what, Shigi and Maru were also poisoned?"

"Yes," Kayu Saitoh said with an assured nod. "Let me ask you—how long have their bodies been left there? When did they die?"

"It was right after the bear fled," Hotori Oze said, moving to sit in front of Kayu Saitoh. The woman had more reason than anyone to want to know the truth—to identify what lurked in her body. "They vomited blood not long after. I remember the order too. First was Shigi Yamamoto, that night. Maru Kusachi and Hogi Takamiya were the next morning. I don't know about Shijira Iikubo. By the time we noticed, she was already unconscious. All of them died soon, one after the other."

"Those three aren't relevant. What order they died in doesn't mean a damn thing."

"What? What do you mean that they aren't relevant? They threw up blood and died—Maru Kusachi and all of them. How can you say that when I'm going to die vomiting blood too?"

"You're right. What matters…is you." Kayu Saitoh said, trying to take control of the conversation. "You, and Nokobi Hidaka…Shigi Yamamoto's victims."

Hotori Oze furrowed her brow in bewilderment. "Shigi Yamamoto's…victims?"

"Tell me, Hotori Oze, did Shigi Yamamoto give you any food?"

"Any food? No."

"Then what about Nokobi Hidaka? Did she give you any potatoes?"

"We were both on guard duty the same day, and she gave me some potato soup, but…"

"Wait a minute," Hono Ishizuka said, cutting in. "How did Nokobi have any potatoes? Dendera is practically without food. I can't believe that Nokobi had enough potatoes to share."

"Shigi Yamamoto had the potatoes," Kayu Saitoh said.

"Shigi?"

"Nokobi Hidaka received her potatoes from Shigi Yamamoto—poisonous potatoes."

Hono Ishizuka said, "Kayu, you're talking as if you saw it for yourself, but you didn't, did you?"

"You're right, I didn't see it. But I'm convinced it's what happened."

Sounding unswayed, Hotori Oze asked, "Where's your proof?"

"Shigi Yamamoto's body was in front of the stone pot. Potato soup was inside the pot. If any of you want to eat it and see if you throw up blood, you'll have your proof."

Hono Ishizuka narrowed her eyes condescendingly. "Don't be ridiculous."

But Hotori Oze laughed. "That's a good one. Hey, Hono Ishizuka, why don't you try eating it? You're only going to starve to death or be killed by that bear anyway, so what do you have to lose?"

Hono Ishizuka gave no response, save to extend that condescending gaze to Hotori Oze.

To both of them Kayu Saitoh said, "Of course, we're not going to try to prove it that way. But since both Nokobi Hidaka and Hotori Oze ate the same potatoes at the same time and became ill at the same time, you have to admit I'm not being unreasonable. Nokobi Hidaka never gave up on attacking the Village, and she was conspiring with Hotori Oze. If Nokobi Hidaka got potatoes from Shigi Yamamoto, it's plausible that she would share them with Hotori Oze, and it's plausible that only those two became ill."

Kayu Saitoh had never tried to use reason to explain something before, and as she spoke she felt muddled, but she had somehow managed it. She looked to the other women to see how she did. By their expressions they didn't appear convinced, but neither did they obstinately reject what Kayu had said. The women seemed to be deep in their own thoughts.

"For now, let's accept that part of it," Hono Ishizuka said, wiping sweat from her forehead. "But the main question remains. Where did Shigi get the potatoes? She certainly couldn't have kept a secret field somewhere."

"I doubt she did. That's why she waited sixteen years." Kayu Saitoh nodded. "I thought about how the plague happened sixteen years ago. Shigi Yamamoto was already in Dendera by then, right? Remember, her family had an herb garden, so I think she would have known it wasn't a plague. And I think she recognized it was poison. She might have even slipped poisonous potatoes into the food of some of the victims in order to confirm it. Either way, Shigi Yamamoto saw with her own eyes a great number of people dying because of poisonous food. And in that moment... she realized she could bring about her aspiration."

"And what exactly is that? What was this aspiration?"

"She wanted to go to Paradise."

The firewood crackled in the hearth.

No one opened their mouths. Kayu Saitoh surveyed the silent room, recognizing the weight of her words. Partly due to the tense atmosphere, she was suddenly aware of and irritated by her bangs. She tried to brush them aside, but they refused to move. She thought this was peculiar, but then she realized her right arm was gone, so she used her left instead. Then she spoke again.

"Shigi Yamamoto obviously never told me directly, but she wanted to go to Paradise. She had never wanted a new life in Dendera. But when she was Climbing the Mountain, you all saved her. That's what drove her to commit such evil."

Hono Ishizuka leaned forward. "Shigi wanted to go to Paradise? She wanted to die?"

"I think so. She had so much vitality in the Village, and yet the moment she came to Dendera, she became as lifeless as a corpse. She came into Dendera, and in Dendera she would die." Selfishly, Kayu Saitoh sympathized with her. "I think she must have been crestfallen. She had resolved herself to Climb the Mountain and find her noble death. But she was rescued by women who she believed had died noble deaths ahead of her. And they prattled on and on, boasting about how they were alive, *they were alive*, and I think she felt let down. Like I did."

When she said, "Like I did," the other five women—that is to say, all the surviving women of Dendera—reacted, turning their eyes to her. Kayu Saitoh again felt the weight of what she had said, and she added, "Some of us weren't looking to escape death."

Hikari Asami had been listening quietly, but now she spoke. "Shigi Yamamoto . . . wanted Paradise." She began taking slow steps toward the entrance. "She witnessed the turmoil sixteen years ago and saw that it was really food poisoning. I get . . . the gist of it."

"Well then, I'm *so* glad you get it," Hotori Oze growled. "*I* was the one who was made to eat those damn potatoes."

Hotori Oze jumped to her feet and began to charge, fist raised, at Hikari Asami, but she suddenly began vomiting blood, and Hikari Asami ended up holding her. As the blood came up, Hotori Oze moaned painfully, "Damn you."

Kayu Saitoh said exactly what was on her mind. "You all had your bigger purposes. You killed others to further the preservation of Dendera. You killed others to further the raid on the Village. All Shigi Yamamoto did was act on her own larger purpose."

Hotori Oze yelled, "She should have left us out of it!" She pushed Hikari Asami aside and returned to where she had been sitting.

"I don't think that was an option. Shigi Yamamoto wanted to bring all of us to Paradise with her." Kayu Saitoh watched over Hotori Oze. "Shigi Yamamoto saw your slovenly existence in Dendera, and she was revolted by it. Wanting not even to talk with you, she lived as if she were already dead."

Kayu Saitoh understood better than any of the others what it was like to simultaneously have a reason to live and a reason to die, and she understood that those who sought only their own death pursued their path with just as much tireless effort as those who sought to live.

With a few coughs, Hotori Oze said, "Does that mean Shigi Yamamoto was putting on an act? She hadn't gone senile?"

"I think it was an act. Throughout her deathlike existence in Dendera, she waited for the plague—no, the poisoning—to come about again. She was waiting for her opportunity to kill everyone."

With despair in her voice, Hono Ishizuka moaned, "And once Makura came down with the symptoms, then Shigi took action."

"Makura Katsuragawa's symptoms were likely identical to those of the women's sixteen years ago. Once Shigi Yamamoto knew it was another outbreak of food poisoning, she acted. It had happened during a momentary lull in events, but we were in an uproar over the bear, and I was even locked up in a cage. No one would have noticed her stealing the poisonous potatoes from Makura Katsuragawa's hut. Besides, Shigi Yamamoto was as active as a corpse; none of us would have paid her any attention."

Hotori Oze wiped her mouth and said, "When we learned that Makura Katsuragawa had come down with the symptoms, and that Tsugu Ohi had died, we all gathered in the clearing, clamoring for the poor woman's death. All of the huts were empty. That must have been when she did it."

"No, Shigi Yamamoto wasn't that careless." Kayu Saitoh shook her head, thinking of the timing of Soh Kiriyama's and Somo Izumi's decline. In the end, Soh Kiriyama had died as clueless to the circumstances of her illness as her sister had been. "She would have acted immediately. Since no one paid her attention, it would have been easy work. Soh Kiriyama and Somo Izumi were unmistakably her doing—and Kushi Tachibana and Ire Tachibana too."

Kayu Saitoh admitted finding Kushi Tachibana and Ire Tachibana collapsed in their own blood. Since it was in the past now, none of the women rebuked her and Hono Ishizuka's decision to hide the truth. Rather, the women asked her to continue her explanation.

Hotori Oze said, "All right, if she wanted to kill everyone—if she wanted to bring all of us to Paradise—couldn't she have fed us all the potatoes at the same time? After Soh Kiriyama staged her revolt, and Masari Shiina became Dendera's leader, nothing happened for a while."

"That answer I really can't know for sure, but between the bear and our infighting, maybe she thought it was easier to let us die on our own. My guess is that she didn't have enough potatoes to kill everyone."

"Kayu," Hono Ishizuka said, "why, after the long respite, did she make Nokobi eat the potatoes?"

"It's because of me," Kayu Saitoh declared. "Nokobi Hidaka was starving and miserable, so I told her my plan to resettle. I told her that I wanted to leave Dendera and take everyone with me. Shigi Yamamoto lived with us, so she of course heard us talk."

"And so," Hikari Asami said softly, "she had to rush it."

"She figured that if we all moved, it would become harder to kill us. So, first she put the rest of her potatoes in our hut's cooking pot. Unaware, Nokobi Hidaka shared them with Hotori Oze. But they were intended for me." Seated directly in front of Hotori Oze, Kayu Saitoh bowed her head to the woman in heartfelt sincerity and said, "I'm sorry."

"Hey, don't apologize." Hotori Oze snorted. "Say you're sorry again and I'll give you a thumping."

Kayu Saitoh gently lifted her head. Hotori Oze regarded her with a stern expression but one without any signs of anger or ill will.

Hikari Asami spoke. "Kayu Saitoh . . . despite all this being nothing more than your speculation, I think you're right. But I still have to ask. Why would Shigi Yamamoto choose to die when she hadn't yet killed us? She left it unfinished... when she could have killed us."

"Who can say? She may have judged that we wouldn't be able to survive anyway."

Kayu Saitoh hadn't thought it through that far, and so she had only said the first thing that came to her mind. But she suspected she wasn't far from the truth.

"All right," Hikari Asami said. "What about Maru Kusachi's circle? Why did she kill those three, but not us?"

"Maru Kusachi, Hogi Takamiya, and Shijira Iikubo killed themselves."

"They killed themselves?" Hotori Oze repeated.

"Those three—neither Hawks nor Doves—they, like Shigi Yamamoto, wanted to die. They wanted Paradise. This too is only speculation, but I don't think I'm wrong."

Kayu Saitoh recalled every word of her short conversation with Maru Kusachi. The woman had said she was going to a place without the bear, the plague, or starvation. She had said that Kayu Saitoh knew the place better than anyone. Outside of Paradise, Kayu Saitoh knew of no such place.

Hono Ishizuka narrowed her eyes, seeming to extend her condescending look to the three women who were no longer with them. "So that's what they were doing when they were sluggardly skulking about. They were trying to die, were they?"

"I have my doubts about whether or not they knew it was food poisoning, but they did suspect something about Shigi Yamamoto's potatoes." She sent a fruitless glance to her missing arm. "When Soh Kiriyama led her revolt, we all took positions at the storehouse. With free run of Dendera, Shigi Yamamoto fed her poisonous potatoes to Ire Tachibana and Kushi Tachibana. One of Maru Kusachi's three must have witnessed her doing it. Then, sometime later, the twins died. That would be enough to arouse plenty of suspicion."

"Those asses!" Hotori Oze let her anger speak. "They didn't attack the Village, and they didn't defend Dendera. They just died."

"Unlike Shigi Yamamoto, those three women didn't involve anyone else in their deaths. Don't be too angry with them. Who can scoff at those who have left for Paradise?"

When Kayu Saitoh was taken to Dendera—not that she had asked for it—she gave up on death because she had been tainted. She had decided that once she had been rescued, Climbing the Mountain was lost to her. She condemned the women of Dendera, who were directly responsible, but never searched for a different way to die. From that perspective, she viewed the actions taken by Shigi Yamamoto and Maru Kusachi's group with envy. Though she did of course have her share of disagreements with the methods they employed, she had to admit that they found the deaths they had sought.

Hotori Oze, who had placed the attack on the Village above all else, said with total contempt, "*I'll* scoff at them!"

Capping the discussion, Kayu Saitoh said, "That's all I have to report. That's what I came up with from my suspicions and conjecture. There was never a plague in Dendera. So don't fear. The rest of us won't die from it—although, just to be safe, we might want to burn what potatoes we still have."

"What does that matter now?" Hono Ishizuka muttered. "We have no future. We can't change the fact that Dendera is in ruins—not with only six of us left, and not with Masari dead." Tears came to the corners of her eyes. "Without Masari, Dendera can't carry on. No one cared about Dendera as much as she did."

"Masari Shiina," Kayu Saitoh said. "Tell me, what was going on inside that woman's head? What happened to her in the Village was terrible. She had hardly anything to do with what happened, and yet she was publicly humiliated and lost her eye. She had every right to hate the Village more than any of us."

"Did she hold a grudge against them?" Hono Ishizuka said. "Of course she did. Masari did hate the Village more than anyone."

"Then why did she never come around to the Hawks' side?"

"Masari thought in the long term. She thought about what would happen after she died." A fire came into Hono Ishizuka's words. "She *was* striving to carry out her hatred—her revenge—against the Village, not through violence but through the land."

"Through the land? What's that supposed to mean? Tell me in a way I can understand."

"She wanted to make Dendera more prosperous than the Village. That was Masari's true goal." Hono Ishizuka turned her watery eyes on Kayu Saitoh. "She took root here, in this land, refusing to run away, and she was building a utopia solely for those who had been abandoned. By saving the abandoned women, and the abandoned women who came after, and the generations of women who would live long after she had died, she was making this a wonderful place where all could live in peace and bounty."

At that, her tears overflowed, and she broke down crying.

Now, finally, Kayu Saitoh understood Masari Shiina's true feelings. She found the idea far more graceful than raiding the village, but at this point, nothing was going to come of any of it.

"It doesn't matter now," Kayu Saitoh said, because it didn't. "She died, and that was the end of it. It doesn't matter how much you concern yourself with other people, when you die, that's the end. That's the limit to what you can do on behalf of others."

"When you die, that's the end," Hotori Oze mocked. "She gave her life leading that bear into the trap, but the bear still lives."

"That's right," Hikari Asami said softly, "the bear still lives. And with how badly we hurt it, it must be in a terrible rage. It'll come back for sure. And when it does, the six of us will have to face it. And when we do, we'll lose. We'll die."

Kayu Saitoh thought the same thing. It was the truth. Clearly, whatever stratagem they might employ, they couldn't defeat the bear in a fight. The six surviving women had to find a different path. They would have to choose one of only four options: defeat the bear in some new and different way; flee the area; not flee the area, fight the bear, and die; or not fight the bear and die. All six women knew this, and they shared the same weary expressions.

Hotori Oze said, "If we're going to die, I'd still rather not become that bear's dinner. Don't you have any ideas, Kayu Saitoh?"

"I do, of a sort."

"Tell us, please. Dendera has no leader. And I don't have much time left. I guess I just don't have the energy to use my head anymore."

"My idea is not something we do together. No one will be helping. It will be lonesome."

"As long as it's something," Hotori Oze said, "I don't care what it is."

"We disband," Kayu Saitoh offered. "It's like you say, Hotori Oze—Dendera lost its chief. And with only six of us, we can't call it Dendera any longer. And worse, that bear will return. So we must disband. Those who want to remain, remain. Those who want to resettle, resettle. If you want to attack the Village, attack. If you want to fight the bear, fight. If you want to die, die."

Hotori Oze harumphed. "So what then, anarchy?"

"You know, I hadn't realized it, but we *are* free. We were free the moment we were cast out of the Village. There's nothing keeping us in Dendera. All of us here, myself included, are free. So why don't we disband already and do as we please? Well, how about it?"

Kayu Saitoh directed her words equally among the five women. Some appeared amused, and others frightened. Hotori Oze wore a gleeful smile, while Usuma Tsutsumi and Ume Itano had turned incredibly pale, seeming anxious over the uncertain future.

Hono Ishizuka wiped her teary eyes. "After we disband, what will you do, Kayu? Will you choose to run? Will you choose to die?"

"No, I will fight. I will kill the bear."

"You'll kill the bear? Don't be absurd."

"I'm serious. I will kill the bear. I'll do it alone."

"Do you not realize how absurd that is? Have you lost your mind?"

"Maybe I have," Kayu Saitoh said with a self-mocking smirk. "But I'm serious."

"Kayu..."

"I don't want to build a utopia. I don't want to keep living. I don't want to be the foundation for future generations. I'm not interested in any of that. From the beginning, I've only wanted to die. That's my aspiration. No matter what I've been through, that has ultimately remained unchanged. I will find my peaceful death."

Reading into her words, Hikari Asami said, "You... sound like you have a plan. Tell us."

"Sure," Kayu Saitoh said with a nod. "I think this is the only way that bear can be killed now. First, I'll..."

2

In pain, Redback rolled her bulk in the snow to soothe her burns, but she was full of vigor and strength. The burns had scarred her front legs, her rump, and her face, and her oozing, exposed flesh stung badly, but her wounds only affected a small portion of her giant body. Even the red fur on her back remained mostly unharmed. She felt confident in her coming victory and satisfied by her decisive attack against the Two-Legs. She hadn't been able to have a leisurely meal, but she had been able to pack in enough meat to fill her belly. Knowing that there was more meat waiting for her if she went back to the land where the Two-Legs dwelled, she was able to relish her certain victory.

Having fully regained her once-lost confidence and pride as the ruler of her territory, her rage toward the Two-Legs had dissipated. That constant thought, *Kill and devour,* occupied a large portion of her thoughts, now as always, but the underlying reason had largely shifted to the simple acquisition of food. Moreover, Redback understood that her body was in full working order. She had been burned, but she had put much distance between herself and death; no longer did she sense its presence. Savoring elation at being the sovereign ruler of her territory, she knew she would birth another cub, and this time, for certain, she would provide her child with the upbringing necessary to succeed her as the new ruler.

Then something warm flowed into her nostrils.

Sunlight streamed through a break in the clouds and reached softly to Redback's face.

This light was manifestly of a new kind—not the one that had spurned life through this cruel winter, but one that completely enveloped her. Redback reached out her tongue as if to eat the sunlight itself. The light had no taste and no mass, but her stomach responded nevertheless, and immediately she knew it to be a sign of the coming spring. Bears, as a species, were highly sensitive to spring. Typically, bears spent the winter holed up in a den. There they remained at rest, neither asleep nor awake, but passing through the boundary between. When the world outside had turned fully to spring, they knew it without being told. Slowly they awoke, then emerged from their den. This was certainly her first time spending a harsh winter out in the elements, but she hadn't lost her sensitivity to the signs of spring. She stretched her scorched body and savored spring's coming.

3

"Preposterous," Hono Ishizuka said. She again had been the first to respond. "You *are* trying to get yourself killed! That's no plan—it's merely desperation."

"No, it's a great plan," Hotori Oze said, her voice elated. "Although it *is* desperate."

"Are you serious?" Hikari Asami asked. "Are you seriously going to do it?"

"Of course I am," Kayu Saitoh said with a nod. "I don't see any other way to kill that thing."

Hotori Oze clapped her hands. "Kayu Saitoh, I'm in. I may be dying because I ate that stinking potato, but I can still show you the trails. Take me with you."

"Impossible."

"What?"

"Weren't you listening? I'm the only one who can do this." Kayu Saitoh regarded Hotori Oze's carefree attitude with a reproachful stare. "You've been in Dendera for a long time. The people in the Village might figure it out."

"So what? Dendera is destroyed, and we're all dying. What does it matter now?"

"Come on, Hotori," Hono Ishizuka said, regarding the woman with a defiant expression, "that's enough of that claptrap, all right? I'm going to rebuild this place. I'll turn Dendera into Masari's utopia."

"You're the one spouting nonsense. What are you going to rebuild? Don't make me laugh. Wait... you're not actually serious, are you?"

"Our first chief, Mei, built this place alone. I'm simply going to do the same thing she did. It's not nonsense."

The tears were gone from Hono Ishizuka's eyes, and only determination was in their place. Seeing the woman's expression, Hotori Oze shrugged with disinterest and muttered that only fools had survived.

"Listen to me, Hotori Oze," Kayu Saitoh said. "We're going to split up and each go our own way, but we mustn't trouble each other. Find your own aspiration, and find your peaceful death."

"I already have, and you know it—it's to destroy the Village. The Village is as foul as dung, and its inhabitants even fouler. All I have left is to kill them all!" As she spoke, her lips sprayed a mist of blood and spittle. "I can't think of anything else. That's why you need to take me with you."

"But I'm not—"

Hotori Oze cut her off. "If I can't go with you, I'll attack the Village alone. And they'll beat me, and they'll torture me, and I'll spill everything, crying. That'll mean trouble for the rest of you."

"What I was trying to say," Kayu Saitoh said with great patience, "was that I'm not out to attack the Village in particular. I'm going to kill the bear. That's all I want to do. That's all."

"Kayu Saitoh."

"What?"

Suppressing her fervor, Hotori Oze asked, her tone insistent, "Do you really want to kill the bear?"

"Why are you asking me that?"

"You don't have passion for Dendera or the Village. You don't have a reason—even a misguided one—to kill the bear."

Kayu Saitoh wanted to give her some kind of quick response, but she just couldn't find the words. Inside her, her thoughts and views were real and in order, but very little of it could she clearly express through her language or demeanor. And even that small fraction was so fragile it would scatter as soon as she tried to put it into words. She had no response for Hotori Oze.

In any other time, once faced with this dilemma, Kayu Saitoh would have ended the conversation, but she thought of the bravery it had taken to suggest disbanding Dendera and the responsibility that had placed on her, and she endeavored to speak her thoughts.

"Of course I have a grudge against the bear. It killed Kura Kuroi. It killed Mei Mitsuya. It killed so many of us. It's only natural that I should hate it. Hotori Oze, you said I don't have passion, but I do have a head, and it has some thoughts for the Village and Dendera. It's true that I don't hold a deep resentment for the Village, and my interest in growing Dendera pales compared to Hono Ishizuka. But I have my own mind and my own thoughts. As meager as they may be, as laughable as you all may find them, I have thoughts formed of my own mind. But… that said, I do wish for death. And in that case, fighting the bear is the quickest way. If by doing so, I kill the bear, then isn't that better than anything? That was my thinking. Can you understand?"

Seemingly unconvinced, Hotori Oze arched her eyebrow and said, "Like hell I could."

"I…understand," Hikari Asami said, nodding. "Kayu Saitoh, I understand that you don't want to use your head. I understand…that you don't have true grit."

"What did you say?" Kayu Saitoh began to get angry but couldn't muster the energy, and in the end, she grinned. "You're right. Hikari Asami, you may be right. I don't have grit. I don't have a conscience. And so I don't give any of you any particular consideration. I don't care what happens to the Village or Dendera. All I want is to die."

Hono Ishizuka regarded her with a look of heartfelt pity. "Kayu, you are a strange woman. How have you lived this long without anything inside you? I just don't understand you."

"And I don't understand the way you think. What is it that's so different about us when we were both raised the same way in the same place? I don't understand why you all have so much hate for the Village. Were they so bad to you? Was life there so terrible? Were the men that terrible? Or is it all about Climbing the Mountain? Because we all Climb the Mountain, each and every one of us in the Village is able to die together. And you, Hono Ishizuka—neither can I understand why you want to sustain Dendera. You should have died already. You should have died when you Climbed the Mountain. But you live this forced existence, and it forces you to want to keep living. I just don't understand you."

"Well, my reasoning is simple. Unlike you, I don't believe in Paradise or any such twaddle."

"I don't believe in it either."

"You . . . don't? But you—"

Kayu Saitoh cut in, surprised by the conviction in her own voice. "I'll repeat myself. I just want to die. I abandoned my aspiration of going to Paradise. I failed my Climb, so I'll never get there. And if that's the case, I give up on Paradise. Instead, I'll just die. I'll free myself from any other efforts, and I'll die alone. If I manage to take the bear with me, no one will be able to complain."

"I'll complain!" Hotori Oze asserted angrily.

Kayu Saitoh merely sidestepped the woman's comment. "We've talked enough. My aspiration won't change. You all should fulfill yours. Today, we disband. Do whatever you wish. But don't ridicule anyone else's aspirations. Don't laugh at those who want to sustain Dendera. Don't laugh at those who want to flee. Don't laugh at those who die."

Resentfully, Hotori Oze said, "You're only saying that because you get to die the way you want."

But the dissolution proceeded. One of the women suggested that if this was the last day that Dendera was to be Dendera, then they should have a celebration, however modest it might be. Only six women survived in Dendera, and their food reserves were practically gone—and the potatoes were too unsafe to eat. But in talk of a celebration, the women's disparate beliefs and opinions found unity. Hono Ishizuka and Usuma Tsutsumi gathered together the corpses scattered around the settlement, while Kayu Saitoh with her one arm and Ume Itano with her injured hips scoured the huts for food. As thoroughly as they searched, they still didn't find much that could be called food, but they did come across some cornmeal, flakes of dried fish, some rabbit meat one of the women had hunted and dried in secret, and a few other such things.

By the time each woman had finished her task, night had fallen, and soft moonlight illuminated Dendera's ruins. Working together, the six buried the remaining bodies—those of Kotei Hoshii, Ate Amami, Kyu Hoshina, Nokobi Hidaka, Tamishi Minamide, Shigi Yamamoto, Masari Shiina, Hogi Takamiya, Shijira Iikubo, and Maru Kusachi. As Kayu Saitoh dug through the dirt with her only arm, she tried to come up with some thought about how the dead outnumbered the living, but she didn't find any insight. Hono Ishizuka began to cry again as she carefully placed Masari Shiina's body—now nothing but charred bone and festering flesh—into the grave, but Kayu Saitoh couldn't connect with the dead in that way. When she looked at Nokobi Hidaka's exposed, shriveled intestines, or Kyu Hoshina's perforated corpse, she felt nothing. Neither did Hotori Oze, judging from the way the woman hauled the bodies much the same as she would bundles of wood. Kayu Saitoh deemed death in this place to be entirely without meaning.

After their work was done, the six old women gathered in the clearing. They all had felt that the center of the grand destruction was the proper place to celebrate, rather than one of the desolate, stranded huts. The women used pieces of the manor's former walls to construct a makeshift fire pit, in which they began heating a stone pot. Before long, the broth began to smell of dried meat and fish. When they added in the cornmeal, the sound of the simmering soup made their stomachs growl. Then, in the sparkling moonlight, they began their meager feast. Around the fire they ate meat and gristle, and sipped hot, starchy cornmeal porridge. As they chatted and slurped, they polished off the rest of the stone pot's contents. With their stomachs full for the first time in a long while, drowsiness and fatigue washed over them, and in moments, exhaustion took hold. This time, they had used up almost every last scrap of food in Dendera, but no woman complained.

"This is nice," Hono Ishizuka said. "It's so very nice to eat this much." With the preservation of Dendera her aspiration, the woman typically would have taken a position against such reckless overeating, but her expression was one of true contentment.

Adding wood to the fire, Kayu Saitoh said, "Once I kill the bear, you'll be able to go into the Mountain again. If I do, I bet you'll be able to find much more food than this. You'll again be able to find the abandoned women too. Dendera will be vibrant once more."

"Yes, that will be my duty to fulfill," Hono Ishizuka said. She lifted her head, seeming to imagine Dendera's future. "Now that Kayu mentioned it, will any of you help me to rebuild? Do any of you wish to remain here?"

Usuma Tsutsumi and Ume Itano's expressions were a little conflicted, but they both volunteered their names. This seemed not to be out of a personal aspiration, but rather a lack of any other path to follow. Kayu Saitoh felt a pang of guilt for single-handedly declaring Dendera's dissolution, but she knew there hadn't been a choice. She also understood that the more freedom a person had, the harder it was to choose a course of action. But Usuma Tsutsumi and Ume Itano seemed to have realized that nothing would come of life in Dendera as it was now, and they didn't seem unhappy with the disbanding or with staying to help in Dendera's reconstruction.

The one to display clear displeasure was Hotori Oze. Even during dinner, she hadn't spoken much, her expression that of a sulking child who had been left out of the group, and she stared in silence at the Mountain looming over the night. But Kayu Saitoh knew she couldn't take the woman with her.

Kayu Saitoh looked to Hikari Asami, who was sitting beside her, and asked, "What are you going to do? Will you remain here? Will you go somewhere else? Or will you die?"

"I think... I'll be leaving the Mountain. The food is poisonous, and this land is without hope. And there's that bear. So I'm going somewhere far away from the Mountain... though I don't know how far I'll make it."

"I'm going to kill the bear."

"Even so... Even so, I'm going far away. I *want* to go far away."

"I understand." Kayu Saitoh nodded. "I'll say nothing more."

"So, Kayu," Hono Ishizuka said, "when are you going to leave?"

"I'm planning on being gone in the morning. Why?"

"We're counting on you to deal with the bear. Usuma, Ume, and I are staying here in Dendera. If the beast attacks again, we'll be defenseless."

"I knew I hadn't felt that pain in my ass for a while. Listen, Hono

Ishizuka, if you don't have faith in me, you can go somewhere else with Hikari Asami."

"If I went far from the Mountain," Hono Ishizuka said, her voice level, "finding the women Climbing the Mountain would be tough. We don't want long lives—we want to rebuild Dendera."

After a moment, Kayu Saitoh said, "It's all starting to sound the same to me."

"The same?"

Kayu Saitoh decided to speak what she was thinking. "Me, you, and all of us—what we're saying is all starting to sound the same to me."

"To die or to live? Those sound like opposites to me. Of the two, I'll pick a long life. You can laugh at me all you want, but I'll live a long life."

"Good. And I..."

"What's that?"

"Never mind." Kayu Saitoh stood. "I'm going to sleep."

No one watched her go. She hadn't expected otherwise. She was now a stranger to Dendera. If she wouldn't be seeing them off, no one would be seeing her off. The women had come from solitude, and to solitude they were returned. There was no sisterhood now, only solitude. Kayu Saitoh had simply been the first of them to experience it.

Kayu Saitoh went to the easternmost hut in order to sleep alone. It was the same hut she'd been sleeping in, night after night, since she came to Dendera. Shigi Yamamoto's corpse had been taken away, and the room felt too large for Kayu Saitoh alone. Unsure of how to handle all the space, she nevertheless spread out some straw and lay down to sleep. With her full stomach, sleep soon came, melting into her. In her head were not thoughts of the dead, or of Dendera, or of the day to come. She slept without dreaming.

When she forced herself out from that deep slumber and pulled herself out of the straw, a fair amount of time had passed, and darkness surrounded her. She stirred the hearth to feed the fire, producing a dim light for the room. Still feeling half asleep, she stood, rubbed her eyes, scooped water from the water jug, and took a drink. The cold water froze her insides and banished the remnants of sleep. She took the several cooked potatoes from the hearth, put them in a basket, and tied the basket to the sash of her white robe. Then she lit a torch from the hearth's fire, put on her straw coat, and went outside.

The night had not yet lifted, with inky darkness spreading out before her, but still she walked. Having to hold the torch in her left and only hand, she was without a spear to lean on. Moving was a fair challenge, but her steps were brisk. She walked with the lively, cheerful steps of an animal that had just learned how to walk. Soon, her walk turned into a run. As she was enjoying the sound and sensation of the snow crunching beneath her straw sandals, she noticed that the snow was firmer than it had been before. Its surface had melted in the day's heat and frozen at night into a texture like granulated sugar. She ran, sinking her feet into the sugary snow. As her eyes adjusted to the darkness, the white expanse seemed to glow pale blue. Kayu Saitoh's plan was to leave Dendera before dawn and without anyone noticing her.

But when she saw two torchlights ahead she knew that wouldn't happen.

Hotori Oze and Hikari Asami stood near the boundary between Dendera and the Mountain.

Each held a wooden spear, wore a straw coat, and carried a basket from which wafted the smell of food. Hotori Oze wore a smirk as she silently watched Kayu Saitoh approach. Hikari Asami wore no expression as such and held her torch aloft to provide Kayu Saitoh light.

Kayu Saitoh stood before them and said, in a tone emphasizing admiration over disapproval, "You figured me out."

Hotori Oze said, "Only every thought in your head."

Hikari Asami lowered her torch and said, "Kayu Saitoh, I know you want to go alone, but it's too reckless. You should take us with you."

"But..."

"We won't be any trouble," Hotori Oze said with a grin. "Not to Dendera, and not to you. Surely you can't complain then."

"You won't listen to me no matter how many times I say it, will you? Not when you've headed me off like this."

"Good. I'm glad we could keep this short. All right, let's go up the Mountain." Hotori Oze turned toward the Mountain. "I'll lead the way."

"And I'll find the bear for you," Hikari Asami said, facing the same way. "I know the creature better than anyone."

"But Hikari Asami, are you sure? I thought your bigger purpose was to get far away from the Mountain."

"After I find the bear, I'll do just that," she replied. "Once I find the bear, I'm leaving the Mountain—because I'm not like you. I don't intend to die. Don't assume everyone wants to die."

4

The three women stepped onto the Mountain at night. Kayu Saitoh felt calm and without fear. Emotionally, she had returned back to when she first began to Climb the Mountain, when she clasped her hands tightly and listened to the night ravens flapping their wings. Some might call this regression, but Kayu Saitoh felt blessed. She knew that if she told her feelings to her guides, Hotori Oze and Hikari Asami, the women would laugh at her, so she held her tongue and walked in silence. The Mountain was as steep as ever, and the snow deep, and the farther they walked, the less use their straw sandals were. Dragging their sore, snow-soaked feet, the women kept moving.

Hotori Oze pointed at a patch of snow no different than the rest and began her babbling. "At the right time of year, a lot of grapes grow over there. I didn't give a damn about Dendera, and I was so angry all the time, but when the grape season came, I always felt just a little bit better. Just a little bit, yeah? And over there, way back that way, it's covered in snow now, but the ground gets wet there, and it's full of snakes. They're black, and only little things, but they'll bare their tiny fangs and jump right at you. They've bitten me many times. Many times, on my feet."

As the woman cheerfully chatted, they entered deeper into the Mountain. The slope grew gradually more severe, and without a spear to use as a walking stick, Kayu Saitoh kept losing her balance. When Hikari Asami noticed this, she snatched Kayu Saitoh's torch and handed her her own spear. In time they reached the narrow animal trail where the bear had killed Itsuru Obuchi and the others. With the path barely visible in the darkness, Kayu Saitoh proceeded with great care. Hotori Oze had taken the lead. The woman seemed untouched by fear of any sort and walked in her typical jaunty way. But suddenly, she stooped over and began puking blood. Nothing could be done to help her, and Kayu Saitoh and Hikari Asami waited wordlessly for it to pass. And when it did, Hotori Oze stood as if nothing had happened, laughed, and said, "I guess I ran out of blood," and started walking again.

The women made it through the ravine, but the steep slope continued. The Mountain was still, the trees only visible in hazy outline. Kayu Saitoh noted, with great impatience, that they weren't even halfway up the Mountain. Soon the night lifted. The world was tinted blue, becoming a little more visible. The women pressed on into the blue Mountain. When the sunlight reached them, however weak it yet was, the women decided to rest. They tossed aside their burned-out torches, spread their straw coats out on the snow, sat, and removed their sandals. Their feet had turned a deep purple color and could barely feel the straw. Enduring the jabs of pain in her feet, Kayu Saitoh pulled a potato from her basket. When Hotori Oze and Hikari Asami saw it, they yelped in surprise.

Hotori Oze stared at the potato and said, "Where…did you get that?"

"What do you mean, where? It's one of Shigi Yamamoto's potatoes."

Without peeling the skin, Kayu Saitoh bit into the potato. She could feel its coldness in the roots of her teeth.

"What are you doing eating that? Do you want to end up like me? Do you want to puke blood?"

"I'm going to play tag with a bear. I should fill my stomach first."

"But..."

"If the food poisoning kills me, the result's the same," Kayu Saitoh said, chewing on the potato. "I'm going to die. It's what I intend to do."

"That's some resolve," Hikari Asami said, taking out the last of the dried fish from her basket. "I don't intend on dying here. I'm eating the safe food."

"As you should."

Kayu Saitoh forced down the cold potato.

Hotori Oze watched her for a while, then clicked her tongue, swiped a potato from Kayu Saitoh's basket, and stuffed it in her mouth. She chuckled and said cheerfully, "It doesn't matter if *I* eat it!"

When the morning brightened, the women resumed their march. Their bodies were frozen to the core; their noses had gone numb as if someone had given them a good, hard punch; and their hands were stiff; but the women didn't—and couldn't—let that stop them. They pushed through bamboo grasses and climbed over haphazardly growing bushes. Kayu Saitoh had never been this deep into the Mountain. As she gazed around at the unfamiliar scenery, she ran her tongue along the inside of her mouth, still able to taste the potatoes, and knew that she could never go back to Dendera. The Mountain became ever more steep, now absent of anything that could be called a path. The uneven ground hid beneath the snow, and each time she stumbled over an indentation or a break in the rock, she tumbled and hit the ground hard. But no one criticized her, for Hotori Oze and Hikari Asami also struggled, even with the benefit of all four working limbs. To her irritation, Kayu Saitoh realized that her forehead and arms were bleeding from various scrapes, but she didn't stop moving. Punishing her body, she climbed and climbed along paths that weren't really paths, with no end in sight, when suddenly the women reached an open space. Kayu Saitoh gasped.

They had reached the Destination, where all who turned seventy were abandoned.

Kayu Saitoh had never seen the Destination in broad daylight like this, but that wasn't the only difference. With few trees providing cover to the open space, the direct sunlight had melted most of the snow, revealing countless bleached-white skeletons scattered about.

Though some bones stood out, namely skulls and ribcages, there were many she couldn't identify, including some crushed into a fine white powder that blanketed the earth in place of the snow. Her breath caught at her first true sight of the place where she had awaited death. Something in the shade of a fir tree caught her eye, and when she looked she saw it was a skeleton seated in a formal position. Its hands seemed to be clasped in prayer.

Kayu Saitoh's feet moved mechanically into the center of the Destination. Bones cracked and popped beneath her feet. Though worried that she might step on the skeleton of someone she knew, she nevertheless proceeded into the clearing, when something else caught her eye, this time in the shade of a rock. It was a fresh corpse, and one that Kayu Saitoh thought had come after her Climb. She tried to get a look at its face, but wild animals—maybe even the night ravens—had picked it apart and left nothing recognizable.

The women put the Destination behind them. Kayu Saitoh and

Hikari Asami remained silent, but anger had stirred Hotori Oze into becoming even more talkative than before. The woman's earlobes turned red from more than just the cold air, and she bellowed and yelled.

"How can this happen? Climbing the Mountain always makes me mad, but I've never been this furious in my life. It's unforgivable. Isn't it?" Her breath huffing and white, Hotori Oze struck a fir tree with her spear. "To abandon us...to abandon us...it's insane! It makes me sick. Everyone in that damn Village makes me sick. What's wrong with their heads?"

"I understand how you feel," Hikari Asami said calmly, "but be quiet. Someone from the Village might be nearby, Climbing the Mountain."

Hotori Oze shouted louder. "Then we'll kill him! Unbelievable. I can't understand it. What is it with that place—that Village? Where I used to live, yeah, we didn't do anything like this. Do you know why everyone from the Village is crazy? Because you're all destitute. Every single person in that Village is mad. It's nothing like where I used to live. What a sorry and pathetic excuse for a village. That's why you've all lost your minds!"

Seeing tears begin to glimmer in Hotori Oze's sharp, hawklike eyes, Kayu Saitoh and Hikari Asami swallowed their own emotions and waited for Hotori Oze to calm down.

Once she had done so, the women proceeded again, but now it was different.

Now they were searching for the bear.

Compared to the vastness of the Mountain, even the bear's massive form was a mere speck, making the search one of great difficulty. But

Kayu Saitoh's plan required them to find the bear, so they all searched intently for any trace of the creature. Hikari Asami's knowledge and experience with the bear was a boon. The woman had assured them that they would find a place where the bear had torn strips of bark from a tree or where it had lain to rest in the snow. But Kayu Saitoh and Hotori Oze hadn't her skill and could hardly expect to notice such minute clues. Time passed with no progress, and when night came upon them, the women had nothing to show for it. The three women tucked themselves away in a natural hollow formed by the roots of a tall tree, and there they hastily took their cold, paltry dinner. Darkness covered the Mountain, and the women gave up their search for the day. To conserve their strength, they tucked themselves in their straw coats and lay down inside the hollow. Kayu Saitoh groaned. Exhaustion tormented her with a numbness that ran from the top of her head down to her toes. Their hollow didn't provide complete protection from the Mountain's harsh winds, and the women had no fire. As they endured the biting cold, they forced themselves into slumber. Kayu Saitoh never felt like she had gone to sleep, but at some point she noticed that dawn was approaching, and she arose to see how her body was doing. Her joints hurt as if they had all been broken, and her throat was swollen. She decided that the swelling was an ignoble thing and kept it to herself.

Their second day on the Mountain began. Yet neither on this day did they find any sign of the bear. Time kept on passing. Kayu Saitoh was getting anxious. She started to worry that she might die on the Mountain without ever finding the bear. At her core, that didn't particularly bother her, but somewhere within her, some part of her she didn't have the words to describe forcefully rejected that end. She felt exasperated by this stubborn part of her, but rather than fight it, she accepted it and kept on searching for the bear.

After some time, Hotori Oze vomited blood.

She coughed and coughed and then collapsed on the spot.

Kayu Saitoh and Hikari Asami ran over to her but could do nothing aside from support her back and feed her snow. Hotori Oze threw up a mixture of blood and snow and told the others to leave her be.

"What are you doing?" she said, clearly in pain. "Hurry up and find that bear. You don't have time to look after me. You know you don't. Right?"

With Hotori Oze unable to walk, Kayu Saitoh and Hikari Asami carried her to the hollow before again setting out to wander the Mountain. Then, Kayu Saitoh found an odd-looking fir tree. The hard, dark-brown outer bark had been torn away, and several claw marks had been gouged into the softer inner layer. Kayu Saitoh hurriedly fetched Hikari Asami, but the woman hardly glanced at the fir tree before announcing that it was an old mark. But then Hikari Asami ran her hand along the wood, said that the splintering on the underside of the claw marks meant it was the work of a bear, and offered some encouragement to Kayu Saitoh that the bear could be nearby. The trail ended there, however, and the following search was fruitless. The sky, glimpsed through the gaps between the trees, had turned to orange, and the wind of the Mountain spurred on the night. Thus did the second day end with still nothing to show for it.

"That damned bear," Kayu Saitoh muttered impatiently. "It shows up whenever it damn well pleases, but when we go looking for it, it's nowhere."

Matter-of-factly, Hikari Asami said, "That's...how animals are apt to be."

"What should we do? We could go back to Dendera, but I don't want to."

"If we ration our food, we can last for several days. Our strength is the problem. Can you still move, Kayu Saitoh?"

"Don't mock me." Kayu Saitoh swung her left arm around wildly. "Hotori Oze is the one who can't move. I don't think she has much time left."

"We can't do anything for her. There's no way to save her." Hikari Asami kicked at the snow at her feet. "At least we were able to bring her a little closer to the Village...I think, to her, that's better than dying in Dendera."

"Do we really have to leave her there?"

"It's what she wants of us."

"Let's go back to the hollow for the night," Kayu Saitoh suggested. "It's too dark for us to find anything out here—and I want to check in on Hotori Oze."

Back at the hollow, Hotori Oze was lying where they had left her. Traces of frost ran along her face, where it stuck out from the straw, but she was breathing, albeit shallowly, in her sleep. Careful not to wake her, Kayu Saitoh and Hikari Asami quietly began to eat. The potatoes were too frozen to bite through, so Kayu Saitoh angrily hurled them away. The potatoes vanished into the mountainside and the quickly encroaching darkness. Merely throwing the potatoes had left Kayu Saitoh out of breath. When Hikari Asami had asked if she could still move, Kayu Saitoh had blustered, hoping to mislead the woman, but in truth her strength was almost entirely gone. Her throat's swelling had worsened, the stump of her right arm hurt, and her legs were exhausted, puddlelike and unresponsive. Even if they could find the bear, her plan wouldn't work if she didn't have the stamina to carry it out. She exhaled into her cupped hand in an attempt to keep herself warm, but it had little effect.

Night fell. Waiting for sleep that wouldn't come, Kayu Saitoh curled up inside the hollow. The tips of her gray hair and her eyebrows were frozen stiff, and her fingernails had started to crack, possibly from the cold.

Hikari Asami said, "So you're still awake," and sat down beside her. "If you don't sleep, you'll die."

"I'm scared to die."

The words came out of their own accord.

"Is that so," Hikari said with only a nod. "You're scared?"

"I'm scared," Kayu Saitoh repeated, still curled up in a ball. "I've never really used my head for much, so I don't know much about Climbing the Mountain. I don't know much about Paradise, either. All I want is to die. And yet I'm afraid of dying."

"You're...stating the obvious. Everyone's afraid to die."

With newfound surprise, Kayu Saitoh said, "Yeah, I suppose I am stating the obvious."

Kayu Saitoh and Hikari Asami didn't say anything of note after that. Having abandoned the possibility of sleep, the two simply watched the dawn's gradual arrival.

When the first light came streaming in to dispel a part of the darkness, Hotori Oze awoke. Staggeringly gaunt, her face had lost so much color that the crevices of her wrinkles now stood out in harsh contrast.

Her eyes slitted, Hotori Oze mumbled as if in delirium, "I'm back... Wonderful. Wonderful. I finally made it back. I made it back..."

"She's hallucinating," Kayu Saitoh said, dispirited. "She's done now."

"Hmm? Kayu Saitoh, what are you doing here? What's going on?" Hotori Oze's eyes squinted with incomprehension as she looked at Kayu Saitoh. "You can't be here. This is where I used to live."

"She's having a dream—a dream of when she was happy," Kayu Saitoh said, realizing that with the potatoes in her own stomach, the time would come when she would meet this same fate. "A shameful thing, but there's no shame in it now."

"I don't think she's looking at us."

Hikari Asami was right; Hotori Oze's eyes were moving randomly, and it was hard to tell if she was seeing anything or not.

"Take a look, Kayu Saitoh," Hotori Oze whispered faintly. "What do you think? It's beautiful, isn't it? This, this is how bountiful the place I lived was. It's nothing like the Village. Listen to all the birds. And we have squirrels and rabbits in abundance. Even the moles are fat... making all their holes in the dirt. Just a little farther ahead, there's a little field, where in the spring, butterbur and horsetail and plants of all kinds grow in plenty. Fish swim in our mossy river—lots of them, and all of them big. Carp with bright green scales, plump redfin... Look, you can see them over there. I really enjoy trying to catch them as they splash about."

"She's completely lost it," Kayu Saitoh muttered hopelessly. "Carp and redfin don't swim the same waters."

"My home...is not like your Village. It's not squalid." Hotori Oze's vacant gaze roamed about. "Even the mud has turtles and eels. When you step in it, it's funny how they all scatter. That's in the place I lived. Your Village doesn't have that. And everyone wears beautiful kimono, and they're always smiling. Always. And in the spring, the butterbur bloom red and blue flowers, and..."

The talk of her dream was interrupted when she vomited blood. It came in a retching fit, sullying her own face with splashes of red. Kayu Saitoh and Hikari Asami tried wiping her clean but had to give up when the blood kept coming.

Hotori Oze's face twitched into something of a grin. "Kayu Saitoh, I'm glad...I was able to show you. How about it? What do you think of my old home? It was beautiful, right? It was truly beautiful, right?"

"I know. Don't say another word."

Hotori Oze likely didn't intend on obeying Kayu Saitoh's command, but she closed her lips until only her front teeth showed, and she took several deep, loud breaths, and then moved no more.

Hikari Asami watched over her until the end, then said, "We're burying her. If anyone Climbing the Mountain finds her...it'd mean trouble."

The hollow was free of snow, and burying her wasn't that difficult in and of itself, but it was gloomy work, and one that required perseverance.

When the two women had scooped out just enough soil to fit Hotori Oze entirely, they lowered her body and covered it with dirt. Kayu Saitoh wished she could have left a gravestone or wooden marker, however makeshift, but she had to abandon the thought. As Hikari Asami had said, someone Climbing the Mountain might find it. When the two women finished their work, Kayu Saitoh, completely exhausted, slumped back down to sit, even though this was only the beginning of their third day on the Mountain.

But Hikari Asami didn't do the same. Her eyes were bright and earnest, and her expression was one of caution. She slowed her breath until she hardly breathed. Her ears twitched, the sensitive movement animal-like, and she began to sweat despite the cold of the Mountain. The muscles around the base of her neck were taut and trembling.

"What's wrong?" Kayu Saitoh asked.

"Hush," Hikari Asami whispered.

Kayu Saitoh understood what that meant, and in the next moment, her mouth had gone completely dry, and her inflamed throat felt hot.

Hikari Asami stepped out from the hollow. Remaining on alert, she looked all around, turning her head like a restless little bird, then motioned for Kayu Saitoh to come. Kayu Saitoh moved, remaining cautious herself. Hikari Asami seemed to be mindful of the wind's direction, and she opened her mouth a crack and motioned with her head. Kayu Saitoh nodded her understanding. The woman crouched and went on the move, with Kayu Saitoh following after. Hikari Asami scrambled up the Mountain's slope on her hands and feet, and Kayu Saitoh, with only one arm, had to do all she could to keep up. Still facing ahead, Hikari

Asami impatiently admonished her to stop making so much noise. Kayu Saitoh wished she could, but with one arm, moving silently proved a difficult task.

The two elderly women scrambled up the Mountain and dove into a thick growth of bamboo grass to hide. Hikari Asami carefully poked out her head and looked all around. Not wanting to get in the way, Kayu Saitoh crouched down and kept quiet, but when Hikari Asami told her to look too, she lifted her head and saw a sweeping vista of the Mountain glittering in the morning sun.

And there, in the distance, she saw the bear.

The creature was roaming majestically through the Mountain—through its domain. Four stout legs powered the ambling beast's bulk, which was peppered with festering burns and scars. But judging from the healthy, rippling movements of the muscles on its shoulders and rump, and the bushy luster of the red fur on its back, the bear hadn't lost its vigor or will. Hikari Asami must have noticed it too, because she let out a disappointed sigh.

The bear roamed about, twitching its ears and nose, seeming to make more use of those senses than its vision. Every now and then, it stopped to brush its paws on the ground while its red fur swayed.

Hikari Asami whispered into Kayu Saitoh's ear. "It seems to have noticed us... but it doesn't know where we are. But... it's only a matter of time. We moved downwind, but we can't escape the bear's nose."

"Will it find us?"

"It's only a matter of time," Hikari Asami repeated. "Kayu Saitoh, it's up to you now."

Her parched throat trembling, Kayu Saitoh stared at the bear. Inside, she was shaking, but outside, her body was as stiff as a dead dog. Her eyes wavered not one iota as she stared steadily at the bear and the bear alone.

But Kayu Saitoh was preternaturally calm and quiet. One could even call her relieved. Outside of fairy tales, a person could never become a bear, but Kayu Saitoh felt attuned with the bear's emotions and senses, and in her thoughts a single scene came into view.

5

Redback sensed that the Two-Legs were somewhere near, but she couldn't see where. Maddened, she brushed her front paws on the ground and made a threatening sound. Meanwhile, she sniffed and sniffed and moved her soft, furry ears about. Redback—and all bears for that matter—relied on their senses of hearing and smell to find their prey. Redback focused her attention on the smells wafting around her. She opened her mouth a little, stuck out her tongue, and sucked in the cold air. This way, she could smell the very currents of the wind, but the stink of the Two-Legs was now absent. She knew this meant her prey had escaped downwind, and it was there she narrowed her gaze.

She saw the familiar mountainscape.

She'd seen it—this domain she ruled—enough to grow tired of it.

And Redback saw the Two-Legs blended into it. Their faces were sticking out from the bamboo grass. And they were facing her direction.

They had noticed her too, but she didn't shrink back, instead turning to face them. The two Two-Legs had hidden themselves in the bamboo, and when she met one of their gazes, an unfamiliar sensation came over her. The sensation was so alien that she nearly lost her balance. She remembered when she had seen those eyes before. The second time she had attacked the place where the Two-Legs dwelled, her gaze met one of theirs, and in those eyes she had seen something kindred.

Redback didn't understand the Two-Legs.

She didn't understand what they thought and why they lived.

She didn't understand for what purpose they existed.

But in those eyes staring back at her, she saw a deep and almost impudent understanding. To Redback, this was displeasing, but more than that, it was an enigma.

Redback had known caution and worry, but this sensation that now assailed her was something new. She felt her feral intellect ill-suited to deal with this situation. Her life had one course: live in solitude, give birth to a cub, and raise it. To deviate from this path was beyond her capabilities. And so when Redback decided to stop thinking, she did so with immediate success. Rather than go through the pretense of agonizing over the differences between herself and the Two-Legs, she chose simple faith in her claws and fangs. She chose to obey her instinctual imperative: *Kill and devour.* Redback was a creature of the wild; such was her limitation, and also her strength.

She needed to survive. She needed to live; to overcome the cold and barren winter, to recuperate in the warmth of spring, to rule over her domain, to raise her next-born cub to be the next ruler. Those were her only reasons to live, but to Redback—and to every wild animal—they were enough. The reasons were as unyielding as they were simple.

Strength coursed through Redback's massive body.

When the muscles in her legs and shoulders and abdomen and rump were brimming with power, she released the energy in a mighty roar. The trees shook, snow falling loose from their branches. It was a threat and a declaration of war. Upon hearing that roar, any creature smaller than her on the mountain would spring into flight, but the Two-Legs remained motionless as they stared at her. Though she had spurned any thought of the Two-Legs, her fear returned anew. She couldn't comprehend why these creatures, weaker than any other animal on the mountain, didn't run. The sound of her cry should have filled them with overwhelming terror. Staring at her like they did was an agreement to battle. Redback discarded all doubt. With the red fur standing along her back, she advanced, closing distance with the Two-Legs. They remained still within the bamboo grass.

With survival of the winter at stake, she launched herself at them.

6

"It's coming," Kayu Saitoh said when she saw the bear begin its charge. "I'll take it from here. Hide yourself, Hikari Asami."

Kayu Saitoh leaped out from the bamboo grass, and after a moment's hesitation, ran in the opposite direction from the bear. A rush of exhilaration filled her, and blood pumped into her eyes, as she numbed to the noises and sights of the world around her. Running was all to her now. She didn't even notice the branches and bamboo stalks tearing at her white robe, and it took some time for her to realize that Hikari Asami was running directly behind her.

"Why are you following me?" Kayu Saitoh shouted, running as fast as she could. "I thought you wanted to live. I thought you wanted to go far away. You'll get killed!"

"The bear will catch up to you too quickly alone. You should know by now how powerful its legs are."

"But—"

"Let me help you."

"Do what you want, you fool!"

As she shouted, she leaped down a drop-off and twisted her ankle on landing, but she ignored the pain and took off running again.

The two women sprinted down the Mountain.

Kayu Saitoh hurdled over fallen trees, strode across hollows, and seemed to skate atop the snow, but as the Mountain sights flew past in a perpetual, turbulent whirl, she lost sense of where she was going.

Hikari Asami grabbed her left arm and pulled her along.

"This way," she said, keeping ahold of Kayu Saitoh's arm as she ran ahead. "You really couldn't have done it without me."

Thankful for Hikari Asami's decision to help, she shook free from the woman's grasp and kept on running.

At the speed the two women were sprinting down the Mountain, one tiny mistake would send them tumbling. Yet still they had no hope of outrunning the bear. The beast's odor, its bloodthirsty growls, and its tangible rage pursued them. But Kayu Saitoh couldn't spare a glance over her shoulder. Focused on what was ahead, she ran. But the view around her was unchanging. The trees stood densely, and deep snow blanketed the earth. Gritting her teeth, Kayu Saitoh squeezed every bit of strength from her body as she ran. Each time she sucked the cold air in through her nose and mouth, her lungs protested in pain. Her wide-open eyes had thoroughly dried out, bulging nearly out of their sockets. Her feet had long since gone numb, and she couldn't tell when they were on the ground. And yet she kept on running. But the bear had closed in, and Kayu Saitoh could feel its breath hot and wet on her back.

"Keep running this way," Hikari Asami said from ahead. "Run straight forward. When the woods open up…the Village will be right in front of you."

Then Hikari Asami stopped on her heels and lunged at the bear.

The beast hadn't been able to react to this sudden movement, and the two of them rolled down the slope and crashed into a large fir tree. Hikari Asami was wedged between the bear and the tree, and the impact had split open her head, but she had tangled herself up in the bear's front legs. The beast moved its limbs about and managed to sink one set of its glistening claws into the woman. Kayu Saitoh thought only of reaching the Village. She ran with her mind cleared of anything else.

This was her plan.

If the few remaining old women weren't strong enough to defeat the bear, they could lead the bear to the Village. The people of the Village might kill the bear. Or, the bear might kill everyone in the Village. But for the plan to work, someone had to lead the bear to them. And no one could do this but Kayu Saitoh. If any other of the women did it, any survivors would find her presence suspect and would come looking in the Mountain. And they would likely find Dendera. But unlike the other women, Kayu Saitoh hadn't been on the Mountain long. The people of the Village would simply consider her a coward who, unable to face her death, had come back. She didn't care if they butchered her. She didn't care if the bear devoured her first. And even if she somehow survived, the potatoes were in her stomach.

She would be able to die.

Kayu Saitoh kept on running. Swinging her remaining arm, she gave herself to the run. She didn't see anything. She didn't feel anything. With her sandals shredded, her gray hair frozen standing, blood streaming from her nose, her straw coat blown away, and her white robe flapping open, Kayu Saitoh looked like a monster. She shot across the Mountain with the ardent wish to die not as a monster but as a person. She wanted to die as a human being.

Suddenly, she could again sense the bear's presence.

Thinking she had built up a little distance between herself and the beast, she looked over her shoulder and saw it chasing after her, its red fur, bathed in Hikari Asami's blood, glistening even more redly than before. Its stout legs moved with terrific speed, and it kicked up snow as it gave chase, its single eye glittering with pure rage. A single thought materialized inside Kayu Saitoh's mind: *Kill and devour,* and she knew the bear's creed had jumped into her thoughts. She shook her head to dispel the image, then looked forward again as she glided down the Mountain's slopes. A change had come to the Mountain's scenery. It was nothing dramatic, merely a slight alteration, but the scenery now felt familiar to her. She was convinced this feeling was no mistake. She had seen this place when she had Climbed the Mountain. She had seen it while her son carried her on his back. Her lips broke into a smile, and the air rushed into her mouth and puffed out her cheeks like those of a frog. But meanwhile the bear was catching up to her, its growls coming from close by now, but Kayu Saitoh kept on running.

She was running as hard as she could when she noticed that she was approaching the tree line. And she saw that the snow had melted in patches, exposing the bare soil. But more than that, the slope had eased up, and the ground was flat underneath her feet. She was nearing the Village. Nearly half naked, nearly a monster, but wholly human, Kayu Saitoh held nothing back as she ran. From behind, she could still hear the bear gaining on her. As she kept running, she became aware of a rich aroma she hadn't smelled in some time. It was the smell of wet earth. The snow had melted, bringing the hidden earth to the surface where it released its pent-up aroma. Kayu Saitoh felt as if she could cry out in elation, but she wasn't out of danger yet. The bear too was desperate; desperate to carry out that single-minded thought—*Kill and devour!*—desperate to continue its bloodline. Kayu Saitoh sensed this, herself desperate to die and desperate to find her ending. She picked up her speed, for death right here and right now was the only outcome she could not permit. But she had pushed her body beyond its limits. Her entire mind was occupied with putting one leg in front of the other. Blood seeped from her cracked lips, wind buffeted her swollen eyelids, a sour taste spread in her mouth, her heartbeat thundered in her ears—in other words, she was near death—but her legs alone were in fine function. And yet even they had become a struggle.

Then Kayu Saitoh's feet, which had been almost completely numb, suddenly stepped on something. She felt a soft, springing sensation she hadn't experienced in a long time. This was no time to concern herself over such things, and she ignored it and kept running, but then she felt it again, and she permitted herself to lower her gaze, just a little bit, and looked at the ground.

The adonis flowers had begun to sprout.

Startled, Kayu Saitoh broadened her view. New buds dotted the ground where the adonis had broken through the thinning snow. The yellowish buds spread out atop their leafy stems, pushing aside the snow to poke their heads out of the ground. They were little things, but they made a grand statement. Kayu Saitoh saw the many buds that would soon be blooming in abundance, and she knew that spring was coming. Spring began with the adonis flowers; spring was coming. She felt strength flooding through her. She was, of course, not completely healed, but she would at least be able to run at her fastest for a little while longer. She ran through the adonis, their buds beneath her feet. Those round buds came up everywhere, and beneath them, their thick roots must have extended far.

Kayu Saitoh, and the bear, ran through this landscape. She could count the fir trees, and only a thin layer of snow—and the adonis buds—covered the ground. The Mountain was behind them now. Kayu Saitoh, and the bear, were running almost on top of each other. Kayu Saitoh, and the bear, ran as if it were only natural. Kayu Saitoh looked up from the adonis flowers, and there, not that far away, she saw the Village.

END

ABOUT THE AUTHOR

Yuya Sato, born 1980, is a writer of "strange fiction," which features fantastic or horrific concepts treated in a refined literary style. Some of his short work has appeared in English in the mixed manga/prose anthology series *Faust*. His novel *1000 Novels and Backbeard* won the Yukio Mishima Prize.

HAIKASORU

THE FUTURE IS JAPANESE

PHANTASM JAPAN—NICK MAMATAS AND MASUMI WASHINGTON, EDITORS

The secret history of the most famous secret agent in the world. A bunny costume that reveals the truth in our souls. The unsettling notion that Japan itself may be a dream. The tastiest meal you'll never have, a fedora-wearing neckbeard's deadly date with a yokai, and the worst work shift anyone—human or not—has ever lived through. Welcome to *Phantasm Japan*.

Nadia Bulkin
Gary A. Braunbeck
Quentin S. Crisp
Project Itoh
Yusaku Kitano
Jacqueline Koyanagi
Alex Dally MacFarlane
James A. Moore
Zachary Mason
Miyuki Miyabe
Lauren Naturale
Tim Pratt
Benjanun Sriduangkaew
Seia Tanabe
Joseph Tomaras
Dempow Torishima
Sayuri Ueda

ASURA GIRL—OTARO MAIJO

Seventeen-year-old Aiko lives a life of casual sex and casual violence, though at heart she remains a schoolgirl with an unrequited crush on her old classmate Yoji Kaneda. Life is about to get harder for Aiko, as a recent fling, Sano, has been kidnapped, and the serial killer Round-and-Round Devil has begun slaughtering children. The youth are rioting in the streets, egged on by the underground Internet bulletin board known as the Voice from Heaven. Expecting that Yoji will come and save her from the madness, Aiko posts a demand for her own murder on the V of H, but will she be left waiting... or worse?